Ellie Darkins spent her formative years devouring romance novels and, after completing her English degree, decided to make a living from her love of books. As a writer and editor, she finds her work now entails dreaming up romantic proposals, hot dates with alpha males and trips to the past with dashing heroes. When she's not working she can usually be found running around after her toddler, volunteering at her local library or escaping all of the above with a good book and a vanilla latte.

Susan Meier is the author of over fifty books for Mills & Boon. *The Tycoon's Secret Daughter* was a Romance Writers of America RITA® Award finalist, and *Nanny for the Millionaire's Twins* won the Book Buyers' Best award and was a finalist in the National Readers' Choice awards. She is married and has three children. One of eleven children herself, she loves to write about the complexity of families and totally believes in the power of love.

PRINCE'S CHRISTMAS BABY SURPRISE

ELLIE DARKINS

REUNITED UNDER THE MISTLETOE

SUSAN MEIER

MILLS & BOON

First Published in Great Britain 2021
by Mills & Boon, an imprint of HarperCollins*Publishers* Ltd,
1 London Bridge Street, London, SE1 9GF

www.harpercollins.co.uk

HarperCollins*Publishers*
1st Floor, Watermarque Building,
Ringsend Road, Dublin 4, Ireland

Prince's Christmas Baby Surprise © 2021 Harlequin Books S.A.

Special thanks and acknowledgement are given to Ellie Darkins
for her contribution to the A Wedding in New York miniseries.

Reunited Under the Mistletoe © 2021 Harlequin Books S.A.

Special thanks and acknowledgement are given to Susan Meier
for her contribution to the A Wedding in New York miniseries.

ISBN: 978-0-263-30000-0

11/21

MIX
Paper from
responsible sources
FSC **FSC® C007454**
www.fsc.org

This book is produced from independently certified FSC™ paper
to ensure responsible forest management.
For more information visit www.harpercollins.co.uk/green.

Printed and bound in Spain using 100% Renewable Electricity
at CPI Black Print, Barcelona

PRINCE'S CHRISTMAS BABY SURPRISE

ELLIE DARKINS

MILLS & BOON

For Betty Darkins

1928–2020

Thank you for letting me borrow your books
and your name.

CHAPTER ONE

IF SOMEONE HAD told him that being best man for his old university friend would mean being dragged to a freezing cold floristry studio less than an hour after his plane had touched down in New York, Gio might have reconsidered his answer.

He caught the florist's eye and stifled a yawn as he followed his friend Sebastian, Sebastian's fiancée, Ivy, and their wedding planner, Alexandra, into the freezing cold studio-slash-workshop where they were to inspect the proposed floral displays for the upcoming wedding. He glanced over the arrangements that the florist had laid out for them and had to admit to being slightly impressed. He knew nothing about flowers, but these seemed bold and artistic, and would not have looked out of place alongside the Dutch masters that graced the walls of the palace in Adria. He could tell from their spellbound expressions that Sebastian and Ivy were impressed too, and that was good enough for him.

He watched the florist speaking to Ivy and Sebastian and tried to catch her eye again, but she was focused entirely on his friends, which gave him an opportunity to get a better look without giving himself away. She was cute. Very cute. More than a head shorter than him, with a soft, wavy bob that finished just below her jaw and a fringe that framed her face, highlighting pixie-like features and a delicately pointed chin. There was something about the soft roundness of her petite frame that made him want to pick her up and tuck her into his pocket. And something about the determination in her face as Alexandra quizzed her on the costings and the details of delivery and timings that told him for sure that she'd kick him if he even tried it. Intriguing.

He tried to concentrate on what she was saying, but he knew he was fighting a losing battle with fatigue. He was aware that his shirt was still creased from where it had got crumpled in his bag, and his stubble was about a day and a half beyond actually being stubble. The time difference between New York and Adria meant that he had been awake way into the night, and he'd only had just enough time to throw himself into the shower when Sebastian had hammered on his door a few minutes before they were meant to be leaving for their meetings with various wedding suppliers. Sebastian had insisted that Gio be in on all the details so he could step in if there were any problems on the big day. Not that he could possibly anticipate any, given the fierce efficiency of the wedding planner. But when things went wrong it was altogether unsurprising that a crown prince could get results just by asking nicely.

His mother would be horrified if she could see him now, and no doubt would have all sorts of things to say about how, as Crown Prince of Adria, he was representing their tiny nation on the world stage and he should occasionally present himself as if he remembered that fact. It was a shame, really, for all involved, that the more his mother seemed to remind him of things like that, the more he wanted to act like a teenager and ignore her just to make a point.

He hadn't asked to be a crown prince. No one would choose to have their life mapped out from the day they were born: where they would live, what they would do every single day of their lives...who they would marry.

He looked at Ivy and Sebastian, both of them glowing in that wholesome way that they had whenever they were talking about the wedding, which considering it was in just over ten weeks' time was pretty much all they had talked about since he had arrived in the country. And he contrasted that warm glow with the haughty iciness that his parents exuded in their wedding photos—a wedding, and a marriage, that had been planned to suit the families involved rather than the individuals who were taking the vows. An uncomfortable foreshadowing of his own future.

He tried to shake off the feeling of dread, because so far he'd managed to deflect all suggestions from his parents that he really should be married by now. Neither of them was exactly delighted with the shambolic state of their union, after all, and perhaps they had the good sense to try and protect their firstborn from sharing their fate for as long as possible. But he knew that it couldn't last for ever. Eventually, he would have to marry, and he wouldn't be the one choosing the 'lucky' woman. The best that he could hope for was that he didn't entirely hate his partner, the way his parents had come to hate one another.

A shiver passed through him at this portent of his future, and he looked at the florist again. Was she the sort of girl that he would marry if he had the choice? He tried to imagine it. A future where he got to choose what he wanted. *Who* he wanted. And found that he couldn't. He'd spent so long resigned to the fact that he wouldn't get to choose his life partner that he couldn't imagine what he would do with free choice even if he had it.

That shiver of dread had kicked off some sort of chain reaction in his body and, before he even knew what was happening, somehow a yawn was creeping up on him and, although he fought it hard, it escaped him, stretching his jaw out of shape and drawing the attention of everyone in the room.

'Oh, I'm sorry, are we keeping you awake?' the florist asked, and he was torn between amusement at the expression on her face and mortification that he'd just yawned during what could potentially be one of the more important meetings of her life.

'I'm so sorry, Miss...'

'Ms,' she supplied. 'Thomas. Hailey Thomas.'

'I'm so sorry, Ms Thomas,' he started again. 'The blame lies entirely with me and my jet lag and not with your delightful...' He had to think for a moment to find the right word in English, a language he had been speaking every day since he had gone to boarding school in the UK at eleven. It was simply fatigue that had scrambled his thoughts, he told himself. Not the presence of Ms Thomas. 'Creations,' he finished, limply.

'You're a fan of my work?' she asked, her hands planted on her hips and her mouth quirking up at one corner, just enough for him to see that she had a sense of humour, and somehow he was hitting her buttons. Well, that was an interesting development. Because, as he looked her up and down, he was certain that there were a couple of other buttons he wouldn't mind uncovering.

'They're very beautiful,' he said, honestly appraising what he could see of her work. Not that his opinion should count for much—he was hardly an authority here. This was entirely her field, and he wouldn't dream of trying to explain it to her.

'Thank you,' she said, turning back to Ivy, Sebastian and Alexandra to continue their meeting, and he considered himself dismissed. He slunk at the back of the room, his eyes never leaving Ms Thomas as she talked them through various options, pulling flowers out of arrangements and offering them up for Ivy's inspection, occasionally sketching something on her notepad, and listening thoughtfully to the feedback from the couple.

He could just go to bed, he told himself. If he did that, there was a small chance that he would sleep right through to tomorrow morning and wake up feeling human again. Or, on the other hand, he could stay here watching Ms Thomas spilling Latin flower names picturesquely from her lips: a hitherto unknown turn-on. They were wrapping things up, he realised, snapping his mind to attention, and out of the fantasy of Hailey Thomas whispering into his ear.

'Ms Thomas,' he said, rather louder than he'd intended, and the four other people in the room all snapped their heads to look at him.

The woman he'd been addressing merely raised her eyebrows a fraction in response.

'I was wondering if you'd allow me to take you to dinner,' he said, the first idea that popped into his head. 'As an apology for my lapse in manners.'

She stared at him for a moment, her eyes appraising. 'Wouldn't you rather go to bed?' she asked, and for just a moment the room was in perfect silence as they all absorbed what she'd just said, and then all started speaking at once.

'Well, of course I considered that too, but—'

'Gio!' Seb cut in.

'I… I meant…' Hailey stuttered. 'I meant jet lag! Because you *yawned*—'

She stared at him as they all paused in the heavy, uncomfortable atmosphere. 'Thank you, I'd be delighted,' she said at last in a frostily professional voice, and then snapped her notebook closed and turned on her heel to address Ivy, Seb and Alexandra. 'Ms Jenkins, Mr Davis, it's been a pleasure. Please let me know if you have any more questions; otherwise, I'll see you just before the big day.'

She turned, more slowly, to him. 'Mr… I mean, Your Royal…' She trailed off, and he realised they hadn't even been properly introduced.

'Gio,' he said quickly, wanting to slice through the formalities. 'I'm Gio to my friends.'

'Gio, then. I'll meet you in the lobby of your hotel at eight.'

He nodded. 'I'm staying at the Ritz-Carlton.'

And with that Hailey swept from the room and left everyone in it—himself very much included—more than a little in love with her. If only he had the sort of life where falling just a little bit in love with someone made a blind bit of difference to his future, he might have been a little excited.

CHAPTER TWO

WHAT THE HELL had she just agreed to? And why? Dinner with a prince? In public—because there was no way that she was meeting up with him in private after both of them seemed to have lost their wits in that meeting with Sebastian, Ivy and Alexandra.

This was going to be a nightmare. She had already embarrassed herself spectacularly—there was no good reason to give herself the opportunity to make things worse. Well, she supposed things *couldn't* get much worse than accidentally propositioning him.

She took a moment to wonder how accidental that had actually been. Because, while of course she didn't mean to suggest that they should go to bed together in front of her clients—his friends—she would be lying if the thought hadn't been there in her mind and then just slightly…escaped. She couldn't help but wonder either what exactly his reaction would have been if she *had* propositioned him. If, for the sake of argument, they had been alone in the room and able to explore that idea properly.

She shook her head. That was never going to happen. She wasn't in the habit of going around propositioning princes of tiny European countries she'd barely heard of, and she wasn't going to make a start now. It didn't take a genius to see that that could lead to nothing but complication and heartache. She had had a simple start in life, had already reinvented herself once with her big transatlantic move, and the last thing that her life needed was another sphere where she didn't belong.

But it was one dinner—she was hardly signing herself up for a lifetime of public appearances. All she had to do was eat one meal, accept his apology for yawning— *yawning*—while she was trying to pin down the details of the trim for Ivy's bouquet, and that would be that. She'd never have to see him again, not unless he sought her out to go through the arrangements for the flowers the weekend of the wedding, and she somehow predicted that that wouldn't be high on his list of priorities.

Hailey strode into the hotel lobby at a minute past eight, determined not to be caught fidgeting or awkwardly waiting for Gio. If he wasn't here, she'd simply turn around and walk out again. One chance—that was all he was getting. And half a dozen times in the past few hours she had decided that she wouldn't even give him that. She would have cancelled, had he not been a friend of her clients. This job was the biggest of her career, and she wasn't going to risk upsetting the bride and groom by standing up the best man.

Of course he was there. Because the sight of him unnerved her—and it seemed he could always be counted on to unsettle her as much as possible. He did it on purpose, she was sure. She couldn't explain *why* she was so sure. It was only that…surely no one could have this much of an effect on her by *accident*, simply by existing in proximity to her.

She saw the moment that he spotted her across the room and tried not to read anything into the gleam in his eye. It was just a flicker of light. There was nothing to interpret there. This dinner was just as he had said: a formality to excuse his lapse in manners when he'd yawned during their meeting. He wasn't…interested in her. That much was made clear in the collective mortification and embarrassment in the room following her gaffe about him going to bed.

He was a prince—and she didn't belong in his world any more than he belonged in hers of 4:00 a.m. flower markets, thermal base layers and hands chapped from bleaching buckets in the cold. With Ivy and Sebastian, her place and her role were clear. She was the hired help. And she was comfortable and secure knowing that. But this development was throwing that security on its head and leaving her uncomfortably adrift. She hated that feeling. Had run from it, all the way from West London suburbia to New York.

Because, strangely, so far from home, she knew that she *shouldn't* belong. After a childhood spent moving from family to family, children's home to children's home, she had tried over and over again to feel as if she was a part of something. As if she truly belonged with the family she had been placed with this time. And she'd smiled and tried so hard to be good. It had been exhausting, and it had never worked, so that by the time the revolving door of foster homes had stopped—and she had finally been adopted by a kind, loving couple who had tried everything to make her feel a part of their family—she was beyond it. Perhaps, when her birth parents had given her away, it had severed any chance that she would feel entitled to have a link to any place, any people, that would be hers.

New York had been such a relief. A place where she was declared a misfit by the stamp in her passport.

Where she didn't have to try and belong any more. She could just be herself in a city filled with misfits. And so she had relaxed into it. Into her art history studies, for which she had moved halfway across the world. Into her talent for floristry, which she had discovered when a part-time job had overlapped with her art course and created something quite magical. And marketable. And in her boss, Gracie, she had made a dear friend, who felt more like a mother than the circus of people who had played a part in her childhood.

She wouldn't fit into Gio's world, but that didn't matter for the space of a dinner. She'd had plenty of practice not belonging. It was only a night, and she did know how to be a tourist.

'You came,' Gio said, greeting her with a dazzling smile and a kiss to both cheeks.

'I thought that was the general idea,' she said, raising her eyebrows a fraction and stepping half a pace back. Preserving her personal space. Because standing too close to Gio had an effect on her that she didn't want to think too much about. The sort of dizzying, pulse-racing, thought-distracting effect that made it hard to remember not to be swept away by those Mediterranean good looks and impeccable manners, no doubt polished at a finishing school somewhere—or whatever wood-panelled, cigar-smoke-fugged, whisky-soaked men's club princes were sent to, rather than a school that taught young ladies how to get out of cars without flashing their knickers.

At least, that was what she assumed royalty did. Her upbringing hadn't exactly given her a great view of the curriculum of European finishing schools.

'Well, I'm delighted to see you,' he said, smoothing

over her prickliness. 'I booked a table at the restaurant here. If that suits.'

Dinner at the Ritz-Carlton, and Prince Charming for company? She supposed it suited.

He offered his arm as a formal invitation to accompany him and she took it, momentarily dizzy at the feeling that she was walking into someone else's life. She shook it off, as she had so many times before.

'Your displays this afternoon were very beautiful,' Gio said as they were seated, and the eye-roll escaped her before she could help it. 'You don't believe me?' he asked, raising an eyebrow, the corner of his mouth turning up in a smile.

'Oh, I think you made your feelings very clear.'

'Ah. The Yawn.'

'The Yawn.' She smiled despite herself, because the abashed look on his face was anything but princely. 'But you gave me the gift of your company by way of apology, so how can I possibly be cross?'

His eyes widened. 'Why is it that every word you speak gives me the impression that you mean the exact opposite?' Gio asked as a waiter arrived with a bottle of champagne that he must have ordered in advance and poured two glasses.

She suppressed a smile because this evening was already proving more enjoyable than she had imagined it might, and the surprise threatened to throw her off-guard. It seemed as if there was a chance that Prince Giovanni of Adria was more than just a pretty face: he could make her laugh too, and wasn't that a dangerous combination...

'Well, if we're not going to discuss your work—'

'And you don't work,' Hailey cut in without thinking, the words slipping from her lips as she concentrated on her menu. She looked up as soon as she realised what she'd said, her lips a small O of surprise.

Gio was grinning at her, and the sight made her stomach flip. He smiled with his whole face. Not just the curl of a lip or a crinkle at the corner of his eyes. She was talking wide smile, dimples, deep crow's feet. *Twinkling* eyes. The whole works. So bright that she suspected that some of it was reflected in her own face.

And she knew she was in so much trouble.

His cheeks hurt. Which was the strangest way to measure the success of a date, but there they were. Three hours into dinner with Hailey Thomas and he had spent every moment of it absolutely delighted. She made him laugh with everything she did. Everything she said. She made him smile most when she was actively trying to annoy him, which had been her default setting for the first half hour or so, until she had seen how much it had amused him and she'd reined in her claws and conceded that she wasn't going to get a rise out of him.

They'd quickly run out of small talk about the wedding and Ivy and Sebastian, and she'd seemed averse to talking about her life. So he'd answered her questions about Adria, told her of its sparkling lakes in the summer and ski resorts in the winter, how they spent early December at the ski lodge in the mountains, before returning to the palace for Christmas. How his father had fought to keep its independence. He'd asked her what he should see while he was in New York, and she'd answered with the names of parks and galleries he'd never heard of.

And the teasing and the eye-rolling and the gentle laughter between them had felt so *easy*, so natural, that he could let himself pretend for a minute. Pretend the fact that he was halfway besotted with Hailey actually mattered outside of this moment. That anyone in the palace, in the entire kingdom of Adria at all, cared about whether this was a good date or a bad date, for that matter.

Any feelings he had for another person would always come second to the demands of his family. His position. His parents would select a bride who would strengthen Adria's place in Europe, and the best that he could hope for was that it wasn't someone he hated on sight. That it wasn't someone he would come to hate. At the very least, he had to hope he would be happier than his parents, who had despised one another for as long as he could remember.

He shook his head—the last thing he should be thinking about was the myriad ways his parents had conspired to make one another miserable. No. Right now he was only interested in Hailey. And—if he was reading this situation right—all the ways they might be able to make each other happy. Just for tonight.

She was here, for a start. Sending him interested, heated glances any time she thought that he wasn't looking. It was amazing, the things she could do to him with just a flicker of her eyes caught in his peripheral vision. He leaned forward, resting his elbows on the edge of the table, trying to follow the movement of her hands as she told him about the first time that she had visited a flower market.

She used at least a dozen words he had never heard before. At least a dozen more in Latin, and he wanted to ask her what each and every one of them meant. Wanted to watch the plump curve of her lips as she explained them to him. He imagined trying to make her come apart as she did so. How he would tease her while she explained the different varieties to him. She would fight hard to keep her head, not to lose control and give in to the pleasure. She'd resist out of principle, wanting to be the one in command, and he would savour every loosening bond until she was incoherent and coming against his mouth.

He realised he had lost the thread of conversation when she cleared her throat.

'Am I boring you?' she asked him, her eyebrows raised in challenge. 'Again?'

'Not at all. I just find myself momentarily distracted.'

'By?' Hailey asked, with an arched eyebrow to accompany that single word that suggested she knew exactly the direction his thoughts had taken.

'By you.'

'Ah.' She stared at him for a moment, seemed to be considering her options. 'What was I doing?' she asked sweetly.

'I don't think it's wise to tell you,' he said honestly, feeling suddenly flushed. Like a schoolboy who'd been caught doing something he shouldn't.

'I think I like distracting you,' Hailey said, sitting back in her chair and taking a sip of wine, fixing him with an assessing glare.

'I think I like it when you look at me like that,' Gio said in a low voice. Her gaze stripped him bare. Bare of his skin, as if she could see every one of his secrets. He had no doubt that he could keep nothing from her if he allowed her into his life. So thank goodness he was safe in the knowledge that he could give her no more than a night. If she wanted even that from him.

'I like looking at you,' she admitted, this time not darting her gaze away.

'Hailey—' He realised he didn't know what to say

to her. How to ask for what he wanted, but not all of it. That he wanted tonight, and if things had been different he would probably want many nights after that, but that wasn't his to offer.

'Do you want to go upstairs?' she asked.

He was undoubtedly the most beautiful man she had seen in her life. She had suspected it that afternoon, when he had been stubbled and crumpled and jet-lagged, yawning through their meeting. In a clean shirt, freshly shaved, hair swept back off his forehead, he was devastating. And looking at her as if she were dessert.

She didn't have the chance to bed a living god very often. It seemed churlish to turn down the opportunity when it presented itself. When she'd been telling him the names of the flowers she had seen at her first flower market, his eyes had burned with intensity as she'd named more and more obscure specimens, exaggerating the shape of her lips around the long, twisting words. He could be a gift to herself, she reasoned. A little bonus for landing the biggest job of her career. For making a life for herself here in New York. She could play fairy tale princess with this beautiful man just for one night, knowing that was all it was. He could hardly be free to date a glorified flower seller, so there was no risk in taking what she wanted, just this once.

But he hadn't answered her. She looked across and felt the first pang of doubt. Had she misread this entirely, and he didn't want her after all?

Until he spluttered, 'Yes,' and stood abruptly.

She laughed into her wine. 'I didn't mean right this second.'

But he held his hand out to her. 'What's wrong with

right this second?' he asked, and Hailey had to concede that he'd made a very good point.

She calmly set down her wine, pushed back her chair and stood. 'Lead the way then. We can order dessert upstairs.'

It was still dark when Hailey woke and eased out of Gio's arms, desperately tempted to stay under the blankets with him and say a proper goodbye. But she had to be at her workshop by seven or her team would have to condition that morning's delivery of flowers by themselves, and she'd always sworn to be the sort of boss who remembered how to roll up her sleeves and do even the least glamorous jobs herself.

Gio blinked sleepily a couple of times as she pulled on underwear and searched the suite for her clothes. 'Are you leaving?' he asked, his voice rough from lack of sleep as he levered himself up in bed and rested back against a heap of crumpled pillows.

Hailey smiled and crossed back to the bed, giving in and allowing herself to be pulled back down beside him, moaning lightly when his hands slipped into her hair and he pressed a gentle kiss to her lips.

'Good morning,' she said softly, between kisses. 'Sorry, I was trying not to disturb you. I have to get to work.'

'I don't mind you disturbing me like this,' Gio said, his hands sliding up her thighs. She smiled, not sure whether she should be more happy or sad that Gio had turned out to be an absolute sweetheart, who she wouldn't ever see again.

'Mmm…' she agreed, before pulling herself away again. 'But any more of that and I'm going to end up being late.' She glanced at her watch. 'Later than I already am. I'm going to have to go back to my place and change,' she observed, zipping up the black shift dress that she had worn to dinner last night.

'Here,' Gio said, snagging his shirt from the floor by the bed. 'How much time does it buy me if you wear this?' he asked. Hailey rolled her eyes but smiled as she pushed her arms into the sleeves and tried to roll up the cuffs, giving her wrists up to Gio to finish the job when he tugged at her hands.

'Find me something warm to wear over the top and you've got yourself twenty minutes,' she told him as he rolled the second one into place, only half joking. But Gio seemed to take it as a challenge. He kissed her hard once, and then disappeared into the walk-in closet.

'What are you doing?' she called out to him, resenting the fact that he was spending the last few minutes they had together separated by a door, rather than carrying on kissing her. She was on her way to tell him that when he emerged from the closet with an ice-blue sweater that looked so soft it had to be cashmere. He held it out to her and she hesitated for a moment before taking it. A swiped shirt was one thing—a classic walk of shame move. But this…this felt too much like a gift. Too intimate. But Gio slipped his fingers between the buttons of his shirt that she was wearing and pulled her to him. She looked up as he slipped the sweater over her head and tweaked the collar out of the neckline.

She pushed her arms in and pulled the body down— it slouched over one shoulder and hit mid-thigh—fitting better than any sweater dress she'd worn before. 'I can't take this,' she told him softly, rubbing the hem between thumb and finger. It was just as soft as she had imagined, and must have been more expensive than anything she owned.

For a moment, standing there in his clothes, enveloped in his scent, the morning light creeping through the window hitting cheekbones and jaw and early morning stubble all just right, she wished—just for a moment—that this could be the start of something. That she could promise to return his sweater that night, the perfect excuse to see him again. And at the same time she knew that she absolutely could not do that. She didn't belong in his world any more than he did in hers, and she was kidding herself if she thought that things could ever be any different.

'It's a gift,' Gio said, tilting her chin up so that she met his eyes. 'Looks better on you than it does on me anyway,' he said, giving her such a boyish grin that she couldn't help the chuckle that escaped her.

'Fine then,' she said. 'You've got yourself twenty minutes. What are you going to do with them?'

CHAPTER THREE

It WAS STUPID to be awkward, after everything, Hailey told herself as she stood outside the door to Gio's hotel suite two months later. She'd had to send a very awkward text to Alexandra, Sebastian and Ivy's wedding planner, to confirm that Gio was staying in the same suite as the last time he'd been in town. Knocking on the door couldn't possibly be any worse than that, she told herself. After all, things hadn't been awkward when she and Gio had parted after the night they'd spent together. Far from it: they'd exchanged kisses but not phone numbers, both sleep-deprived but deeply satisfied, with no plans to see each other again, except in a strictly professional capacity.

And that was exactly how things would have stayed, if she didn't have this one, fairly important, piece of news to share with him. She should really knock on the door. The wedding was in three days, and she had no idea how long he would be in town after that. She needed to tell Gio face to face, before he left and she never saw him again.

She lifted her hand and rapped her knuckles on the wood before she could change her mind. As she waited for him to answer, she steeled herself for the surprise she'd see on his face. It had been so obvious to them both that they could be nothing more than a one-night stand that they'd never even felt the need to spell it out. And now she was showing up on his doorstep with news that would change his life. One way or another.

She knew how that felt—the experience was still raw. It had been only ten days since she had taken the pregnancy test, after a mad scramble back through her diary had shown her she'd missed not one but two periods since that night with Gio. She'd been so busy with all the preparations for Ivy and Sebastian's wedding that she hadn't even noticed.

Ten days was not enough time for the shock to fade. Not enough time to prepare herself for this conversation. But she'd seen the schedule for the wedding party between now and the big day, and there wasn't a minute free after this morning. And the news that you were going to be a father needed more than a minute to process. It needed more than ten days—she could attest to that— but she would take what she could get. He was going to take this badly, she knew, but she'd deal with that when the time came.

She rapped on the door of his suite a second time and could barely take a breath while she waited for him to answer. She wasn't even sure what she would do if he wasn't there. If someone else answered the door. If he had company. At least she knew he didn't have a date for the wedding—not that she'd looked at the guest list *just* to check that fact.

But he answered the door before she could have second thoughts and it was as if they had been cast back two months in time to that first afternoon they had met, when he had been rumpled and jet-lagged. This time he was barefoot and still had the creases from his pillow on his cheek, and he looked so…soft that she wanted to reach out and touch him.

But she mustn't. Because this situation was going to be difficult enough to negotiate without letting sex get in the way of things. Again. Nothing about their relationship had changed. Apart from the fact that they were having a child together. She had considered whether continuing with the pregnancy was the right choice, but after being abandoned as a baby by parents who didn't want her she couldn't imagine doing anything but meeting her baby with love and devotion.

She didn't expect Gio to feel the same way.

She didn't have to be told that a prince didn't get free choice over his life. And that an illegitimate child conceived during a one-night stand was the sort of thing that one covered up rather than celebrated. But he was the baby's father and it wasn't her place to make that decision for him, just to brace herself for it when it came and devote herself to loving her baby so much that it would never feel the lack of its other parent.

Gio's eyes widened as he rubbed sleep out of them with the heel of one hand. 'Hailey? What are you—?'

He seemed to remember those impeccable manners of his and pulled himself more upright before standing to one side, gesturing into the room with one arm.

'Come in, please. This is a pleasant surprise,' he lied, a polite, false smile on his face. He obviously thought that she was here to pick up where they had left off. Which under other circumstances would be somewhat mortifying. But, as it happened, was just… Yes. Still mortifying. She straightened her spine and walked into his suite.

'So, Hailey, to what do I owe the—?'

She turned to look at him, standing in front of the door that he'd just closed behind her, and she took a moment to feel sympathy for him. Standing there in all innocence, with no idea of what was coming, thinking that this was just an awkward encounter with a ghost who hadn't understand his very clear message about their lack of future.

'I'm pregnant,' she blurted. She had planned to lead into it a little more gently, but he was looking at her as if he was preparing himself to put her out of her misery, and she couldn't bear to be the subject of his pity. Not even for a moment.

'You...' His stance was suddenly rigid, his body a stiff line in front of the door. 'You're pregnant?' he asked, and she nodded, giving him a moment to process the news.

'With my baby?' Fair question—he barely knew her. Had no reason to know that he was the only man she had been with in the last half a year, never mind in the last two months.

'Yes,' she said, holding her ground in front of the table in the lobby of the suite. The freesias were fresh, she noted out of habit, their scent familiar and comforting.

'I think we had better sit down,' Gio said, as shell-shocked as she had expected him to sound. She gave a sharp nod and followed him through to the sitting room, where she perched on the edge of an antique sofa, waiting for him to speak.

'This is a...surprise,' he said at last, and she couldn't help it, she laughed.

'For me too,' she offered, and for the first time a smile turned up the corner of his lips. It wasn't one of the grins that she'd basked in that night, a grin that used every facial muscle and left her somewhat dazzled. But it was something.

'How long have you known?' he asked.

'About a week and a half,' she said, her voice flat. 'I would have called, but I didn't have your number.'

'No. I suppose it's the sort of news one is meant to hear in person.' He nodded, and she wondered how much of this was sinking in and how much he was simply on autopilot. 'Thank you for telling me. I'm assuming you want to—'

'Keep it?' she interrupted, not wanting him to think that the alternative was on the cards. 'Yes, I do. I am. Of course, I understand that you probably don't want...'

'I do want,' he said, before she could outline exactly how she thought that he was going to let her down. And she was speechless with shock. He rubbed his face with his hands and there it was again, that sympathy for the fact that she was upending his world when he was jet-lagged and rumpled from sleep. If there was any good time to deliver news like this, this definitely wasn't it.

'I will be a father to the baby,' he said decisively, sitting on the sofa beside her and reaching out a hand, before seeming to change his mind and resting his fore-arms on his knees. 'Please do not doubt that.'

'I... I'm surprised,' she said, not thinking, and Gio narrowed his eyes at her.

'I didn't realise you thought so little of me.'

Hailey shook her head. 'I didn't. I don't,' she said, backtracking. 'I'm sorry for making assumptions. But in the circumstances...'

'What circumstances?'

There he went again, making her laugh when she had every intention of being serious. 'What circumstances? You mean apart from you being a prince, so not exactly the master of your own fate. You have obligations. You don't need to tell me that you're not free to... The baby was conceived during a one-night stand we had no in-tention of repeating. Oh, and we live on different con-tinents. Other than those circumstances, you mean?'

He smiled, and she fought against the dazzling effect,

knowing that those instincts weren't remotely helpful or relevant to this conversation.

'But we're going to have a baby,' Gio said, a touch of wonder making it through the shock in his voice.

She nodded, feeling slightly shell-shocked herself.

'We're having a baby,' she repeated, the first time that she'd said the words out loud. The first time the pregnancy had felt real.

'Then everything else comes second to that,' Gio said. 'Second to you, and the baby.' He reached for her hand, and this time she let him take it. 'We deal with this together,' he said, his voice low. 'We're a team now. A family.'

A family. He had wondered all his life what a family life would mean for him, and never once had he imagined this, that it would mean having a child with a partner he had chosen himself. Of course, they hadn't precisely chosen this. This was a wonderful accident that in an instant had changed the direction of his life. But he couldn't tell Hailey that. Couldn't tell her that having a baby with her undid all the plans that his parents had ever made for him. All the expectations that they had for his life. All the things that he was meant to do out of duty for his country, his family.

Well, everyone at the palace was simply going to have to come to terms with the fact that he wasn't going to be told how his life unfolded any more. He didn't know what the future looked like, but for the first time in his life he had the feeling that he could actually be the person who got to decide on its direction, and that was more than he had ever hoped for before.

'And are you well?' he asked Hailey, trying to remember that the fact that she was carrying his baby didn't change anything between the two of them. He had no right to expect that there would be any repeat of the night that had got them into this situation. Heaven knew she had made it clear enough the morning after that she didn't want to see him again, except in a professional capacity at the wedding. But surely a baby changed things? He had been equally sure that they would go their separate ways, no matter how often his thoughts had strayed in her direction in the weeks since they had been together.

So now what? His first thought had been that his parents couldn't force him into a marriage now—who would take him with an illegitimate child in tow, complicating the succession as well as his private life? His brain caught on the word illegitimate. A bastard child would be shunned by his family, would have no claim to a part of its father's life.

He thought about that for a moment. How his life might have been different if he had been able to grow up away from the palace, and all the pressures it brought with it. And then he remembered the stark loneliness of his childhood—the feeling that he'd had every time his nanny had told him that his half hour with his parents was up and it was time to go to bed. He wouldn't do that to his child, leave them wondering whether their parents even loved him. He would make sure there was always a place in the palace for his child. That they always knew that they were loved. He wouldn't repeat his parents' mistakes.

'I'm fine, Gio,' Hailey said, and he remembered he had asked her that question. 'But are you?' Those pixie-like eyes were assessing him carefully, and he wondered how much the wounds of his childhood were on show.

'I'm fine,' he said automatically, because he wasn't

sure he had the vocabulary to tell her how he was really feeling. It was hard enough to understand, never mind explain, either in her language or his.

'I should give you some space,' Hailey said gently. 'It's a lot to take in, I know that. You probably need some time to get used to the idea.'

He nodded, because there was nothing that she had said that he could argue with. He could hardly gather his thoughts just now; there were too many of them, sprinting off in different directions.

'Let's talk tomorrow,' he said, because there was no way that he could wait longer than that to see her again.

'I've seen the schedule for tomorrow,' Hailey said, shaking her head. 'You can't possibly have the time.'

'I'll make time,' Gio said. 'This is more important. Tell me when is good for you and we can meet here.'

Hailey nodded and he breathed a sigh of relief; he hadn't realised until that moment that he'd been worried that she wouldn't agree to see him again.

Well, that could have gone worse, she supposed as she walked away from the hotel. He at least hadn't thrown her out of the room or refused to believe that the baby was his—or existed at all, all of which had crossed her mind. Turned out having a baby with a man you barely knew was full of unknowns, and it was hard to see where the next strike might be coming from.

But she had seen from the expression on Gio's face that he wasn't ready to talk about this yet—they had seven more months to get on top of the practicalities, so they could wait until tomorrow to start talking about it, if that was what he needed.

CHAPTER FOUR

GIO STRAIGHTENED THE cuffs of his shirt while he waited for Hailey to arrive. He had never felt this nervous before in his life but, then again, he had never had so much riding on the answer to one single question before either. His jet lag had kept him awake long into the night, and he'd had ample time to think in the silent small hours about how he could do right by both Hailey and their baby. And after following their choices through twisting labyrinths of possible futures it had become clear what he needed to do next.

He heard Hailey's efficient knock at the door—two sharp raps of her knuckle on the wood, and something deep in his stomach lurched with nerves. This was fine, he told himself. This was his choice. This hadn't been forced on him by Hailey, his family or anyone else. He wasn't trapped—he was choosing this for himself. If he told himself that often enough, maybe he'd even start to believe it. Because he might be choosing this *now*, but it was hardly a free choice, not now the baby was on the way. Without that complication, he'd chosen the exact opposite, walking away from Hailey and everything that she had made him feel. The melancholy he had felt, knowing that he could never live a life where he was in control of his destiny. Where he could make actual choices about his future, free from the constraints of his position.

'Come in, you look lovely,' Gio said as he answered the door to Hailey, remembering at the last moment that this was supposed to be a happy occasion. He'd added the compliment on autopilot, but as he said it he realised how true the words were. Her cheeks and lips were rosy pink, her hair framing her face in soft, shiny waves. And she glowed in the way he'd heard expectant mothers did, but had never actually seen for himself before.

'So, I suppose we have a lot to talk about,' Hailey said over her shoulder as they walked to the same sofa where she had sat yesterday. Hailey perched on the edge, her posture the very definition of composed. The whole scene couldn't be more different to the night that they had stumbled up here from the restaurant, when the only things that had landed on these seats were items of clothing tossed there en route to the bedroom.

Life would be so much easier if he could simply forget that night. If they could approach this impending co-parenting without all those memories muddying the water. But his brain had the unfortunate habit of throwing graphic memories at him at the most unhelpful moments. Like now, when he was meant to be proposing, and instead he was remembering the taste of the skin on Hailey's neck, warm and salty with perspiration.

'I appreciate that the distance is going to make things complicated, but I'm sure that we can work out a way for you to have regular visitation with the baby.'

'Visitation?' he asked, taken aback by Hailey seeming to already be half way through a conversation.

'Yes,' Hailey said, and he saw her composure falter for a second before she reined herself back in. 'Yesterday, you said that you wanted to be involved in the baby's life. Of course, if you've changed your mind...'

'I've not changed my mind,' Gio said quickly, because that was the furthest thing from what he wanted. 'I don't want to just "visit" my own child. I want... I want to marry you, Hailey. I want you to come back to Adria with me.'

She wasn't sure how long they sat there in silence while she sorted through the various warring thoughts clamouring in her brain. The idea that she should marry Gio was ridiculous, of course. For so many reasons that she couldn't just this second decide which of them she wanted to remind Gio of.

They lived continents apart.

He was a prince. She was a commoner.

It was meant to be a one-night stand.

They barely knew each other.

He was clearly acting out of some well-intentioned chivalry, which was admirable but not the recipe for a happy marriage. Not if he felt that he was being strong-armed into it.

'I don't want to,' she blurted out, a little more directly than she had intended. And she was surprised to see his face fall with disappointment. Did he actually want to do this?

Even if that was the case, it didn't make the idea any less absurd. You didn't marry someone you barely knew just because you'd got pregnant. This was the twenty-first century.

And yet. There was something so appealing about the thought. Nothing to do with the palace or the money. Or, God forbid, the interest from the press. No, it was the idea of them being a family—the type with two parents and a baby they desperately loved. All living together, all wanting to be together. She didn't want to be a princess, she didn't want to think about the implications of joining a family like Gio's, but she did want…that.

The problem was, she couldn't have one without the other.

'Gio, I'm sorry, that came out more bluntly than I'd intended. I only meant to say that I don't want to marry out of obligation. Or for convenience. I… The thought of being a proper family for this baby is incredibly tempting. And I'm touched that you would want that enough to propose. But let's be sensible. I don't fit into your world. I'm never going to fit into your world. It just makes more sense for us to go about our lives as before. I know that you will make time for the baby. I trust you to be a good father.'

Gio leaned forward, elbows resting on his knees. 'I want to be more than a good father,' he said. 'I want to be *there*. I don't want to miss any of it. And the only way to do that is to live together. I understand that you have a life here and I respect that. But if you come to Adria we can make opportunities for you there too. I can help with that, with connections. Or if you don't want to work you don't have to—or we'll divide our time between Adria and New York, until…until my obligations mean that I can't be so often out of the country. Just…think about it. Please?'

She thought about it for a second, her eyes fixed on his clasped hands. 'We could do all of that without being married,' she pointed out, and he dropped his head into his hands.

'But I have to marry,' he said, his voice muffled before he looked up and met her gaze. 'I've always known that. Discussions about who I would marry started before I could walk. My parents will be no less firm on the issue even if I have a baby with you. Adria will need a legitimate heir…'

'What, and I'm the brood mare? How flattering.'

'No, that's not what I mean at all. But my parents won't stop their pressure just because we have a child together. The thought of marrying for Adria has always been…'

She watched him search for the word, and felt a wave of sympathy for him.

'Challenging. The thought of having to do it while you and our child are treated differently would be unthinkable. But, given your condition, my parents can't object publicly to our marriage without causing a scandal. And if we are married they can't force me to marry anyone else.'

'Gio,' she said softly, reaching for his hand. 'No one can force you to get married.'

'No,' he agreed. 'But they can make their disapproval clear if I do not go along with their intentions.'

'And is their disapproval so important, if they don't care enough about your feelings to recognise that they are hurting you?'

'They're my family.'

She nodded. She'd never thought that she could feel sorry for a man raised in a palace but, from the sound of it, his childhood had created emotional wounds every bit as deep as the ones that she had been carrying.

It was all too much—too much to think about and too much decide while she was sitting here looking at him. This close, it was hard to know what she was thinking and feeling, never mind making a good decision about her future. Especially as it wasn't just *her* future at stake. She was a mother now, and she had to make the right decision for her baby too.

'I… I need to think about this, Gio. I didn't expect this.'

'You're pregnant with my baby and it never occurred to you that the sensible thing is to get married?'

'No.' She shook her head and sat up a little straighter. 'Because I don't live in the nineteenth century. I'm not some fallen woman you need to rescue.'

'No. But I'm a public figure with a country's reputation depending on my choices and my decisions.'

'Wow. An obligatory proposal. You do know how to make a girl feel special. So how does it work?' she asked. 'We smile for the cameras on our wedding day, then go to our separate wings of the palace while you discreetly smuggle a mistress in through the kitchens?'

'I would never…'

'Never? Really? Because, if not, you're making a lot of assumptions about what would be included in this marriage of convenience. How long do you normally go without—?'

'No one said anything about a marriage of convenience.'

His words fell into heavy silence.

'Of course you meant a marriage of convenience,' Hailey said, refusing to let her voice shake. 'You only asked me to marry you because I'm pregnant.'

'Yes,' he agreed. 'Of course that's true. But you're pregnant because…we had a connection. More than a physical connection, I mean. We spent the night together because we were enjoying each other's company at dinner. I just think that we should remember that, if we can. But, right now, we have to decide a few things. We need to think about how this will look to everyone,' he said, changing the subject. 'If we don't make a pitch for how this story is reported then someone else will. And they won't run it past us first.'

'Your family?'

'Perhaps. If we're lucky. Depends on how quickly they move and whether the press pick up on it from somewhere else first. Does anyone else know?'

'You're the first person I've told,' she said.

'Good.'

'Good?' Hailey stiffened. 'Good because you're going to be a father and you're happy that you're the first to know it? Or good because I haven't pre-emptively scuppered your public relations campaign?'

He sat up straighter, his tense posture mirroring her own. 'You're being naïve,' he told her.

'Excuse me?' Hailey spluttered, unable to believe he could accuse her of that. '*I'm* being naïve? You're the one who thinks that getting married is going to solve this, rather than making it a million times more complicated.'

Shaking his head, Gio said, 'I apologise. I shouldn't have said that.'

'If you're already thinking it,' Hailey said, 'whether you say it out loud or not is neither here nor there.'

Gio collapsed against the back of the sofa and ran a hand through his hair, leaving it more dishevelled than ever. 'I feel very much that we have got off on the wrong foot,' he said, his voice softer and more conciliatory than she had heard it before, and she cracked a little smile.

'*I* feel we got off very much on the right foot and that's what got us into this situation in the first place.'

Gio returned her smile and his face was transformed

by it, every muscle working to show her exactly what he was feeling.

'Yes. Well. That much is true, I'm sure,' he said.

'I'm flattered, Gio, that you think I could be a part of your world. But it wouldn't work. And I'm sorry that I can't accept your proposal.'

She watched him in silence for a moment, and then two, as her words struck home, and wished she could know what he was thinking. His feelings played out so clearly on his face when he was pleased; his smiles were illuminating in so many ways. But his other feelings were too well masked, too disguised for her to be able to interpret them.

'I think, Hailey, that whether you accept my proposal or not, you're a part of my world now. You're the mother of my child and that makes you family. And, while I wouldn't wish my family on anyone, here we are. Of course you need time, I understand that. But I'm not sure how much we have to work with. I fly back to Adria the day after the wedding.'

'That's three days,' she reminded him. 'We can't make a decision like that in three days.'

'Then come to Adria,' he protested. 'Spend some time with me. See how things are if we get to know each other. At least give it a chance before you rule it out completely.'

'What are you thinking?' he asked after a long silence, and she wondered what was showing on her face.

She took a deep breath. 'I was just thinking…it would be nice for the baby, you know. A nuclear family. I wish that was something that we could give him. Or her.'

Gio grimaced, the expression so different from one of his smiles. 'You've not met my parents. There's not a lot in my experience to recommend the nuclear family.'

'Yes, well, I can only attest to the opposite, and that didn't have much going for it either.'

She stood abruptly, not wanting to delve into her family history with Gio as a witness, and aware that she had already said too much.

Gio stood, following her, and the action brought his body to within a stride of hers. It would be so easy, so comforting, to take that step and rest her head on his chest. She could accept his proposal and ignore the fact that it was just for show and give her baby the family life that she had never had. Or maybe he would take a step towards her and take the decision out of her hands.

'Hailey, I've upset you. I apologise,' he said, not coming any closer.

She shook her head and fought to regain her composure. 'No, you haven't. I just need to go. I have a lot to do for the wedding.'

Gio reached out a hand and brushed it, just briefly, against her elbow. 'We need to talk again.'

She nodded. 'We will. Of course. Let's just take a couple of days to gather our thoughts. Decide what we want.'

'And in the meantime—'

'I know. Don't tell anyone.'

'No. That's not what I was going to say.' And he took just half a step. Coming too close, but not close enough. Standing near enough to her that she had to tip her head back to look him in the eye, but not offering the oblivion of burying her face into his body to block out the rest of the world. 'In the meantime, if you need anything... if you're not well or you need to talk. *Anything*, Hailey, promise me that you will call me.'

He pulled out a card from the inside pocket of his jacket, scribbled a phone number on the back and passed it to her. 'We're together in this, okay? I don't want you to question that, whatever happens. I am truly delighted by this news. I hope you know that, however complicated it may feel at this moment.'

Delighted. Such a word, and he was; it showed in every muscle on his face. She wondered if that smile would ever not dazzle her. Would her—their—baby inherit that smile? She could imagine a very spoiled child in her future if it did.

'I'm happy that you are. And I am too.' She smiled back at him, though it was a poor reflection of his.

Hailey watched from a shadowy corner at the back of the ballroom as Gio gave his toast to the happy couple. She should probably have left already—once she had checked that the table centrepieces were perfect, there was nothing flower-related left for her to do. And yet here she was, watching Gio and the rest of the wedding party, surrounded by fairy lights and her beautiful flowers and the shimmering Christmas decorations that had transformed the room into a fairy tale, and she couldn't walk away.

Parker and Parker had been at the top of her list of dream venues to work with since she'd heard that it would be hosting weddings, and it was decorated beautifully for Christmas. From the towering trees, dusted with snow and strung with ice-white lights, that lined the steps up to the entrance of the building, to the crystal chandeliers in the grand foyer, garlanded with pine and white poinsettias, and branches strung with lights, like stars seen through the arms of bare winter trees, every inch of it had been transformed into an opulent Christmas fantasy.

The elegant design of every aspect of the day tied together perfectly, from the hand-tied, lace-trimmed bouquets that Hailey had passed to Ivy and her brides-maids that morning, to the towering arrangements in the ballroom and the carefully designed centrepieces for the tables, which added texture and drama without getting in the way of the conversation the room now hummed with.

The bride swept through the crowd in her floor-length white gown, bewitching everyone who looked in her direction. Not least of whom her groom, with his immaculate tuxedo and besotted expression. They held the attention of every person present. Except Hailey, who had spent half her afternoon watching out for Gio and the other half chastising herself for doing so.

But when Gio stood up to give his toast and the eyes of the whole room fell on him, she gave herself permission to fall in with the crowd. To look properly at him, just for a few minutes. And once he started speaking she couldn't help but wonder what he might say on their wedding day, if she accepted his proposal. Certainly he wouldn't be speaking about love, as he was able to about the couple beside him, who were looking at each other adoringly.

Perhaps he would mention duty or obligation. Family and country.

And she had to stop a sigh escaping, knowing that their marriage could only ever be a shadow of the happiness that she had witnessed today.

Hailey finally sank into bed at midnight, with tired feet and an aching back, and it felt as if she had barely closed her eyes when she heard a rap on the door. She glanced at the clock beside the bed. It was somehow six in the morning. She shook her head, trying to shake the fatigue that seemed to have settled into her bones this week. She stumbled to the door and opened it a crack, realising too late that she was wearing an oversized man's shirt that barely skimmed her thighs.

'Gio?' she asked, confused, as she took in the sight of him on the other side of the door. 'It's six in the morning.' Either it was six in the morning and a crown prince really was standing outside her front door or she was dreaming. The dreaming seemed so much more likely, but the gust of cold air on her legs felt all too real.

'I'm sorry,' Gio said. 'Jet lag. I thought I would have heard from you before now and I was going a little crazy. We have so little time. I fly back to Adria tonight and couldn't go without knowing…'

'I've been so busy…' she said, as if that was the real reason she hadn't been in touch.

'I know.' Gio nodded. 'I understand. But I have to get on that plane tonight and I can't bear the thought of doing that without more certainty. I want you to come with me. Just…will you come for a walk with me? I brought coffee. There's regular or decaf. I didn't know which you want.'

'At six in the morning? You can keep your decaf.'

'Understood. Please, I think it might snow. I've been here four days and haven't seen anything of the city. Will you show it to me?'

She glanced past him up and down the street, to make sure they were alone. 'You should come in. I'll get dressed.'

'I'll wait here. Give you some privacy.'

'And have someone see you hanging outside my apartment? I don't think so. Come in. But turn your back.'

She tugged the hem of her shirt down, hoping that he wouldn't notice it was the one he had given her, which had somehow become her regular nightshirt, as she opened the door a fraction wider and took the coffees from him.

'You know, I think I'll need both of these,' she said as a waft of coffee reached her.

'Maybe we should do this later,' Gio said, hesitating on the threshold.

'You already woke me. I'll never get back to sleep. The least you can do is entertain me.'

She disappeared into her bedroom and returned wearing jeans that wouldn't quite button—for a very obvious reason—and swathed in layers, more than ready for anything that a New York winter could throw at her—the snow had been coming down heavily when she'd gone to bed last night—because what she was wearing was something that she could control.

Hat, scarf, mittens? Check. Decisions about her future with the father of her child? No idea what she was doing.

From the corner of her eye she caught Gio smiling at her and threw him a look. 'What?' she asked.

'Nothing. You're just…' She raised an eyebrow, waiting. 'I feel like there might be a strong reaction if I say adorable,' Gio went on hesitantly.

'There will be a violent reaction if you say adorable,' she confirmed, tossing cushions and looking for her phone before finding it plugged into her charger, right where she'd left it the night before.

Gio took a step towards her as she slipped her phone into her pocket, and when she looked up he was close— very close. She craned her neck to look up at him.

'You are very…little,' he said with a quirk of his lips, tucking a strand of hair behind her ear. 'I could just pick you up and…'

She took a step backwards, raising her eyebrows at him. 'Too complicated,' she said firmly. 'I can't think and make decisions if you're saying things like that. If you're looking at me like that.'

Gio shook his head, taking a step away too. 'I'm sorry. I wasn't thinking. You're right. That would be very complicated indeed.'

She agreed, trying to convince herself as much as him. 'If we're going to get married, I don't know if I can handle any more complications on top of that just now.'

'*If* we're going to get married?' he asked, and she couldn't decide if he sounded more shocked or hopeful.

She pulled the door to the apartment building open and gasped as the cold air from outside hit her. A flurry of snow blew into the hallway before she managed to pull the door closed. She took one of the coffees from Gio and warmed her hands around the cup as she crunched through a pile of ice on the sidewalk, carefully watching where she was putting her feet. If she looked at Gio directly, she wasn't going to be able to do this.

'Yes. I want this baby to know its family,' she said. 'To be a part of it. Properly. And if family means parents who are married to each other then that's what is going to happen.'

She had gone round and round in circles, trying to think of a way to give her baby everything that she had missed out on in her childhood, and hadn't been able to come up with anything other than this—marry Gio, give her baby what it deserved and worry about her own feelings for the father at some unspecified point in the future, which she was sure would be simpler and provide more opportunity for introspection. Surely, visiting the country of which the father of your unborn baby was Crown Prince would provide ample opportunity for quiet contemplation.

They stopped to cross the road and she had to squint through the snow to see the light on the other side of the crossing. Gio's hand came to rest on her elbow and she fought down her instinct to shake him off, reasoning that it was sensible to accept help when she was walking through snow in the dark.

Pulling her hat lower on her head, she led him through the park on the corner of her street, with its railings lined with fairy lights, bows hanging from the lamp-posts and a towering Christmas tree in the centre.

They walked in thoughtful silence through the quiet early-morning streets, only stopping to admire an illuminated courtyard in the narrow space between two buildings which had been decorated with multicoloured strings of lights and an illuminated wreath on the gates.

'I'll need some time to pack,' Hailey said quietly as they stood at the railings and took in the festive display. 'And I'll probably have to run to a store for a few things, depending on how long we'll be staying. Oh, I have an appointment scheduled with an ob-gyn next week.'

Gio turned to look at her, his hand slipping from her elbow to her hand, and she forced herself to take a step away.

'Of course,' Gio said. 'I need to fly out tonight. You can take all the time you want. But anything you need I can arrange for you in Adria, including a doctor, if you wish. I don't want you to be…inconvenienced.'

A laugh burst out of her. 'Inconvenienced?' she said, her voice bordering on wild. 'You got me *pregnant*, Gio,' she said, still trying to get her breath back because she was laughing so hard. 'You don't want to inconvenience me?' she repeated, wheezing with laughter.

Gio stepped in front of her and crossed his arms, staring down at her. 'You're laughing at me.'

'I'm not, I'm not,' Hailey said, trying to get her breathing—and her laughter—under control. 'I'm laughing at the situation. It's absurd. You said it yourself. And tonight we're going to get on a plane and nothing is ever going to be the same. How do we do this? Will we see your family tonight? Go straight to the palace?'

Gio thought about it for a moment. 'Yes,' he replied eventually. 'If you agree. We should tell them as soon as possible and I want to do it in person.'

Hailey nodded and Gio reached for her hand, brushing the back of it with his thumb before pulling away. He took a deep breath and forced it out through his teeth. 'They're going to be angry,' he said, and her stomach lurched even as she was grateful for his honesty. 'Don't misunderstand me; they will be unfailingly polite to you. It's me they'll be disappointed with. But they won't let anyone else see that.'

'I'm not worried about how they are with me,' Hailey said, feeling brave. 'They're nothing to me, to be perfectly honest. I've never been interested in their opinion of me before, and I haven't heard anything that makes me think their good opinion is worth having. It's not me I'm worried about. It's you.'

'You don't have to worry about me,' Gio said as they turned and walked on, and he forced a smile that was almost painfully lacklustre. They had reached Twenty-Eighth Street and Hailey couldn't help but be happy to be around the familiar sounds and scents of the flower district. She felt more at home in this short stretch of New York City than in any home she'd ever occupied in the UK. Every time she walked these sidewalks, she knew exactly who she was and what she wanted for her life. Except now, with Gio beside her, all those old certainties were gone.

'I might not have to worry, but I'm going to anyway,' Hailey said, sidestepping around a pile of planters and pots, forcing her closer to Gio's side. She made her voice soft, despite the anger that she felt. 'Because, frankly, it sounds like your parents are cruel.'

Gio shook his head. 'They're not cruel.'

She felt her heart ache for him a little, that he could be treated so badly by the people who were meant to love him the most and not even recognise how much they were hurting him. 'You're scared to tell them that you're having a baby,' she told him gently. 'That doesn't sound like a loving and supportive relationship.'

'There's a difference between difficult and cruel.'

'Making you doubt that they care about you is cruel,' she told him. 'I've barely known you five minutes and I already know you would never treat our child like that, no matter the circumstances.'

'I'm glad you know that,' Gio said, stopping to let the fronds of a fern slip through his fingers, knocking away the flakes of snow they had been collecting. 'I know that this is unconventional,' he said. 'And I'm sure that there are a thousand reasons why we should be second-guessing ourselves. So really it's remarkable just how happy I am about this baby. Please try and remember that when we're in the midst of family politics.'

Family politics. Unfortunately, in his family, family politics tended to stumble into the arena of fragile international diplomacy, which he suspected he'd just thrown a brick through.

And his parents were going to treat him like a wayward ambassador rather than a cherished son who was delighting them with news of their first grandchild. He'd spent his whole life being treated as a slightly disappointing subject and was well able to handle it, but it wasn't fair to expect Hailey to have to put up with their nonsense. His parents had perfected the art of freezing someone out without ever, for a moment, breaching the rules of polite conversation. He would protect Hailey from it the best he could because he hadn't forgotten what she'd said about her own family, and how the lack of one had caused her pain. He knew that she was coming into this situation with scars of her own, and he wasn't going to let his parents hurt her.

CHAPTER FIVE

'So this is your world,' Gio said, looking around the market. It was still snowing, though more lightly now, and flakes were catching in his hair and eyelashes. Prince Giovanni in the snow. It would be a fairy tale if there wasn't so much of her real life at stake.

He'd visited her in her workshop near here the first time she'd met him, but that had been late afternoon, which might as well have been the middle of the night as far as the early risers at the flower market were concerned. The stalls and stores had been practically deserted then, rather than how she loved them, how they were now, packed with people and flowers and foliage.

'This has been home, really,' she said, picking the stems of fern he'd been fingering from the bucket, adding some seeded eucalyptus, myrtle and cascading maidenhair fern into a tumbling bouquet of greenery. The store owner emerged from the building and handed her a length of twine with a raised eyebrow but without asking questions, and she wrapped it around the stems, fingers working with muscle memory, even through knitted mittens. She paid and thanked the store owner and then handed the bouquet to Gio, trying not to think too hard about what she was doing. For a moment, he just stared at her.

'I don't think anyone has ever given me flowers before,' he said, looking between the tied bundle and her face, a little dazed.

'Technically, it's just foliage,' Hailey said, deflecting. 'And you have good taste,' she added, feeling her cheeks pinken up. 'These ferns are lovely. Call it an engagement present.'

He almost stumbled at that, and she had to laugh softly as she grabbed his elbow. 'Having second thoughts?' she asked, not entirely sure that she was joking.

'No, absolutely not. It just reminded me, I wanted to talk to you. About a ring.'

She stopped and turned to him, her feet suddenly taking root. 'Oh, you don't have to… I wasn't hinting…'

'I didn't think for a second that you were,' Gio said, smoothing over her stumbling words. 'I really *have* been wanting to talk to you about it but I didn't want to press you. It's tradition to choose a family piece for the engagement ring. But I don't want to—'

'No, you're right, of course. This isn't even real. It wouldn't be appropriate—'

'Hailey. Stop. Please. Let me finish. Of course this is real. It may not be entirely conventional—though, given the history of European royal families, I rather think that the statistics might be on our side. We are the ones who decide what "real" looks like for us. I only brought it up because I want you to be able to choose. I don't want to stick you with some antique if it's not what you want. We could choose something new, either here or in Adria. Or something from the family collection together. I want to give you choices, Hailey.'

'Because you've never had any,' she said, seeing the root of the issue although she suspected he wasn't even aware of it.

'I didn't say that.'

'Seems you don't have to say things out loud for me to know what you're thinking.' Which was terrifying, for many reasons. Mainly because it was true, and a result of the absurd intimacy that had been so characteristic of their relationship from the start.

Which she really shouldn't be dwelling on. She had said that things were too complicated, and she was right. She had to concentrate on the baby. Work out how she was meant to live in Gio's world. How she was meant to raise a baby in a world that she didn't understand. She'd thought she was done with that—with figuring out the rules of someone else's family and trying to make herself a part of it. She'd come here to New York, where she'd known she would stick out, where no one would expect her to know the rules. And somehow she'd found her place, found her people. Here on these streets that woke before dawn and were packing up for the day before noon. She'd found Gracie here, or Gracie had found her.

'There's someone I need you to meet,' she said suddenly. Before she could overthink it.

'Now?' Gio asked, laughing and looking at his watch. 'It's eight a.m.'

'So Gracie will be on her third pot of coffee. With any luck she'll be brewing number four and we can share.'

'Okay, pre-breakfast meeting then,' he said gamely. 'And Gracie is…?'

'She was my boss at my first job in New York. I worked part-time as a florist while I was at college. Gracie taught me everything I know about floristry, and most of what I know about myself. She's a…she's a really good friend.'

Though of course 'friend' wasn't nearly a big enough word for someone who meant so much to her. It was unthinkable that she could leave for Adria without telling Gracie her news. All of it.

She led Gio across the road and then pulled him through the door into Gracie's store. 'Gracie?' she called, guessing her friend was in the small room at the back where she hung the aprons and kept the coffee pot.

'Hailey, honey, is that you?' Gracie shouted back, before emerging through the curtain over the door, wrapping her arms around Hailey and squeezing her in a bone-crushing hug. 'This is a wonderful surprise! How did the wedding go yesterday?' the older woman asked. And then she looked past Hailey to Gio, who was still standing by the door. 'And who's this?' She held Hailey away from her by her upper arms and gave her a rather knowing look.

Hailey cleared her throat awkwardly. 'Yes, of course. Gracie, this is…' She hesitated over how exactly she was meant to introduce the Crown Prince who had got her pregnant. Until she remembered how simply Gio had introduced himself to her. 'Gracie, this is Gio.' She paused. 'We have a little news.'

Gracie glanced away from Hailey, over her shoulder to Gio, before her eyes locked back on Hailey's face. 'You have some news, huh?' Her eyes flicked down to Hailey's midriff, and she knew her friend had guessed correctly.

'We're expecting a baby,' she said quickly, getting the words out there. 'And we're getting married. I'm flying out to Adria tonight.'

'Well, honey, that's quite a *lot* of news,' Gracie said, her glance over Hailey's shoulder rather more suspicious now. 'If you'll excuse us…'

'Gio,' Hailey prompted her.

'If you'll excuse us, Gio, I need to speak to Hailey alone for a moment.'

Gracie's firm grip on her arm slipped down to her wrist as she tugged her into the back room.

Gracie fixed her with a look from which Hailey knew there was no escape. 'What's going on,' she demanded.

'I mean, I think I gave you the highlights,' Hailey said, trying—and failing—not to meet her eye.

'Uh-huh. You did. And now I want the small print. Is this what you want? I never even heard you mention this guy and now you're getting married. Leaving New York. Sweetheart, if you need help, you only have to ask. Not even that. Give me any sign that you want me to step in here and I'll keep you safe. You have options.'

Hailey let out a deep breath, because she knew Gracie meant it. If she was in trouble, Gracie would burn down buildings to get her out of it. Knowing that lifeline was there made it a little easier to breathe, even though she didn't need it.

'I know it's unexpected,' Hailey said, taking a seat on one of the stools by the counter, pouring them both a cup of coffee and opening the bag of pastries she knew she'd find in the drawer. 'It was the furthest thing from planned. But we're both excited about the baby, and we both want to try being a family.'

'Oh, honey, there are a lot of ways to be a family,' Gracie said, laying a hand on her arm. 'I know you know that.'

'I do, and I've tried many of them—including finding my own family in the New York flower district—and it's made me feel happier and more loved than I ever have in my life. But the only one I haven't tried is a family with a child being brought up by its birth parents, and this is my only chance to find out what that feels like.'

Gracie sighed. 'Just because that is more traditional it doesn't mean it's better, or that it will make you happy. You and Gio can make a good family without you giving up your life here.'

Hailey nodded, because she knew that Gracie was right. She also knew that she couldn't give up this opportunity to try. 'I know that. But we're still going to try.'

'Okay.' The older woman nodded thoughtfully. 'Then you should know that you have my full support and you always will, whatever happens.'

This time it was Hailey who hugged Gracie to her. 'Thank you. You have no idea what it means to me to hear you say that.'

Gracie sniffed, and Hailey wondered if she was close to tears too. 'Should we put the boy out of his misery? Or leave him to stew a little longer?' Gracie asked.

'Let's go back out there,' Hailey said. 'I'm half terrified that he's going to come to his senses and take it all back.'

'He'd have to be criminally stupid to do that. The way he looks at you, I don't think you have anything to worry about.'

'Oh, it's not—' she started to say, before she stopped herself. She had been going to say that this wasn't a real marriage. She didn't even know what it was. All she could be sure of was that she had to marry him, and it seemed safer altogether if she kept her feelings out of the equation. Falling for Gio could only make things more complicated, so she was simply going to forbid herself from doing so. 'We're very happy,' she said weakly.

When she returned from the back room, Gio was pacing with hands clasped behind his back, and Hailey was surprised and a little touched to see he looked nervous.

'Everything all right?' he asked Hailey, with a nervous glance at Gracie.

'Everything's great,' she told him, leaving Gracie's side and coming to stand beside him. And then, suddenly, it wasn't. She felt tears pricking the back of her eyes and she fought to keep her chin from juddering with held back tears. Because she was leaving. And as much as she wanted to give her child the family it deserved—and that meant Gio—it meant leaving the family she'd found here, after looking for so long.

'We don't have to go,' Gio said gently, tilting her face up with a knuckle under her chin.

'You already told me that you do. Your family.'

He brushed her hair back from her face, cupped her cheek gently. 'So I'll call them. They'll get over it.'

She laughed a little at that. 'I know you don't mean that and we both know it's not so simple. But I appreciate the sentiment.'

'I do mean it. We've never really talked about what your leaving New York means. That was unforgivable of me.'

'So we'll talk about it in Adria,' she said. 'But we should go, tonight. Your parents are expecting you.'

'If you're sure.' He was focused one hundred per cent on her, his hands cupped at her cheeks, and it was hard resisting the urge to turn her head and nuzzle into his palm.

'I'm sure,' she said, her voice steadier. 'We can always come back. I hear those planes fly both ways across the Atlantic.'

He huffed a little laugh under his breath. 'Well, I flew back to you, didn't I?'

Hailey stared at him, aware that her expression

must be turning goofy. But there was something about the way he'd said those words that made her stomach tighten. It almost sounded as if he meant it, that he was here with her because he wanted to be and not because the New York social calendar and a glitch in her contraception had forced them back into each other's lives.

She heard Gracie clear her throat behind her, and remembered that they weren't alone. When she turned around, Gracie was giving her a look that made her blush.

'You know, I don't think I need to worry about you after all. Enjoy your trip, honey. And let me know the minute you're back in New York. I want to know everything that happens with this baby. And I'm always at the end of the phone. If you need anything, you call me. You understand?'

She was gathered in to Gracie's chest for a hug and took the opportunity to surreptitiously wipe away a tear with the heel of one hand.

'I'll call. I promise. But you don't have to worry about me. I'm fine—I'm happy,' she said again with a self-conscious glance at Gio.

They left the store, back out onto the street, bracketed each side by towering bamboos and ferns, surrounded by blooms in holiday reds and whites and greens, all covered in snow. She had no idea what she was going to do away from this place. She had worked too hard to set up her business to just let it go because she was going to be a mother. And she couldn't just shut up shop in New York and start afresh in Adria. She had no clients there. No contacts. No suppliers. She employed a team of assistants here and she couldn't just fire them all because she'd decided to torch her life in New York.

She was going to be a princess, she reminded herself. She wasn't exactly an expert on European royalty, but she didn't know of any who were running their own business. As far as she was aware, if you didn't want to work for the family firm you got thrown out. They would have to talk about this, and soon. But they had to get the small question of telling his parents out of the way first. They'd deal with the practicalities of their lives first.

'So that went… Did that go well?' Gio asked. 'I feel like I'd need to know Gracie better to judge.'

Hailey smiled, bumping herself against his side. 'It went fine. I think she liked you.'

She stopped walking suddenly, as she spotted a poster on the building in front of them. It was for an exhibition at The Metropolitan Museum of Art, a painting that she had studied for her art history major, and that had inspired her first solo attempts at floristry. She remembered the first time that she had seen it, in a library book at her art school: there had been something about the way that the light caught on the flowers, the contrast of rich colours against a dramatically dark background, that had inspired something deep inside her. It had seemed magical. Otherworldly.

She had thought, *I have access to light. I have access to flowers. I want to make something that moves me like this painting does. But I want to be able to walk all around it. I want to be able to touch it, to smell it.* And she had worked with Gracie to find the flowers that she needed, and the best way to display them, and find the light that picked out their colours and their shadows.

'What is it?' Gio asked, interrupting her memory.

Hailey hesitated, not sure how honest she should be. She forced a smile and kept her voice light. 'Nothing, just an exhibition that I'd hoped to see. It doesn't start until next week and it's only running for a few days. There's a painting that I loved when I was at art school; I've never seen it properly. But it's fine. I'm sure I'll get another chance.'

She looked up at Gio, who was frowning.

'You definitely have to fly out tonight?' she asked, already knowing what the answer would be.

'My parents are expecting me.'

She shrugged off her disappointment and stopped outside another couple of stores as they walked along Twenty-Eighth Street. 'What time is the flight?' she asked. 'And how long should I be planning on staying? I need to know what to pack.'

'I'll have the car pick you up at eight to give us enough time to get to the airport. And as for how long? That's up to you. I'm inviting you to Adria. To visit. To live. But I don't want to force you into anything. We can decide together how long you want to stay. And if you change your mind and want to come back, you come straight back. If you haven't brought something that you need, then we'll get it for you in Adria.'

She nodded again. 'It's Christmas in ten days,' she said, trying to keep her voice casual. 'It'd look strange if we spent our first Christmas apart.'

Gio stopped, touched her hand lightly until she turned to him. 'We could fly back here if you want,' he said, his eyes serious.

'And have you take four transatlantic flights in less than a fortnight?' Hailey forced a smile. 'You'd be wrecked. No, we'll spend Christmas in Adria. Do we have to spend it with your family or...?'

'There's tradition. Church for Midnight Mass. Balcony photocall in the afternoon. Dinner with the family, of course.'

She nodded. It was what she'd expected. 'Okay, so we're going to be seeing a lot of them.'

'Normally I would. This year...' Gio ran a hand through his hair.

'You think we're going to be banished?'

'I think maybe we'll want some space from them,' he said diplomatically. 'Six hours around a dinner table might be a little much.'

'It's going to cause enough waves, me turning up pregnant, out of wedlock.'

'Not for long,' Gio argued.

'Excuse me?' Hailey frowned, unsure of his meaning.

'You're not going to be out of wedlock for long,' he clarified, running a hand through his hair.

'Right.' Hailey nodded. 'Of course.'

It still felt surreal. Not only was she pregnant, but she was going to be married soon. Married into a royal family, at that.

'We didn't really talk about a timescale for that,' she observed.

'Soon,' Gio said quickly. 'I want to do it soon.'

'Right. The closer to nine months after the wedding the baby arrives the better, I suppose. Though you know that I'm two months gone already.'

Gio's eyes met hers. 'That's not the reason.'

CHAPTER SIX

HE PROBABLY SHOULD have lied and said that of course
that was the reason he wanted to marry quickly. She'd
given him the perfect excuse, and he'd discarded it on
an impulse. Now he was left trying to hide the truth of
the matter. He wanted her to be his wife and, knowing that was going to happen, he didn't want to wait.
It was just because of the baby, he told himself. He
wanted his family settled. He didn't want his parents
to be able to get in the way of this. He wasn't sure that
they could stop him marrying, but he wouldn't put it
past them to try.

'I don't want my parents interfering,' he said, wondering if that sounded as unconvincing as it felt. It didn't
matter as long as they were clear about why they were
telling themselves they were getting married.

And the reason didn't have anything to do with the
night they had spent together. It couldn't, because that
was too complicated—Hailey herself had said so. She
was only marrying him out of obligation, and that was
fine. He'd come to terms with the fact already. It was
more than he had hoped for that *he* got to choose his
wife, rather than his parents or a council of politicians.
But that didn't make it a love match. Hailey didn't love
him. She didn't even know him, and he'd spent enough

of his life giving love without it being returned to expose himself to that sort of hurt again.

Whatever seeds of feelings he might have for Hailey, he had to tamp them down and remember that the choices that they made should be based on what was right for their child, not about their personal feelings.

'So we should move quickly if we want to do this,' he said, wanting to move the conversation to practicalities.

'How quickly?'

'How do you feel about New Year's Eve?'

Hailey stopped walking abruptly. 'The New Year's Eve that's on December the thirty-first, two weeks from now?'

Gio nodded, sliding his hands into his pockets and hoping that he hadn't given away that his heart had stopped beating when she had stopped walking. 'That's when it usually falls.'

'Two weeks is *not* enough time to arrange any wedding, Gio. Never mind a royal one.'

Gio held her gaze, trying to keep his expression free from emotion. 'The longer the planning goes on, the more complicated it'll get,' he countered. 'I want to keep things simple.'

There. They were back on track. That was a perfectly reasonable explanation for why he wanted to do this quickly, which had nothing to do with how he felt when he looked at Hailey or thought about the fact that she would soon be his wife.

But this wasn't a normal marriage. Pursuing this attraction would only make things exponentially more complicated. They had to concentrate on the most important aspect of their relationship, and that was as parents, not lovers. Hailey had made that much clear to him.

'I should be getting back,' Hailey said, glancing at the time on her phone. 'I've got a lot to organise if we're flying tonight.'

'Is that a yes to New Year's Eve?' Gio asked. He was well aware that it hadn't been but, as much as he didn't want to press her, he wanted to know that she was going through with this. That in two weeks he would be able to call her his wife.

'It's an *I'll think about it* to New Year's Eve,' Hailey told him with a slight frown.

'Then that will have to do, for now,' Gio conceded.

'It's all there is on offer right now.'

He nodded. 'I understand. I do. I won't pressure you.'

'You just want me to marry you and move halfway across the globe on half a day's notice.'

Hailey shook her head, because this wasn't Gio's fault. Now she was pregnant, all these complications were inevitable. That had been the risk she'd taken when she'd gone to bed with him that night. When she'd decided to keep the baby.

'I'm sorry,' she said, reaching out a hand to him in an attempt to find the ease between them that she'd taken for granted earlier. 'None of this is your fault. It's the universe that has made this complicated. You're just suggesting solutions—albeit somewhat radical ones.'

'I want to do the right thing,' Gio said with such earnestness that she had no choice but to believe him. No one proposed to a practical stranger for any other reason, especially when someone like him proposed to someone like her.

'I know. And I'm sure we are doing the right thing. Just let me get my head round it in my own time.'

As she threw clothes into her suitcase several hours later, she could only be thankful that she'd scheduled a break in her calendar following Ivy and Sebastian's big society wedding. There was nothing between now and January that her team couldn't manage without her, and by then she had to hope that she'd come up with a solution for how to run her business from Adria. She knew she could rely on Gracie to step in and help out with any crises. Except, that was, the crisis right in front of her—what to pack to meet your royal future in-laws, who were almost certainly going to hate you.

She could call Gracie and ask her advice, but she wasn't sure that she could talk to her again without spilling all her misgivings about the decisions that had led her here, and she couldn't be sure that if she did that she wouldn't change her mind and back out of the whole arrangement. For the sake of her baby, she had to hold her nerve, give her child the chance to know its family, its place in the world, in a way that had always been denied to her.

She hadn't thought that she'd ever have to do this again, stand over her suitcase and prepare to shift her life into someone else's family. But this was the price that she had to pay so that her baby never had to feel this. And she would pay it gladly for her child to have a better start in life than she'd had, so they could reach adulthood and find love on their own terms, secure in the knowledge that their parents had cherished them from the moment that they knew a baby existed.

In the end she went with practicality, throwing in thermals and knitwear, and some of the nicer outfits that she'd acquired for blending in at society weddings. The maternity jeans and leggings that she'd picked up last week, in anticipation of the day when leaving her top button undone was no longer a universal solution to what to wear.

She was never going to belong in Gio's family, but

she'd try and hide that fact behind designer shirts if she could. She threw things in without looking, averting her eyes from the growing pile of clothes in the case. If she didn't look at it directly, it couldn't hurt her. Couldn't call back memories she'd long since buried—and she wanted it to stay that way. The knock at the door made her jump, and she wondered how long she'd been standing by her case, trying not to look at it.

She pulled the zip closed and answered the door, expecting to see Gio on the other side. But instead she was faced with a uniformed driver who gave her a professional nod at her look of surprise.

'I'm here to drive you to the airport, Ms Thomas,' he said. 'Can I help you with your bags?'

'It's just this one case,' she said, fighting down her disappointment that Gio had sent a driver for her rather than collecting her himself. It was foolish, she told herself. The man had asked her to marry him; she shouldn't be questioning his commitment to her. But there was a difference between commitment and…what? Personal interest? Was that what she wanted from him? They had both been very clear that they were only marrying for the sake of their baby. This arrangement was perfectly in line with what they had agreed.

She grabbed her bag herself, forcing a smile for the driver, and then surrendered it, throwing a handbag over her shoulder and pulling the door shut behind her. She turned the key in the lock, wondering when she would be back in her own space again. When she would be back in her own life rather than someone else's.

She shook her mind clear and followed the driver down the stairs and into the car. Scrolling through the news on her phone, she smiled when she stumbled across pictures of Ivy and Seb's wedding, seeing how beautifully Ivy's opulent vision of the day had materialised, and how proud she was of her team for their part in it. And she resisted the ever-present urge to open her messaging app to see whether she had missed a text from Gio, letting her know that he wouldn't be collecting her in person. He didn't owe her an explanation, and she figured she'd see him on the plane soon enough.

As the car passed through a gate into a private airport and then pulled up alongside a private jet, she decided there were going to be some things about living in Gio's world that she wouldn't exactly hate. She was glancing back down at her phone when the car drew to a halt and the door was opened for her. She looked up to see Gio standing at the top of the steps to the aircraft, and then he jogged down to the tarmac and held out a hand as she stepped from the car.

'Hailey,' he said, swooping in and kissing her on both cheeks. 'I'm sorry I couldn't collect you in person. There was something of a crisis and my father has been on the phone all afternoon and evening.'

She smiled, accepting his apology, and refusing to let her body react to the scent of him when he leaned in to kiss her. Following him up the steps, she lost the thread of what he was saying as she took in the luxurious interior of the cabin. Reclining leather chairs faced one another across the space, and a crystal decanter and glasses sat on a side table. Through an open door, she could see a separate cabin with a large bed, made up with acres of white cotton and monogrammed pillows. She looked away because she hadn't been in such close proximity to Gio and a bed since he'd got her pregnant, and that knowledge was doing something to her body that was very inconvenient, considering she was meant to be keeping this all about the baby and nothing else.

'It's fine,' she told him, bringing herself back to the present moment. 'I understand that you're busy. Is this crisis anything to do with…?' She raised her eyebrows, not wanting to speak out of turn in front of the cabin crew, knowing that people like Gio set store by confidentiality.

'No, that crisis won't be landing until tomorrow. Which is why I wanted this sorted today. I do try and keep Adria to one at a time.'

'Well, sorry to have made that more difficult for you,' she said, taking a seat when he gestured her towards one.

The cabin crew closed the door of the aircraft and then melted away with a discretion she assumed must be normal around the passengers of private jets.

'It's not like you got yourself pregnant,' he said with a smile. 'I should probably warn you, though, if things are a little…tense when we meet my family, it's nothing about you personally.'

'Well, that doesn't exactly fill me with confidence,' she said with a wry grin, trying to hide how horrifying the thought of being rejected by another family was for her. Fortunately, she interrupted herself with a yawn.

Gio smiled. 'You should take the cabin. Rest. I woke you at an unreasonable hour. You can try and get ahead of the jet lag.'

'Ha, in the life of a florist six a.m. is nothing, trust me. I'll hold out a little longer. You're the one who's still on European time. You should take it.'

'Take the only bed when my…' his pause was every bit as pregnant as she was '…fiancée,' Gio finished at last, and they both sat there with the word ringing in the air around them. That was truly going to take some getting used to. 'How about neither of us sleeps, and we have a drink and talk instead?' he suggested. 'What can I offer you?'

'Am I a terrible British cliché if I say tea?' Hailey asked.

Gio laughed. 'I should have thought of that before I brought you coffee this morning,' he said, calling over a crew member and ordering their drinks.

'Oh, no, that was definitely the right call,' Hailey said, taking a seat on one side of a highly polished side table. 'But I think we're out of New York airspace and that changes things. So,' she went on. 'Family politics. Give me the primer. I want to know what I'm letting myself in for.'

Gio sighed, sat opposite her and ran a hand through his hair.

'Is it that bad?' Hailey asked, looking at him with concern.

'Bad isn't the right word,' he told her as one of the cabin crew brought her tea on a silver tray, and a tumbler of some amber liquid for Gio. 'My family is… complicated,' he said, taking a sip and letting his eyes close for a second. 'I'm not just a son to them; I'm a junior partner in their firm. And that relationship always seems to be the one dictating how things are between us.'

'And that's why they think they have a right to choose who you marry?' Hailey asked, pouring her tea and stirring in milk.

'That's why they emphasise that I have responsibilities to consider before making big life decisions.'

'Which is why things are going to be frosty.'

He shrugged. 'I don't know. Maybe.'

She watched him carefully as his forehead creased and he took another sip of his drink. His head fell back against his seat and he closed his eyes. 'It's not too late to change your mind if you're having second thoughts,' she told him, more concerned in that moment about the tension that she saw on his face than their plans for the future.

'You're literally on the plane,' Gio said, opening his eyes and giving her a weak smile.

'I don't think that's legally binding,' Hailey said gently. 'We don't have to get married just because we shared a private jet.'

'Now you tell me.' She was relieved to see the corner of his lips quirk a little higher, but she was still waiting for one of those truly dazzling smiles of his. She wasn't sure when she had started to measure the mood of a room just by the breadth of his smile.

'I'm not having second thoughts,' Gio said, reaching for her hand, squeezing it and then leaving his palm covering hers. 'I know we are doing the right thing. But I also know that it's going to take some work on our part—on *my* part—to make my parents see it the same way.'

We're doing the right thing.

She repeated the words to herself as the plane taxied to the runway, trying to understand why they made the bottom of her stomach fall. Why they left her feeling so flat when it was the exact thing she was telling herself about why they were getting married. Fair enough... This whole thing would be more fairy tale if they were to fall for each other. But she wasn't in this for the fairy tale, no matter how her heart might give a little stutter at the thought of it. This relationship was about giving her child the best start in life. Nothing to do with how she had felt that night with Gio, or how her skin felt against his now. She drew her hand away.

'We *are* doing the right thing if it means you choosing the future that you want. We'll make sure your parents see tha—' Her last word was interrupted by another jaw-stretching yawn. When she opened her eyes, it was to find that Gio had fixed her with a stern look.

'You're going to bed,' he said, standing in front of her and offering his hand. She shouldn't take it. But the thought of those crisp white sheets and pillows—the idea of sleep—dragged her under. And if she was meeting the hostile in-laws tomorrow, she could at least do it looking more rested than she was sure she did right now.

'Okay. You're right,' she conceded. 'I had no idea growing a baby took so much energy. I mean, I'm not even really doing anything yet; it's barely more than a dot.'

She took Gio's hand and let him pull her up, neither of them moving when her change in position brought her body up against his. She craned her neck to look up at him and remembered how good that had felt. To have him above her and around her and inside her. How the real world had faded away out of respect for his—frankly perfect—frame. She cleared her throat, knowing that letting this moment draw out would cause nothing but trouble for them both.

The sound seemed to snap Gio back to his senses and he took a step back from her. 'I'll show you the cabin,' he said, and Hailey took the very grown-up decision to see absolutely no innuendo in that.

She followed him through the door, where he started pulling throw pillows off the bed and pulling back the sheets. 'The bathroom's just through there,' he said, indicating a door across the other side of the bed. She slid it open and found a small but immaculately appointed space, complete with shower, soft monogrammed towels and a counter stocked with luxury toiletries.

When she turned back, Gio was in the doorway to the cabin and the bed was turned down for her and looking more inviting than any horizontal surface with Prince Giovanni of Adria *beside* it instead of *in* it had any right to.

'Thanks,' she said, trying to keep her voice casual. 'Could you have someone wake me well before we land? I want the rest of that briefing before I meet your family.' She glanced back into the bathroom. 'And to try out that shower.'

Gio half smiled. 'Get some sleep, and do *not* worry about my parents. They're my problem.'

She held his gaze for a breath. 'I'm fairly sure that marriage makes things *our* problem. Otherwise, what's the point?'

Another almost-smile. What was a full one going to cost her, and could she remotely afford to pay? she wondered.

'Goodnight,' Gio said softly, and the intimacy of it sent a dangerous shiver up her spine. It was only because they were thirty thousand feet in the air in a glorified tin can that he was having this magnetic effect on her, making her question whether she had made the right call making their relationship all about the baby she was carrying, and not at all about the wild chemistry that had dragged them up to his suite that night and kept her pinned to his mattress—well, to various places, actually—until the sun had risen the next day.

As she slipped between the sheets, Gio started to turn away.

'Wait, where are you going to sleep?' she asked, suppressing a yawn.

'I'm fine,' he said, turning back towards her. 'Don't worry about me.'

'Too late for that.' She gave a dramatic sigh. 'Come on, you look exhausted. If I get to sleep, you get to sleep. The bed's plenty big enough and we're both too exhausted to do anything irresponsible.'

He stood looking at her in the doorway for long enough for her face to turn red and to wonder whether she'd just made a huge mistake. Well, she couldn't pretend she hadn't said it now. 'We're telling people that we're getting married,' she reminded him. 'We *are* getting married. People are going to find it strange if we act like polite strangers. And sleep in separate beds.'

'In the palace—'

'We're not in the palace. If there was another bed on this plane I'd be pushing you into it, but here we are. Okay, I'm going to sleep now. I'm leaving it up to you.'

She turned her back to the door, pressing her cheek against the cool cotton, hoping it would calm the hot flush of her face.

And then, above the noise of the aircraft engines, was the sound of leather-soled shoes on thick carpet. A pause as Gio stopped by the bed, and a dip and roll of the mattress as he slid in behind her.

A soft tapping brought Gio to wakefulness, and he pulled the warm body beside him close as he tried to work out where he was. Not his rooms at the palace. Not the hotel suite in New York either. Hailey gave a soft moan as she stirred, and it was as her eyes opened and her wide green gaze met his that he remembered.

'We'll be landing in fifteen minutes, Your Royal Highness,' the flight attendant called through the door.

Right. He had asked to be woken before they landed,

back before he'd decided that caution and sleeping in a chair were overrated and he'd accepted Hailey's invitation to sleep beside her.

This could, technically, just about, be considered 'beside her', he supposed. If one discounted the arm around her midriff and the way that he had used it to pull her tight when they were in that space between waking and sleeping. And the fact that he hadn't yet let her go.

'We should—' she started to say, and he sat upright in an instant, snapping back to reality, gathering the sheets around them. 'I'm going to…the bathroom,' Hailey said, her words faltering. 'Freshen up— No time to shower, but…' Her voice trailed off as she stood beside the bed.

'I'm sorry,' he said. 'I was asleep and I—'

She waved a hand, in a gesture he thought was supposed to look more casual than it actually did. 'It's nothing. Let's not mention it. I guess it's just something we're going to have to get used to.'

Get used to? he thought, as she slid closed the door to the bathroom. There was no way he was ever going to get used to being so close to her and not being allowed to touch. It made so much more sense to think about their marriage in platonic terms. Something that they were doing for their baby, rather than examining the way that they felt about one another, or exploring the chemistry that kept pulling them together. There was enough going on without throwing sex into the mix. And there was no way he was going to risk falling for her when she was so clearly only doing this for the baby's sake.

If she accepted, their wedding would be two weeks away. That meant that he had two weeks to work out how he was meant to spend a lifetime alongside Hailey without falling for her.

Hailey emerged from the bathroom with her pink cheeks still damp from being splashed with water, and Gio clenched down on the lurch of his heart at the sight of her. He had to remember that this wasn't a fairy tale. He might have chosen Hailey himself, but this was no more a love match than if he'd accepted one of the suitable young women his parents had been pressing on him since he had turned twenty-one. It would be just as foolish believing Hailey could love him as it would have been to assume the same of any of that parade of convenient minor European princesses. The lines in their relationship could hardly be more blurred. But that didn't mean that he could let his emotions get confused. This was a sensible decision. The least bad course for his future was to spend it with a woman who he was already tied to for the rest of their lives. It wasn't the most generous assessment of their situation, but he had to remember that Hailey wasn't doing this because of her feelings about him.

Much like his parents, she was tolerating him. Tied by blood to one another's future. He already knew what would have happened if it wasn't for the biological glitch that had led to her pregnancy. She would have walked away from him—she *had* walked away from him—that morning in New York. No doubt she resented the fact that she was stuck with him, when she'd wanted to cut all ties—forget him as soon as that night was over. Or if she didn't now, she would eventually.

The plane touched down with barely a skitter on the runway of the private airfield, and he just had a chance to spot the anxious expression on Hailey's face.

'Hey,' he said, reaching out a hand and laying it on her arm. 'Are you okay?'

'Nervous,' she admitted, though the anxiety on her face was quickly replaced with fierce determination.

'It's still just us,' he said, suddenly feeling awkward and withdrawing his hand. 'The airfield is private, and I asked that no one meet us but the car. The family will be waiting for us at the palace.'

She let out a relieved breath. 'Okay. Stay of execution. How long until we meet them?'

'Twenty minutes?'

'Twenty minutes of real life left. Got it.'

'Sorry you have to spend it in the back of a car with me.'

She gave him a heated look. 'You know, I can think of worse ways…'

He grinned at her. They really had to stop flirting like this. Had to remember that this was no normal relationship. He had to stop this turning into a situation where he found himself wanting something that he knew he could never properly have.

His own parents had never loved him. He'd known a long time ago not to expect love in a royal family. He would settle for someone who liked him. And, to do that, he had to manage his expectations and make sure he didn't give away more of himself than he was ever going to get back in return.

The back seat of the car saw absolutely no action besides Hailey carefully knitting her fingers together over and over, until he reached out and laid his palm over them, stroking the back of her hand with his thumb. 'I promise it'll be okay,' he told her, wishing his words alone would be enough to soothe the worried lines from her forehead.

She gave him a weak smile. 'You've changed your tune.'

'I never said it wouldn't be okay. It might get a little… awkward, at first. I grant you that. But it will all be okay in the end. I promise.'

She snorted lightly. '*In the end…* You do realise that leaves quite a lot of scope for how long things can be "awkward", as you put it. Are we talking ten days or ten years for this *in the end*? Roughly speaking.'

'Roughly speaking? I can't be sure.'

He stepped through the door of the palace, acknowledging the doorman with a nod, and laced his fingers through Hailey's as they headed towards his parents' rooms. He had no doubt that his parents would be waiting for him there.

The ceiling soared twenty feet above their heads, greenery was wreathed around every horizonal surface and quite a few vertical ones too. A fire roared in the grate, surrounded by a collection of furniture that was worn in the very expensive way that only the truly wealthy managed to achieve. Gio had stiffened beside her, and his tight grip on her fingers tugged at something in her heart. Because she was the one who was about to come face to face with her royal future in-laws, who she was fairly sure were going to hate her. And yet he— Crown Prince Giovanni of Adria, their cherished son and heir—was the one who was nervous.

'Mother,' Gio said as they walked into the grand reception room, and Hailey stood rooted to the spot, waiting for the drama to begin.

'Giovanni, you're home,' said his mother, Queen Lucia. An elegant woman dressed all in black, she sat with ankles crossed and tucked demurely beneath her,

her hands folded tightly in her lap. 'You've brought a guest,' she added, looking pointedly at Hailey in a way that made her wish she wasn't currently encased in a thick parka.

Hailey's heart stuttered and she forced herself not to turn to look questioningly at Gio. He hadn't *told* them she was coming?

The squeeze of Gio's hand stopped the words in her throat. He hadn't given her any reason not to trust him. If he hadn't told his parents she was coming, she was sure that he must have had his reasons.

Queen Lucia rose to stand and stalked towards them at such a glacial pace that it had to be a deliberate power move. In sleek black cigarette pants and a fitted sweater, her hair caught up in a chignon that would put any Parisian coiffeur to shame, she barely looked old enough to be Gio's mother. When she reached them, Gio stepped forward and kissed his mother on both cheeks.

'Mamma,' he said, 'may I present Ms Hailey Thomas?'

Hailey fought the sudden urge to curtsey.

'How do you do,' the older woman said, her eyes barely leaving Gio's long enough to flicker disapprovingly over Hailey.

'How do you do, Your Majesty,' Hailey replied. Thanks for *that*, *Debrett's* etiquette section, she thought, seeing a flicker of approval on the Queen's face. Well, she'd got one thing right, at least. But they'd see soon enough how far that approval stretched when she found out about the baby. And the engagement.

'You should have let us know that you were bringing a friend,' the Queen admonished her son. 'I shall have to speak to the housekeeper.'

'There's no need. Hailey will share my room.' So

much for that talk about separate rooms, Hailey thought, trying not to let her surprise show on her face.

The Queen's eyes, however, widened just a fraction before she regained that tiny fraction of composure.

'Of course, if you wish. Come, sit by the fire,' she said, gesturing formally as a maid came to relieve them of coats and their luggage disappeared upstairs.

'Is Father here?' Gio asked as he took a seat on a stiff-backed sofa and pulled Hailey down beside him with their linked hands. His fingers were still tightly threaded between hers, and she couldn't help the feeling that he was holding on for dear life.

As he spoke, King Leonardo emerged through a doorway in the corner of the great hall. Gio's back stiffened further—something that Hailey hadn't thought was possible—and he made as if to stand until his father waved his hand.

'No need to get up, son. I heard you arrive.'

'Father,' Gio said, as the King took a seat opposite.

'Have you introduced your guest?'

They went through the formalities, Gio's voice becoming more strained the longer that they sat there.

'Well, Giovanni. You said on the phone that you needed to speak to us in person.' The royal couple both shot Hailey a questioning look. 'I suggest you tell us what this is about so that we can deal with whatever needs dealing with.'

It didn't take a genius to work out that *she* was what needed dealing with in this situation, and if Gio's parents hadn't guessed the full extent of the trouble, they had to be at least halfway there.

Gio fixed his eyes on his father, gripped Hailey's hand a little tighter and spoke with a tense jaw.

'Hailey and I are expecting a baby,' he said without

a hint of emotion in his voice. 'We're also engaged. The wedding will take place on New Year's Eve. I would like it if you could congratulate us.'

The four of them sat in silence, the hoped-for congratulations conspicuously absent. The Queen cleared her throat as the King's face grew red.

'Are you asking for our permission or our blessing?' Queen Lucia asked eventually.

'Neither,' Gio replied, his voice as cold as his mother's. 'I'm informing you of our plans. I'm an adult—I don't need your permission to marry.'

'You're the Crown Prince of Adria,' his father countered.

Hailey had to fight the urge to roll her eyes. Did he think that Gio could possibly have forgotten that fact? But it didn't stop him droning on.

'You have responsibilities. Your marriage is a question for me, your mother and our advisors. Do you have any idea how difficult this is going to be to undo? Who else knows about this?'

Hailey couldn't help but notice it was the same question Gio had asked her when she had told him that she was pregnant, and wondered whether Gio had realised it too.

'I don't think you understand, Father,' Gio said, and she could hear in his voice how much this steady control was costing him. 'Our wedding will take place in two weeks' time. Our baby will be born in the summer. I'm informing you as a courtesy only because this is happening whether you like it or not.'

That 'or not' was somewhat redundant, wasn't it? Hailey thought. They couldn't have been any clearer that they absolutely did *not* like this.

'Are you sure she's pregnant?' Queen Lucia asked,

speaking for the first time since Gio had shared their news, and staring at her son as if Hailey wasn't sitting right there in front of her. 'And that the baby is yours?'

'I'm sure. We're delighted,' Gio replied, honestly sounding nothing of the sort, but she appreciated the gesture nonetheless.

'Then I have nothing more to say to you,' Queen Lucia said, standing and brushing down her already immaculate trousers. She had left the room before Hailey had a chance to close her mouth. She glanced across at Gio to see how he had taken her rudeness and found his face a blank indifferent mask.

Gio's father followed his wife out of the room, leaving the two of them sitting beside the fire in a space that could grace any Christmas card, with its looping pine boughs, bright silver bells and sprigs of berries. And yet the mood was decidedly more frosty than festive.

'Well, that went well,' Hailey said with an ironic smile, giving Gio's hand a squeeze before dropping it— no need to keep up the pretence that they were in love with one another now they didn't have an audience.

Gio let his head tip back against the back of the chair and rubbed a hand over his face. 'I'm so sorry I subjected you to that,' he said, muffled slightly by the hand that still half blocked his face.

'No,' Hailey said gently. 'I'm sorry that they spoke to you like that. Are you okay?'

'Yes.' Gio emerged from behind his hand. 'I'm fine. That's almost exactly how I expected it to go.'

'Then I'm sorry for that too,' she said. She'd spent her life longing for a family, and had never considered that you could be just as lonely in the heart of one as you could be on the outside looking in.

'What happens next?' she asked. 'Do we just leave things like that?'

'Next, we arrange the wedding,' Gio said, sitting forward and resting his elbows on his knees.

'Without their blessing?'

He shrugged. 'I have my own office. They'll take care of the arrangements.'

'That's not what I meant,' Hailey said.

Gio let out a breath. 'I know it's not. But I'm not going to change how they feel. We make our plans and we make the best of it.'

'"We make the best of it"?' she repeated. 'I'm not sure a happy marriage has ever followed those words.'

He fixed her with a piercing look. 'A happy marriage has never been an option for me. Not the way that you mean.'

'Then why are we doing this?' she asked, trying to protect herself from the hurt that threatened at his words.

'For the baby,' Gio said, his eyes narrowed slightly. 'I thought that's what we were doing.'

'Yes. When I thought that was what you wanted. That it would make you happy, even if not in the hearts and flowers way some people might want.'

'You don't want hearts and flowers?' Gio asked.

Hailey rolled her eyes. As if the answer to that wasn't obvious. 'I agreed to this, didn't I?'

'I'm sorry,' Gio said, shaking his head. 'I know it's not enough.'

She reached for his hand. 'It's not too late to change your mind,' she told him again, though each time she said it, it felt less and less true.

'I could say the same to you,' Gio replied, squeezing her fingers.

She laid his hand on her belly and looked up at him.

'It's too late for me. I want this baby to know its family. To belong. I have to make it work.'

'Even though it's *this* family?'

'You don't get to choose your family.'

'Never was a truer word spoken,' Gio said, turning up the corner of his mouth, but the strain around his eyes prevented it from turning into a real smile. She wondered if she would see the real one again.

'I don't want to change my mind,' he said. 'I want you. This. I want *us* to be a family.'

'Then you'd better start making some calls. New Year's Eve is only a fortnight away.'

Gio's parents didn't join them for dinner, and as the evening wore on it became apparent that they weren't going to join them at all. Hailey sat and watched as Gio grew tenser and tenser, sipping at a single glass of whisky, his knuckles white on the cut crystal.

'If they're going to snub us, we might as well call it a night,' Gio said eventually, after they'd passed the evening in a formal drawing room in silence, watching the fire burn low.

'Fine by me,' Hailey said, interrupting herself with a huge yawn. 'This baby hasn't got the jet lag message. I could definitely sleep.'

'Good.' Gio stood and reached out a hand to help her up. 'I'll show you our rooms.' He kept hold of her hand as they climbed the stairs. The words were on her lips to tell him it wasn't a good idea to share a room. But she remembered the look on his face when his parents had let him know what they felt about their first grandchild and, whether it was a good idea or not, she didn't want to leave him alone with whatever thoughts were causing that pained expression.

Gio opened a door into a comfortably furnished sitting room, the walls covered with an elegantly mismatched collection of bookshelves and one wall with windows out onto the snow-covered gardens. Through an open door she could see a bedroom beyond, and through another a small kitchen. Stepping through into the bedroom, she sighed with satisfaction. It was lit by flickering firelight, the walls were panelled in warm old wood and the floor was scattered with thick, plush rugs. The four-poster bed was hung with tapestried curtains and piled high with embroidered, tasselled cushions in warm colours.

'You take the bed,' Gio said, pulling cushions from it and tossing them onto the antique-looking sofa on one side of the open fire.

'Not this again,' Hailey said, pulling open the wardrobe and finding her clothes pressed and hanging inside.

'The rest of your things will be in the drawers,' Gio said, clearly spotting her wide-eyed awareness that her clothes had been magically unpacked and pressed.

'We're going to be married in a fortnight. We need to learn to sleep in the same bed. I'm going to be wearing at least three layers of flannel and I think I can trust myself,' Hailey said.

'Who said it was you I was worried about?'

Gio looked her straight in the eye for so long that she felt her cheeks warm.

'Come on, Gio, don't tease. We're being sensible about this.'

'I'm sorry. Okay, we'll share for now. But I'm arranging for you to have your own rooms in case you change your mind. I shouldn't have told my parents we would share without asking you first. And you don't have to worry. It's perfectly usual for royal couples to have separate chambers.'

'All those generations of unhappy marriages,' she mused.

'I don't want to be one of them,' Gio said, sitting on the edge of the bed and gesturing for Hailey to sit beside him. She perched up on the mattress, and when it gave way beneath her, pitching her closer to Gio, she didn't fight it and let the side of her body rest against his.

'I know that we wouldn't be doing this if it wasn't for the baby. But I want to try, Hailey. I want to try and be happier than my parents are. There was something between us, that night. Wasn't there? And I'm not talking about the sex, I'm talking about us. Is that enough to base a marriage on?'

'It's enough to be a start, at least,' she said. 'And I want to try too. Let's try and build a friendship. By being there for one another. Let's see where that takes us.'

She let her head come to rest on his shoulder. 'Okay, but I'm still wearing the flannel.'

He laughed against her cheek. 'I'm all out of flannel.'

'Well, find something to sleep in because I want this friends thing to work, and I'm only human.'

'I didn't realise I was so irresistible.'

She looked up at him with a grin. 'Yes, you did. You absolutely did. And I'm not going to massage your ego any further.' She got up from the bed and found her pyjamas in a drawer of the enormous bureau.

In the bathroom, she removed her make-up and splashed cold water on her cheeks, hoping it would cool the hot pink flush she could see in the mirror. This was perfectly fine. This was sharing an enormous bed with someone who was going to be a friend. The fact that their relationship had started with a fiercely hot one-night stand didn't have to come into it.

When she got back into the bedroom, the sheets were turned down and the lamps by the bed were lit. The curtains were all closed against the cold night and the overhead light was off, bathing the whole room in a warm orange glow.

She climbed into bed with her pyjamas buttoned to the neck, and was immediately swallowed up by the soft mattress and the heavy layers of blankets and quilts.

Gio emerged in the doorway of the bathroom and Hailey turned her head on the cold pillow, wondering if the circulation in her face was ever going to feel normal again. Was she really signing up for a lifetime of this? she asked herself. Of being so distracted by her husband—her *husband*—that she could barely look him straight in the eye?

It would fade, she promised herself. This feeling. This need for him. It was pure lust, and if they ignored it for long enough it would fade. When that happened, they would work out some friendly arrangement so that they didn't spend the rest of their lives celibate. Maybe they'd stay married in name only, with a discreet arrangement for their future love lives.

Except…except she couldn't see that happening. Not for her, at least. She simply couldn't imagine a life with Gio in it where she wanted someone else more than she wanted him.

So perhaps, in time, when the intensity of their first meeting had fully faded, they'd fall into bed again in a safe, companionable, married sort of way that wouldn't have the power to hurt her.

She felt Gio slip into the bed beside her and turned to look at him, one hand tucked under her cheek, the other under her pillow. 'Managing to resist so far?' he asked, a curve to one side of his lips as he mirrored her body language, his cheek to the pillow, hands tucked beneath them. And she realised how impossible it was to imagine feeling 'companionable' about him.

'The whisky breath is helping,' she said, knowing that it would make him laugh.

'I say,' he objected, nudging her knee with his. 'I brushed. And flossed.'

'Such a good boy,' she said mockingly. 'So wholesome.' Though the words died in her mouth because they both knew he was nothing of the sort.

'It's nice, having you here,' Gio said out of nowhere, and that blush was back on her cheeks.

'I like it too,' Hailey admitted. That was safe, surely. They were going to be married by the end of the month. It was safe to say that she liked being here. It didn't say anything that she hadn't already implied by accepting his proposal. Just so long as she didn't lose sight of the fact that liking it here didn't mean that she got to stay. Didn't mean that she'd been accepted. One day, when their baby was settled and in no doubt about where they belonged, she and Gio would move on. She was just the vessel for the baby's place in this family. She would never belong. Not properly. And that was fine. She'd spent her whole life on the periphery of families she didn't quite belong to. She had plenty of practice at not letting that hurt her. As long as she remembered what this was. As long as she remembered that her place here was only temporary and that Gio and his family couldn't hurt her if she remembered that fact, then she would be fine.

'Where did you go?' Gio asked, and when she looked across at him she found his brow slightly furrowed.

'Just thinking,' she said, her voice quiet in the scant inches between them.

'About?' Gio prompted.

She sighed. Where could she start?

'Nothing important,' she lied. 'Just wondering where all this will end up. The wedding. Then the baby. Then parenting. And then what? What comes next?'

'Whatever we choose,' Gio said, as if it would all be as simple as that. Perhaps it would. Perhaps, one day, he would simply choose someone who wasn't her and she would go back to her safe old life in New York. Become a peripheral part of a royal family. Third wheel to a more prestigious circle than her childhood foster families, but ultimately no more wanted than she had been then.

'Try and get some sleep,' Gio said, pressing his lips to her forehead. 'Tomorrow's going to be a busy one, and our baby could change its mind about the jet lag.'

CHAPTER SEVEN

GIO WATCHED AS Hailey's eyes closed, watched on in wonder as sleep dragged her under as easily as she drew breath. Despite the tiredness he could feel in his bones, the sleep he would have welcomed with open arms never came. He would have liked to chalk it up to the change of time zones, and yet he knew that would be a lie.

It was the fact that he was lying next to the woman he'd barely been able to stop thinking about since the night that they had spent together, knowing that his baby was growing inside her. That in two weeks he would call her his wife. And at some point after that they would have to work out what being married would actually mean for them. Not love, of course. He knew better than to expect that to grow out of what was an arrangement rather than a relationship. But friendship, perhaps. Respect. Companionship. That could be enough, he told himself.

He couldn't even face the question of where that would leave their physical relationship. Would Hailey want that, one day? he couldn't help but wonder. He knew she was attracted to him. And they'd proved well beyond doubt already how good it was between them.

How complicated could it be, sleeping with his wife?

Endlessly complicated, he acknowledged, if he had to stop himself from falling for her. He wasn't sure he could trust himself to do that.

He woke the way he had finally fallen asleep, his nose mere inches away from Hailey's, her hands still tucked beneath her cheek, as if she'd moved not an inch since he'd finally closed his eyes. He turned away from her slowly, reaching for his phone to check the time and then sliding out of the bed, deciding to leave her to sleep. She still looked tired, the shadows beneath her eyes not quite faded. And even if it weren't for that, he didn't want her to have to hear what he was sure his parents would have to say to him.

He found them at the table in the formal dining room, sitting opposite one another in silence, each of them sipping coffee and reading a newspaper. His mother looked up from hers as he stepped into the room, before placing it carefully beside her plate.

'Are you alone?' she asked.

'Yes,' Gio said. 'I didn't want to wake Hailey.'

'Good. Because we should talk before this goes any further.'

Gio nodded and took a seat beside his father. There was no point trying to stop them saying their piece. Perhaps once they'd done so, and they'd aired their concerns, they'd be able to leave him alone, knowing that they had at least tried.

'I know you think you're doing the honourable thing in marrying the girl,' his mother said. 'And I can respect that. But I think what would be best for the whole family is if she simply went back to America. If the child is born out of wedlock it won't impact the succession, and I'm sure we'll be able to find you a more suitable bride who will be understanding about these things. You could still take care of them financially, of course.'

'"The girl"? "The child"?' Gio said, anger making his words sharp. 'That's *my* child you're talking about, and the woman *I'm* going to marry. If they go back to America, then so do I.'

'You're being ridiculous, Giovanni,' his mother said dismissively, gesturing to a footman to pour her another cup of coffee. 'The Crown Prince of Adria cannot simply move to another country. You need to be here, where you can get to know your people and they can get to know you.'

'Then I won't be Crown Prince anymore,' Gio said, looking his mother straight in the eye, his voice perfectly calm now. 'If you're going to make me, then I choose them. A normal life. A normal family.'

'Now you're being rash,' his mother said, stirring cream into her coffee and looking at him over the rim as she took a sip.

'You're forcing me to be. I'm going to make this very clear for you. You welcome Hailey. You make sure the whole world sees that you are delighted for us. For your first grandchild. Or I'm leaving. It's as simple as that.'

They both stared at him in silence as he reached for the coffee pot and poured himself a cup with a rock-steady hand. He sat, sipped his coffee. Waited.

He felt no pressure because, quite honestly, he couldn't care less what they said. If anything, it would be a relief if they turned him away and never wanted to see him again. But he didn't have to think too hard to know that was never going to happen. He was their only child, the sole heir to the kingdom, and they wouldn't risk the succession over his choice of wife. Over the mother of his child.

His father broke first. Taking a sip of his coffee, he fixed him with a seemingly casual look over the rim of his cup. 'If she's your choice, then of course you have our support, son.'

Of course. Classic parental move. To make him feel as if he were the one who had caused the conflict rather than them.

'Mamma?'

She looked up at him, feigning surprise. 'Of course we'll support you,' she said with a raised eyebrow. 'If you're certain you're not making a mistake.'

And that was the best he could hope for, he supposed, in terms of parental support. Really, he couldn't have asked for clearer proof that he was making the right decision, that he owed it to himself, and to Hailey and their baby, to make his own family in his own way.

'Wonderful,' he told them, his voice heavy with sarcasm. 'We'll begin making plans today.'

'We'll wait to hear from your office what is expected of us then,' his mother said, reaching for her newspaper again, and he knew he was dismissed. He plucked a croissant from the basket at the centre of the table, wrapped it in a heavy linen napkin and left the room, coffee in hand.

'Is that for me?' Hailey asked, pushing herself up on her elbows as Gio walked into the room, and he passed the croissant over without hesitation.

'It is. I can have something else sent up if you want.'

'No,' Hailey said, sitting up properly now and taking the pastry from him, suddenly realising she was famished. 'This is perfect. Is the coffee for me too?'

He passed over the cup. 'As long as you don't mind sharing.'

'We've shared more.' She smiled. 'Sorry, that was crude.'

But Gio grinned as he sat on the side of the bed. 'Don't apologise on my account. I rather liked the things we shared.'

She grinned at him over their shared cup of coffee.

'Did you talk to your parents again?' she asked, feeling the carbs and coffee hit her system, restoring some sense of normality.

'How did you know?'

'You have a look.' Lines on his forehead, tense muscles in his jaw, ramrod-straight spine. 'How did it go?' she asked.

'As well as one could have hoped,' Gio said, and she wondered whether he really thought that she would fall for that kind of polite evasion.

'Terrible, then?'

Gio nodded. 'I threatened to renounce my title and leave the country. That sorted things out.'

Hailey froze, her cup halfway to her lips. He couldn't seriously have threatened to do that for her. For the baby, she corrected herself. 'You didn't,' she said.

'Actually, I did.' For the first time the muscle in Gio's jaw eased slightly.

'Why would you do that?'

'Because I don't want to be part of a family that doesn't welcome my wife and child.'

Well, didn't that just hit her right in the centre of the chest? Because perhaps it was the two of them, standing on the edge of this family, not quite accepted at the centre.

'And what did they say?' she asked.

'That I was being rash.'

She snorted. 'Well, they weren't entirely wrong.'

'I meant it, though,' Gio said, reaching for her hand, his face earnest. 'I'll move to New York, if that's what you want. If you want a normal life for this baby. My family—it's…far from ideal.'

'But it's your family,' she said. 'And our baby's too. I don't want to take them away from the place where they belong.' Was that really what was most important, she had to ask, even if it wasn't where Gio wanted to be? But she had to try—belonging to a family was what she'd wanted her whole life, and she couldn't just decide for her baby that they wouldn't have that—even if it hurt Gio.

'The baby belongs with your family too,' Gio said, which was her cue, she supposed, to confess to her lack of one.

'Ah, well,' she said, trying to keep her voice casual. 'I don't really have a family.'

'I'm sorry,' Gio said, reaching for her hand. 'Do you want to talk about it?'

'There's not really much to talk about. But I suppose I should tell you the whole story, because we'll have to think about how to handle the press. I don't know my biological parents—they gave me up for adoption when I was a baby. After that there were children's homes and foster families. I was adopted as an older child, and they were nice people, but it was too late for them to feel like *my* family.'

'I'm sorry,' Gio said earnestly. 'That sounds…lonely.'

Hailey shrugged. 'It is what it is. But I don't want our baby to be…rootless, like I am.'

'And that's why you agreed to the marriage,' Gio said, realisation clearly dawning.

'I don't want you cutting off your family just because they don't like me,' she said with a sudden pang of guilt.

Gio shook his head. 'It's not that they don't like you. They don't know you. They just have their own ideas for my future, and they think they should be the ones making decisions for me.'

'I don't care if they like me. I wouldn't expect them to in the circumstances.'

'If I walked away from people who don't support me it wouldn't be the same thing. I don't want you to worry about me.'

'But I do.' She reached out a hand and stilled him with her palm on his cheek. 'I do care, Gio.'

He forced a smile. 'Of course you do. For the baby's sake. I do understand, you know.'

'No, you don't. I care for your sake. I don't like seeing you hurt.'

And she didn't want to think too hard about why that was. But she'd had years to accept that her parents had hurt her. The wound was healed—scarred, and angry, but no longer open. Gio's wounds were fresh and she couldn't bear to see how it was hurting him.

He turned his face into her palm until his lips brushed the heel of her hand. Then, with a sigh, he pulled away, wrapped his fingers around hers and let their joined hands fall to the blankets.

'I'm not hurt. And you don't have to protect me.'

She could accept the second half of that declaration. And he might be able to hide his hurt from himself, but she could see it clear as day. But if he wasn't ready to talk about it, she didn't have any choice but to accept that.

'What time is it?' she asked, feeling a strong need to change the subject.

'Nearly ten,' Gio replied, looking relieved. 'I have a meeting with my chamberlain in an hour to start making arrangements for the wedding. In the meantime, what would you like to do—a tour of the palace? A more substantial breakfast? A longer lie-in?'

'How about another cup of coffee and a tour?'

'Perfect. I'll have a tray sent up and let you get dressed. Just come through when you're ready.'

'Gio…' she said as he was about to turn away. He raised an eyebrow. She looked him up and down—well-pressed shirt and trousers. His hair neater than she'd ever seen it. 'What does one wear to tour a palace?'

He smiled. 'Whatever you're comfortable in will be perfect.'

She nodded, not sure if she should say what she was thinking. That she couldn't care less whether she was wearing the right thing in the eyes of his parents, but he so obviously cared about their good opinion and she didn't want to add to his distress. In the end, she pulled out a pair of black jeans and the cashmere sweater she'd 'borrowed' after their night together. Perhaps she'd feel a little more as if she belonged here. In the closet she found that her black leather boots had been cleaned and polished and she pulled them on.

When she left the bedroom Gio was waiting for her in the living room of their apartment. He smiled at the sight of her, and she knew that he recognised his sweater but didn't say anything. He just poured her a cup of coffee from the silver tray that had appeared on the coffee table and held it out to her. His expression was carefully guarded, the result, she was sure, of her gentle probing into his feelings about his parents. So she kept their conversation on safer ground as they toured the palace, asking questions about the portraits hanging along the walls in their gilt frames. Gently teasing him about why a palace required a Crystal Ballroom *and* a Gold Ballroom, and how one decided which of one's ballrooms to use when one was throwing a ball. As Gio told her the stories of his forebears in the palace, she watched his shoulders drop, his gait loosen and the hint of a smile return to his mouth.

'You don't want a ballroom for our wedding?' Gio asked. 'You can choose Crystal or Gold. Whatever your heart desires, Princess.'

'I thought you wanted to keep things simple,' Hailey said with a startled laugh.

'I do,' Gio replied. 'But I realise I never actually asked if that's what you want, which was unforgivable of me. If you want a ballroom, of course you can have a ballroom.'

She shook her head. 'Small and simple suits me just fine. I'd feel a little awkward not filling my half of a ballroom.'

'I'm sorry; I didn't think,' Gio said. 'But if there's anyone you would like to invite, you should. I know it's short notice, but one of the benefits of marrying into my family is that we are good with the logistics of flying people around.'

She shook her head. 'Really, there's only Gracie, and I couldn't ask her to disrupt her holiday plans.'

Gio frowned at her. 'I don't know. I got the feeling that she would disrupt just about anything if you asked her to.'

'Which is why I'm careful about what I ask for. I wouldn't want to put her out.'

Gio looked at her long enough that she shifted in her boots, until she rolled her eyes, breaking their eye contact and turning away from him. 'Then let's go look at the morning room. It's beautiful with the low sun at this time of year. I think you'll like it.'

He led her through a series of opulent chambers, the names and functions of which she couldn't hope to guess at, until Gio opened the door to a small room with walls lined in cream silk, the sun slanting in low through windows that reached from the distant ceiling to the tops of the baseboards.

A small cluster of silk-upholstered chairs was arranged around a roaring fire and a pretty writing bureau faced the windows out onto the snow-covered formal gardens.

'What do you think?' Gio asked, hands clasped behind his back.

'I think it's beautiful,' Hailey said. Because what other word could she use to describe such a fairy tale location?

'How many people will be attending?' she asked, suddenly realising she had no idea what a 'small' royal wedding looked like.

'As many or as few as we want,' Gio said. 'Though my parents will expect certain dignitaries to be on the guest list. I have an inconvenient number of cousins. I'll keep it as small as I can, but it would make life easier if we give in on a few of the more senior names.'

'If it makes things easier with your parents, then of course do what you have to do.'

He smiled and nodded. 'I have friends too, from school and university, that I'd like to invite. But the timing will make it awkward so hopefully a lot of them won't be able to make it. I quite like the idea that this is something for us. Not some grand performance.'

'I agree. And in the circumstances… I moved around a lot as a child and didn't make any friendships that survived my move to New York. Things with my adoptive parents are… This is rather *a lot* to have to explain to them. Never mind expecting them to come here and be a part of this circus. I know I should tell them, but I honestly don't know…'

She turned to look out of the window and her shoulder bumped against Gio's side. She should move away from him, but the feel of him beside her was comforting and she would take whatever reassurance she could get at the moment.

'I can't wait to see these gardens in the summer,' she said. 'They must be spectacular.'

'Remind me to introduce you to the head gardener,' Gio said, leaning back into her just a fraction. 'I'm sure you two would have a lot to talk about.'

'I'd like that,' Hailey said, thinking. It was only just starting to sink in how much she had left behind in New York, with no idea if she was ever going back.

She had built her business with her own cold, red, chapped hands. Bleaching buckets in Gracie's shop at five in the morning. Putting in eighteen-hour days in the run-up to weddings, conditioning flowers and putting in the extra effort to deliver anything her clients demanded. Eventually, she'd outgrown Gracie's business and, with her friend's support and the growing reputation of her fine art style, had branched out on her own, building her client list for high-profile events, with her own team of assistants, hand-picked and trained by her and Gracie until they worked like a well-planned, well-executed machine. Sure, they would be able to handle the events she'd already designed without her. The designs for the next two months were already signed off with the clients. She could absolutely trust her team to bring them to life.

God knew she could do with a break from her endlessly freezing cold workshop, snipping stems and sweeping away the forest carpet of foliage that gathered as they trimmed away leaves.

But the designs? She had never considered giving that up. When she had met Gracie, discovered the art she could create, the emotions she could evoke with her floral installations, she had finally found her place. She had built her whole adult life, her whole adult identity, around her love of art, her job and her business. Without those, who was she? Was she the lost, rootless girl she had been when she'd landed in the United States for the first time?

She remembered the lonely young woman she had been back then and shivered.

'Are you cold?' Gio asked, pulling her into his side with an arm around her shoulder, but she shook her head and stepped away from him.

'Just wondering how my team are getting on without me. I have a lot of decisions to make about what to do with the business. I don't see how I can continue to run it if I'm living here.'

'I'm sorry. I hate how much you're having to give up to be here.'

'You don't need to apologise,' she told him. 'Give me enough credit to know that I can make my own choices. I want to be here. I just don't know enough about what my life will be like here to know if I can run a business. I've got no contacts. No clients. No suppliers.'

'You have talent and experience, wherever you decide to use it. And a royal household at your disposal.'

'And while I'm grateful for that, I'm not sure that I want my business relying on inherited privilege.'

Gio crossed his arms and faced her. 'Like my life is? Like our child's life will be?'

'I don't know, Gio! I want to be here. I want to be

with you! I just don't know how any of this works in practice. I'm going to be a princess, for goodness' sake. I don't know *how* to be a princess.'

'You want to be with me?' Gio said, taking a step towards her so that she had to crane her neck to look up at his face, and her whole body hummed with awareness of how close he was. But she had to concentrate on what they were talking about here.

'For God's sake, Gio. That's the part of this you hear? This whole situation is so confusing. I have no idea what my life is going to look like a month from now. And it's making me want to hold onto those things that I *do* know extra hard. And that's one of them. I don't know where that leaves us.'

Gio's body language relaxed and he turned back towards the window.

'It leaves us with the things we can control now,' he said gently, and she took solace from the calm competence in his voice. 'Which right now is the wedding, where we want to spend Christmas and keeping you well and the baby well. Would you like to meet with the palace physician?'

'Do we have a choice over where we spend Christmas?' she asked.

'If we want to,' he told her. 'We have a ski lodge up in the mountains. We could escape, just the two of us. Leave all the rigmarole of the royal stuff behind.'

God, that was tempting. Dangerous, but so very, very tempting. But a sure-fire way of pissing off the in-laws and guaranteeing tension in their future relationship. 'That isn't exactly going to endear me to your family,' she told him 'Stealing you away for my first Christmas here.'

'I don't care what they think,' he said with a shrug.

'Well, I do,' she said. She didn't have the luxury of not caring, like he did. 'I'm going to have to live with their opinion of me, and it's low enough as it is. I don't want you shielding me from them.'

'Then we'll spend Christmas here,' he said. 'But trust me. Give it a week and you'll be begging me for a break.'

CHAPTER EIGHT

THE TEN DAYS until Christmas had stretched before her like an eternity, making her wonder how she was going to fill the time. For a 'small' wedding with only a handful of guests, it seemed to require just as much planning as the largest society wedding. And as much as she and Gio had told his parents and their staff that they didn't need to sign off on every detail, still the questions kept coming. About menus, vows, music, candles. The only area where Hailey truly had an opinion was, of course, the flowers.

She sat with the head gardener and the palace florist, talking about what was in season locally, what was flowering in the greenhouses, what displays had already been planned for the holidays and could be adapted for a wedding.

She walked in the forest with the groundskeepers, pointing out foliage for garlands to be strung, wound and arranged around the morning room where the ceremony would take place and the stairs where the Queen was insisting that they had formal photographs taken. They had at least managed to draw the line at a press conference on the wedding day itself. Instead they had promised official engagement photographs in exchange for an embargo on the news until Christmas Eve and the press keeping their distance from the wedding itself.

She had a video conference with her ob-gyn in New York and a local specialist she and Gio had chosen, to ensure her continuity of care whether they were in Adria or New York.

She now stood looking at the rail of dresses that Gio's private secretary had sent over for approval. It was Christmas Eve, snowing, below freezing outdoors, which meant it was barely above that temperature in the vast formal rooms of the palace. How was she meant to choose what to wear? This was more than just what she liked and what was comfortable. The dress she chose today would be photographed and shared around the world in an instant. This outfit was going to be all that people knew about her. If she chose a designer outfit, would she look out of touch? If she went high street, was she going to be the commoner who was dragging the royal family and the whole of Adria into the gutter she'd emerged from?

She flicked through the rail: navy trouser suit, emerald shift dress, a deep ruby wrap dress cut on the bias, with a cascade of pleats to the front. Well, that would solve the baby bump issue, she supposed, which had suddenly decided to make itself known on the morning of the photoshoot. She checked the notes that Gio's chamberlain had provided with each outfit, with the details about where each item had come from.

This one was from an up-and-coming Adrian designer. A one-off piece. She held the dress up in front of her in the mirror and smiled at how the colour added roses to her cheeks and brought out the chestnut tones in her hair.

She turned her head at a knock at the door and raised an eyebrow at Gio in question when he walked in.

'It's beautiful,' he said. 'Is that the one you've chosen?'

'I think so. What do you think it says about me?'

He smiled. 'That you look great in red?'

She rolled her eyes. 'I know you're more savvy about the press than that. Does it send the right message?'

'This sends the message that you are beautiful and smart and accomplished.'

Which were all the right things to say, of course. Which made it more than a little suspicious.

'That's a talkative dress,' she observed, her voice sardonic.

'To be fair, it's your face that's saying most of it.'

'You're an exceptionally smooth talker, you know that?'

'How else would I have got you to agree to marry me?'

Hailey laughed, hanging the dress back on the rail. 'Do you really want me to answer that?'

He shook his head, smiling. 'No. I want you to come here and look at this. It's a good thing. I think. I hope.' He sat on the love seat in front of the window and patted the cushion beside him. 'Come, sit. Please?'

He pulled a small leather box from his pocket and for a moment she forgot to breathe. This was the part in the fairy tale where she was meant to swoon. And it might be clichéd, but she couldn't help but be slightly overwhelmed at the thought of him dropping to one knee while holding that tiny box.

'We talked about a ring,' he said, 'and if there's something in particular that you want then you only have to say. But I saw this in the family collection and it seemed so perfect for you...'

He looked up at her, and she recognised hope in his eyes. She took the box from his outstretched hand. The leather was warm from his skin and she turned it over a couple of times, not sure how she felt about it.

'You didn't have to do this,' she said. They'd talked about a ring, once, briefly. But, in the grand scheme of things, it just hadn't seemed important.

'We're about to announce our engagement. Trust me when I say you need a ring,' he said.

'But a family piece…'

'Is entirely appropriate for a woman who's about to become my family.'

She shook her head because there was just no chance that he could understand what she was feeling.

'What about my background?' she asked. Because he might think that it didn't matter, but he was wrong.

'What about it?' he asked, proving her point.

'The press are going to have a field day,' she said. 'Digging around. All those foster parents to pay for their stories. All those kids I shared children's homes with. My birth parents, wherever they are. My adoptive parents. I know I should have told them already. But it's too late for a Christmas card and I haven't picked up the phone and called them in over a year. I just can't do it.'

He reached for her fidgeting hands. Closed his around them, trapping the ring box inside.

'Does a family ring change that? Because we can absolutely choose something new. No weird family connections involved. But…'

'But?' she asked, not sure how he could possibly make wearing a piece of jewellery from the royal collection feel right on someone like her.

'But all of those things you're worried about would still be the case, regardless of which ring you choose. We've spoken to the press office about your past. They're handling it. Would you like to talk about it again?'

'No, no. That's not what I mean. It's just… I'm not

the sort of person who's meant to wear a piece from the royal collection, am I?'

'You're the woman I'm marrying,' Gio said, pulling her closer, 'which is precisely why you are the right woman to wear a family ring.'

'This is precisely the problem, Gio. You're marrying me, but I'm not the sort of woman you *should* be marrying. And you know that your family agrees with me.'

'You're the woman I *want* to marry,' Gio argued. 'I feel like that should count for more than what my parents think. Isn't what *we* want more important?' he demanded.

It was so easy for him to say that. He wasn't the one who was going to be curtseying to the wrong duchesses and turning up to the polo match in the wrong shoes. If he thought that didn't matter, then he was being either hopelessly obtuse or naïve.

'I think that it will matter to the journalists who are going to slate me for every mistake. It matters to your friends and family, who will be laughing at me behind my back.'

Gio ran a hand through his hair again, a sure sign that he was reaching the end of his patience. 'Hailey, did you forget how we met? You know my friends. And you know that Sebastian thinks you're great.'

'Sebastian isn't your mother,' she pointed out.

'Why is my mother's approval so important?'

He *was* being obtuse, because there was no way that Gio could possibly be unaware of the answer to that question.

'Because she's your mother, Gio, and the *Queen*.'

'You're having doubts.' Gio said, which was quite the leap from what she had said. And a convenient way to turn this conversation back on itself.

'No, I'm not.' She couldn't have doubts because she

wasn't marrying Gio for herself, which meant that her
feelings about his mother didn't come into it. She was
doing this for their baby. 'I'm just starting to realise what
I've let myself in for. I thought I was done with feeling
like this,' she added with a sigh. Because she might have
no thoughts of backing out but that didn't mean that she
was blind to the challenges that lay ahead of them.

'Like what?' Gio asked.

'Like the one who's always going to be on the outside
looking in. Always trying to look like I belong when
everyone knows that I don't.'

'That's not how I feel,' Gio argued, taking her hand.

Hailey shook her head because that really wasn't the
point. 'It's not about feelings, Gio. It's about facts. And
one fact that we can be certain of is that I'm never going
to fit in with your family. It doesn't change my mind.
I still want to marry you. I suppose I'm just realising
what that's going to mean for me.'

'My family isn't *our* family,' Gio said with an edge
to his voice. '*Our* family is the three of us, and if being
in Adria makes you feel that way then maybe we should
think again about living somewhere else. Or maybe
you really should reconsider whether marrying me is
the right thing to do.'

'If I do that, our baby is going to grow up as an out-
sider too, and I can't do that to them. No. I know what
I have to do, and I'm sorry for the wobble.'

'What you *have* to do? Hailey, you don't have to do
anything that you don't want to. I don't want to marry
someone who's only doing it because she feels she has
no choice. Call me old-fashioned but I'd rather have
someone who *wants* to marry me, even if it's not for
romantic reasons.'

Hailey stared at him. 'But you're doing this for the same reason, let's not pretend that—'

Before she could finish her sentence, Gio had pulled her to him and slid his fingers into her hair. He tilted her face up to his and she resisted the urge to turn her cheek into the heat of his palm. Instead, she tipped her chin up, just a fraction, so that she could look him in the eye.

She took a breath, determined to finish her sentence, but before she could speak Gio's eyelashes swept closed, his chin dipped and his lips pressed hard against hers. She shivered as his fingertips curled into the short hairs at her nape, and wound her arms around his neck, pulling herself higher as Gio deepened the kiss, licking into her mouth, wrapping an arm tight around her waist and pinning her to his body, any thought of keeping her feet on the ground—either literally or metaphorically—long forgotten.

When he pulled away, taking in a great, heaving gasp of air, she realised that she was as far gone as he was, could feel the hot pink flush of her skin, the rapid beating of her heart and the gasp of rapid breaths.

She raised her eyebrows at Gio, not trusting herself to speak just yet.

'I'm marrying you because I want to,' he said by way of explanation. She had yet to find the capacity for speech, so had no choice but to let him go on. 'The fact that you're pregnant is part of that, of course it is. But you seem to have this idea that I'm acting out of some disinterested sense of duty. And, as I think I have just made painfully clear, that couldn't be further from the truth.'

She stared up at him as he slowly loosened his arms but kept her close. 'But I thought… I didn't think that we were…' She floundered, unable to form a sentence. Because this was everything that she had told herself not to want. If they were going to add their *feelings* into this situation then she had no idea where it was heading. If she could tell herself that they were both doing this for the baby, then she could let herself believe that it was a good idea. That there was some version of the future that ended with a happy family life, rather than with her heart broken, piecing together the parts of her life that remained when Gio burned it to the ground.

But if this was going to get personal, if Gio was saying that he wanted *her*—just her, not her baby, not her as a mother to his child, or even a princess to his prince—if he wanted her then it was personal. It would be her, personally, who would be left broken when it all went wrong.

'We don't have to,' Gio said, his voice low and rough, almost breaking with barely contained emotion. 'If I misread things and this isn't what you want... If you want to pretend that this never happened and you're happier with the idea that I've not thought about you that way since that night, then fine. I can give you that. But I couldn't just let you make assumptions without... correcting them.'

'Consider me corrected,' she breathed, still not able to commit to a decision one way or another. On the one hand was Gio, and kissing, and the fact that she might expire from frustration if she didn't get him into the nearest bed very soon. And on the other...her heart. Which had been bruised so many times before that she couldn't bear the thought of exposing it again.

'So,' Gio asked gently. 'Is that what you want? To pretend this never happened? To go back to assuming that I'm doing this out of duty and nothing more? That I'm not thinking about leaning down and kissing you again right now?'

She shook her head because she couldn't deny what her body so clearly wanted. She didn't have it in her to lie at this moment. 'No. I don't want that,' she said. 'But that sounds a lot simpler than whatever it is you're suggesting.'

He nudged his nose against hers and she drew in a sharp breath at that intimacy. 'I'm suggesting we give this a try,' he murmured.

'Marriage,' she clarified. 'A real marriage. Not just…'

'Yes. Given that we're about to announce our engagement, and you're expecting my baby, resisting this attraction brings to mind sayings about horses bolting and stable doors.'

Attraction. Right. Of course. Hailey gave herself a mental slap to the side of the head. Not love; that would be ridiculous. Or affection, which would have been nice, she supposed. But at least attraction was simple. Straightforward. Gio was making it clear from the outset that this was about sex, and that was fine. That was as simple as duty, really, if she squinted at her own thoughts. This wasn't a love match and it never would be. She didn't have to worry about whether Gio was going to fall for her, because it had never been on the cards. But attraction—*that* she could return, safely, without risking anything getting broken. In that they were equal.

Her hands had come to rest against Gio's chest and she let them drift down to his hips, following the jut of his waist around to his back. She arched back against the arm at her waist, looking up at him thoughtfully.

'Resisting has been rather…energy-intensive,' Hailey conceded, as if the way she had bowed her body towards him at the first brush of his lips hadn't been perfectly eloquent without her saying a word. 'And as the pregnancy goes on, I can't imagine I'm going to have all that much energy to spare. So it would make sense, really...'

Gio raised an eyebrow at her. 'From a purely practical standpoint?'

'Right. Yes. From a purely practical standpoint I think that more—' she looked them both up and down, gestured between their bodies '—more of this would be acceptable.'

Gio huffed out a little laugh, hands coming to her cheeks, tipping her face up until she was looking him in the eye again.

'Acceptable,' he repeated, his voice breaking into a gravelly lilt that did something dangerous between her thighs. 'Are you quite sure that was the word you wanted to choose? Not, perhaps, irresistible, or something similar?'

Her lips quirked up in a smile that she tried to tamp down. There was no need to feed his ego any more than necessary. 'I think "acceptable" just about covers it,' she said, though it would have been more effective if her voice hadn't dropped to a breathy whisper.

'Then I see I need to try harder to impress you.'

Gio gave her one of his full-on smiles, and just like the first time she was lost in those wrinkles around his eyes, the lines bracketing his wide mouth and his even white teeth.

'Try as hard as you like,' she invited, tipping herself up towards him and letting out a groan as his lips came down to meet hers.

CHAPTER NINE

Attraction. That was safe enough, Gio told himself. He'd been dreaming—literally and metaphorically—about having Hailey back in his arms ever since that first night in New York. It couldn't be any more dangerous to claim her, surely.

He just had to remember that they were only talking about attraction here. No one had said anything about emotions being involved, and he knew better than to think someone might love him just because he loved them. So he would stop fighting this need he had to put his hands on Hailey, to have her lips on the stubble beneath his jaw or her breath in his ear as he kissed his way along her neck.

He just had to remember not to fall for her, because she couldn't have made it any clearer that she wouldn't be here at all if she hadn't been pregnant. She hadn't chosen him, or this life. She was making the best of it in order to give their baby the family she thought it deserved. He couldn't expect her to love him when not even his own family had managed that. Realistic expectations were the only thing that were going to keep his heart safe.

Hailey eased herself away from him just a fraction and they both glanced down at the dress that she was somehow still holding, which had been crushed between their bodies.

He loosened his arm around her waist and she took half a step back, away from him.

'I'm going to have to get this pressed,' she said with a look that caused a very self-satisfied grin to light up his face.

'I'm sorry if I inconvenienced you,' he said, and Hailey hit him gently in the chest, rolling her eyes.

'Don't fish for compliments. It's not dignified.'

He laughed, taking the dress from her, shaking out the worst of the creases and hanging it back on the rail.

'How are you feeling about the photographs? Is there anything else you need?'

'Can you get me a lifetime of experience in the public eye so that I don't feel quite so terrified?'

He smiled a little wistfully. 'I wouldn't wish that on you, darling.'

Darling? He didn't know where the endearment had come from. And it shouldn't have felt so natural on his lips. He refused to overthink it. It was just a word. Generic and impersonal, the sort of word anyone might use with a woman they had just thoroughly kissed. There was absolutely no reason for the hook he felt in his stomach.

'Then I suppose I'm as prepared as I am ever likely to be,' Hailey said, with no mention of his verbal slip. Perhaps she hadn't even noticed it. Perhaps she just assumed it meant nothing.

'You approve of the dress?' she asked.

'You don't need my approval.'

Hailey made a little huff of frustration. 'I'm asking you as an expert on press relations. Not as my fiancé.'

'Well, then,' Gio replied. 'In my role as your unofficial press advisor, I would say that the dress is an excellent choice. As your fiancé I would say that you look glowing and beautiful, but we both know that my opinion isn't important.'

She reached up and kissed him on the lips. A touch gentler, more comfortable, safer, than the one they had shared before.

'Thank you. Then I've got everything I need.'

They both looked around at the sound of a knock at the door.

'Hair and make-up are ready for Ms Thomas,' the chamberlain said when Gio called for him to enter.

'We just need a few minutes,' Gio said, glancing over his shoulder. 'We'll call you when Ms Thomas is ready.' He had almost forgotten that he had come in here with a task to accomplish, and he couldn't leave until it was done.

'Was there something else?' Hailey asked, her expression quizzical as the chamberlain snicked the door closed behind him. Gio picked up the ring box from the coffee table, where it had sat, forgotten, while they'd thrashed out how they felt about one another.

Dropping to one knee, he opened the box, held it up to Hailey and said, 'This is how I should have done this in the first place. Hailey Thomas, would you do me the great honour of agreeing to marry me?'

Hailey took the ring from the box, turning it over in her fingers as she followed the winding fern engraving around the delicate gold circlet.

'Gio, it's beautiful. Perfect. I love it.'

He smiled again, broadly, with a deep glow of satisfaction that he knew her well enough to anticipate her reaction.

'When I saw it, I thought it could have been made for you. I hope I wasn't presumptuous.'

'Not at all,' she said, watching his face as he slid the ring onto her finger. 'I'm touched that you chose something so perfect. Yes, of course I will marry you.' He stood and glanced down as she let her hand rest on his chest, and the sight of the ring on her finger, a visible sign of the commitment they were making together, made something feel tight behind where her hand rested.

'I really do have to get ready,' Hailey said, looking him in the eye and letting her tongue flicker over her lips in a way that was absolutely not going to help that happen any time soon. He groaned, pressed a quick kiss to her lips and stepped away.

'I'll leave you to it,' he said. 'Have someone call me if you need anything.'

Hailey turned her hand in the light from the window. She had meant what she'd said to Gio just now—the ring was perfect. If he hadn't told her that it was a family piece, she could have believed that he had had it made for her.

Suddenly, with Gio's ring on her finger, this whole thing felt real in a way that even having his child growing inside her hadn't yet achieved. When she walked out of the palace wearing his ring, that would be all anyone would be interested in. She was setting herself up for a life that was Gio-adjacent, and everything she did from that moment on would be judged on how well she integrated herself into his family. Well, she considered, at least she had already fulfilled her first obligation as a princess by getting pregnant. There was one thing, at least, that she couldn't be accused of failing at. Though no doubt once everyone realised that the date of conception roundly coincided with the date that she had met Gio, the tabloid press—and Gio's family—would have plenty to say about how a royal baby *should* be conceived.

Which, she was sure, would be right about when Gio changed his mind and started wondering how he could get himself out of the situation they were in. It had happened again and again through her childhood, sometimes after the first sleep-deprived night, when the nightmares that had followed her through a succession of homes had caused her to cry out in her sleep, waking other children, babies, pets. Foster parents who thought that taking in an older child would mean avoiding the night-time waking of an infant. Only to find by morning that an emotional, traumatised child was not the easy option.

Sometimes it had come after a month, or three. For a million reasons she'd forced herself not to care about because they all amounted to the same thing: none of them had wanted to keep her.

She had every reason to assume that her relationship with Gio would follow the exact same pattern. If she hadn't got pregnant their first night together, she would never have seen him again—she would be long forgotten by now.

She had tried to warn him off rushing into this marriage. But if he was going to insist on giving their baby everything that she wanted for it by marrying her and making them a family then she was going to take him up on it.

But she wasn't stupid enough to think that it would be for ever. Sure, there might never have been a divorce in the Adrian royal family, something that Gio had explained was the reason his parents were still married—and still miserable—but there were plenty of ways for Gio to send her back to New York without legally end-ing their marriage. He could stop coming home. He could simply just stop caring.

Whatever happened between them, wherever that kiss just now was heading, the most important thing she had to do now was remember that.

She could enjoy this now—she *should* enjoy this now. How often did you actually get to marry Prince Charming? But she could never lose sight of the fact that his feelings for her were only temporary.

She could give up a lot—her home, her business, her privacy—but she wasn't stupid enough to give up her heart. Protecting that was her last line of defence.

The photographs were being taken in the morning room, where they would be getting married in just a week. It was heavily decorated for the Christmas season, with boughs of greenery around the mirror behind the writing bureau, swagged pine wreaths across the fireplace and branching candelabras on side tables. An enormous tree had been erected in the corner beside the French windows and the natural light caught in the silver and crystal decorations.

A brocade-upholstered chaise had been pulled in front of the window, the low winter sun picking out the silver in the ivory fabric. Hailey hesitated after a footman showed her into the room, watching Gio where he was talking with the chamberlain and the photographer. He had had his own encounter with the hair and make-up team, it seemed. His curls were tucked neatly back after she had mussed them earlier, his stubble trimmed as short as she had seen it.

His suit was a sober charcoal three-piece, with a silver silk tie and snowy-white shirt that had been pressed to within an inch of its life. In short, there was nothing about him that would possibly betray the fact that there was a human under all that tailoring rather than something chiselled from cold, hard marble.

That was until he looked up and saw her, and one of those devastating grins spread across his features and her mind was cast dangerously back in time, to the night that they'd first met, when that smile had been her undoing.

And then she remembered. This was showtime. The photographer was here to capture the happy couple with their whirlwind romance—a much better cover for a shotgun wedding than a drunkenly and accidentally conceived illegitimate prince or princess. That was the reason for Gio's smile—he was playing the part of an adoring fiancé, she reminded herself, and he was waiting for her to do the same. She crossed the room to him and accepted his kiss on both cheeks, before his fingertips found her chin and tipped her face up to his until she met his gaze. She felt her cheeks flush with heat at the look in his eyes.

'What's wrong?' Gio asked, clearly picking up on her discomfort, his hand on her cheek now.

'Nothing,' she said, wiping her face clear of whatever it was giving away. 'Just nervous, I suppose.'

'Don't be,' Gio said, his voice low. 'Just be yourself. That's all we need to show everyone.'

Not true, her brain protested. They needed to show the people what they wanted to see. Not the messy, real-life problems beneath it all.

Being herself had never been enough in the past, and it certainly wasn't going to be enough to navigate through this new royal life. What she needed to do was fake it. Because perhaps if she did that for long enough, this life would start to feel real and she could kid herself that she belonged in it. Maybe one day she might start to believe it.

She pasted a smile onto her face that she hoped looked more genuine than it felt, and met Gio's eyes before very deliberately stretching up onto her toes to kiss him on the lips. 'I'm fine.' She turned her smile onto the photographer. 'Should I sit?'

The photographer, his assistant and the hair and make-up team bundled her to the chaise and spent an inordinate amount of time tweaking pleats and placing hands and checking light levels. She was aware that she was sitting as if she had a stick up her arse, and that in this position her dress probably wasn't doing a great job of hiding their little secret.

Every time the camera clicked she flinched, and her grip on Gio where their fingers were entwined went a little more white-knuckled.

Until Gio lifted their linked hands to his lips while the photographer checked something on his laptop.

'You either need to tell me what's wrong or find me a paramedic, darling,' Gio said quietly in her ear. 'Because if you squeeze any tighter, bones are going to start breaking.' She tried to snatch her hand away, but Gio captured it in his, pressing a kiss to the centre of her palm.

As she tried to process his words, from the corner of her eye she caught sight of a bare patch in one of the garlands. The mistletoe had lost its berries, and leaves had been crushed where someone had been heavy-handed when it was installed.

'What's wrong?' Gio asked, following the line of her gaze to the fireplace.

'Nothing's wrong,' she said on reflex.

Gio arched an eyebrow. 'Are you sure about that? You seem to be staring.'

She grunted quietly with frustration. 'Okay, fine. There's a bare patch in the garland over there. It's annoying me and I can't concentrate. But it's fine. Probably no one else would even notice.'

'But you've noticed, and it's bothering you,' he said, his voice maddeningly reasonable.

She shrugged. 'It's fine, okay? Just drop it.'

'Look, if you want to fix the garland, you should fix the garland,' Gio said.

'We're in the middle of a photoshoot,' she hissed from the corner of her mouth, trying not to move from the position the photographer had finally deemed acceptable. 'I just want to get this over with.'

'They'll wait,' Gio said, his voice terse. 'You just said yourself you're not happy with how it's going. The great thing about marrying me—'

She snorted half a laugh—she couldn't help it.

'The great thing about marrying me,' Gio went on, though with a twinkle in his eye, 'is that you sometimes get things to be just how you want them. Take advantage of that. If you want to fix the garland, we'll put things on hold while you get it how you want it.'

She glanced at the photographer and then rolled her eyes. 'Fine, well, if I am marrying you, there should at least be some perks.' But she couldn't deny that the corners of her lips were turning up.

'We're taking a break,' Gio said, standing from the chaise and holding his hand out for Hailey. She slipped her hand into his and followed him across the room to the fireplace.

With the grand dimensions of the room, the garland was at head height and she had to strain her neck to properly see the strands that were bothering her.

'Need a hand?' Gio asked.

'Something to stand on,' she said, looking around.

'Aha,' Gio said, before returning with an upholstered footstool.

She raised a brow at him. 'I'm not standing on an antique.'

'It's fine. It's ugly and I don't want to inherit it anyway,' he said, making her laugh.

She wavered, but then kicked off her shoes. She tested the surface with her toes before tentatively stepping up, before Gio's hands came to rest on her waist.

'What are you doing?' she asked, spinning on the spot and nearly toppling off the stool in the process.

'Making sure you don't fall,' Gio said, his face straight. 'And a good job too, by the looks of it.'

'That was only because you—' she started, before Gio interrupted.

'I'm not risking you falling—not risking you or the baby. I'm planning on being horribly over-protective of you both; you'd better get used to the idea.'

She snorted at his overreaction but didn't move away. And it took probably more moments than it should for her to realise that she was still standing with her body pressed against his, with no real inclination to move. Not when the heat had returned to Gio's eyes and she felt herself warming under his appraisal.

'I should...' she started, but she couldn't really find the motivation to finish the sentence, not when she was doing what she had been thinking of doing since that kiss earlier, and with the audience still on the other side of the room there was no reason not to indulge the impulse to be close to him. They were meant to be madly in love—pressing herself against him and not denying how irresistible he was to her was practically her job now. As long as she didn't start to believe it herself, she was fine. She could play with it, and why not play with something that felt so good?

For the first time she was eye to eye with him, and suddenly the stool didn't seem so bad after all. She decided she quite liked it as she let herself drift towards him, let her lips brush against his. He smiled against her mouth and she took in his expression as she pulled her body away from his.

'I need to fix this garland,' she said, her voice soft.

'Uh-huh,' Gio managed, looking a little dazed. She turned and his hands stayed on her hips as she re-threaded the strands of the greenery that made up the bough, borrowing a sprig of berries from further along the garland and twisting leaves and stalks to hide the areas that had been crushed. She leant away from the fireplace and into Gio's shoulder to take in the effect.

'Better?' she asked.

'Much,' Gio answered, his lips close to her ear as his arms wrapped around her waist.

She snorted a laugh at him, but relaxed against his body as she took in her handiwork.

'You're meant to be looking at the garland,' she reminded him.

'Of course.' But his arms tightened around her waist and his lips pressed to her neck, and she suspected that he had about as much interest in the greenery as she did right now—which was close to zero.

A subtle clearing of throats from behind them snapped her out of whatever trance being so close to Gio's body had provoked. And if it hadn't been for his steadying hands on her hips she was quite sure that she would have lost her footing while performing an inelegant leap down from the stool. Somehow, despite the fact that having an audience had given her permission to let her feelings for Gio show for once, she'd quite forgotten that they were there once his body was close enough to hers that she could feel the heat of it even through the layers of starched cotton and brushed fine wool he was wearing.

'I'm sorry,' she said, walking back towards the chaise. 'Should I sit back where—?'

'Actually, Your Royal Highness,' the photographer said, addressing Gio, 'if you'll forgive me, I took the liberty while you were adjusting the floral arrangement, and I thought you might like to take a look...'

With more than a little trepidation, Hailey looked at the photographer's laptop as he drew up a couple of the shots. There was no denying that they were... compelling.

The red of her dress against the green of the pine boughs was undeniably festive, and the natural light combined with the candelabras either side of the fireplace was beautifully soft and atmospheric. But that was nothing compared to the warmth that was so obvious between her and Gio. As she'd leaned back against his shoulder and they'd shared a heated look. The way he'd watched her, hands anchoring her as she'd leaned to tweak the garland. The way that her body had been plastered against his from shoulder to knees, when she'd turned in his arms and he'd lowered her to the floor.

They looked very much...into one another. They were almost too revealing, Hailey thought, studying the expression on the face of the Hailey on the screen. The one who was staring into Gio's eyes as if no one else in the world existed.

But that was the story, she reminded herself. She and Gio might not have exactly worked out how this marriage of theirs was going to work, but what they had agreed on was that they wanted his family and the rest of the world to believe they were madly in love. And these photos…well, they certainly got the job done. And if it meant that she could get on with the rest of the day without having to sit stiffly on that chaise for a moment longer, then she was going to jump at the opportunity.

'These look wonderful,' she said, glancing up at Gio to make sure that they were on the same page. 'I'm happy if you are,' she added, waiting—and waiting—for him to respond. His gaze was fixed firmly on the screen, and in the end she resorted to slipping an arm around his waist in a less than subtle attempt to get his attention.

'Yes. Perfectly fine,' he said at last. 'I think we can wrap things up here.' And with that he strode from the room, leaving her bewildered in a room full of strangers.

'If you'll excuse me,' Hailey said to the photographer, hoping that she didn't sound quite as abandoned as she felt.

She walked from the room, wondering whether she should try and find Gio—what she would say to him when she did. Was he afraid, as she was, that those pictures had revealed too much? That in an unguarded moment they had revealed that this marriage was more real than either of them had intended? And if that was the case—if the feelings were real—where did that leave them? Because this had seemed so much simpler when they were both telling themselves—and each other—that they were only doing this for the baby's sake.

Before she had seen that look in Gio's eyes in the photos, so similar to the expression in her own. It made it so much harder to remember that this was all temporary—the attraction and, she didn't know, affection—that was between them, even if the legal marriage part meant that she was signing up to be around for the long haul. But the only way she could make that work was by making sure that she remembered that whatever Gio thought he might be feeling for her now, it wouldn't—couldn't—last. But if those pictures had been of anyone else—if they had been strangers, rather than herself and the man she was about to marry, she would have said that the feelings she could see between them looked very much like love.

But that was absurd. She couldn't love Gio. She'd only known him a few months, had spent barely a month of that time in his company. She lusted after him, sure. Fantasised about him. Thought about the night they had spent together and dreamed about it happening again. But she couldn't love him. *Couldn't.* Because this marriage was supposed to be simple—a way of giving her child the family life she wanted it to have. It was not meant to have anything to do with how she might feel about Gio personally.

The best thing that she could do about those feelings was bury them as deep as she could and pretend they'd never existed. And as for the rest of it—the kiss they'd shared earlier that day, how she'd felt with Gio's body hard against hers... Well, she'd not had feelings for Gio the one night they'd gone to bed together, any more than he'd had feelings for her. So there was no reason to conflate the two. They could kiss, or more, if they both wanted, without it meaning any more than it had that first night. And, hell, maybe it would make things easier if they weren't trying to deny what they wanted on that front. They were going to be married. She wanted that marriage to last. And she knew that she could do that without Gio loving her—she had never expected that in the first place—but she wasn't sure that she could be married to him without wanting him.

And it seemed as if they were reaching their limits on how long they could ignore that want.

She retraced her steps through the palace and found the door to their bedroom ajar, Gio sitting on the edge of the bed with his jacket discarded, tie loosened and hair curling rebelliously around his ears again.

'Hey,' she said from the doorway, and Gio looked up, clearly startled.

'Hailey,' he said, his voice cracking.

'Everything okay?' she asked. 'You left so quickly...' She crossed to the bed, planning on sitting beside him, but Gio caught her by the hips and pulled her between his legs, bringing them eye-to-eye again.

'I think we need to talk about how this marriage is going to work,' he said gruffly.

'Funny,' Hailey said, cupping his jaw and moving closer. 'I was thinking the same.'

'I want you,' Gio said bluntly, as if she didn't know it already. 'And when I saw those photos, I don't know... Maybe I'm just seeing what I want to see, but I think you feel the same. And that makes it so much harder to hold back from what I really want to do.'

'And what is it you want to do?' she asked, letting her hand stray round to his hair, where it was coming undone, threading her fingers into his curls and turning his face to her.

'This all started with me wanting you,' he said. 'With not being able to follow what was going on in that meeting because I couldn't stop looking at you.'

'Oh, and here was me thinking that this started with you yawning through my very important client presentation.' Hailey tried to make light of it, but her voice shook, and she knew there was no way of avoiding the conversation they were about to have.

Gio pulled her even closer, wrapping his arms around her waist and letting his forehead rest against her collarbone. 'Please, don't remind me. I thought you'd forgiven me for that.'

'Oh, I don't know,' she said, turning and pressing a kiss to the side of his head. 'If this is the reaction I get, I might bring it up more often.'

He pressed a kiss against her collarbone and she gasped. She felt his lips curl into a smile against her shoulder and didn't have to look down to know how his expression would have changed into something dangerous.

'We're getting married next week,' he said, brushing a kiss against the side of her neck that drew another gasp from her as she dug her fingers deeper into his hair.

'We are,' she agreed, tipping her head to one side to grant greater access where his lips were tracing up the side of her neck. His grip around her waist had loosened, and one hand ran down the smooth satin of her skirt, fingering the pleats until his fingertips found the hem at her calves and slid the fabric up, up, until he reached the bare skin at the top of her thigh and he groaned.

'Gio,' she said, her voice sounding distant, even to her own ears.

'Hmm,' he replied, and she felt it as a hum against her skin.

'I think maybe we were talking.'

'Mmm…' he said, and she felt the vibration of his lips all the way down to her thighs.

'And I think we should maybe finish that conversation before this goes any further.'

He paused, and her skin felt chilled where his lips had touched. He glanced up and met her eyes. 'Is that conversation going to conclude that we both want this to go where it is clearly going?'

'Well, yes, but—'

'Then isn't *afterwards* as good a time as any to have that conversation?'

Did he know that the soft touch of his fingertips around the top of her stocking was making it completely impossible to think? She had to suspect that he did, and yet she found no interest in stopping him. He was right. If this was inevitable, it didn't really matter whether they talked before or after.

Several hours later, as she tucked her chin onto his chest and struggled to stop herself falling asleep, she wondered why they had waited so long to do this again. Surely nothing that felt so good could be a mistake. And yet…

That was the problem, wasn't it? Because some parts of their life *did* feel so good, and yet others…too good to be true. Bathed in sweat and hormones and after-glow, and without the conversation she was sure that they needed to have, it would be too easy to forget all the things she'd been reminding herself of since she had got here. That she couldn't let herself fall for Gio. No matter how good or how right it felt lying here, with his shoulder for a pillow and his child growing inside her. Sooner or later, his affections would falter and the only way to survive that would be to protect herself from feeling too much. Now was the time she had to fortify those walls, make sure that she was strong enough to be with him, to give their baby the family it deserved, without letting herself get too hurt when it all ended.

CHAPTER TEN

HAILEY WOKE TO a light knock at the door, and a morning greeting from a maid, and as she was pushing herself up on her pillows and rubbing the sleep from her eyes she remembered that it was Christmas Day. She crossed to open the curtains. And a moment after that she remembered that she and Gio shared a bed now, and realised that on their first Christmas morning together they weren't waking up together.

They'd eaten supper in their apartment the night before, once they'd dragged themselves out of bed, eschewing the big family feast, knowing that they would be spending hours around the table today. And Gio had even skipped out on midnight mass, which she was sure they would pay for when they saw his parents today. But it had been inevitable really, that one time together wasn't going to be enough, and that it would be worth paying the price of skipping out on royal engagements as long as they were there for the *cenone* tomorrow—the big meal that the day revolved around. Today. Just a whole afternoon and evening with her soon-to-be in-laws, who she was pretty certain hated her already, and who she knew treated Gio so poorly. But this was the price she paid for giving their baby a family with a mother and a father and a safe home and a place in the world.

The whole point of being here was to be *with* Gio. So why wasn't he here? It wasn't exactly something she could ask the staff, and the very fact that she even had staff was something she could never get used to.

She showered and dressed slowly, not sure whether she was missing some important family breakfast or something, but there was no way she was leaving this room without Gio by her side to protect her.

Just as she was about ready to renounce their engagement and run off back to New York, Gio turned up with a tray full of toast and tea, and if she wasn't already planning on marrying him in less than a week, that could have been the deciding vote.

'Thought you might want something to eat before you have to face my family, so I raided the kitchens,' he said, placing the tray on her dressing table and catching her by the hand. He reeled her in, slid a hand to the short hair at the nape of her neck and pulled gently. She looked up and melted. It was unfortunate to have a fiancé so irresistible, even when you were mad at him.

'I was cross with you,' she murmured against his lips.

'I'm sorry. I didn't think you'd wake before I got back,' he said. 'You were sleeping so deeply when I left.'

'Well, I was tired, for some reason.' She gave him a smirk and was rewarded with a boyish grin.

'Will I be forgiven if I give you your Christmas present? We usually exchange gifts after lunch, but I'd rather it was just us here.'

'A gift?' Hailey asked, surprised. Between the baby and the wedding and moving halfway across the world in the space of a couple of weeks, Christmas presents had been so far down her agenda that they had fallen off the bottom completely. 'You can't, Gio,' she exclaimed. 'I haven't got you anything. I didn't even think.'

'Would it make you feel better if I told you that it was more of a…a loan than a gift?'

She frowned, both confused and intrigued. 'What do you mean?'

He grabbed her hand and pulled her into their sitting room, where a cloth was draped over something that could only be a picture frame, standing on a very dignified-looking gold easel.

'Gio…what have you done?' she asked nervously.

'It's just a loan,' he reminded her, pulling her by the hand until they were standing in front of the easel.

She reached out slowly for the gold draped cloth and pulled. In the second before it fell she knew what painting it was going to be, and her heart dropped into her stomach.

'Gio, you didn't— You can't— What did you do?' Because this painting was supposed to be in New York, at the exhibition she'd wished she'd been able to attend before she'd left. The one that she'd mentioned in passing to Gio, and she'd had no idea that he'd remembered.

'I didn't buy it,' Gio said ruefully. 'The museum wouldn't sell,' he told her, and at the thought that he'd even tried to buy it for her, something in her brain exploded. 'But we have it on loan, for our apartment. For a year. I had to promise that it could feature in a few exhibitions, but for most of the time it's yours to look at whenever you want.'

She glanced between the painting and Gio; neither seemed quite real in that moment. She reached out a finger to feel the brush strokes in the oil paint, but pulled herself back at the last moment, remembering that this was a priceless four-hundred-year-old masterpiece.

'I don't think I'm ever going to be able to stop looking at it,' she said, as tears filled her eyes and Gio's arm found its way around her waist. She leaned into his side, letting his arm take the weight of her head as she gazed at the painting. 'How did you know?'

'The way that you looked at the poster in New York. The way you so carefully tried to hide how much it meant to you. It was just a suspicion, but I'm glad that I was right. Merry Christmas,' he added, dropping his head to kiss her.

She groaned into his mouth and deepened their kiss, her arms coming around his waist as he lifted her closer. 'You like it?' Gio asked, and there it was; the doubt in his voice was what it took to tear her gaze away from the most beautiful thing she had ever seen.

'Gio,' she said seriously. 'I love it. It's the most astonishing thing I've ever seen. It's the most astonishing thing anyone has ever done for me. I *love* it,' she said again, her words heavy with emotion.

'So, is there any fallout from yesterday?' she asked when they eventually broke apart. 'Are your parents angry that we didn't come to dinner? Or church?'

He nodded. 'Yes. But I don't regret it. They'll have plenty of us today.'

She stifled a groan at the thought of it. 'I'm glad you don't regret it. I don't either. But is this where we have the conversation we didn't finish yesterday?'

'If you want to.' What she really wanted to do was spend the day gazing at her painting, but unfortunately they were living in the real world, with Gio's real family to face, and she didn't think she could do that until they knew where they stood with one another. 'I think we both need to know what this means to us, but there's no point having that conversation unless both of us want to.'

'Then yes. I want to. I'm sorry I didn't say that,' Hailey replied, and then took a deep breath. 'Was yesterday just a physical thing for you?'

'I don't see that it can be just physical,' Gio replied. 'Not when we're getting married in less than a week.'

'So it's more than that?' she asked.

Gio pulled them over to sit on the couch. 'You're asking a lot of questions and not offering much in return,' he observed, which was a fair observation, but he wasn't exactly being forthcoming about his feelings either.

'Yes. Well. Not knowing what to say is an unfortunate side effect of not knowing what I'm thinking,' Hailey told him. 'Or feeling. Everything seems so complicated.'

'So let's make it less complicated,' Gio suggested, as if that was something that they could realistically do. 'If I weren't me. If we didn't have to worry about my family trying to marry me off to the nearest available countess, then what would we be doing right now?' he asked.

'We already know the answer to that,' Hailey reminded him. 'We wouldn't have seen each other after that one night in New York.'

'We would, because of the baby. I wouldn't want to change that.'

'Then...' Hailey thought about it, tried to remove some of the complications of their situation to see what would be left if she and Gio were just... Hailey and Gio. 'I suppose we'd have got to know one another. Tried to be friends,' she said.

'And when those friends realised that they both still...*wanted* each other?'

She tried to remember how this worked in the real world. In her real life. In the before times. 'Then I guess... friends with benefits,' she said, her eyebrow raised.

'Not dating?' Gio clarified, in a cold, tense voice that made her wonder whether she'd just made a mistake.

'I never really did the dating thing,' she offered by way of explanation. But she could see the hurt in Gio's eyes, and didn't know how, or if, she could fix it.

'Is "friends with benefits" compatible with marriage?' Gio asked, still with that strained quality to his voice.

Hailey shook her head, not sure that this conversation was going how she'd intended, and equally unsure of how to get it back on track. 'A married couple who are friends is probably not the worst basis for a relationship,' she suggested, trying to look for the positives.

The *best* start to a marriage was probably 'madly in love, can't live without you', she supposed. But that didn't seem to be on the cards for her and Gio. So maybe they could make this marriage work like this. By being friends, and not fighting the fact that they wanted to fall into bed together at the end of the day. Or the middle of the day. Or—she glanced at the clock on the mantelpiece, wondering at what time they would be expected to make an appearance—at the start of the day, for that matter.

She placed her cup of tea carefully on the table beside the sofa and reached for Gio, pushed him back, settling herself comfortably across his thighs. 'I think I like being your friend,' she said with a tentative smile, hoping that The Talk hadn't spoilt things between them. She leaned down and kissed him. 'I love my gift. I'm sorry I didn't think to get you one.'

Gio arched an eyebrow, palms smoothing up her thighs. 'Merry Christmas to me,' he said, the start of a smile turning up the corners of his mouth. 'If you want to give me a last-minute gift, I'm sure we can think of something.'

His palm found the curve of her bottom, pulling her down more heavily on top of him.

'Shouldn't we...' she asked between kisses '...be going downstairs?'

'I think this would be awkward with an audience,' Gio said, pulling her close by the nape of her neck and kissing her until Hailey sat up abruptly, pulled her dress over her head, and found his mouth again with hers.

By the time they made it downstairs, Gio's family were sitting around the Christmas tree in the drawing room, sipping coffee and making polite conversation.

She had no doubt that his family knew exactly why they had missed breakfast that morning. Why they had missed dinner last night, and midnight mass too. She searched for something to say to the people who would become her family in less than a week. How many times had she done this before? she wondered. Met a new family at breakfast and found that she had no idea what to say to them. No idea how to belong. No idea how to make them love her. To make them want to keep her.

It was only the warm, smooth slide of Gio's fingers tangling with hers that reminded her that there was one very important difference now—this time she wasn't alone.

Gio wanted her here. For now, at least, she belonged with Gio, even if she didn't feel at home in the palace yet. And Gio would help her.

She squeezed his hand in silent thanks as Gio wished his parents a Happy Christmas and engaged them in small talk as Hailey looked on, happy to be on the edges of the conversation. To observe Gio and appreciate the way he tried to make her comfortable here in her new home, with her new family.

She refused the cup of coffee she was offered, mentally calculating how many cups she'd consumed in the last twenty-four hours, and had to suppress a smile as Gio pulled aside a member of staff and instructed them in how *exactly* she liked her tea prepared. She hadn't even realised he had been paying attention.

There was a warm glow in her chest at that knowledge—that didn't seem to fit with either 'convenient marriage' or 'friends with benefits'. Something that felt bigger and scarier than either of those and—accordingly—she planned to ignore it in perpetuity.

When they all moved to the big table in the dining room, with crystal, polished silverware and floral arrangements just a little higher than she would have designed, she realised with a sudden flash of horror that she and Gio hadn't been seated together. Of course, she remembered, it wouldn't do for the aristocracy to sit next to their own spouses at the dinner table.

But, with a squeeze of her hand, Gio pocketed the place card of the cousin who had been seated beside her.

'Gio,' she hissed under her breath. 'You can't.'

'I'm not leaving your side. Not with these sharks circling,' he whispered, pulling her into her seat, throwing his arm across the back of her chair and easing her closer to him with his fingertips on her shoulder.

'Tell me about the centrepieces,' he said, and her eyes snapped to his with surprise.

'Why do you want to know about the centrepieces?' she asked, suspicious—she could feel her own frown, the crease between her eyebrows.

'I don't care about the centrepieces,' Gio said. 'I want to see you talk.'

He wanted to watch her mouth. She remembered now that he'd done that the night they'd met. Well, how could she refuse an invitation to be worshipped doing something that she loved?

'Oh, you want to hear all about the *lisianthus* and the *zinnia*, do you?' she asked, over-enunciating and rolling her eyes as he set his elbow on the table, rested his chin on his hand and settled in to watch her talk.

She explained the different blooms and foliage, the meanings of each, which had to have been imported or grown in hothouses. She knew that Gio couldn't have developed a sudden interest in floristry, and yet his eyes were fixed on hers with unwavering focus. She flushed at the knowledge of how much he plainly desired her. The novelty of that hadn't worn off, and she didn't expect it to any time soon. She had barely got started with exploring Gio's body, with fully exploring all the things that he could do with hers.

Gio was her friend—he had every right to look at her that way after everything they had done over the last twenty-four hours, full of promise of what would come later. After denying how much she wanted him, she was suddenly intoxicated with the knowledge that she didn't have to any more. She could look. He could look. They could make all sorts of promises with their eyes, with every intention of collecting—and delivering—just as soon as they were alone together.

It was only when she realised that the room had gone quiet that she glanced around and realised that their conversation had not gone unnoticed. She felt heat rush to her cheeks again.

Sure, it worked in their favour for Gio's family to think that they were enamoured of each other. They were meant to be so in love that they couldn't wait to be married. But she had a more than sneaking suspicion that what was showing on her face wasn't exactly 'romantic'.

Well, it was too late to worry about that now, she told herself. His parents already knew she was pregnant. It wasn't as if she was planning on playing the blushing virgin on her wedding day.

CHAPTER ELEVEN

HE DIDN'T HAVE to pretend any more. The thrill of that had been coursing through his body since yesterday. A heady, potent force that held as much sway over him as the knowledge that he was going to be a father.

All he had to do now was keep their new 'friends with benefits' arrangement clear in his mind and ensure that he didn't start to kid himself that Hailey felt more than friendship towards him. Married or not. They weren't… romantic with one another. He had to remind himself that whatever this looked like from the outside—whatever they *had* to make it look like from the outside—Hailey didn't feel that way about him. Wasn't going to fall in love with him.

When they'd had their long-overdue conversation about what they were to each other in private, behind the public façade of their marriage, she hadn't even been able to go as far as dating. She'd gone straight to 'friends'. Sex, yes. Feelings, no. Which was absolutely acceptable, because it would never occur to him to hope for more. Even his own parents had been unable to form an emotional attachment to him. He supposed he should be grateful for the circumstances that meant Hailey would be bonded to him—committed to a life with him, even if only for the baby's sake. Because he knew he didn't have any chance of keeping her without it.

For the first time in his life he had a view of the future that was less lonely than the life he'd led until now.

But that didn't mean he could let his guard down. He'd learned over the years how to protect himself. Which barriers he needed to build and later reinforce if he didn't want his parents' indifference to his happiness to hurt him at every turn.

He had managed to thwart his parents' plan to have the choice of his spouse made by the royal council. And, against the expectations he'd had all his life, he'd chosen the woman he wanted to marry. But that didn't mean it was going to be smooth sailing from here.

The first, and most prominent, problem was the fact that he had no idea how to be a husband. A father. All his life he'd watched his parents fulfil their duties—to their country, to one another, to him—and in none of it had he ever seen an example that he wanted to follow. How to balance the obligations of state and family. How to maintain a cordial, affectionate relationship. How to treat the person your life was tied to when your relationship was based more on obligation than love.

He'd dreaded being forced to marry someone he didn't like, or barely knew. But he realised now, too late, that he'd never given enough thought to what came after. To what made a good marriage. All he knew was what he *didn't* want. So perhaps they got to start this with a clean slate. They could choose what would make their marriage happy. Right now, he couldn't think of anything that he wanted more than to watch her talk about flowers. The way her eyes lit and her words flew from her lips as she described what she would have done with the table. The work of art she would have created if this had been her commission. Until suddenly the joy faded from her eyes, and it didn't take thirty years of marriage to guess why.

'You're thinking about your business,' he guessed.

She nodded. 'I know I'm hardly the first person to have to give up her business because she got pregnant. I knew when I accepted your proposal what it would mean. But I just don't know what I'm meant to do with myself. At least until the baby comes.'

'I never said you have to give up your business,' Gio pointed out.

'No, but I don't see a solution for how I'm meant to run it from three thousand miles away. I keep going round and round in circles without finding a solution. I think maybe I should just give the business to Gracie. She's the only one I would trust to look after my clients.'

'You're aware that we have flowers in Adria.' He glanced at the arrangement in front of them. 'I never expected that you would give up work. If you want to, that's one thing. But you shouldn't have to make a sacrifice like that if it's not what you want.'

'I don't know what I'm going to want when the baby arrives. But I've spent a decade building that business. I can't just…forget about it. No matter the obligations I have here.'

Obligations. Well, that told him everything he needed to know about what this marriage was to her, and he felt a sinking sensation in the pit of his belly. He tried to avoid the—

'So, Gio, Hailey?' His mother's voice cut through his thoughts and, for the first time in what felt like an hour, he tore his eyes away from Hailey and glanced down the dining table to the Queen.

'How are the wedding plans going?' she asked, and he suppressed the urge to roll his eyes.

He swore, from the minute they had announced their intention to marry, no one had shown the least bit of interest in any other part of their lives. It didn't matter how many times they'd asked them their preferences— how many times they'd told everyone around them that they didn't mind about the details as long as they were married at the end of the day, no one seemed to engage Hailey in conversation about anything other than the wedding.

'No change from yesterday,' he told his mother, trying to keep the annoyance out of his voice.

'I hear you are doing the flowers yourself. It's such a novelty to have someone with a trade join the family,' Queen Lucia said to Hailey, who looked startled at being addressed directly. She opened her mouth, closed it again, and Gio laid his hand over hers as he addressed his mother.

'That's enough,' Gio said, sending a sharp look at his mother. 'Hailey is a world-renowned floral artist. She just did the flowers for Sebastian's wedding—it's how we met. No one could do a better job.'

He stood abruptly, his chair toppling behind him. 'I was very clear when Hailey and I arrived,' Gio continued, 'that my continued presence in this family is dependent on you both treating her with kindness and respect. I will not tolerate her being spoken to like that.' When he glanced across, it was to find Hailey standing beside him, wide-eyed with surprise. He reached for her hand. 'If you're finished, darling,' he said to her, 'I think it's time we retired.'

Her cheeks flushed and she nodded. 'Let's go.' He kept hold of her hand as they walked slowly from the room, not betraying the strength of his anger at the way his family had treated them. But as soon as they were out of sight of the dining room, he pulled them through a door hidden in the panelling of the corridor and crowded her up against the wall.

'I thought we were going back to our apartment,' she said, but let her head drop back against the wall as his hands came to land on her hips and he allowed his body to bow into hers until she was pinned by his weight.

The blaze in her eyes was hotter than ever, and she curled her fingers into the front of his jacket, leaving him in no doubt that her thoughts matched his entirely.

'I'm not sure I can wait,' Gio said, aware of the crack in his voice, not caring that it exposed exactly how much he wanted her.

'For what?' Hailey asked with mock innocence. The tight grip of her hands on his lapels pulling him down to her told a different story. She let her head fall to one side, exposing the long elegant line of her throat, and he couldn't resist dropping his lips there, letting them linger, brushing them against the sea of goosebumps that spread across her skin.

'Mmm…' she moaned, one hand leaving his sweater to thread in his hair, holding his lips to her skin, and gasping when his teeth and tongue followed the path of his lips.

'We should really be somewhere more private,' she said, and he nipped at her and smiled.

'That sounds promising. I want more than just the privacy of our apartment, though. Let's get away from here for a few days.'

She laughed, pushing him away. 'What are you talking about? We can't just disappear.'

'We can be in front of the fire at the ski lodge, completely alone, not another human in sight, in less than an hour if we take the helicopter. Say yes. Please?'

The corners of her mouth twitched up, and he knew that he had her. He wrapped his fingers around her wrist and pulled her behind him as he made his way through the dark corridors without a moment of hesitation.

Later that night, with Hailey's head cushioned comfortably on his shoulder, blankets, throws and furs pulled around them in the nest they'd made in front of the fire, Gio thought back to that expression on her face when his mother had been so cutting to her at the dinner table. How it had made him realise how little he knew her. How hard it would be to be a good husband to her if he didn't rectify that.

'I'm sorry about my mother,' he said, coiling one of her curls around his finger. Letting it slip from his grip as she looked up and propped her chin on his chest.

'It was nothing.'

He frowned. 'I don't think it was. It upsets me that she hurt you.'

'She didn't,' Hailey said, but from the tone of her voice it sounded as if the words came more from habit than honesty. He wanted her to be honest with him— needed it, if he were honest. If they wanted this marriage to turn out better than his parents' had.

'I want to know you better,' he told her, and felt the muscles of her back stiffen under his hand. 'I want to be a good husband,' he pressed on. 'I'm not sure that I know how to do that, if I'm perfectly honest. But I do want to try. I hate seeing pain in your eyes and not understanding it. Not knowing how I can help.'

Hailey was silent, and for a moment he worried that he'd pushed too far. Maybe with their whole 'friends with benefits' agreement he shouldn't be pressing for deep and meaningful conversations. But eventually Hailey settled down into his shoulder again and he held his breath, waiting for her to speak.

Form factor of pionium bound state by perturbation
theory methods applying the Jost function formalism
has carried through to his structure...Applying the Jost function
for their various further Fermi region

CHAPTER TWELVE

HAILEY HADN'T REALISED that Gio had seen her reaction when his mother had spoken to her as if she were some sort of interloper—the help who had somehow found herself invited to dinner. She'd done it with all of Gio's extended family looking on. And it had reminded her of every family meal she'd had to grit her teeth and get through before.

And Gio had seen, but not known what had caused it. He wanted to know, wanted to know her, and it struck her suddenly that she could just…tell him, share with him what she had felt. And have someone on her side. Someone who would go out of their way to make her welcome. Someone who she knew belonged on her side.

She closed her eyes and trusted herself, trusted Gio, and started to speak.

'It reminded me of being a child,' she said, but then faltered. She still wasn't sure how to tell this.

'Can you tell me more?' Gio asked gently, his hand stroking slowly up and down her back, stopping occasionally to ease a knot in her muscle, or tuck the sheets and blankets a little more snugly around her shoulder.

'I lived in a lot of different places. With a lot of different families,' she told him. 'And… I never belonged. To start with, I would try so hard. Then I'd give up.

Then I'd try twice as hard to be good.' And it would hurt twice as much when that still didn't work and she was still on the outside, trying to work out what it would take to actually belong in one of those families.

'It never worked. Even when I was eventually adopted I… It was too late. I'd never had a family of my own. I'd grown up without one, and I couldn't make myself fit. So when your mother looked at me like that, and spoke to me like that, it just brought back memories. That's all.'

She tucked herself into his shoulder a little tighter, although the fire was still burning hot beside them and their blanket nest was more than a match for the chill in the air. He wrapped his arms around her waist, pressing a kiss to the top of her head. He wanted her to be in no doubt that she belonged here, in his bed, in his arms, no matter what they called it, either to themselves or to the outside world. They were a family, the three of them, and they belonged together.

'I'm so sorry,' he said. 'That sounds hard, and I'm sorry that my mother made you feel like you don't belong here.'

If only it could be like this all the time, just the two of them in an isolated lodge, unreachable except by helicopter, not a parent or politician in sight.

'It's hardly news,' Hailey said, and he could feel her forcing her face into a smile. He looked down at her, at the warmth of her skin in the reflected light of the fire, and cupped her cheek with his hand until she looked up and she met his eyes.

'You belong here,' he said, and the resolution in his voice hit her somewhere deep in her chest. So she forced out a laugh because that was easier than acknowledging how she was really feeling.

'Right. The orphaned flower-seller from the city, installed in the royal family. I remember that one.'

'The princess and her husband in their lodge,' Gio countered. 'The mother of the heir to the throne of Adria in the country that's going to love her.'

'Come on,' Hailey said to Gio seriously, turning in his arms and letting in the cool air. 'You can't really believe that. They'll love the fairy tale wedding. They'll love the baby photos they'll expect us to release. Will they love me when I don't lose the baby weight as fast as they expect? When I want to prioritise our baby's privacy over their desire for access? Will they love me when they're faced with a choice between respecting my privacy and a salacious magazine article about the broken homes and grubby people in my past?'

'None of that is real,' Gio said, tucking a curl behind her ear. 'Those people don't know you.'

'But your mother made it clear that I don't fit in this family and she's right. Don't give me hope or false expectations when we both know the truth. It's not fair to me, Gio. It's cruel. Even my own biological parents didn't love me. They can't have, to have given me up. To have been happy to leave me with strangers. To never try and find me.'

'Do you want to find them?' he asked, and Hailey shook her head.

'No. Not any more. I can't see what good it would do now. It's too late. Too much damage has been done.'

'Is there anything I can do? I can't change my family. Who I am. But I can speak to my mother and make sure she never says anything like that again.'

Hailey shook her head again. 'No. It's not worth it. I just want to leave it. Honestly, Gio, I've felt like this all my life. One conversation with your mother isn't something worth making a fuss about. But…' She hesitated, worried that this, of all things, was going too far, showing too much of her heart.

'Go on,' Gio encouraged.

'But…thank you. Knowing that you see me—that you see when I'm hurting—that means more to me than you know.' He turned onto his side, drew her close so that they were nose to nose. 'I meant what I said,' he murmured, his voice barely needing to be more than a whisper when they were this close. 'We're a family. The three of us. It might not look like any other family. We might be friends rather than the fairy tale. But we belong together.'

Hailey closed her eyes and let her lips meet his, melting into the kiss as his words hit home. She might not fit in at the grand palace, with the King and Queen and the ballrooms and state functions. But with Gio, wherever they found themselves, for once this felt as if she was living her own life. Claiming the things that *she* wanted.

CHAPTER THIRTEEN

WITH SPACE AND time away from Gio's family, Hailey felt herself starting to relax for the first time since they'd arrived in Adria. With walks around the frozen lake, long evenings in front of the fire and lazy mornings in bed, she and Gio finally had the chance to get to know one another. Sharing stories of their pasts—her struggle to find where she belonged, his to put off his parents' need to control his future. And somewhere in the middle of it, her life had stopped feeling so much like a role that she was playing and more like something that she was choosing for herself.

She couldn't imagine choosing better than Gio. He had been attentive to the point of devoted since they had escaped the palace, and she had to admit that she could get used to the idea of being worshipped, if Gio was the one doing the worshipping.

But their isolation couldn't last because, as part of their deal with the press to keep the wedding day private, they had agreed to a brief press conference on the steps of the palace. The day before their wedding she awoke in their palace apartment to clear skies and a fresh layer of powdery snow that had fallen in the night.

The engagement pictures had been released on Christmas Day, probably right about when she and Gio had been sneaking off to the ski lodge, provoking further ire from the Queen. The clamour and excitement from both the press and the public had been as ebullient as they'd expected, and she was glad of Gio's foresight in isolating them from it all at the lodge. By the time that they had arrived back last night there was barely any time to feel nervous. The palace press team had assured her that the journalists who would be attending had been warned that questions about her family or history were entirely off-limits for any publication that wanted any sort of relationship with the palace in the future.

She had chosen her outfit with a team of press officers and aides from Gio's office yesterday. Her hair and make-up team were primed yet again to transform her into a princess. All she had to do was plaster on a smile, answer the pre-approved softball questions, and then get a good night's sleep. That last one might be harder than it sounded, she considered, glancing across to where Gio slept beside her. Perhaps she could call on tradition and insist on separate bed chambers tonight if she didn't want to yawn through her own wedding.

She hadn't seen the Queen or the King since Christmas Day and had no expectation of that relationship thawing any time soon. Her relationship with Gio though…warm wasn't the word. They weren't even newlyweds yet, and they had barely seen fresh air or daylight in the last five days. As a princess, she might never be good enough. Never really belong in this new life. But if she made her world small—if she could shrink it down to fit in the confines of their apartment, their bedroom, their bed—then she knew where she belonged. She could feel comfortable there. If it wasn't for the fact that Gio had a country to help run, she would be blockading the doors and insisting that they never leave.

She hummed with pleasure as Gio woke and wrapped his arms around her, and then let her eyes close as the smell and feel and heat of him attacked her. It would be so easy if they could just stay like this, she managed to think before Gio's lips found the spot where her shoulder met her neck and she lost conscious thought altogether.

She was still grinning when she emerged from the bathroom a couple of hours later to find her hair and makeup team already in her bedroom, making themselves at home at her dressing table.

'I'm sorry, Ms Thomas,' one of them said, 'but we were running out of time and His Royal Highness said we could get set up.'

'No, it's fine,' she said, pulling her robe tighter around her as she shivered. Even if she never left these rooms, the real world would always have a way of finding her. She had no right to a truly private life any more. That was the cost of a life with Gio in it. Make-up artists and hairdressers in her bedroom, and her discomfort with that a constant reminder that she hadn't been born into this life and would never truly belong in it.

Gio emerged from his dressing room as she took a seat at the dressing table and came across to kiss her gently on the lips. Somewhere behind her, a comb started teasing out the knots from the back of her hair.

'Sorry,' Gio said as he pulled away. 'The chamberlain was stressing about the time.'

'It's fine,' she lied, aware that her smile probably looked a little tight. She couldn't say anything—not least because there were staff present. She wasn't so ignorant that she didn't know not to speak about private things in front of them. But later, when they were alone, she would have to. She had to have a safe space. Somewhere she didn't have to *try* all the time.

She smiled as she was transformed into her photo-ready self, and she wondered who had given the instructions for how she should look. She had been so distracted that they were halfway through her make-up and had teased volume into her hair before she realised that they hadn't asked for any direction in what they were doing. So had it been the chamberlain, Gio or his mother who had decided what her hair should look like today?

There wasn't a good answer to that question. Being dressed up like a doll by any of those people was an unpleasant thought. Though she supposed there were different levels of fallout for each if she failed to live up to their expectations.

But there was no time to discuss it because she was being ushered out of her seat at the dressing table and clothes were being pressed into her arms and she was hustled into the bathroom when she insisted that really she *did* mind changing in front of the team, even if they had already seen it all before, as they so delicately put it.

She just had to go along with it today—this might be her engagement, her wedding that they were talking about, but this wasn't her party. Gio, the chamberlain and the Queen had taken it all in hand, and she'd watched it all go on around her, waiting for her cues and looking for her marks. And it made her feel like a child again.

From the time that she'd landed in New York, she'd made her own future. Her art history studies. Her move into floristry. The business and career she had spent her whole adult life building—and which she was about to lose, giving it up for a life of being told where to stand and what to wear and what to say. She had known that accepting Gio's proposal would launch her into a new life. But she hadn't known it would feel so much like her old life. How quickly her brain would fall back into old patterns.

Gio's hand found hers as she stood in front of the grand double doors and gave it a quick comforting squeeze. 'Ready for this?' he asked.

Her well-rehearsed smile didn't falter. 'Of course.'

Smile. Wave. Tell them how much she was in love with Gio. Back indoors. She could do this.

The noise started as soon as the door clicked open, shouted questions and requests to look this way and that. She straightened her back as she walked out to the top of the steps. She smiled to the left and the right. Waved when Gio did and answered the questions the journalists shouted from behind their microphones.

'How are you finding Adria?'

'It's very beautiful.'

'How did you meet?'

'At a friend's wedding,' Gio answered.

'What do the royal family think of having a commoner join the family?'

'Tell us what it's like going from children's home to a palace?'

'Is it true you're only getting married because you're pregnant?'

'Why aren't your parents attending the wedding? Do you think they are more angry or heartbroken?'

Hailey froze. Those hadn't been on the list of approved questions. Someone had obviously got wind of her background and decided to take a chance that she'd answer. And had they worked out the pregnancy for themselves? Her hand dropped to her stomach. Or had she just confirmed it for them?

'That's enough,' Gio snapped, a harshness in his voice she hadn't heard before. His arm came around her shoulder and he steered her inside, kicked the door closed behind them and forced her to sit on an upholstered bench just inside the door.

She opened her mouth, and realised she didn't know what to say. Because, despite everything the press office had promised her, this had always been inevitable. She was always going to face these kinds of questions, behind her back even if not always to her face. She had *warned* Gio that this would happen, and yet she'd still stood there and stupidly thought that she could be protected from the reality of their situation.

When the journalists had mentioned her parents, she couldn't even be sure which ones they were talking about—her birth parents? Her adoptive parents? She had been an idiot not to tell her adoptive parents, and she felt a sudden pang of guilt. Somehow, she'd managed to convince herself that they wouldn't hear the news. They deserved better than to hear it from this pack.

'I... I...' she started, but couldn't seem to find the next word. She closed her eyes, trying to shut out the clamour from outside.

'Deep breaths,' Gio instructed, kneeling in front of her as she kept her eyes tightly closed, concentrating on drawing in even, measured breaths as the shock started to fade.

She shivered. Somehow, on the steps outside she had been able to ignore the biting cold. But, even though they were indoors now, a draught crept around the doors and her arms wrapped around herself were not enough to keep out the cold.

'Hailey, I'm so sorry,' Gio said. 'I know for a fact that the chamberlain is on the phone yelling at a newspaper editor right now. They'll never get near you again.'

'Do you think it's true?' Hailey asked. 'That my parents are upset I didn't invite them to the wedding?' She focused on that because it seemed simpler than unravelling the fact that she shouldn't even be here in the first place. That she didn't belong and never would.

Gio clasped her hands in his, chafing them between his palms to try and get some heat into them.

'I think you know the answer to that better than I do,' he said. 'But you never once mentioned wanting them here. I think you can trust yourself to know what you want. What you need. What's right for you.'

'I don't even know who they meant,' Hailey confessed. 'My adoptive parents...' She trailed off.

'I can find out, if it will help...' Gio offered.

'No,' she said, her body loosening at last, but her mind still stuck in the hurricane that had started with the journalist's intrusive questions. 'At least not yet. I have to concentrate on getting through—'

She stopped herself, realising too late that those weren't exactly glowing terms with which to speak about their own wedding. Had she thought about it that way before? As something to get through?

The engagement photos.

Dinner with Gio's family.

The press conference.

Anything, really, that wasn't being holed up together had been something to endure, rather than enjoy.

But their wedding? Their marriage? That was meant

to be her choice, what she wanted. So why was it feeling like a trap, something she had to 'get through'...?

She pulled her hands away from his with no more conscious thought than that it felt wrong in the moment.

'Hailey?' Gio asked, his eyes still full of concern. 'Is there anything I can do to help?'

She drew herself a little more upright, opening her eyes and bringing herself back to the present moment.

'No. Thank you.' Her voice sounded stiff, forced. But she couldn't seem to soften it. 'I think I just want to go back to our room.'

'Of course, I'll cancel—'

'No,' she said quickly. 'I just need some space. Some time alone,' she told him, wrapping her arms back around herself.

Gio watched as Hailey walked away from him, with the certain sinking feeling that something had just been broken that would be extremely difficult to remedy. He could murder whoever had asked those questions. He hadn't recognised the journalist so they must be new on the beat—well, he hoped it had been worth it, because he would make sure they never worked again.

But that wouldn't fix the situation with Hailey, who had retreated from him ever since they had returned to the palace.

At the ski lodge, where they could pretend they were just a normal couple, she had been open and relaxed with him. But once they'd returned to the palace he'd seen the change. The stiffer line of her spine, the tight pull of her smile. The waver in her voice. As if she wanted to be anywhere but here, with him. The one saving grace of the situation was knowing that they could recapture a little of that isolation by retreating to their apartment and shutting the door behind them.

Now she was locking herself in alone, and he didn't know how to reach her.

They were getting married tomorrow. Right now, he couldn't even be sure that Hailey would turn up. He had a sudden nauseating vision of waiting for her at the altar with a gradual realisation that she wasn't coming.

A stab of pain hit him right in the chest, and he had to raise a hand and use the heel of his palm to force away the feeling, the sudden certain knowledge that if she didn't marry him tomorrow his heart would break. And that could mean only one thing—despite everything he'd told himself, every stern warning he'd given his heart, he had fallen in love with her. He had handed over his heart little by little, so he'd barely noticed that he was doing it. And now it was entirely at her mercy.

He shivered at the thought, not comforted in the least. He'd known all along that the very worst thing that he could do in this situation was fall in love, and yet here he was.

All he could do was trust Hailey when she'd given him her word that she would be there tomorrow. If he couldn't fully believe that, how could he even hope for happiness after that? A year of happiness. A decade. Would he find himself, twenty years from now, in the same unhappily married state as his parents?

No. He couldn't think like that. He had to trust in the promises that he and Hailey had made to one another. They had agreed that this marriage was going to be based on friendship. A commitment to their child. It was something they had chosen for themselves. Not out of a sense of duty to others, but a commitment to what they wanted their lives to be.

So he gave Hailey the space she had asked him for.
Had to trust that she would come back to him. And if
she changed her mind? If she decided that she'd made
a mistake in coming here, and wanted to be on the first
flight back to New York? She would need support. He
sat with his fingers hovering over his phone screen,
wondering if he was about to overstep the bounds of
their relationship. Whether this was as meddlesome as
the journalists' questions had been earlier. But there
was only one person he was sure that Hailey needed.
Who he was sure would jump on a plane in a heartbeat
if Hailey asked her.

He picked up the phone and dialled.

CHAPTER FOURTEEN

HAILEY SAT IN front of the mirror, make-up brush in hand, wondering why she couldn't seem to lift it to her face. She had dismissed the hair and make-up crew, not able to stand the thought of them buzzing around her this morning. There was enough turmoil in her mind without additional external influences.

She had been doing her make-up to her liking her whole life. There was no reason why she couldn't paint her face today. She only wanted to look like herself, after all. But she had been sitting here for half an hour now, her robe tied tightly around the ivory silk underwear that had appeared in her dresser that morning, and she hadn't even started.

It wasn't that she didn't want to marry Gio. It was just that, for some reason, she couldn't seem to make her body go through the motions to get herself to the altar.

She thought again about the press conference the day before—she had been pitched back into that unmoored, unrooted time in her life, when she had lingered on the boundaries of the families she'd lived with, and how everyone knew that she didn't really belong. And now here she was, in what should have been the first flush of public and press adoration for a new princess, and already her past was overshadowing her happiness.

She shouldn't be worrying about that today. If anything, she should be worried about the fact that Gio hadn't come to bed last night. Sure, he was probably trying to be a gentleman and respect tradition. He had sent her a beautiful bouquet—no other man had ever dared send her flowers—with a note that somehow managed to be both funny and tender.

But she couldn't help but wish she'd had the already familiar comfort of his arms, the warm press on his lips on her skin to get her through this morning. Her eyes widened at the sound of a gentle knock at the door. Her heart leapt for a second, thinking that it might be Gio, breaking with tradition. But, knowing her luck, it would be her hair and make-up crew, no longer content to leave her to her own devices.

She called for them to come in, lounging against the back of her chair, resigning herself to losing her peace and privacy. When she glanced in the mirror and saw who was waiting for her in the doorway, a great heaving sob escaped her with such force that she wasn't sure how she'd ever been capable of keeping it in.

'Gracie? What—? How—? *Gio*,' she realised with another sob. 'Oh, I'm going to—'

'Marry him?' Gracie asked with an amused expression.

Hailey laughed. 'If I don't kill him for keeping secrets.' She let out a long breath as Gracie folded her in her arms. 'I'm so, so glad you're here,' Hailey said, gulping for air between words.

'Then why didn't you call me?' Gracie asked, holding her out by the upper arms and giving her a chastising look. 'You had to have known I would come.'

Hailey shook her head. 'It's New Year's. You've been working all through the holidays. I didn't want to pull you away and subject you to jet lag when you should have been catching up on sleep.'

'Pfft. That's bull,' Gracie said, giving her a gentle shake. 'Inconvenience me all you want. You're family. That means I get to put you first, regardless of how tired I am. Gio knew that I should be here. So why didn't you?'

Hailey shook her head. 'It's not that I didn't want you here, Gracie. I did, so badly. I just didn't know how to ask.'

'Of course you didn't,' Gracie said, pulling her into another tight hug. 'Because you never learned that that's what you do with family. That the people who love you will be there for you, regardless of what is going on. That you can ask for help when you need it.'

Hailey looked up at the ceiling and blinked, trying to stop another wave of tears.

Gracie took a step away, folded her arms and looked at her critically. 'Excuse me, miss, but aren't you supposed to be getting married in two hours' time? Don't even try telling me that unbrushed hair and a shiny nose are what passes for bridal fashion in Adria.'

Hailey broke into a smile, for what felt like the first time in days, and Gracie picked up a silver-backed brush from the dressing table and wielded it at her menacingly until she sat back in front of the mirror. Gracie pulled the brush through the rogue waves at the back of her head, bringing out the natural shine that came easily to her dark hair.

'So, are we getting you ready for this wedding? Because, if not, I'm telling you I'd be very tempted to take your place. I don't know where this fairy tale prince of yours suddenly appeared from, but he seems like the real deal.'

'He's certainly very charming,' Hailey said carefully. 'And honourable. I'm lucky that he's prepared to do all this to give our baby the best start.'

Gracie's hand stilled and Hailey couldn't avoid her disbelieving look in the mirror. 'Honourable? Doing the right thing?'

Hailey nodded, aware from her reflection in the mirror that her smile was a little too tight. 'I know what this is, Gracie, and it's not a fairy tale. If Gio hadn't got me pregnant we wouldn't have even seen each other again, never mind anything else.'

Gracie shook her head as she started to brush through Hailey's hair. 'Yes. But that was months ago now. Are you telling me it's been all honour and duty since then?'

'Well, not exactly…'

Gracie cocked an eyebrow, the hint of a smirk around her mouth. 'Meaning?'

'Well…we're going to get married. And obviously we're attracted to each other, otherwise…'

'So you're sleeping with him?'

Hailey nearly strained a muscle in her neck snapping her head round to look Gracie in the eye. 'Gracie!'

'I'll take that as a yes,' her friend said, laughing, with a very self-satisfied expression on her face. 'So,' Gracie recapped, 'you're sleeping with this gorgeous, honourable man who shares your values and wants the same things for your family as you do. Can you please tell me what the problem is? Because I'm not seeing it.'

'He doesn't love me,' Hailey said simply, because there was no point sugar-coating it. 'So I can't let myself love him, however easy and tempting it might be to fall, because it can only possibly end with me getting hurt.'

Gracie sighed and let her hands rest heavily on her shoulders. 'Are you sure about that?' she asked gently.

'Me loving him or vice versa?'

'Either. Both.'

Hailey turned on the stool until she faced Gracie, and accepted her hug when the older woman squeezed her to her middle.

'We said it was just…friends with benefits,' she admitted to Gracie's well-tailored shirt. 'But I don't know… I think I've been kidding myself that it's not more. But what's the point in deciding I feel that way if he doesn't? I can't imagine that loving him and not having him love me back would be much fun.'

'I don't think loving each other and never admitting it to yourselves would make for a happy marriage either.'

'You're saying we shouldn't go through with it?'

'I'm saying you should marry him, if it feels right. But don't let that stop you talking. Keep talking. Be honest with each other and see where your marriage could go. Don't decide at the outset it's already everything it could be. Don't make self-fulfilling prophecies because you're scared to be honest with him. And if you can't be honest with him…' she went on, looking at Hailey sternly in the mirror '…if that's something you think can never come—if you want to call things off and come back to New York and raise this baby living with its Aunt Gracie—then I will take you home and keep the world away. It's your choice, honey. You decide what you feel for Gio. What you think your future together might look like and I will support you.'

'You're being too nice,' Hailey said, pushing Gracie away so that she could look up at her. 'I'm whingeing that a prince and the father of my baby wants to marry me. I should be on cloud nine this morning.'

'You deserve someone to care what you want and

love you whatever you choose. You have that in me. I'm sorry for all the things that happened in your life that make it hard for you to believe that. But it's true. I love you. And there's no reason that Gio won't love you like that too, if he doesn't already.'

'He doesn't. It's not the same thing.'

'Maybe not. But the fact that you have someone who loves you—me—is. And if that disproves some of the things that you tell yourself are true, then good.'

She used the brush to neaten Hailey's fringe. 'Now, get yourself ready and tell me what you want to do. I'm going to get some coffee and give you some time to think.'

When she was alone Hailey fixed herself with a serious look in the mirror. If she was going to change her mind, she should do it now. She wasn't so cruel that she could leave it till the last minute. She imagined Gio standing in the sunlight-filled morning room, waiting for her, and her heart clenched at the thought of anything hurting him.

'So, we're doing this,' she said, reaching for her foundation and make-up brush. 'I'm doing this,' she said again as she started to apply her make-up.

By the time Gracie came back, bearing coffee and pastries, she was brushing pomade through her eyebrows and pressing her lips together to blot the soft rose lipstick that made her mouth look just bitten, just kissed.

'You're going through with it?' Gracie asked as she took in her made-up face.

'If you know someone who can help me into the dress.'

It was a simple slip of ivory silk with little cap sleeves and a bias-cut skirt that spilt around her legs and moved like water. At the back, a row of silk-covered buttons followed the line of her spine to where the neckline scooped down low, framing her shoulder blades and the pale skin of her shoulders.

She'd chosen it with indifference the day after she'd arrived at the palace, jet-lagged and shell-shocked from the rapid succession of events that had brought her halfway across the world and circling the most exclusive of families, terrified that she was never going to belong.

She smoothed her hands down the silk, where it swelled over her slowly growing baby bump. She wasn't sure about the rest still, but she belonged in this dress. It was more beautiful than anything she'd ever worn. It followed every line of her body, even the ones that were still new and unfamiliar to her. She looked like a bride. And, she realised, she felt like one as well. Not like someone playing dress-up. Not like someone playing princesses. Not even like someone who was about to walk into someone else's life.

Just her. With her plans. With her reasons for marrying Gio and making the future they wanted together.

'So, are we ready?' Gracie asked.

'We're ready,' Hailey declared, sliding each foot into ivory silk shoes which somehow fitted perfectly without her ever having tried them on before. She had known there must be perks to being royal, but it wasn't until she took her first steps in made-to-measure shoes that she realised just how comfortable life as a princess could be.

An aide stepped into their reception room and she raised her eyebrows in question. 'Excuse me, miss,' she said, her face a little tight. 'There's a slight delay.'

Oh. Her lips made the shape, but no sound escaped.

'What's the problem?' Gracie asked with the characteristic directness of a New Yorker as she came to stand behind her.

'It's…er… We can't quite find His Royal Highness.'

Hailey dropped her bouquet on the table beside her and Gracie tutted, picking it up and placing it gently in the dry vase it had been sitting in all morning, the stems drying out so they wouldn't drip down the front of her dress.

Gracie's hands settled on her shoulder. 'Stop whatever you're thinking. Right now.'

'He's gone. He's changed his mind,' Hailey said, her voice shaky. She could feel the blood drain from her face, leaving her faint and wobbly.

Gracie steered her into a chair. 'You're overreacting,' she told her sternly. 'This is a goddamn palace. *Literally* a goddamn palace. You could lose someone here because they've found a new bathroom on the fifth floor and have decided to keep the knowledge to themselves. Are you telling me the two of you haven't been sneaking around this place, making out in secret passageways?'

The corner of Hailey's mouth turned up and she felt a little blood return to her cheeks.

'Exactly. He's taken a shortcut or something. He's not leaving you. He hasn't abandoned you.'

'You can't know that. You can't promise that,' Hailey said.

Gracie sighed, coming to sit beside her and taking her hand, realising the extent of her power to reassure. 'You're right. I can't make promises on his behalf. But I can make them on my own. I won't abandon you. Whatever happens, I'll be here with you. You won't be alone.'

Eventually, there was another knock at the door and Gracie went to open it, using her body to shield whoever was on the other side from view. But her hissed whispers weren't effective and Hailey already knew in her gut who it was. It was Gio, of course, here to break things off, unable to go through with marriage to a woman he didn't love. Not willing to sacrifice his future to give her child the security she'd never had in her own life.

'Let him in,' she told Gracie. There was no point in delaying the inevitable. The sooner she could get out of this palace and back to her real life the better. Delaying this wasn't going to change the outcome.

Gracie stood to one side and Gio appeared in the doorway. The perfect fairy tale prince in a dark suit and perfectly white shirt. But his hair gave away his thoughts. It was messy and unkempt, the waves combed through by fingers that never could stay still when he was troubled.

'Hailey,' he said, his voice low and gravelly. 'I think we should talk.'

Hailey let out a resigned sigh. 'I don't think we need to,' she said.

'You don't?'

She shook her head, unable to drag her eyes up from the floor. 'No. I think if we're calling this off, the less we say the better. This was always a crazy idea. I'm sorry that it took me this long to see that clearly.'

She glanced up, only to see that Gio's face had hardened, his eyes and mouth pinching, a deep furrow appearing between his brows.

'You're calling off our wedding—' he ground out the words '—with fifteen minutes to go? Just like that? Are you serious?'

Her eyes widened a fraction—wasn't that what he wanted? Why else would he be here? 'That's what you came here to say, isn't it?' Hailey said. 'What does it matter which of us says the words?'

'You're so sure, are you? And you're okay with that?

Sending our guests away and just pretending there isn't an officiant waiting for us in the morning room.'

'I don't have any guests here,' she reminded him.

'I can't believe that is the part of what I just said that you're taking issue with,' Gio snarled.

Hailey threw her hands up, so far out of her depth that she didn't know which direction to start swimming. 'What do you want me to do?' she asked. 'Weep and beg you to change your mind? What would be the point?'

Gio glared at her, and she shrivelled under his gaze. 'Oh, I don't know, perhaps to fight for this relationship?'

'And that's what you were doing here, was it?' She was angry now, and didn't care who saw it. 'When I had my bouquet in my hand and was on my way to you. If you were really interested in this relationship, we'd be married by now.'

'But we aren't,' Gio said slowly, stalking towards her, 'because I was worried that you were having second thoughts and I needed to make sure that this was really what you wanted.'

'I haven't seen you in twenty-four hours—'

'Because you wanted space!'

She laughed at that. 'And *this* is the time for you to question that? Not last night? Not first thing this morning? When I'm in the dress and am halfway out the door. You choose the very *last* minute to break my heart?'

His eyes snapped up to hers. 'What do you mean, break your heart? You've been very clear all along that you're only doing this for the baby.'

'*I'm* only doing it for the baby? *You're* only doing this so your parents can't force you to marry someone else. I have the great honour of being the least bad option once you'd got me pregnant, so you were stuck with me anyway.'

Gio shook his head, as if he couldn't believe what he was hearing. When he spoke, it was slowly and deliberately. 'I proposed because I liked you, Hailey. Because, baby or not, you were someone I could see myself spending a life with. A marriage of laughing over dinner and sharing our days and, yes, raising our child together in the life that we had chosen. I fell for you—as much as I tried to resist it every bloody day—because of the woman you are. The way you marched into this circus of a family and stared down my mother and—'

She stared at him, trying to process his words, trying to square them with the certainty she'd had just moments ago that he had come here to call off their wedding. 'You've been trying not to fall for me?' she asked, certain that she must have heard him wrong.

'That's what I just said.' Gio's words were careful and measured, and gave away nothing of the emotion behind them.

'And...how did you get on with that?' Hailey asked, still unsure about how to take the swerve this conversation had just taken.

'Without great success,' Gio said. 'Clearly.'

She stared at him, wondering if that meant what she thought it might mean. It was hard to know, when she'd had so little practice with people loving her. The disconnect between his unintelligible declaration and his stern expression wasn't exactly helping.

'So you weren't coming here to break things off with me?' she asked again, still not entirely certain whether this wedding was going ahead.

'I was coming here because I was worried about you,' Gio said, his voice softening now as he took a step towards her. 'Because I care about you.'

'So you still want to marry me?' Hailey said.

Gio pushed his hands through his hair and Hailey's hands itched to smooth it. To take Gio's hands in hers and soothe him. 'Do you *want* me to jilt you?' he asked, his frustration evident again in the growl of his voice.

'No!' Hailey protested, finally taking a step towards him, closing the remainder of the distance between them and catching his hands in hers. She pulled them towards her and held them against her middle, craning her neck to look him in the eye.

'I wasn't trying to put you off,' she said earnestly. 'I thought you wanted out and it was easier to push you away than to admit how much the thought of that hurt me. I still want to marry you,' she said emphatically.

'Erm...not to kill the mood here...' Gracie said behind them, and Hailey jumped—she'd forgotten her friend was there. 'But there's a fairly significant crowd the other side of this door who want to know what the hell is going on. I don't want to rush you, but are we having a wedding here or not?'

Hailey widened her eyes at Gio in question. 'I want to marry you. I'm sorry I freaked out.'

He looked at her for a long, slow minute, a shadow in his eyes that had darkened rather than lifted since he had walked into the room.

'Okay,' he said, with a smile that didn't reach his narrowed eyes. 'Let's get married.'

Gracie handed Hailey her bouquet, and she had to look down at her hand and force herself to relax her knuckles before she crushed the delicate stems. Her other hand gripped Gio's with no such consideration as they walked from their apartment, past an assortment of panic-stricken aides and towards married life.

CHAPTER FIFTEEN

GIO HELD HIS body straight throughout the ceremony, repeating the familiar words of the liturgy and holding onto Hailey's hand as if she might disappear if he didn't. He wasn't convinced that his heart rate had recovered from the horror of Hailey trying to break off their marriage. Even now, in front of the judge, he couldn't be entirely sure that this was really what she wanted.

True enough, she hadn't seemed to want to call things off—but who would want to cancel a wedding with minutes to go? That didn't mean that she wanted the decades of marriage that he had been hoping would follow.

When they were pronounced husband and wife he leaned in and kissed her, the dutiful husband. But her lips felt foreign, as if something had broken between them and marriage vows hadn't been enough to fix it.

Because he had laid it all out in front of her. His constant struggle to not fall in love with her. His total failure at the task. And she had stood there and listened to him and taken his hands. She had even married him. But she hadn't suggested in even the mildest terms that she shared his feelings. That she might even want to one day. And so, moments before his marriage, his worst fears for the future had come true. He was in love with someone who didn't love him back. In a marriage that he was sure would turn sour one day, and he would one day find himself in a marriage that looked too much like his parents' for comfort.

'Is everything all right?' Hailey asked in the first quiet moment they had, as the photographer adjusted some lighting and they had half a room to themselves. It was the closest thing to privacy they'd had since they had left their apartment.

'Fine,' Gio said, his voice flat.

'Really?' Hailey raised an eyebrow. 'Because you've barely said a word all afternoon.'

'I feel like I've done nothing but talk,' he said, distracted.

'You've barely said a word to *me*,' Hailey clarified.

'There are a lot of people here,' he pointed out.

Despite their decision to go through with the wedding, the air was far from clear between them. They had left a lot unsaid in their apartment that morning and, once they got started, things could get heated. He wanted privacy for that.

A line appeared between Hailey's eyebrows and he couldn't help but lift a thumb to rub at it. He couldn't bear to see her looking unsure—unsure of him.

Her face turned into his palm, her cheek a perfect fit in his hand, and for the first time since they had been pronounced husband and wife he allowed himself a full, deep breath. This was still right. And easier than talking. This was something they could still rely upon. They couldn't be sure that it would last, but there was no denying it was there between them right now. His love might be unrequited, but in this, at least, he knew that his feelings were returned. This need to be near. To feel skin on skin. To ground themselves with the other's body.

He stroked his thumb over Hailey's cheekbone, feeling the hum of appreciation through his fingertips and the hollow of the centre of his palm. He stroked down further, his thumb finding the corner of her mouth, and then the velvet of her lower lip. His other hand came up in a mirror of the right, and he turned her face up to his, thumb still caught on the jut of her lower lip, fingertips in the short, soft hairs at the nape of her neck.

'We got married,' Hailey said, her voice somewhat dazed as he continued his exploration of her mouth, her jaw, her nape.

'You're my wife,' he replied, feeling a fierce possessiveness in his chest, which apparently didn't care whether she loved him back or not, only that she was his, and close enough to him that he could count each of her eyelashes.

He leaned down and brushed his lips over hers, softer but more sensuous than their first kiss as husband and wife. Softer, that was, until Hailey sighed, wrapped her arms around his waist, leant her body into his and opened her mouth to him.

He kissed his way into her mouth, one hand staying on her jaw, tilting her head so he could kiss her deeper. The other was hard around her back, pulling her up and into him, the hard swell of their baby pressed safe between them. One of Hailey's hands unhooked from his waist and wound around his neck instead, pulling herself higher, and he straightened his body, keeping Hailey pressed against him with one hand on her backside as her toes brushed and then left the ground.

'I can't wait to get you upstairs,' Gio breathed against her mouth when they finally broke apart, and he lowered Hailey carefully to the ground. She looked up at him, wide-eyed, the swell of masculine pride he felt at her blown pupils and flushed cheeks for now soothing his hurt that she hadn't reciprocated his declaration of love earlier.

That didn't seem to matter as much just now. Because, even if she didn't love him back, he was hopelessly lost to her. He couldn't imagine ever wanting anyone else. It was Hailey for him or no one. He had her in his arms, and he wasn't strong enough to let her go, even to save his own heartbreak.

If she was indifferent, then he was the one who stood to get hurt. And he could live with that.

'Your Royal Highnesses?' said the photographer from where he had finished setting up the lights. 'We're ready for you now.'

But he wasn't quite ready to let her go. He looked at her for a moment longer before he was able to drag his gaze away, though he had no intention of his arm leaving her waist. He wanted her by his side, her body pressed against his, for the rest of the day. Just until he could be sure that he hadn't dreamt it all. That Hailey was his and he was going to be allowed to keep her.

He didn't have to fake a smile for the photographs, as he'd feared he might. He was all too conscious of the stupid grin on his face. And exactly what—who—had put it there.

His heart was on show for the whole kingdom to see, and there was nothing now that he could do to protect it.

By the time they made it back to their room that night, Hailey's head was buzzing in a way that sadly had nothing to do with the large amounts of champagne that had been consumed that afternoon, not a sip of it by her.

No, her brain was a whirling round of wedding vows, Gio's declaration that he loved her, and small talk with an array of foreign dignitaries she could neither name nor distinguish from one another. And she hadn't had a single moment of quiet to process any part of it. The moment with Gio, the kiss, didn't count because she'd been so overwhelmed by sensation that she couldn't think.

She was alone with Gio for the first time. In the silence she could feel the knowledge of what they had done soak into her mind, her body. They were *married*. They had tied their lives together—publicly, lavishly— and it couldn't be undone. Oh, they could separate, of course, but that wasn't the same thing at all. That wouldn't mean they hadn't made promises to one another, in front of both Gio's people and the law.

He was her *husband*—her heart stuttered at even the thought of the word. He was her family. The father of her child. Her legal spouse. And he loved her. At least that was what she thought he'd been trying to say. Except she'd been so dizzy with thinking that she was about to be jilted, and then somehow making Gio think that she was jilting him. The rush of relief that she'd felt when she'd realised that he still wanted her…she'd been flooded with adrenaline and could hardly think, never mind untangle Gio's tortured confession that he'd been trying not to love her, and had failed.

He'd not left her side since that kiss, and throughout the day she'd felt the insistent press of his fingertips at her hip, her waist, on her collarbone, as if he was still worried that she was going to bolt. If she had thought that a wedding ceremony was going to dispel the tension that had boiled over that morning then she would have been sorely disappointed.

By the time they reached their bedchamber that

night it was positively combustible. Gio kicked the door closed behind him, and before Hailey knew what was happening she'd been spun around against it, trapped between her husband and the hard wood of the door.

'Hello, wife,' Gio said, his voice barely more intelligible than a growl. Hailey squeaked as he started kissing her neck, her ear, her collarbone. But there was something important that she needed to ask him before this went any further, because she'd spent all day turning it over and over in her mind, asking herself whether she had imagined it.

'Er… Gio?' she asked as his hands went exploring, and she had to talk herself out of letting him do what he liked on their wedding night and having this conversation at a later date.

'Mmm…?' Gio grunted, doing nothing for her resolve, nudging her legs apart, and making her thankful for the generous cut of her skirt, that meant that the silk spilt around their bodies rather than constricting her.

She pulled him closer with a foot around his calf and let her head tip to the side even as she tried to continue the conversation they'd cut short earlier.

'Gio, I need to ask you something important,' she said.

'Ask away,' Gio replied, though not stopping his attentions to her breasts.

'Did you tell me that you loved me, earlier?'

He looked up, a startled expression in his eyes, and with the sudden lack of urgency and attention on his part she cursed herself for not waiting until *after* to ask the question. Because, if she'd read this wrong, she couldn't exactly see them picking up where they had just left off. And she really didn't want to leave what they had been doing unfinished.

Gio looked at her, his breath catching in his throat, for so long that she was convinced that she had made a mistake. Then he started to speak, his voice hesitant, and she felt a thrill of anticipation.

'I...can't believe you have to ask me that.'

Hailey tried to find the ground with her feet, feeling suddenly vulnerable.

'Well, I'm sorry, but things were all rather confusing. And I thought that you might have said something that meant that you did, but I wasn't sure and...now I wish that I had never brought this up. Can you just forget that I said anything and get back to doing what we were doing?'

'I've told you that I love you once today without hearing it back, Hailey. I don't think that I can stand to do it again.'

She looked at him in shock. 'So I was right. You do love me.'

He shook his head, his face a picture of resignation. 'Of *course* I love you,' he groaned, resting his forehead against hers. 'I've probably loved you all along, much as I tried not to. But, really, I know that you don't feel the same way, and there are things that I would much rather do than talk about that right now.'

'What do you mean, you know I don't feel the same way?' Hailey said, her hand coming up to his cheek. '*I* don't know how I feel ninety per cent of the time these days, so I don't know why you get to be all certain.'

'Well, the evidence was quite clear,' Gio replied. 'For example, there was the time I declared myself on our wedding day and you didn't say it back—'

'I didn't know that's what you were saying!' Hailey protested.

'And there was the time after we made love and I

asked you what you wanted this to be and you said that you didn't date.'

'I *didn't*. I don't!' Hailey cried. 'That doesn't mean that I wasn't falling in love with you. Just that I didn't know how to stop and I was terrified because I've known all along that you were only doing this because you didn't want to have to be forced into something by your parents.'

'That was weeks ago,' Gio replied. 'And I was in shock. If you think that I haven't been falling in love with you every day since I met you then you haven't been paying attention.'

Hailey pushed him away gently with a hand on his chest, just so that she could get a better look at him, to be sure that he wasn't playing with her. Or had been replaced by an imposter.

'But really,' Gio went on, 'like I said, it's really not enjoyable talking about this when you don't—'

'Of course I bloody love you back!' Hailey declared, realising at last why Gio had been so hesitant to talk about his feelings. 'I left behind my life and my business and my apartment and my friends to move halfway across the world and live under the same roof as your awful, *awful* parents. How could you doubt how I feel about you, you great idiot?'

'Because…you were doing it for the baby?' Gio said, with what sounded like a hint of reluctant hope in his voice. 'I mean, that is what you told me.'

'Only because that's what I was telling myself,' Hailey said with a groan. 'Because, in case you hadn't noticed, falling in love with someone you think doesn't love you back feels quite inconvenient in the moment.'

'So you love me,' Gio clarified, his hand coming up to cup her chin.

Hailey rolled her eyes as she grabbed him by the shirt and pulled him closer. 'I love you,' she said, looking him hard in the eye. 'I fell in love with you a long time ago, and I don't have any plans to stop loving you for the rest of my life. And you married me this morning so I'm afraid you're stuck with me and you are just going to have to get used to it.'

She was rewarded with one of Gio's life-changing smiles, a smile that could rival a sunrise and compromise the political integrity of entire kingdoms.

'Well, isn't that convenient,' he said with a smirk, 'because I love you too.' And with that he brought his mouth down on hers. 'And I'm never planning on letting you go.'

Later, lying in rumpled sheets and blankets, Gio twisting her wedding ring around her finger, Hailey couldn't help but be aware of the extremely smug grin she was sure that she must be wearing.

'I can't believe we made this so complicated,' she told Gio's chest, where her cheek was pressed comfortably against his warm skin. Gio mumbled his agreement, and she chuckled at the knowledge that she had robbed him of the power of speech.

'We were lying like this three months ago,' she observed, remembering that night together in New York, how comfortable they had been. How right it had felt. How bittersweet the morning after had felt, when she had wanted so much to have more of him but had been too afraid to ask for it. 'We could have just…not stopped,' she observed, wondering how things could have turned out differently if they'd just recognised what they were feeling right from the start.

Gio gave another grunt, let go of her hand and rolled

on top of her, his hands brushing her hair out of her face. 'I wouldn't change a thing,' he said, kissing her gently, 'not one thing, if it meant that we ended up somewhere other than here.'

She thought about it as he kissed his way down her body, the utter perfection of sharing a marriage bed with Crown Prince Giovanni of Adria, and found that she couldn't fault his reasoning. In fact, if she didn't know better, she'd say that they'd somehow—blindfolded, directionless and hindered by several key moments of stupidity—stumbled on a fairy tale after all.

* * * * *

...in one of her limbs during the night out of the fire
...while I ... She had once been careful to keep warm
as much for the sake of her ... as for ... of warmth
once she felt ...

She thought to herself she feared the way in which
both ... he rather rather unconscious responses that she
...and forget ... as if ... she had found that she
could stand it even if it was ... he ... she didn't know
better ... she saw that they ... somehow ... she might
...and that ... as he ... to say ... to ... moment or
...suddenly ... as a new tide swept of.

REUNITED UNDER THE MISTLETOE

SUSAN MEIER

MILLS & BOON

CHAPTER ONE

"THE QUEEN SENDS her regrets."

The Queen?

Autumn Jones stifled a laugh. She knew Ivy Jenkins's society wedding would be packed with a who's who of guests...but the Queen?

She glanced around the office of Ivy's Park Avenue townhouse. Decorated for Christmas, the whole place could have been taken from the pages of a high-end style magazine because Ivy was Manhattan royalty. Autumn, the most average woman on the face of the earth with her mid-length auburn hair and hazel eyes, should have felt out of place, but because of Raise Your Voice, the charity where Ivy volunteered and Autumn worked, she and Ivy had become close. Not just friends. More like sisters.

As Ivy's assistant handed a Tiffany's box to her, a gift in lieu of the Queen's appearance, dark-haired, green-eyed Ivy arched one perfectly shaped eyebrow. "She's seriously not coming? Are you kidding me?"

This time Autumn couldn't hold back the laugh. Sometimes Ivy's life amazed her. "You weren't actually expecting *the* Queen to come to your wedding?"

"No. I just thought she'd RSVP by the November twenty-eighth deadline. Not two days after. For Pete's sake, where is her staff?" She pointed at the seating chart she and Autumn had been reviewing in front of a marble fireplace rimmed with evergreen branches and bright red ornaments. "Look, she has a seat…two. One for her. One for her guest. Because Alexandra, the wedding planner, made this chart based on RSVPs."

Autumn shook her head. It was exactly two weeks until the wedding and though Ivy was as polished as ever, her nerves were beginning to fray. Not a lot. She'd been one of Manhattan's elite her entire life. She knew how to be a lady, and she liked to throw a party— two reasons why Autumn and Ivy had bonded at Raise Your Voice, a charity created to assist underprivileged women who needed help climbing the ranks of corporate America. Ivy had the connections and Autumn had the skills to host events that raised millions.

As Ivy handed the Tiffany's box back to her assistant who walked it to the table with the other wedding gifts, the office door opened again. Sebastian Davis, CEO of one of New York's most exciting tech startups and Ivy's fiancé, entered. Wearing a dark suit and white shirt with a thin gray tie, he looked ready for the board meeting Autumn knew he had that crisp Saturday.

"Good morning, everybody."

Ivy and Autumn said, "Good morning."

He bent down and bussed a quick kiss across Ivy's cheek. "More gifts?"

Ivy rolled her eyes. "And late RSVPs. We're looking at the seating chart before I approve it for Alexandra." She took a quick breath. "Did you know the Queen wasn't coming?"

He winced. "No. But it takes a lot to get her to travel to America these days. Besides, the royals from Adria are coming. That's enough royalty for anybody's wedding." He headed for the door again. "I'll see you at dinner." But he stopped suddenly and pivoted to face them. "By the way, Autumn, your partner for the wedding is having dinner with us tonight and I was hoping you would join us."

Ivy clapped. "Oh, great idea!" She turned to Autumn. "I cannot wait for you to meet Jack."

Autumn happily said, "Okay. I don't think I have plans on my calendar for tonight, but even if I do, I'm sure I can reschedule. Anything you need in the next two weeks, I'm your girl."

"Good," Sebastian said.

Ivy smiled.

She rose from her chair, grabbing her purse and briefcase from the floor beside it. "I should get to work, too."

Sebastian waited for her at the office door. "You're going into your office on a Saturday?"

"Most of our clients have Monday through Friday jobs. Saturdays are when they have time for appointments with our mentors."

Sebastian smiled. "Makes sense. Can I give you a lift?"

"No. I'm fine."

They walked into the main foyer, a space so elegant it could have been in a museum. The sound of their heels clicking on the marble floor echoed around them.

Sebastian opened the black and etched glass front door for her. She stepped out with a murmured, "Thanks," for Sebastian, but when she looked toward the street, she blinked and did a double take.

Leaning against Sebastian's black limo was a big, fat unresolved piece of Autumn's past—

Jack Adams.

Tall and thin and wearing a dark suit and black overcoat in the cold last-day-of-November air, he looked every inch a mogul like Sebastian.

His blue eyes met hers across the sidewalk. He pushed off the fender of the limo.

Sebastian said, "Hey! You're here!"

"I wanted to catch a ride to the board meeting. Thought I could run my new management system by you while we drove."

Sebastian motioned to the car. "Great. Get in." Then he faced Autumn. "Autumn, this is Jack Adams, your partner for the wedding."

Jack held her gaze. He didn't make a move to tell his friend Sebastian they already knew each other. In fact, he extended his hand to shake hers, like they were strangers meeting for the first time.

Oh, dear God! Maybe he didn't remember her!

"Jack, this is Autumn Jones."

Their hands met, wrapped around each other and bobbed up and down once. Feeling like a deer in the headlights, Autumn could only stare at him. She'd think she had the wrong guy—Jack Adams was a common name—but she'd remember those blue eyes anywhere. Five years had been very kind to him. Not only did he appear smooth and polished, but also he was just plain gorgeous.

In that second, she could forgive herself for their one-night stand. Because had it been up to her, it would have been more than a one-night stand. But looking at him now, she could see why he hadn't thought of her as anything other than a passing fancy.

He was well dressed, sophisticated, obviously rich.

And she was still Autumn Jones, outreach officer for Raise Your Voice. She had the same car, same apartment, same job… Good God. It was like she was stuck in a time warp.

"It's nice to meet you Mr. Adams…"

He almost smiled. "Jack."

Or maybe he did remember her?

Her heart thrummed as she recalled some particularly *interesting* parts of their encounter.

A blush crept up her cheeks. "Sure. Sure. Jack."

Sebastian said, "Sorry, Autumn. Don't mean to rush off but we've got to get going."

"Me too." She pointed to the right. "I'm picking up a birthday cake at the bakery—"

Her voice trailed off and she fought to keep her eyes from squeezing shut in misery. Her biggest claim to fame was that she was the office birthday girl. She remembered the date, bought the cake, got the card signed.

No fancy job. Not married. Not dating. Still ten pounds overweight.

Yeah, Fate. She got it. No sense in rubbing salt into the wound.

She pivoted to head to the bakery.

"Nice to meet you, too, Autumn."

Jack's smooth voice stopped her dead in her tracks as it washed over her like good whiskey. Which, if she remembered correctly, had been his drink of choice.

Refusing to think about that night, that wonderful night that could have stayed in her memory like the plot of a favorite movie if he hadn't unceremoniously disappeared from her bed, she faced him again.

She said, "Thanks," then quickly turned to go.

Before she got two steps down the block, Sebastian called, "Don't forget dinner tonight!"

This time she did squeeze her eyes shut. Seriously?

She had to endure dinner with him? She groaned. And the *entire* day of the wedding?

She straightened her shoulders. Damned if she'd let that hurt or upset her. She might be stuck in the past, but she was a mature adult. And no matter how successful he was, he was an oaf. He'd swept her off her feet then sneaked out in the middle of the night. No goodbye. No call the next day. Or the next week. Or the next month.

Yeah. She was over him.

She popped her eyes open then faced Sebastian and Jack again with a smile. "I won't forget!" she said with a wave, hoping to speedily spin around and get out of there—

But her eyes met Jack's and she suddenly felt tall and why-hadn't-she-ever-buckled-down-and-lost-those-ten-pounds? clumsy.

Damn it! What the hell was it about this guy that she couldn't step out of idiot mode?

Waking up in her empty bed the day after the most romantic night of her life had been embarrassing and soul crushing, but she'd moved on.

Really.

Seeing him shouldn't even be a blip on her radar screen!

But if the tightening of her chest was anything to go by, it hadn't quite been the nonevent she'd convinced herself it was.

She said, "Goodbye," pivoted and raced away, her heart heavy.

Yeah. It truly hadn't been the nonevent she'd convinced herself it was.

Jack Adams stared out the darkened window of Sebastian's limo.

Of all the people to be his partner for Sebastian and

Ivy's wedding… Autumn Jones? The woman who reminded him of the worst day of his life?

"You wanted to talk about your new management system?"

"Not really the system itself," he said, glancing at Sebastian. "The provider. I've got it narrowed down to three. I wanted to see if you'd heard of any of them."

Sebastian chuckled. "You mean you wanted to see if I knew any dirt on any of them."

Jack snorted. "Yeah."

"Okay, who are you considering?"

Jack opened his briefcase and handed Sebastian his short list.

Sebastian scanned it. "Two are relatively new. But this one," he said, pointing at a name on the list, "has been around forever. That's always a nudge in their favor…"

"That's the group we were thinking about working with." Jack put the list back in his briefcase.

"So, you're good?"

"Yeah, I'm good."

Sebastian eyeballed him. "You don't look good. You look like you swallowed a live fish."

Jack gaped at him. "A live fish?"

"Yeah. Something that didn't go down well."

This was why Sebastian was rolling in success. A genius with a keen business sense wasn't unheard of. A genius who could read people like short books? Not so easy to find.

"Maybe I'm just making too big of a deal about the management system. After all, there are prepackaged systems for restaurants…especially companies with multiple sites."

"Or maybe you're avoiding the subject."

Jack reached for a bottle of water from the small

fridge beside the limo's minibar. There was no way he'd tell Sebastian about his night with Autumn. Partially because he didn't want to embarrass her. Partially because it had taken him years to erase that night from his brain. He didn't want to bring it up again.

"You know that anybody who runs a company is always thinking. Always preoccupied." He opened the water and took a long drink.

"Yeah, I get it." Sebastian nudged Jack's bicep. "But how about being present tonight. Who knows? You might just hit it off with Autumn."

Jack swallowed so hard and so fast, he almost choked. "She seems like a very nice woman but…"

Sebastian frowned at Jack. "But what? She's not your type?"

"I don't have a type."

"Of course, you do. Cool brunettes who don't ever really get to know you because they're shallow and you pretend to be somebody else. And at least two of them were crazy."

"That's not true."

Sebastian only looked at him. "Not even the one who stole from you? Or the one who burned down your beach house?"

Jack grimaced. He had horrible luck choosing women. Everyone but Autumn because she'd only been a one-night stand. She hadn't had time enough to do something egregious like steal from him, cheat on him or burn down his beach house—

Which was why he now only had one-night stands. He'd gotten engaged three times out of a desperate need to feel connected, to feel normal, to have a normal life. He was over that now. Some people simply were made to stand alone. Be strong. Make their mark as a businessperson, not a family man.

"All right. It's a little true. But I finally figured out it's not a good idea for me to settle down. There are temptations in a billionaire's life." Like things to steal. "And I work hard." Leaving at least one fiancée so lonely, she'd cheated.

Sebastian snorted. "And fiancée number three had a temper."

He held back a groan. She sure had. A person had to be really angry to pour gasoline on someone's sofa, toss a match on it and walk away without a backward glance. "Yeah. She had a temper."

"But I do agree that you work hard. Maybe too hard."

"Probably." But he worked hard for his mom. For her vision. To see that vision realized. She'd come up to him the night of his first and only Raise Your Voice gala and told him she wasn't feeling well and would be taking the limo home. He thought of going with her, but he had already spotted Autumn across the room and felt like lightning had struck him. So, he'd kissed his mom's cheek and let her go.

Then he'd turned off his phone and eased through the groups gathered in the crowded ballroom to introduce himself.

While he and Autumn were laughing, dancing and eventually going back to her apartment, his mom had realized she was having a heart attack, called an ambulance, gotten herself to the hospital and ultimately died.

Seeing Autumn reminded him of his biggest failure, his greatest mistake. If getting engaged to a thief, a cheater and a woman who burned down his beach house had been bad, losing his mom because he's been bedazzled by a woman had been the worst.

He'd be a mature adult and do his part for Sebastian's wedding, but he'd limit the time he spent with Autumn. If only to keep her in the category of one-night stand and not give her the chance to prove yet again that he wasn't a good judge of women and shouldn't have relationships.

He also didn't need to be reminded that Autumn had started his run of bad luck with women.

CHAPTER TWO

AUTUMN PULLED FOUR DRESSES from her closet, looking for something to wear to dinner. She didn't want to dress up, but she also didn't want to look out of place. Normally with an impromptu invitation she'd go home with Ivy, borrow something to wear and dress at her house. Easy-peasy.

Angry, confused, and even a little confused about why she was so angry, she couldn't risk slipping something to Ivy about Jack—*the guy who'd pretended not to know her.* Her best friend was getting married. She didn't want to spoil anything about the next two weeks for Ivy. So, she couldn't tell her about Jack dumping her. She had to look normal. Happy.

On the other hand, she didn't want Jack Adams to think she'd dressed up for him. The scoundrel. Make love to her as if she was the woman of his dreams then never call? It would be a cold, frosty day in hell before she'd dress up for him. It would be difficult enough to speak civilly to the oaf.

In the end, she chose a simple black dress, high heels and a sparkly clutch bag that she'd gotten at a second-hand store. She left her apartment, raced to the subway, and headed for the Upper East Side and Ivy's townhouse again.

* * *

Jack exited his limo and told the driver to return for him in two and a half hours. He was tired after the board meeting that had taken an entire day. But he also knew Sebastian and Ivy would be tired. Not only had Sebastian been with him at his board meeting, but he and Ivy were knee-deep in exhausting wedding preparations. He wouldn't overstay his welcome.

Climbing the steps to the townhouse, he also wouldn't let himself think about Autumn. Though he knew she was probably tired too if she'd spent the day at her office, he couldn't handle the feelings that rumbled through him just recalling her name. Anger with himself and grief had almost paralyzed him that day. He couldn't let seeing her bring all that up again.

He rang the bell and Ivy's longtime butler answered. "Good evening, sir."

"What's on the menu tonight, Frances?" Jack asked as he shrugged out of his overcoat and handed it to butler.

"Seared steak and polenta with *chimichurri*."

His mouth watered. "Ah. Is Chef Randolph tonight's chef?"

"Yes. It's Louis's night off. Randolph asked about you. Maybe you could stop by and say hello after dinner."

"I'll do that."

Frances took the overcoat. "Everyone's in the drawing room."

He smiled at Frances, straightened his jacket and tie and headed into the second room on the right. As soon as he stepped over the threshold, he saw her. Tall and shapely in her black dress with her shoulder-length reddish-brown hair curled in some kind of foo-foo hairdo, she looked amazing. Feminine, yet sophisticated.

Sebastian rose from the sofa. "There he is."

Jack glanced at his watch. "I'm not late, am I?"

"No. No!" Ivy reassured as she walked over to give him a hug. "We're just happy to see you."

He shook Sebastian's hand, then—obligated to do so by social convention—he turned to Autumn. "Good evening, Autumn."

She politely said, "Good evening," from her Queen Anne chair across from the sofa. The room had been decorated for the holiday with red and green ornaments nestled in evergreen branches. They sat on the mantel, looped over drapes in the big window and hugged the bases of lamps.

Sebastian walked to the bar. "What can I get you to drink?"

"Whiskey."

Autumn shot him a glance. She knew he drank whiskey. They'd had a night together. She *knew* things about him. Personal, intimate things. Like his ticklish spots. She'd laughed at them…then ran her tongue along them to make him crazy.

He took a cleansing breath. That morning, it had been easy to pretend he didn't know her. Tonight, it sat like a four-ton elephant in the center of the room. Something he and Autumn would have to walk around. Something Sebastian and Ivy would trip over.

Of course, they wouldn't know it. They could say a million embarrassing things, but as long as he and Autumn ignored them, everything would be fine.

Ivy said, "I heard your board meeting went well today."

Jack snorted. "Depends on your perspective. I prefer two-hour board meetings to eight-hour board meetings."

Sebastian handed Jack his whiskey. "Then you shouldn't want to expand and need the advice of your board. A board you chose I might add."

Autumn gave him a sideways glance. "The board meeting this morning was for *your* company?"

Pain rippled through him. Any time anyone called Step Inside *his* company, it was like a knife in his chest. Step Inside had been his mother's dream. His mother's baby. Now he was running it, shaping it, enjoying the benefits of its success.

Still, he faced Autumn with a smile, not showing one iota of emotion. "Yes. We were working out details for expanding." Quickly, to prevent Sebastian from telling Autumn things Jack preferred to stay private, he added, "The original five-year plan finishes in six months, and today I was seeking approval and guidance for expansion in the next five years."

"Your plan is ambitious," Sebastian said. "But I've seen you in action. You can do just about anything you put your mind to."

"Interesting," Autumn said. "In other words, if he sets his mind on something, something he really wants…he goes after it?"

"Yes!" Sebastian wholeheartedly agreed.

Jack worked to stay tall in his chair and not slink down in embarrassment. She clearly assumed he hadn't been interested in her after their one-night stand and that was why he hadn't called her. Which was okay. He'd take the hit. From her vantage point, he had treated her terribly. But hearing her say it, backhandedly calling him out, he had to struggle not to wince.

He'd always believed Autumn had been the first in

his string of bad choices about women…so why did he suddenly feel like the villain?

Autumn said, "That's wonderful."

Before she could ask him another question or toss a barb, he smiled and said, "What about you, Autumn? You work at Raise Your Voice, right?"

She cleared her throat. "Yes."

"That's an interesting charity."

She pulled in a long breath. Her expression became like a thundercloud, as if he'd somehow insulted her.

Ivy said, "She's the go-to girl for everything. She manages their PR and is the public face of the company. She organizes most events. She supervises staff *and* the mentors who have 'office' hours on Saturdays."

A bit surprised, he peeked over at Autumn. They'd spent most of their night together dancing and making love, but he did remember she had organized the gala where they'd met.

A blush crept up her cheeks. Was she embarrassed?

In the five years since they'd seen each other, he'd taken over a company and she was still in the job she'd said was a steppingstone to—

He'd forgotten what it was a steppingstone to, but as he looked into her pretty hazel eyes, more memories formed. He remembered her in bed, naked with a tousled mess of sheets covering bits and pieces of her legs and torso, her eyes shining as she talked about things she wanted out of life. Happiness first and foremost, but also the kind of position that would come with respect.

Since she was still in the same job, he supposed the *respect* aspect of her future might not have materialized.

But all those mundane recollections were edged out by the memory of how soft she was. How touching her had felt like coming home. How she kissed in a way that made him feel he was sinking into something important.

He shook his head to dislodge the images. Those were the things that he couldn't let himself think about. Not merely to prevent the next thoughts—the phone call that woke him, racing to the hospital and being told his mother had died—but also so he wouldn't wonder what might have been.

Like the Prince in *Cinderella*, he'd felt he'd found something special, maybe even the woman of his dreams, but he'd been the one to race away and go back to his real life. Not that it was drudgery—

Frances stepped into the wide doorway. "Dinner is served, ma'am."

Sebastian rose and took Ivy's hand to help her stand. "Thank you, Frances."

With a quick nod of acknowledgment, the butler left.

Sebastian motioned Autumn and Jack to the door. As the foursome walked down the hall to the elaborate dining room that had been decorated with tinsel, and shiny red ornaments, Jack wasn't sure what to do with his hands. Should he guide Autumn to the dining room with a hand on the small of her back? Should he keep his distance?

In the sitting room, actually talking to Autumn, too many memories had assaulted him. Good and bad. Happy and devastating. It was no wonder he'd forgotten common courtesy.

Sebastian seated Ivy. Jack followed suit and seated Autumn, who cast him a confused look. He wanted to tell her he was simply following Sebastian's lead not getting familiar, but that would break their cover.

He took the chair beside Autumn, across from Ivy and Sebastian who had chosen the more intimate seating arrangement rather than sitting at the head and foot of the long table.

Ivy smiled. Looking elegant and sophisticated in her slim red dress and pixie haircut, she lit the room. "No more talk of business. No more talk of companies. We want you and Autumn to get to know each other."

He glanced at Autumn, who smiled at Ivy. "Oh, I think we know each other well enough to be partners in a wedding."

Jack fought back a wince.

"Let's talk about something more interesting than me and Mr. Adams."

The insult of her use of his formal name rumbled through him and he quietly said, "Jack. My name is Jack. Remember?"

She turned and smiled, but if the woman wanted to be on Broadway, she'd never make it. Her smile was so fake it was a wonder her face didn't crack.

"Of course, *Jack*."

Until that moment, he'd never looked at their one-night stand from her perspective. First, he'd been grieving his mom. Then he'd been busy. Then he'd had a string of terrible engagements that had rendered him totally incapable of having a relationship. But tonight, he suddenly realized he'd hurt her.

And why not? They had been like soul mates who'd found each other after a long separation. They'd instinctively known each other's whims and wishes—

Then he'd never called.

A thought hit him like a boulder falling on a road in the Rocky Mountains.

What if that night hadn't just been the worst night of his life?

What if his not calling had made it the worst night of hers?

What if she wasn't the first in his string of bad encounters with women but the last in his string of good encounters?

And if any of that was true, what was he going to do about it?

CHAPTER THREE

AUTUMN WASN'T ENTIRELY sure how it happened. But after dinner and a glass of Cognac, somehow she and Jack announced they were leaving at the same time.

Ivy grinned. "That's great! This way Jack can give you a lift home."

"I'm in Queens," Autumn quickly reminded her. "That's too far. I can take the subway."

"Nonsense," Sebastian said, handing Autumn her black wool coat. "It's not like Jack has anywhere else to go."

Jack smiled stiffly.

And how could Autumn blame him? She hadn't exactly taken *every* jab at him she could, but she'd used more than one of the opportunities presented to remind him he was pond scum.

Watching him try to get them out of this one would be her last mean thing. She swore. On the day of the wedding, she would be nothing but sweet to him. Or at least sort of friendly.

He caught her gaze, and she lifted her chin in challenge. *Go ahead, rich kid. Get us out of this.*

His blue eyes flickered with something that looked like humor and her resolve shook. *Had he gone from squirming to enjoying this? How could he possibly enjoy this?*

"You know what? I'm happy to give Autumn a ride home."

Her eyes bugged. He wasn't enjoying this! He was turning everything back on her!

"That's not necessary."

He smiled at her. "Of course, it is. I'm not totally familiar with the route, but don't you have to take a bus to get to a subway stop?"

"I can get a ride share."

"Don't be ridiculous. What kind of a gentleman would I be to let a lady go through all that this late at night?"

"One who knows that the lady is perfectly capable of getting herself home."

"Of course, she is," Jack said, motioning for her to walk to the door. "But a gentleman still enjoys doing a kindness."

Ivy laughed as he kissed her cheek when he said goodbye. "Such a smooth talker."

Sebastian slapped his back, then hugged Autumn before she stepped out of the townhouse.

"I'll see you on Monday," Ivy called, waving goodbye.

Then the townhouse door closed.

Autumn turned on Jack. "I am not letting you drive me home!"

Jack talked through a big smile he had pasted on his face. "You better. Sebastian and Ivy are at the window, watching us."

"Damn it!"

He waved off his driver before he could open the limo door and handled it himself, directing Autumn to get inside. "Is that any way for a lady to talk?"

"What do you care if I'm a lady or not?" She turned

back to look at the window. The drapes had closed. She was free. She sidestepped Jack. "They're gone. I'll see myself home."

"Wait!"

She ignored Jack's call and headed up the street, pulling her phone from her pocket so she could call a ride share.

The sound of tires crunched beside her. Through her peripheral vision she saw the limo inching along the curb next to her.

The back window lowered. Jack said, "Come on. Get in. Let us take you home."

"I already ordered a ride share."

"Seriously," Jack said as the limo crawled along. "It is no problem for me to give you a ride."

"Maybe it's a problem for me?"

"Really?"

"Maybe I don't want to spend thirty minutes in a car with you trying to figure out what to say. I don't like you. You dumped me. Our spending time together is the definition of awkward."

He said nothing.

Ah. He agreed.

"At least let me wait for your ride share."

"It's a free country, but you look like you're stalking me driving up beside me like that."

"Okay, here's the thing. I know you're mad that I left after our night together and didn't call. But there were extenuating circumstances."

The limo continued to inch along beside her and she sighed. "Don't be so smug, thinking I'm still mad after five years. I'm a mature adult. Sometimes things just aren't what they seem. I have moved on."

"You'd never prove it by me."

"Hey, just because I got past what happened doesn't mean I want to be friends with you."

He winced.

"I'm serious. You played me for a fool."

"What if I told you that had it not been for the extenuating circumstances, I would not have played you for a fool."

Something hopeful rippled through her and she cursed it. Seriously? She could not give him a pass, have fun with him at the wedding then have him drop out of her life again. "What might have happened doesn't matter. What does matter is that you're a scoundrel. An oaf."

"An *oaf*? No one says *oaf* anymore."

She glanced at her phone. "Hey, my ride's around the corner. He must have just dropped someone off."

She stepped back so she could peer down the street to see when the car turned. Within seconds the blue sedan was driving toward her.

She waved her arm and the car eased to the curb. She fake-smiled at Jack. "See you at the wedding."

She got into the car and they sped off, leaving Jack's limo in the dust. Grateful she didn't have to see him until the rehearsal dinner, she leaned back on the seat, and relaxed for the first two minutes. But then her phone buzzed with a message. She glanced down. It was from Ivy.

Hey everyone!
I was thinking about our introduction dances for the reception, and I decided we needed something more special than a plain announcement of your names as you enter the dance floor. So, I've decided that each couple will have a "piece" of a bigger dance routine

to be performed by the entire bridal party. I've hired a dance instructor to do the choreography and he'll also teach each couple the routine. Because everyone's part is different, there's no need to practice together. Each couple only need to learn their segment of the routine! We think it will only take three sessions.

Isn't this fun? Greg will text your practice times. I've given him all of your numbers.

Autumn groaned. She didn't want to be with Jack at all. But three "sessions" learning a dance routine? Being in his arms? Swaying up against each other?

That was one step too far!

If she didn't know better, she'd think Ivy either knew about their one-night stand or suspected something.

But how could she? No one knew. At least Autumn didn't think so.

She swung around in the back of the sedan, spotting Jack's limo behind them before it turned right and disappeared.

Could *he* have told Sebastian?

She groaned. After the way he pretended they didn't know each other when they saw one another that morning, forcing her to follow his lead, she would clobber him if he had!

Jack showed up at the dance studio Monday evening at six. Sunday morning, he'd called Sebastian and as smoothly as possible tried to get himself and Autumn out of this. But happy Sebastian seemed oblivious to Jack's maneuvering.

Sunday afternoon, he'd received a text from the dance instructor with the times of his practices with Autumn. So here he was. He removed his suit jacket and tie, hanging them on a hook near the door and rolled the sleeves of his white shirt to the elbows. He still wore his loafers from work that day, but he decided that was fine. At the wedding, he'd be dancing in a tux and good shoes. His current clothes were close to that. It would be good practice.

Autumn, however, would be dancing in a gown.

He sniffed a laugh. Wonder how she planned to accommodate that?

Not that he'd been thinking about her. At least not too much. And he wasn't thinking about her as much as working to figure out a way that being with her for the entire day of the wedding wouldn't be too awkward.

He'd apologized. He'd told her as much of his story as he was comfortable sharing. He wasn't sure what else to do.

After introducing himself to the dance instructor, Greg, an average-sized, average-looking guy in jeans and a T-shirt, who beamed with happiness, Jack edged over to the balance barre and glanced at his phone. Autumn was two minutes late.

Hope built that she'd talked Ivy out of this idea, but then the glass door of the studio opened, and Autumn blew in with a gust of wind. Snowflakes frosted her hair. Laughing, she brushed them off. Then she saw him and deflated.

His chest tightened. All these years, if he ever thought of Autumn at all it was to consider her the first in his string of bad luck with women. Now that he'd begun seeing things from her perspective, he felt like a crumb, a snake, someone who owed *her*.

"I couldn't talk Sebastian out of this," he said as she approached him.

"I couldn't talk Ivy out of it either."

The normal tone of her voice encouraged him. "At least we agree about something."

She sniffed and removed her wool coat, revealing black yoga pants and a pink T-shirt that outlined her curves. He remembered those curves warm and silky beneath his palms and took a quick breath to dispel the memory.

"Sorry about the yoga pants. I keep them in my office for when I work late." She glanced down at them, then up at Jack. "I should have practiced in my dress. At least that's somewhat like a gown."

"You look…" *Really hot.* Hot enough that his chest tightened and spectacular memories of their night together cascaded through his brain again. "Fine."

She tossed her coat on an available hook and sat on the bench against the wall to remove her clunky boots. Then she rummaged through her huge purse and pulled out…

"Are those ballet slippers?" He caught her gaze. "You took ballet?"

"A very acceptable thing for girls to do when I was growing up."

He frowned.

"What? You think because I'm clumsy I couldn't possibly dance?"

She was not clumsy. Especially not in bed. She was smooth and graceful.

"No. I was wondering what purpose it serves to learn our part in ballet slippers when you'll be wearing wedding shoes when we actually dance."

She rose. "Not if I slip into these under the table before we're introduced."

He laughed, remembering why he'd liked her so much the night he'd met her. Her blissful pragmatism.

Greg ambled over. Glancing at Jack, he said, "This is your partner for the wedding?"

He and Autumn simultaneously said, "Yes."

Autumn added, "I'm Autumn."

Happy Greg grinned. "Then let's get started." He walked to the opposite side of the room and motioned for Autumn and Jack to stay where they were. "Your dance begins with a series of twirls that gets you to the center of the floor."

Jack balked. "I'm twirling?"

"No. You twirl your partner."

He relaxed. "Thank God."

Autumn giggled. "What? Twirling is a threat to your masculinity?"

"No. I don't want to look like a fool. There'll be lots of important people at that wedding. Most of them eat at my restaurants. I don't want to look like the guy who can't twirl."

"*You're* the one worried about being clumsy?"

"Hey, I didn't laugh at you when you insinuated you were clumsy." He hadn't laughed because he'd remembered her in bed. Definitely not clumsy.

"Oh, poor baby."

Another memory shot through him. The night they'd stayed together, he'd complained about a meeting the following afternoon and she'd walked her fingers up his chest and said, "Oh, poor baby," before she'd completely annihilated him with a kiss.

He sucked in a breath. He had to stop thinking about that night.

"Take your partner's hand and raise her arm enough that you can twirl her out to the floor. I'm guessing it will be three or four twirls before you get to the center of the dance area."

Jack did as he was told. He wasn't completely clueless. He'd actually learned the basics of dancing in lessons his mom had insisted on when he was fourteen because she believed a polished gentleman should be able to dance. He'd groaned and argued, but once he'd begun going to charity events, he'd realized how smart of a decision that had been.

He raised Autumn's arm and twirled her three times, mesmerized by the way she sprang to her toes and made the simple movement of twirling look majestic and elegant.

Her ability gave him confidence and they did two more twirls to get to the center.

"Lovely." Greg smiled at Autumn. "You've taken lessons."

"Only every Saturday morning for what seemed like an eternity."

He laughed.

Jealousy crept up on Jack, but he stopped it because it was wrong. There'd never be anything between him and Autumn. She disliked him and three failed engagements was enough to make any man take a step back and evaluate. He clearly wasn't relationship material.

Greg walked over and positioned them. "When you come out of the twirl, I want you to stand like this." He motioned for Jack to stay where he was and turned Autumn to face Jack.

"Now," Greg continued. "I want you both to shift right, then left, as if you're trying to see over each other's shoulder—"

Jack grimaced. "What kind of dance is this?"

"It's free style. Ivy wants us to tell the story of her relationship with Sebastian. Apparently, she and Sebastian were at odds when they first met and had to grow to love each other. Because you two are the first couple, you'll be demonstrating that discord."

Autumn said, "Should be a piece of cake for us to demonstrate discord."

Jack sniffed a laugh.

Greg smiled. "Well, those movements are only about two seconds of your dance. Lean left, lean right, get into the waltz position. Then it's a waltz around the floor until you are beside Ivy and Sebastian where you will stop, and the next couple will be introduced."

"Okay." Waltz? He loved to waltz. "Sounds easy."

Greg faced Autumn. "Agree?"

"Absolutely."

Greg clapped. "Then let's start at the beginning. Twirl, twirl, twirl. Lean left. Lean right. Waltz hold. Then a waltz around the dance floor."

CHAPTER FOUR

AUTUMN AND JACK returned to the side of the room. He took her hand and twirled her to the center of the dance floor, where they stopped and faced each other before they leaned left and right. Then he stepped toward her to get into the waltz hold.

His hand sliding across her back almost made her stumble, but her trusty ballet shoes saved her. Still, that didn't stop the warmth that spread up her spine causing tingles of awareness that spawned a million memories. Mostly of how they'd laughed at the gala where they'd met. He'd snagged champagne for her from passing waiters and bribed one of them to always have a glass of whiskey on his tray. By the end of the night, they were both tipsy. And happy. They'd seemed like two peas in a pod. Especially when they'd danced.

She put her hand on his shoulder and the memories multiplied. She could almost feel them gliding along the floor, gazing into each other's eyes as if they couldn't believe their luck in finding each other. But more than that, she knew what he felt like beneath that shirt. She could picture his muscled shoulders, back and chest.

She swallowed.

"You okay?"

She raised her eyes to meet his gaze. Those stunning blue eyes almost did her in. She glanced away, saying, "Yes. Fine."

Jack took the first step to lead her in the waltz. His feet were sure. His movements balanced.

Greg clapped. "Stop! Stop! Stop!" He ambled over. "Seriously? You had hundreds of dance lessons, but you don't know you're to look your partner in the eye?"

Autumn stepped out of the hold. "Yes. I'm sorry. I'm just a little scattered today."

Jack's head tilted as he studied her.

"Long day at work," she qualified.

Greg sighed. "It doesn't take a lot of energy to look in your partner's eyes."

She took a breath. "I know."

"Good. Then let's start from the top."

She and Jack walked back to the side of the room. Greg said, "Go."

Jack took her hand and twirled her four times to get her to the center of the dance floor. They leaned left, then right. He stepped toward her and joined their hands as he slid his other arm around her waist.

Her palm tingling, she placed her fingers on his shoulder, then raised her eyes to meet his gaze.

The world upended. Memories of dancing together at the gala whispered through her, then making love. They'd been as close as two people could be and now they were pretending not to know each other.

He effortlessly waltzed them in a circle around the dance floor. But with her gaze connected to his, everything inside her shivered. Not merely with remembered sensations. But with the feeling of rejection. With the sense that she wasn't good enough. The sense that— just as her dad always said—she was average, made to be a worker bee. That she should keep her head down and do her job and hopefully find a man who could take care of her.

The thoughts penetrated so deep, she faltered, tripping as she was gazing into the eyes of the man she'd thought she could fall in love with.

Jack covered her misstep and effortlessly got them to their stopping place. Yanking her gaze from his, she jerked out of his arms.

Greg said, "That was lovely. Jack, you waltz like a dream. You have nothing to be afraid of." He turned to Autumn. "Since you'll be wearing a gown. No one will even notice if you bobble a step."

I will.

Jack will.

And he already thinks there's something wrong with me. A reason not to ever call again. A reason to never see me again.

She did not want to be unbalanced or foolish in his arms.

Damn it. She was not what her father thought. She did not want Jack to think she was. She would not trip in his arms again.

She took a cleansing breath and pasted on a smile for Greg. "Thank you. That was fun and honestly I think we have the hang of it."

Jack continued to study her.

Greg glanced at his phone. "Second couple will be here in five minutes. Do you want to go over it one more time or do you think you have it?"

"We're fine," Autumn quickly said, then smiled to take the sting out of it. "I'm tired. I had that bad day, remember?" She smiled again.

"Honestly, you two have the easiest of the dances,"

Greg said. "One more run through on Wednesday and you should be solid."

"Sounds great," Autumn agreed as she headed for her coat and clunky boots. She slid them on and walked to the door. "I'll see you on Wednesday night."

"See you then," Greg replied, but Jack said nothing.

Which was fine. They had one more dance lesson, the rehearsal dinner and one wedding to get through, then they'd never see each other again. She might be in the same job she'd been in five years ago, but she was extremely good at it. The current CEO was getting up in years and would eventually retire and she would step into his shoes.

That was her plan.

She was not less than. She was a smart woman, gifted in fundraising. With a plan. A good, solid plan to move into the job she was born to do.

One guy who dumped her and one misstep on the dance floor changed nothing.

Tuesday morning, Autumn got a call from Ivy, who bubbled over with excited questions. Making a cup of coffee, Autumn told the bride-to-be that the dance lesson had been fine.

"That's all? Just fine?"

"It's a very simple dance," Autumn said, smiling in the hope the positivity of it would translate to her voice.

"Maybe too simple?"

"No. It's lovely. I love to waltz and Jack's a great dancer. In fact, we did so well last night Greg thinks we only need one more lesson."

After a few seconds of silence, Ivy said, "Jack didn't say anything offensive, did he?"

Autumn laughed. "As we were both focused on learning a dance?"

"Jack can be chatty."

"Does he typically say offensive things when he's chatty?"

"No." Ivy's voice turned petulant. "It's just that I thought you'd enjoy the lessons."

"Dancing was fun," Autumn said, scrambling for something positive to say. Everything about the wedding was important to Ivy. She wanted everyone to love every step of the process as much as she did. And Autumn loved how happy Ivy was and wanted to keep her that way. "The dance is going to be really cool. I think it will be entertaining for the guests."

"Good. Great. You'll all have fun and it will be brilliant. I am glad I thought of it and I'm glad you like it."

Autumn frowned. Ivy was babbling and she never babbled. "Is everything okay with the wedding?"

"Yes! Wonderful. Meeting with the florist again today."

"Oh, that's fun."

"Yes. It really is."

But Ivy had that strange tone in her voice again. Still, she didn't probe any deeper about the dance lesson with Jack, so when she said goodbye Autumn went back to dressing for work.

As she walked out the door, a weird sensation spiraled through her and she stopped on the little porch of her second-floor apartment. She'd told Ivy she didn't think she and Jack needed the final two lessons—

Then Ivy had changed the subject even though she'd been asking questions—

Was Autumn crazy to notice that or did that mean something?

She shook her head with a laugh. She was monitoring the bride for signs of nerves, but that subject change had been meaningless.

She hoped.

Because when Ivy had a bee in her bonnet about something she wouldn't rest until she resolved it.

Jack stepped out of the elevator into the reception area for the corporate offices of Step Inside when his phone rang. Seeing the caller was Sebastian, he said, "What's up?"

"I have a favor to ask."

"Anything for the groom to be."

"We're cake tasting this afternoon."

Jack grimaced at his friend's plight. "I thought you'd chosen a cake."

"We thought we had too. Thing is… Ivy's decided everyone should get their own tiny wedding cake to take home and she wants everybody to have a choice of flavor. She's going for goofy things. New flavors designed by the baker. I'm sort of campaigning for just plain chocolate cake."

"Your favorite."

"Is that so wrong?"

Jack laughed.

"We've already chosen four, but up to this point, chocolate never made the grade. This afternoon at the bakery, I want you to help me get chocolate into the rotation."

Jack laughed at the way he said rotation as if the cake was vying to be a starting pitcher for the Yankees, then he realized what Sebastian had said. "You want me to taste cakes?"

"Yes. As a former chef, your opinion holds weight.

If you come prepared to taste the chocolate and say it's the best thing ever created, Ivy will listen."

It was a bit odd. But he'd seen how stressful the wedding plans had become, so Jack could be a good sport and help out his friend. "Okay. I'll be there." He stepped into his office. Furnished in an ultra-modern minimalist style, with a pale wood desk and a buttery brown leather for the chair, the clean lines of both the room and the furnishings forced him to keep his big, shiny desk empty. He walked over to the hidden closet where he stored his coat. "Text me the address."

"Okay. Three o'clock. I'll see you then."

"Right. See you at three."

Turning away from the closet, he stopped as a weird sensation washed through him. He hadn't thought about being a chef in years. When his mom ran Step Inside, he'd been the head chef of their flagship restaurant. That was where he'd created the menu that had made them so successful that they could put restaurants in the five boroughs and expand into New Jersey. Before she'd died, they'd been discussing creating a research and development kitchen where he could create and test recipes to come up with dishes that would rotate, keeping their menu original and innovative.

He shook his head to clear it. That had been the culmination of their dream. His mom running the business end and him creating. But when she died, he'd taken over the business and found a way to update the menu by subcontracting chefs like Randolph to create new meals. It was that decision that solidified his ability to take over the business with the board his mother had chosen.

It was that decision that had made him who he was today. One hell of a businessman.

So why did it feel so odd suddenly? Like Sebastian mentioning he'd been a chef had dragged him further back in time than seeing Autumn had—

Actually, he could probably blame these new feelings on seeing Autumn, too.

That night had changed so much about his life. He stopped being a son, stopped being a chef, literally lost his entire family and had to pick up the ball and finish the game for his mother.

But it had worked and worked well. He wouldn't question it or analyze choices that had succeeded.

With a ton of emails in his inbox, he dismissed his thoughts and spent an hour reading before he met with the company's chief financial officer and his team who would handle crafting the financials for the new five-year plan.

At one o'clock, he had lunch at one of his own restaurants. He'd changed from his suit into jeans and a sweater with a black leather jacket. No one recognized him, so it gave him the perfect opportunity to observe.

And maybe to be a little bit proud that he'd brought his mother's vision to glorious life.

But on the heels of that pride came the sorrow and the longing to have watched *her* live her dream. He recognized that Sebastian's throwaway comment had spawned memories of the years of dedication it had taken to turn Step Inside into something remarkable. But it felt wrong to be proud of himself. Wrong to enjoy the success.

So, he'd forget all that, forget Autumn, forget Sebastian's throwaway comment and focus on the wedding. When his driver arrived with his limo, he texted the address Sebastian had given him to his driver and settled into the backseat, reading emails on his phone during the ride to the cake tasting. Twenty minutes later, the limo pulled up at a townhouse.

"This is it?"

Arnie, his driver, turned around on his seat. "This is the address."

"Stay close a minute while I make sure Sebastian didn't transpose a number or something."

He got out of the limo, walked up to the townhouse door and rang the bell. Sebastian answered. "Come in. We're all in the kitchen."

He waved to Arnie and headed inside. "This is a house."

"The home of the baker Ivy chose to make our cakes."

Sebastian led him down a hall replete with antiques and Oriental rugs. They walked into an open kitchen with stunning white cabinets, quartz counter tops and tall-backed stools around the biggest island Jack had ever seen.

It was also very similar to what he and his mom had planned for his test kitchen. The memory of meeting with the architect and even approving plans rippled through him.

"Here he is now," Ivy said, racing over to kiss Jack's cheek. "I can't wait for you to test the strawberry cream filled."

He shoved the unwanted memories to the back of his mind and returned Ivy's cheek kiss. "Meaning, you're on team strawberry?"

"Yes. We have one slot to fill. I adore the strawberry. Sebastian likes the chocolate. And Autumn is team lemon."

He saw her then. Sitting on one of the tall-backed stools at the island, she had five or six pieces of cake in front of her. But her hair hung straight, almost to her shoulders and she wore a slim red dress that came to her knees and high-high heels that he was positive would make her look tall and sexy.

"Autumn."

She glanced at him. "Jack."

Even after three times seeing each other there was still something off in the way they treated each other. He'd thought dancing together had melted some of the ice between them, but she'd gotten odd at the end of the session and raced away so quickly he hadn't even heard her say goodbye.

Anybody who wasn't wrapped up in wedding preparations would realize they barely tolerated each other—

Or maybe somebody who *was* wrapped up in wedding preparations had noticed. And maybe that's why Ivy kept throwing them together.

Ivy slid her hand beneath his arm and led him to the spot right beside Autumn.

Yeah. She'd noticed.

"Here's your cake set up." The happy bride pointed at the plate holding the yellow slice and said, "That's the lemon."

She then pointed at the pink "strawberry cream," then at two nondescript versions with names like "tangerine torte" and "special birthday," and finally she pointed at the chocolate. "And that, of course, is Sebastian's pick."

Jack said, "Yum. I'm a big fan of chocolate."

Ivy snorted. "You're a friend of the guy who likes chocolate. You don't get to make your choice until you've tasted all of them."

He winced. "Even that special birthday thing that looks like the color of a zombie?"

Autumn laughed unexpectedly and his gaze jumped to her.

"I knew it reminded me of something. I just couldn't figure out what it was."

Jack's lips lifted into a hopeful smile. Maybe some of the ice had melted after all?

The baker sighed. "It's a theme color." Older, stout and dressed in a traditional chef's uniform of white coat and toque blanche, he gave Jack a you-should-know-that look as he ambled over to the island. "It was created for the birthday party of Angelina Montgomery last year. Guests couldn't get enough of it."

"Oh, yes, Mark! I remember!" Ivy said. "Guests gushed about that cake for months."

Mark took a breath, lifting his nose in the air as if he were looking down on them. "They're still gushing."

Autumn pressed her lips together to keep from laughing and caught Jack's gaze again. He was totally with her. He understood the pride of the great chefs and bakers. He'd been proud of every damned thing he'd created. But sometimes the pretense was just a little bit funny.

He rolled his eyes and Autumn nodded. They were absolutely on the same page.

Memories of the click he'd felt with her five years ago poured through him. He hadn't been born into this life the way Ivy had. Neither had Autumn. Both had worked to get here and worked even harder to belong here. But they'd both also hung on to their normal lives, their normal values.

Ivy turned to Jack. "Jack, this is Mark Patel. His cakes are divine."

Jack offered his hand across the big island. "It's a pleasure to meet you."

Stretching forward, the baker took Jack's hand to shake. "A pleasure to meet you too."

Autumn slid one of Jack's slices closer to him. "Try the zombie one. It's actually pretty good."

Mark nodded approvingly. "I accomplish that gray color with blueberry juice which also gives the cake just a bit of a tangy flavor."

"That had been what I thought," Jack said as he took the seat beside Autumn and picked up the fork. He cut a bite of the cake and ate it. Flavor burst on his tongue.

"Oh, that *is* good."

The baker stuck his nose in the air again. "Of course, it is."

"But, Jack," Sebastian reminded him. "You like chocolate."

"I do," Jack agreed, sliding the zombie cake away and reaching for the chocolate. He took a bite. "Oh, my God." He jerked his gaze to the baker. "Are you kidding me? This is the best cake I've ever eaten."

Sebastian leaned in and whispered, "Don't over sell it."

"I'm not overselling." He caught Mark's gaze again. "This is amazing."

"And Jack knows amazing," Sebastian said, glancing over at Mark. "He owns Step Inside."

Mark's expression said he was impressed. "I've eaten there. And also heard good things from your chefs."

Autumn said, "You *own* Step Inside?"

He winced, expecting some sort of wise crack. The ice might be thawing but it hadn't melted completely. "Yes."

"I love those restaurants."

Pride rolled through him. He tried to stop it. After all, he was only following his mother's plans. But it bubbled up. He swore he could feel his chest swelling.

"And I like the chocolate too."

Autumn's voice filled the sudden void in the kitchen.

Surprised that Autumn had sided with him on the chocolate cake, Jack peeked over at her. The click of rightness they'd shared the night they'd spent together tiptoed back. Too busy having fun, they hadn't shared facts of their lives until she'd told him a bit about her job when they were lying in bed together.

But that night, the past hadn't mattered. Only the present had. The connection they'd felt. The fun they'd had being themselves.

Jack was glad when Ivy broke the spell by groaning and Sebastian laughed. "It looks like I get chocolate after all."

Ivy sighed dramatically. "All right. You win. Chocolate it is."

With the decision made, Mark nudged the plates closer to his guests. "Eat! These cakes are too good to throw away."

Steeped in conflicting emotions, Jack quietly said, "You could donate them to homeless shelters."

Mark batted a hand. "Everything but the pieces on the plates can definitely go to the shelters. Pieces on the plates must be eaten." He grinned. "Can I get anyone a glass of wine?"

Sebastian said, "I'd love one."

Ivy agreed. "Me too. Though I'm only eating one piece of cake because I have a wedding gown to fit into."

Autumn seconded that. "I have a dress to fit into, too. I also have a long trip home." She rose from her stool. "So, if you don't mind, I'll be leaving."

Mark jumped into action, scooping up the plate with her slice of lemon cake that had only one bite taken out. "Let me box this up for you." He grinned. "For breakfast tomorrow."

Autumn glanced at the cake with longing in her eyes. "It would make a great breakfast."

Jack almost told her she was perfect just the way she was. She didn't need to diet. She had curves in all the right places. But not only was this the wrong place and time, the urge itself confused him. She didn't like him. He didn't do relationships. There was no reason for them to get personal. All he needed was for the ice to thaw a little more. He didn't even want to be her friend. After this wedding they'd go their separate ways.

"It will make a fabulous breakfast!" Mark slid the cake into a handy takeout container. Obviously, this wasn't the first cake tasting in his house.

Autumn happily took it. "Thank you."

Mark said, "You're welcome."

She turned to Ivy. "If you need me, call."

"Okay."

Then she waved to Sebastian before she left the kitchen, cake in hand, and slipped out the front door.

Jack blinked, surprised at how quickly she was gone and even more surprised no one had asked him to give Autumn a ride home. Then he remembered the cold war feeling he'd sensed he and Autumn were throwing off when he first arrived.

They might have warmed up over her love of his restaurants, the proud baker and the chocolate cake, but she'd barely acknowledged him when she left.

No. She hadn't acknowledged him at all.

She'd thanked Mark, told Ivy to call if she needed anything and waved to Sebastian.

And nothing to him.

He waited for Ivy to say something about Autumn. Maybe to call him out over the way they barely spoke to each other. She didn't. He expected Sebastian to say something twenty minutes later when he walked Jack to the door. He didn't. He simply said a happy goodbye.

Jack walked down the sidewalk to his limo with the godawful feeling that it wasn't other people who didn't like the cold war between him and Autumn. It was *him*.

He'd hurt her. Good excuse or not, he'd hurt her.

And if he wanted the two of them to get along for this wedding, he was going to have to tell her why.

CHAPTER FIVE

AUTUMN STOPPED AT the door of the dance studio and took a long breath. Fat white snowflakes fell to the sidewalk, making the city a winter wonderland and covering the hood of her down jacket. But she needed a minute to remind herself she was a strong woman who refused to be attracted to a man who was probably a player, someone who had lots of one-night stands and countless pretty girls willing to go anywhere he wanted any time he wanted. The man *owned* Step Inside. One of the best restaurants she'd ever eaten at.

He was way out of her league.

Unfortunately, he hadn't behaved like a rich guy at the cake testing. In fact, he'd been the Jack she'd met at the summer gala five years before. He'd made her laugh at least twice. And, God help her, now that she knew he owned Step Inside, she *did* understand how busy and demanding his life had probably been for the past few years.

She couldn't remember him mentioning what he did for a living the night they'd met at the gala. They'd been preoccupied gazing into each other's eyes and having fun. But now that he'd told her he managed a string of highly successful restaurants, the problem was clear.

Of course, she liked him. He was gorgeous, funny, rich.

But she was Autumn Jones. Average at best. Not the girl Prince Charming would choose to dance with at the ball—unless there was no one else around. Historically, young singles were at a premium at a gala planned to entice wealthy people to donate money.

She hadn't been a choice that night. She'd been the only option.

Which was why she needed the minute to regroup. If she continued to think back to the gala and remember how attuned they seemed to be, she could forget that they weren't two peas in a pod. Plus, she wasn't the same woman she was when she had met him. She might have always wanted to be CEO of Raise Your Voice, but now that goal was in reach. Gerry was old enough that he would soon be retiring.

She couldn't afford a misstep. She couldn't afford to become so involved with a man that she'd end up part of his life rather than having her own life. She'd seen enough of that with her parents. Her mom waited on her dad hand and foot and threw herself into making sure her kids had good lives, but she didn't seem to have a life of her own. Autumn wanted a career. She wanted to help hundreds of people achieve their goals. She didn't have time for a man or a family.

Her resolve to keep her distance restored, she entered the dance studio.

Unlike their first lesson, Jack wasn't yet there.

She couldn't breathe a sigh of relief that she wouldn't see him that night. Even if he wasn't available for a lesson, they'd have to make it up. She wanted to get this final session over with. She didn't want any more confusing encounters. Didn't want to understand him anymore. Didn't want to see peeks of the guy she'd met at the Raise Your Voice gala. She just wanted them to do their part for the wedding and never see each other again.

She took off her coat and sat on the bench to put on her ballet slippers. The door opened and Jack walked in. "Cold out there."

"And lots of snow," Greg agreed, ambling into the studio from a door in the back. "I hope you have a dependable way home."

Before Jack could say anything, Autumn said, "I usually stay with Ivy and Sebastian when it snows this much."

Jack said, "There's no need. I can take you."

Now that she had a solid understanding of what had happened between them, she ventured a smile. "Ivy wants to go over some things about the wedding." Thank God. She and Jack might be getting along but that didn't mean she wanted to spend almost an hour in a car with him, trying to think of things to talk about without getting too chummy, causing her to remember how very much she'd liked him that night.

"And speaking of Ivy," Greg said. "She's changed your dance a bit."

Jack groaned. He removed his overcoat and walked it to the row of hooks on the wall by the big window, revealing a dark suit. After he took off his jacket, he turned to face Greg and Autumn's heart fluttered. He looked amazing in the dark trousers and white shirt. He rolled the sleeves to his elbows then took off his tie and he looked even better. Professional sexy.

Walking to Greg, he said, "I liked what we had."

"You pulled off the waltz like a pro—"

"Because I had about six lessons as a kid and learning to waltz took up most of them."

Greg batted a hand. "You'll get this too. Especially

since the new version isn't much more difficult. We're going to add the basic Charleston step right after the look left, look right move."

Her shoes on, Autumn rose from the bench. Greg reached for her hand and guided her onto the dance floor. "So, you're going to look left, then look right," he said as he reminded her of the move that she and Jack already knew. "Then you do a twirling pivot that puts you beside Jack."

He demonstrated the step so that he stood beside Autumn. "Then you do the basic Charleston step. Take a step back with the right foot. Then swing the left leg back in a kicking motion. Bring the left foot forward again and return to the starting position. Then, with the right foot loose, kick it forward. Bring it back. Blah. Blah. Blah. We're going to repeat that step five times. Meaning the left foot gets five kicks and so does the right."

Jack stared at him.

Autumn pressed her lips together to keep from laughing. It was fun to find something he wasn't good at. Though with the way he waltzed, he'd probably get this easily.

Greg smiled encouragingly. "It's really a very simple dance once you master the primary step."

Looking like a deer in the headlights, Jack said, "But I'll be in front of people. Every additional step adds to the potential embarrassment."

"Why don't we try learning the move, before we ease it into the routine?" Autumn asked, taking pity on him. "Plus, I know the Charleston. Just follow my lead."

Greg glanced at Jack. Autumn smiled hopefully. Jack took a breath.

"Okay. Yeah. Sure. But Ivy does realize this could

backfire, right? Any one of us could go on that dance floor and make a fool of ourselves."

"And you know what?" Greg said supportively. "The guests will love it. They will love that you tried. Everyone roots for an underdog."

Autumn motioned for Jack to stand beside her on the dance floor.

He approached, mumbling, "I do not want to be the underdog."

She held back a snort as he lined up beside her. Now that she knew who he was it was easy to see his objections as funny. He could end up on the wrong side of a society page critic's article.

Greg said, "All right. Let's have a go at this. Take a step back on the right leg. Swing the left leg back in a kicking motion. Bring the left foot forward again and return to the starting position. Then with the right foot loose, kick it forward. Bring it back."

Autumn put her hand on Jack's forearm to stop him. "Forget the words. Watch my feet."

He frowned. She motioned for him to look at her feet before she brought her right leg back, then her left, then kicked it forward.

He brought his right leg back, then his left, then kicked it forward.

"I feel stupid kicking."

"Pretend you're playing for the Giants. You've got the center holding the football up for you and you're going to kick it through the uprights."

One of his eyebrows rose.

"I'm serious. You might not want to kick your leg as high as the kicker on a football team does. But it's the same basic concept. It's also a little more manly that way. Something you can sink your teeth into."

She repeated the step and he followed until they were able to string five of them together.

When they were done, Greg clapped. "Very nice. Now, let's try the thing from the top. Go back to the side. Twirl onto the dance floor. Look left, look right. Charleston step five times. Waltz hold. Waltz."

They walked to the side of the dance floor but before he gave them the signal to start, Greg added music. The song began with a gentle gathering of notes that made it easy for Jack to twirl her to the dance floor, then the music changed subtly for the look left, look right, then it shifted again for the Charleston steps, which Jack bungled.

He sighed. She smiled at him and said, "Let's just go over it one more time."

"Yeah. And are we going to go over it at the wedding before we do the dance?"

She shrugged. "If it will help, we can find a private room and go over the whole routine after dinner, before the dance, so it's fresh in your mind."

He ran his hand along the back of his neck. "Actually, that probably would help."

"Then that's what we'll do."

They walked back to the side of the dance floor and Greg restarted the music, but he stopped it again. "What do you say we run through the entire dance. No matter how poorly you think you've done, Jack, I want you to push through it."

Jack took a breath. "You know why he said that, don't you?"

Autumn peered up at him. "To show us that the dance works?"

"No, he wants me to get practice screwing up and

soldiering on. So, when I screw up at the wedding, I'll just keep going."

She laughed.

Greg hit the music and Jack twirled Autumn onto the dance floor. They looked left then right, then she did the Charleston step and he followed as best he could. Then they got into the waltz hold and began to dance.

He relaxed completely. This was the part he knew.

"Look how well you're doing."

"This is the dance I took lessons for, remember?"

She held back a wince. "You did okay on the Charleston steps."

"Not really. But thanks."

The waltz ended and they headed back to the edge of the dance floor. Greg turned on the music and they started the routine from the top.

This time, maybe because the Charleston steps went a little smoother, when Jack took Autumn into his arms for the waltz and looked into her eyes, he felt like he had gone back in time to their night at the gala. His comfort with the waltz meshed with how comfortable he'd been with her five years ago and emotions tumbled around him. He remembered thinking how logical it was for them to go back to her apartment and make love because everything between them was so effortless—

He wasn't the only one who had felt it. She had too. Which was why he owed her an explanation for why he hadn't called.

What they'd had that night was once-in-a-lifetime perfect. Something he hadn't felt before or since and probably wouldn't ever feel again. Technically, he'd ruined what might have been their chance at permanent happiness.

Or maybe better said, Fate had stolen it and she deserved to know that.

Suddenly the sound of Greg applauding filled the dance studio. "That was beautiful, Jack. You certainly have command of the waltz."

He stepped away from Autumn, but their gazes held. Feelings from the night they met swamped him. The sense of finding something that would change his life.

"You can let go of my hand now."

The spell broken, he released her hand. He might be having feelings from all those years ago, but she wasn't. Not only did he have to remember that, and explain what had happened, but also those resurrected emotions weren't valid anymore. They weren't the same people they had been five years ago. They weren't going to pick up where they left off. Especially since neither of them wanted to.

"One more time, then we're done for the night."

They walked back to the edge of the dance floor. Jack twirled her to the center. They looked left and right, did a clumsy version of the Charleston step and began the waltz. Their gazes connected as he whirled them around the floor, and he felt like he could see the whole way into her soul. She didn't have secrets like he did. She didn't tell lies. She'd had a simple upbringing like his and didn't try to pretend she hadn't. She liked who she was. At least, she had liked who she was the night of the highly successful gala for Raise Your Voice that she'd planned and executed to perfection.

Was it any wonder he'd been so drawn to her?

Once again, it was Greg clapping that brought Jack back to the present. He stepped out of the waltz hold, but let go of her hand slowly. As if bewitched, he couldn't stop staring at her, wondering what would have happened between them if that night had ended differently.

"Jack? Are you with us?"

He shook his head and faced Greg. "I'm sorry. I missed what you said."

"I said you're doing very well."

That would have made him laugh if it wasn't so sad that a couple of steps had him tied up in knots. "We both know I'm not."

Autumn said, "Look at it this way. You ace the twirl. Any fool can look left then right. And you are a master at the waltz. You own this dance—"

"Except for the Charleston steps."

"Which you will get. This is only our first day with those steps."

"Yes. But this is our second session. And it's supposed to be our last."

She frowned. "That's right."

Greg said, "Ivy has paid me to provide as many lessons as you want. Technically, Monday was the last lesson Ivy had scheduled for you, the one we thought you wouldn't need. But that's still five days away from the wedding. That gives you a little too much time to forget everything you learned here...or time enough to have another lesson or two."

He glanced at Autumn. "Do you think we can handle one more lesson?"

"Of course we can."

Her easy acceptance relaxed him, reminding him of what a sweet woman she was, and doubled down on his need to tell her what had happened after their one-night stand.

Greg said, "Okay. Monday it is. Now scoot. I have another couple coming in ten minutes."

She changed into her boots then walked to the hooks on the wall and slipped into her coat and gloves. When he saw Autumn wore mittens he smiled.

His resolve to tell her had never been stronger. She also seemed very receptive.

This was his shot.

They stepped out into the falling snow and she laughed. "You know, come February we're going to be really sick of snow, but the first couple of snowfalls are like magic."

He glanced around. "I remember how I used to wait for snow to go sledding."

"My brothers and I did too."

He hit the button on his key fob to unlock his Mercedes. "You have brothers?"

"Two. Both accountants. Both work on Wall Street."

"Yet you chose a charity?"

"For a couple of really good reasons. First and foremost, I couldn't see myself sitting in an office all day talking numbers."

He laughed. "That does get old quickly."

"Second, I like the idea of using my time to help people." Under the light of a streetlamp, she looked up at him. "What about you?"

"Me?"

"How many brothers and sisters do you have?"

He faltered but realized this was actually a perfect introduction to the conversation they needed to have, though chatting on the street wasn't exactly ideal. "No brothers. No sisters. Only child."

"Oh, that must be fun!"

"Yes and no. Look, let me drive you to Ivy and Sebastian's."

She turned her face up into the snow. "Are you kidding? Miss a chance to walk in the snow?"

He couldn't fault her for that. The wet snow indicated that the temps were around freezing. Warmish for a winter night. And the snow was beautiful.

"Can I walk with you?"

"This is a low crime neighborhood. I'll be fine."

"I know you will. There's just a couple of things we need to talk about."

She headed down the street, starting the four-block walk that would get them to Ivy's townhouse. "You mean like how Ivy and Sebastian keep setting us up for things?"

It wasn't what he wanted to discuss, but now that she mentioned it, they probably should talk about that too.

He hit the button on his key fob to relock his Mercedes and fell in step with her. "I think they noticed we were a little icy to each other."

She laughed. "You think?"

He winced. "All right. I *know*."

She laughed again. The sound echoed around them on the almost empty street. "Maybe we should tell them we met before."

"Maybe." Slowing his steps, he faced her. "Not total disclosure though."

"Oh, God no. If we told Ivy we went home together that night, she'd want every detail."

"Could get embarrassing."

She nudged his shoulder with hers. "Or we could twist it into an opportunity to brag."

Her comment was so unexpected, he burst out laughing. "We were pretty good together."

"Pretty good?" she asked, her pace increasing and

her steps getting longer. "We could have done a demo video for YouTube."

He laughed again, his own voice sounding warmer and happier than he could ever remember hearing it. They'd been bold that night. Brazen, really. And so damn happy.

They walked a block in silence. Then she mentioned Christmas shopping she had to do, and he didn't stop her. Didn't try to change the subject. He loved the sound of her voice. He loved the conversation about something so simple, yet so important to someone who had a family.

"My dad is definitely a Christmas sweater guy. I think the new sweater I get him every year is the only update to his winter wardrobe."

"I understand that. I actually have a shopper who keeps my closet full of updated clothes."

She stopped. Looked at him. "Really? You have someone who makes sure you have clothes?"

"Underwear and socks too."

She shook her head and started walking again. "Are you going to come in with me so we can tell Ivy and Sebastian they should cool it?"

"Are we going to tell them we know each other?"

"If you think about it, it's part of the explanation."

"True. So, we say we'd met before at the gala but leave everything else out."

She peeked at him. "The good parts."

"Yeah, no sense making them more focused on us than they already are."

"Or steal the thunder from the wedding."

"I think we'd only steal their thunder if we do the YouTube video."

She chortled and his heart swelled. This was how

they were the night of the gala. Easy with each other. Happy.

"You're so fixated on the video that I have to wonder if you aren't looking for a little validation."

"No. I don't need validation. I just think…" He glanced over at her. "Making the video recreating that night might be fun."

Time stopped. Even the snowflakes seemed to hang in midair. He remembered peeling off her pretty gown the night they met. Remembered kisses so hot and deep his blood had crackled. Remembered tucking her beside him when she began to fall asleep.

Finally, he said, "I thought that would make you laugh."

She combed her fingers through her hair. "I should have laughed."

But she hadn't. For the same reason his heart was thrumming now. That night had not been funny. It had been joyful. If she was remembering any of the things he was remembering, laughter would not be her reaction. Her breath might stall. Her pulse might scramble. A whole bundle of wishes that things had been different also might tiptoe into her mind.

Because right now he wasn't laughing either.

CHAPTER SIX

AT IVY AND Sebastian's townhouse, Autumn took a step away from Jack. His comments had brought back more intimate memories of that night and her body tingled with remembered passion even as her heart swelled with the disappointment of the weeks that followed.

Shaking off the feeling, she headed to the steps of the front door. "Are you coming in with me?"

He took a step back. "This might not be the right time to tell them about the night we met."

She stopped.

Yeah. He might be right. How could either one of them talk about meeting at a gala and spending the night together without thinking about all the things his video comment brought back? She'd stumble over her words. She might even flush.

She walked back to him. "Maybe I'll have a private talk with Ivy."

He caught her gaze. Snowflakes fell around him. The night was so silent she could hear her own breathing. "You're sure?"

"Yes. And maybe you could mention it to Sebastian."

"Maybe." He looked away then met her gaze again. "For what it's worth. That was probably the best night of my entire life."

She almost said, *I doubt that*, then noticed how serious he was. The light of a streetlight softened his features. His eyes searched hers.

She couldn't lie to a man whose eyes were so sincere or avoid the question that hung in the air. "Yeah. It ranked pretty high on my best night scale too."

The cold space between them suddenly warmed. They really were coming to terms with this. Making peace with it. Maybe even getting to know each other in a way they hadn't had time to do the night they'd met.

Time stood still again. Neither of them made a move to leave.

And then the oddest thing struck her. It felt like a moment for a first kiss. Romantic snow. Just enough nervousness to amplify the attraction that wouldn't let them alone. And curiosity. Sweet, sweet curiosity if everything she remembered was true. Seconds spun into a minute with them gazing into each other's eyes. Feeling the connection they had the night of the gala. Remembering things probably best left forgotten.

Slowly, regretfully, he took a step back. "I've got a four-block trek to my Mercedes. So, I'll see you."

"I'll see you." She was *not* disappointed that he hadn't kissed her. That would have only confused things. Made her blood race. Filled her heart with that indescribable something only he seemed to inspire. Caused her to yearn for things that couldn't be.

She knew he was out of her league. And his not wanting a relationship with her had made sense. Still, the best-night-of-his-life comment fluttered through her brain again. The expression in his eyes. The warmth in his voice.

Her resolve weakened. Before he could turn to head to his car, she said, "Monday, right?"

Walking backward up the street, he said, "That's our third lesson."

"We can talk about whether or not we need a fourth."

A solid five feet away from her now, he smiled. "Okay."

"Okay." Before she could do something foolish or say something worse, she raced up the steps to Ivy's townhouse, slipped through the door and walked into the foyer.

Her wishful-thinking soul imagined that Jack stood where he had been, staring at the door.

Her heart warmed again, but she forced herself to remember how excited she'd been the first few days after their night together. Every ring of the phone had her heart racing. But he hadn't called. He hadn't texted. He hadn't emailed. Nothing.

The first week she'd been excited. The second week she'd been nervous, the realization that he probably wasn't going to call following her like a zombie. The third week, she knew he hadn't meant a damned word he'd said.

So, no. She wouldn't let that best-night-of-his-life comment change anything.

Thursday whipped by like a normal day. With Raise Your Voice's Valentine's Day Ball a mere two months away, work had begun to multiply enough that Autumn didn't have time to think about Jack Adams.

And if a wayward thought did slide into her brain, she booted it out, reminding herself that no matter how wistful he sounded, they were wrong for each other.

Friday morning, Raise Your Voice CEO Gerry Harding walked to her desk, tapped his fingers on the rim and said, "How about dinner tonight? I like Becco. It's a casual Italian place. I'll meet you there around…" He pondered that. "Let's say seven."

She blinked. The unexpected invitation threw her. The only thing she and Gerry ever spoke about was work. What could he possibly want to discuss with her for an entire dinner—?

Oh, Lord! Maybe he was retiring?

Her heart sped up. If he was, all those dreams she'd created as a little girl were about to come true. She'd be the boss. And not just of any old company, but a charity that helped people. She'd finally be the person she'd known was inside her all along.

Still, she couldn't panic or look overeager. "Sure. Seven is great and I love Italian food."

He knocked on her desk again. "I'll meet you there. Don't bring your bank card. This is Raise Your Voice business."

"Okay."

He walked away and she took a long, life-sustaining breath. Holy cats. Raise Your Voice business? Could that be anything other than Gerry's retirement?

Oh, dear God, it was happening—

Or at least she thought it was happening. She would not jump the gun. That was another thing Jack ghosting her had taught her. Never, ever, ever make assumptions.

A great debate raged in her head the rest of the day as she worked to figure out anything else Gerry might want to discuss with her other than to tell her he was retiring.

Nothing came.

She stayed at the office until six forty-five and took a ride share to West Forty-Sixth Street. Gerry was waiting for her inside the door of the restaurant. She hung her black wool coat, and a hostess began leading them through the tables. Halfway there she swore she saw the back of Jack's head.

Which was stupid. Ridiculous. *How could she recognize the back of his head?* Still, curiosity had her gaze swinging around after they'd passed his table and sure enough. It was him.

"'Of all the gin joints…'" Autumn mumbled as she seated herself across from her boss and—damn it!—across from Jack.

Gerry said, "I'm sorry. I missed what you said."

"Old movie quote. From *Casablanca*."

"Great movie," Gerry said, opening his menu. "Are you an old movie buff or a romantic?"

"Old movie buff," she said, refusing to let anyone think she might be romantic. That was another notion Jack ghosting her had squashed.

Her phone pinged with a text. Out of habit, she glanced at it.

Dating grandpas now?

Her head jerked up and her eyes homed in on Jack, who sat smirking at her. She didn't know what he was smirking about. He was single, sitting with two couples.

Gerry peeked over the top of his menu. "Everything okay?"

"Yes. Fine." She smiled again, though her nerve endings jangled.

"Is the text something you need to answer?"

"Actually, it is. It's the kind of text you can't ignore."

He chuckled. "Must be your mom."

Not wanting to lie, she only smiled.

"My wife goes nuts if the kids don't answer a text."
He motioned to her phone. "Go ahead."

"Thanks."

The waiter walked up to the table with water and
Gerry told him they needed a few minutes to look at
the menu.

Autumn typed furiously.

Not able to get a date now? You're the only single in
your group.

Across the room, she saw ridiculous Jack shake his
head, looking like he was chuckling.

Gerry rose from the table. "I'm going to make a quick
trip to wash my hands. You finish your discussion."

Her phone pinged with another text. Gerry left and
she grabbed her phone to see Jack's unwanted reply to
her text.

This is actually a business meeting.

She snorted.

Aren't you the boss? Shouldn't you be saying something profound? Instead of texting me?

Actually, everybody's talking about their kids now.

Oh.

She knew better than to rib him about that. Some
people were sensitive about not having kids. Others
didn't want kids and hated being hassled about that
choice. That was a landmine she didn't want to step on.

Then a snarky comeback came to her and she laughed to herself as she typed.

Sad that you can't keep control of your own meeting.

Just trying to be a generous, understanding employer.

Damn him. She laughed. When her gaze rose and met his across the room, he smiled at her.

Her heart thrummed. Her nerves sparkled like happy glitter.

Gerry returned. "Everything okay with your mom?"

Though it was better that Gerry thought her mom had texted her, it wasn't true. So, she sidestepped, explaining by saying, "It was just a check-in text."

He snorted. "I've sent that text." He glanced across the table at her. "It usually means you haven't visited in a long time." Without giving her a chance to answer, Gerry picked up the menu. "Any of their dishes are wonderful."

"I love Italian." She put down her menu. "And for the record Sunday is our monthly family dinner. They know I'll be there."

"Oh, that's nice! I should tell my wife about that. We're hit or miss with our kids. It would be good to get on everybody's schedule at least once a month."

The waiter returned and they ordered dinner. When he left, Gerry rested his forearms on the table and said, "I asked you to have dinner with me to get an update on the Valentine ball."

She frowned. "You're up to date. We had a meeting yesterday."

"That was our weekly general office meeting." He leaned forward. "You always tell us about your work in broad strokes. I'd like to get some specifics. I'd like to get a feel for how much work planning an event really is. You tell me flowers are ordered. But I want to know how much work actually goes into ordering flowers, choosing menus, finding a band, all that stuff."

She sat back on her chair. He did not sound like a man who was retiring. He sounded more like a guy who wanted to replace her.

Uncomfortable, she said, "Everything's sort of intertwined." She paused, trying to think through her answer but her brain was stuck on figuring out why he wanted to replace her.

Unable to come up with a stall, she gave up and decided to tell him what he wanted to know.

"Here's a quick rundown. The staff comes up with a theme for the ball."

"Isn't every Valentine's Day theme love?"

"Yes and no." She fiddled with her napkin. "Remember the one year that everything was silver and white with only red accents?"

He nodded.

"The theme that year was a Winter Wonderland." An idea Ivy had liked so much she decided to use it as the theme of her wedding, except with aqua and blue accents, not red. "The theme determines colors, which determines decorations, which also determines flower choices."

Her phone pinged. She glanced down at it.

Things are getting serious at your table.

He didn't know the half of it.

"After that, the decisions sort of cascade. Once we know the theme, we can determine the menu, choose a band, design decorations and even compile a list of gift bag contents."

He thought for a second. "That makes sense."

Not sure what to say or do, she nodded.

He took a breath. "You came in and took over that position and literally created your own job description."

"You make that sound like a bad thing."

"No. It was a very good thing. But sometimes, like this morning, I realize that most of the time I have no idea what you're doing."

Insulted and confused, she sat up in her chair. "I'm not slacking off if that's what you're insinuating."

He gasped. "Just the opposite. You operate like your own little country." He laughed. "And while that gets great results, if you were hit by a bus or decided to get another job, we'd be lost."

She relaxed, though it did creep her out to think of herself as getting hit by a bus. "I'm not going to leave."

"You say that now, but your events are legendary in the city. I'm surprised someone hasn't approached you with a job offer."

"People have." She shrugged. "I like what I do and want to continue doing it."

Gerry visibly relaxed.

She relaxed.

Her phone pinged.

Everything okay?

The waiter arrived with their food and in the shuffle of plates and bread being set on the table, and water and wine glasses being refilled, she grabbed her phone.

Everything's fine. But this is also a business dinner. I need to focus.

What fun is that?

She looked up from her phone as he glanced over at her, his blue eyes shining. She liked snarky, flirty Jack.

But there was no future for them.

I'm not looking for fun.

Even as she typed those words, she realized how pathetic that sounded.

No wonder he was out of her league. Aside from him, the only thing she ever thought about was work.

CHAPTER SEVEN

SATURDAY NIGHT, JACK unsnapped the cufflinks from his white shirt, then tossed them into the box on the dresser in his massive closet.

Right now, he'd expected to be in Bethany Minor's apartment for after-date drinks that probably would have led to more. But he'd been the worst dinner companion in recorded history. Distracted. Thinking about the texts he'd shared with Autumn at the Italian restaurant. Wondering if she had a date—

It was nuts. And wrong. They'd had their time together. Fate had ruined it…and he'd hurt her. He would not get involved with her again. Period. End of story. Not just because they'd had their one-night stand. But also because he was poison. Not the guy who had long-term relationships. And he refused to hurt her again.

He fell asleep thinking about her and woke Sunday morning restless and bored. After making himself toast and coffee, he pulled out his laptop and started working, but even work couldn't hold his attention.

He thanked God when his phone rang. "Hey, Sebastian! What's up?"

"Ivy's hosting an impromptu brunch. You're invited."

His pulse scrambled. If Ivy was hosting, her best friend would be there.

He told himself not to get excited, then argued that he wasn't going to say or do anything wrong. He simply liked seeing Autumn. He would not make this a big deal.

"Okay. What time?"

"This is impromptu. Put on pants and get here now."

He laughed. "Got it."

He dressed quickly but slowed himself down when he got to the sidewalk in front of his building. He didn't want to look overeager… He was *not* overeager. He just liked her. Liked talking to her. Liked teasing her.

He walked the few blocks to Ivy's townhouse, rang the bell, did a little back and forth with Frances and joined everyone in the big dining room where a buffet was set up along the back wall.

He glanced at the table where a lot of people already sat eating the informal, impromptu bunch—

No Autumn.

Ivy walked over and kissed his cheek. "If you want waffles or an omelet, we can call Louis back to the omelet station. But there's scrambled eggs, sausages, cheese blintzes, toast, bagels in the warmers."

"That sounds great," he said, though his heart sank.

He told himself that was wrong, but it wouldn't lift. He ate some eggs, a blintz and a few sausages, talking and laughing with Ivy's guests and leaving as soon as it was decently polite to do so.

He walked out into the falling snow and looked up. He'd said he'd never be able to see a snowfall again without thinking about her. But he was wrong. He didn't need snow. He simply never stopped thinking about her.

* * *

Autumn arrived at her parents' home in time to help her mom put the finishing touches on lunch.

"Where are Aaron and Pete?" she asked as she tied a bib apron over her jeans and white sweater. She didn't care if she got gravy on her jeans—they were washable—but her mother was a stickler about things like aprons, placemats and spoon rests.

"Aaron's mother-in-law is in from Florida and Pete wanted to watch the game in the privacy of his own home."

Autumn held back a laugh. Her dad had a tendency to get vocal and loud when watching the Giants. Pete, a kind, gentle soul, didn't like it.

"So, it's just us?" Autumn picked up the bowl of mashed potatoes and took them to the dining room table, her mom on her heels, carrying the platter of fried chicken.

"Yes. But in a way that's good."

She peered at her mom. "It is?"

"Yes! You rarely talk at our dinners. Your brothers' lives are so interesting that they drown you out." She set down the chicken and looked at her beautifully set table with pride. "It'll be nice to hear about you."

As her mother walked away, Autumn winced. She liked that her brothers monopolized the lunch conversation. That meant she didn't have to lie or embellish what her parents considered her very dull life.

Especially on a day when she was beginning to agree with them.

With everything ready, her mom called her dad and he appeared at the curved archway between the living room and dining room.

"Well, Autumn. Looks like you have us all to yourself today."

"Yes. How's it going, Pop?"

"Same old. Same old. Looking to retire in five years."

"Earlier than most of the guys he works with." Her mom beamed. "He won't be able to get his pension until he's fifty-nine or government money until he's sixty-two, but we've got savings."

"I know," Autumn agreed, taking her seat in the middle of the left side of the table. With her mom on the right and her dad on the left, she felt like she was in an interrogation room.

Telling herself to shift that focus, she faced her dad. "I've always been proud of your ability to save money."

"Thank your brothers," her dad said, lifting the platter of fried chicken. "They found the investments."

"They're so smart," her mom put in, her face glowing with pride.

In that second, she had the odd urge to brag about how she was so independent at her job that her boss worried she would get hit by a bus, and she couldn't squelch it.

"I had an interesting conversation with my boss the other day."

Her mom brightened. "You did?"

"Yes, he took me to dinner…"

Her dad harrumphed. "I'm not sure I like where this is going."

"Lots of bosses and employees go to dinner. In fact, one of my friends was at the restaurant with two of his vice presidents and their spouses. That was also a business dinner. Happens all the time."

Reminding herself of Jack might not have been the right thing to do. Even though she'd had to shut him down, she'd loved that he'd texted with her. Flirted with her, really—

She'd promised herself she wouldn't make too much of that.

But now that she'd reminded herself of it, her brain smiled.

Her mother said, "Tell us about the dinner. Are you getting a raise?"

Glad to be brought back to the present, she said, "No. My boss told me that I do so much that most of the time he doesn't even know what I'm doing."

Her dad waved his fork. "That happens all the time with secretaries."

Her nerves tweaked. The way he thought she was a secretary made her crazy. "I'm not a secretary. I'm in charge of all the event planning. I supervise the mentors."

The table fell silent. Autumn picked up her fork and snared a bite of her chicken, refusing to get angry. Her parents were old school. If a woman worked in an office, she was a secretary or assistant. They couldn't get beyond that and Autumn couldn't change fifty years of conditioning.

"It doesn't matter, dear," her mom said. "One of these days you'll find a nice young man and settle down."

She took a breath. They'd been over this a thousand times. "Mom, it isn't that I don't want to get married." It simply wasn't in her life plan. "Right now, I'm focused on my career. I know you guys don't understand my job but it's pretty important and what I do makes a difference."

"You know who makes a difference?" her dad asked, stabbing his fork at her. "Your brothers. That's how I got savings enough to retire. That's why Aaron has that big house in Connecticut. That's making a difference."

"And making money," her mom agreed.

Autumn nodded. They might not understand her job, but she did and that was what mattered.

"So, any nice young men in your life?"

She said, "No." But Jack was. Sort of. They had a dance lesson tomorrow and maybe another one before they'd spend Friday night at the rehearsal dinner and Saturday at the wedding.

She didn't want to be excited over that. But, surely, she could admit to herself that she liked him as a friend.

That didn't sound too bad.

And thinking about him, about spending time with him, about how silly he'd been with the texting, was more fun than having her parents diss her job and ask about boyfriends she didn't have.

For goodness sake, she wasn't even looking for a boyfriend. Which might be why Jack was so appealing. He wasn't looking at her as a girlfriend. They'd had their shot and he'd ended it.

There'd never be anything serious between them.

But did that mean they couldn't have some fun?

Her dad went on chattering about her successful brothers as her mom chimed in with other wonderful accomplishments of her two male siblings and she thought about Jack.

And everybody at the table was happy.

When Jack arrived at the dance studio on Monday night, Autumn was seated on the bench changing into her ballet slippers. The door closed behind him and she glanced over. Their gazes caught and held. A million feelings rippled through him, mostly happiness at seeing her. But that was wrong.

He broke their connection and slipped out of his overcoat, then his jacket and tie. As he rolled his shirt sleeves to his elbows, Greg came out of the back room.

"Okay, favorite couple. Are we ready to tackle that Charleston step?"

Jack winced. "Actually, I looked it up on YouTube. I should ace it now."

Greg laughed. "Better to look it up than to worry about being embarrassed."

"Exactly."

"All right then. Let's take it from the top."

Without a word, Autumn lined up at the edge of the dance floor and Jack joined her. Greg started the music.

Jack took Autumn's hand and twirled her out to the center. They looked left then right, did five perfect Charleston steps, then he pulled her into his arms for the waltz.

As Greg had instructed them, they looked into each other's eyes. He told himself they had only done it because Greg had told them they had to, but there was something more in Autumn's eyes tonight. Something curious and inviting.

He waltzed her around the circle of the dance floor, flowing with her as if they were floating, as if they were made to be dance partners. Something deep and profound seemed to connect them. For twenty seconds, there was no one else in the room.

They stopped, but she didn't try to slide out of his arms, and he didn't try to pull away. They simply stared at each other.

Greg clapped. "That was magnificent! My God,

Jack, you were born to waltz and Autumn you were born to twirl."

She pulled away, laughing at Greg. "Born to twirl? Really? You sound like my mom and dad."

"In the world of dance being born to twirl is not an insult. It's me telling you that you probably don't need another lesson."

She walked over and hugged him. "I know. I'm sorry. I had lunch with my parents yesterday and they always make me overthink everything anyone says."

He batted a hand. "I have parents too. I know the drill."

She laughed again as Jack sauntered over to them. "So, should we take it from the top?"

"Only if you want to," Greg said happily. "You two are gorgeous together."

Autumn's face reddened. "I wouldn't go that far."

"I would. But if you want to continue practicing, the floor is yours for fifteen more minutes. If not, I will be rooting for you at the wedding."

"You're going to the wedding?"

"Ivy's a family friend. She and my wife are on some board together."

Autumn glanced at Jack and she smiled an I-told-you-so smile. They'd discussed the possibility that Ivy had looked for ways to force them together. Her connection to Greg just about sealed it.

"I don't think we need to run through it again," he said, peeking at Autumn. "Unless you do."

"No. I'm fine."

"Then maybe we could have coffee. There's a little place down the street." When she didn't reply, he added, "There are a few things I need to tell you."

The curiosity returned to her eyes, but this time there

was no invitation. Only caution. Still, she said, "Okay," and walked to the bench to change her shoes while he put on his suit jacket and overcoat.

This time the tension that skimmed his nerve endings wasn't excitement. It was a day-of-reckoning feeling. He'd hurt her. He owed her an explanation, even though he knew full well telling her the truth about their night together would end their attraction.

But that was for the best.

CHAPTER EIGHT

THE COFFEE SHOP Jack had mentioned was only two buildings down from the dance studio. When they reached it, he pushed open the door and let her enter before him.

Not sure what to expect from this conversation, Autumn began to slip out of her jacket.

Edging toward the counter of the crowded business, he said, "What can I get you?"

The gesture was simple and maybe even okay given that the place was filled with people on phones and laptops and lines for coffee were long. Still, he'd been weird at the dance studio and she had no idea what he was about to tell her. Best to keep their roles clear.

"I'll get my own."

"No. The place is too full. You get a seat. I'll get the coffee. What do you want?"

She glanced around. Technically, there was only one table with two open seats. She'd let him win this one. "Caramel macchiato."

She wove her way between tables and people to the two high stools at the open table and sat, pulling out her phone as he ordered. No missed calls. No voice mails. Nothing to take her focus away from the fact that he'd said he had a *few things* to tell her.

Of course, she hoped he wanted to explain why he'd

left and never called all those years ago. But that was wishful thinking. Lots of time might have passed, but she wanted to know. At the same time, that lots of time had been *five years*. He could think it irrelevant.

Still, if she eliminated that possibility completely, she had no idea what he wanted to talk about.

She groaned at the way her thoughts had become uncontrollable since he'd reentered her life, before she looked down at her phone and began reading the news.

A few minutes later, he appeared at the table.

He set her drink in front of her. "Caramel macchiato."

"Wow. The big one. Somebody's not sleeping tonight."

He winced. "Sorry."

She waved a hand. "Sleep is overrated." She frowned. "Where's yours?"

"Actually, I sort of just wanted to explain something and then leave."

Well, that didn't sound good.

Particularly when his words coupled with the somber expression on his face.

"I wasn't going to explain why I left you that night." He shook his head. "Five years had passed. It seemed… I don't know…irrelevant?"

She'd thought that. But her curiosity spiked, and her nerve endings sat at full attention. "Maybe five years means it won't annoy me as much as it would have if you'd told me right away."

He sniffed a laugh.

Her overly active brain began remembering the conclusions she'd drawn in the weeks after he never called. He'd met someone else. An old love had returned, and he'd realized he still loved her. An old love had returned and told him she was pregnant. An old love had returned holding his baby in her arms—

"I got up in the middle of the night and for whatever reason, I turned on my phone."

So, an old girlfriend had *called* while they'd had their phones off.

"It was the hospital."

That surprised her so much her brain stopped drawing conclusions.

"My mom had been admitted and they needed me to come down immediately."

And, at her apartment, he'd been almost an hour away in Queens.

"What had happened?"

He took a breath and, seeming exhausted, he slid onto the chair across from her. "She'd had a heart attack. She'd already died by the time I called. I don't know if they weren't allowed to tell me that over the phone, or if something had gotten screwed up. But I raced to the hospital."

She could only stare at him. Remorse filled her. Along with nearly overwhelming compassion for him. "Oh, my God, I'm so sorry."

"I was stunned. She was in her fifties. Healthy. No. She was robust. She was one of those people who had tons of energy. She'd started Step Inside. It was her baby. Her vision. I was the chef for the original restaurant, then I eased into research and development, but the day after her funeral, I had ten restaurants to run."

She leaned back on her chair. "That's a lot."

"It was. She had a good assistant and a knowledgeable vice president who operated as chief financial officer. They literally taught me the ropes of the business."

She remembered him saying something about a five-year plan at Ivy and Sebastian's house, and realized that for the past five years he'd been building his mother's dream.

"You sort of dropped off my radar."

She had no idea what to say. He'd been a chef forced to become a businessman and he'd done a great job if the little she knew about Step Inside was anything to go by. But he'd also lost his mom—

And he had no brothers and sisters. He'd told her he was an only child.

"I'm so sorry."

He slid off the stool. "That's it. That's what I wanted to tell you. It's clear that we like each other but I knew we'd never really ever be able to even be friends if I didn't tell you."

Not knowing what to say, she took a breath before she settled on, "I'm glad you did."

He sort of smiled, nodded and headed for the door.

She watched him walk out into the few flurries of snow that swirled in a light breeze. He flipped up his collar and headed down the street to his car.

She stared straight ahead, her caramel macchiato forgotten.

Technically, he was all alone in the world.

Autumn was so gobsmacked by Jack's revelation that she wondered about him all week. Even standing outside the restaurant for the rehearsal dinner, she thought about him while waiting for her parents. It was a tradition in Ivy's family that the parents of the entire bridal party also be invited to the wedding and rehearsal dinner. Her dad had driven into the city and her latest text from her mom said they were walking up the street.

She glanced left and right, then winced. She didn't

want to run into Jack out on the street, where they'd be alone, and conversation would be awkward. She wanted the protection of other wedding participants, so they didn't have that awkward moment where he realized she knew his secrets. She knew his past. She knew his pain.

She wasn't uncomfortable with it. But from the way he'd left the coffee shop, she knew he was.

Her parents came bounding up the street. Her mom's cheeks were red from the cold. Dressed in his best overcoat and only suit, her dad looked like he'd rather be shot than enter the restaurant.

She straightened the collar of his overcoat. "Ivy's parents might be wealthy, but they are very nice."

Her dad rolled his eyes.

"Sebastian grew up middle class."

"Thought his dad was a lawyer."

"He is, but not all lawyers are wealthy." Though Sebastian's company had taken his dad's mediocre law firm and made it great when it became the firm's biggest client.

She decided to change tactics. "This is a totally mixed crowd of people. You're going to love them."

Her mom nodded happily. Her dad sighed.

They walked into the restaurant where the maître d' motioned for someone to get their coats, then led them to the private room for the rehearsal dinner.

Ivy's and Sebastian's parents stood at the door greeting guests. Ivy's mom, Lydia, with the same short black hair and green eyes as Ivy, immediately reached out and took Autumn's hands before kissing both of her cheeks. "It's so lovely to see you again, darling."

"Thanks, Lydia."

Ivy's dad stepped forward, hugging Autumn. "And

who are these two?" he asked referring to Autumn's parents.

"Lydia, Robert, these are my parents. Mary and Jim."

Robert immediately shook Autumn's dad's hand. He motioned to Sebastian's parents, who were chatting with another couple, but turned around when they realized more people had come to the door. "These are Sebastian's parents. Mike and Emily."

Mike and Emily shook everyone's hand. "Such a pleasure to meet you. We've heard a great deal about your daughter from Sebastian."

Another couple entered behind them and Autumn said, "I'm sure we'll have a minute to chat later." Then she led her parents away from the door and into the small group of round tables with elegant white linen tablecloths and centerpieces made with bright red Christmas ornaments arranged in bouquets of white flowers. Some couples had already seated themselves. Others stood between the tables talking.

She immediately homed in on her parents' place cards. "It looks like you're sitting here."

Her mother frowned. "Where are you sitting?"

"I'm in the bridal party. I'll probably be at the main table," she said, pointing to a table at the head of the room.

"We'll be alone?"

"You're sitting with six other people."

"Jim?"

A tall, barrel-chested man approached her dad. He extended his hand to shake Jim's. "What the heck are you doing here?"

To Autumn's surprise, her dad laughed. "My daughter's in the wedding." Jim turned and introduced Autumn and her mom to Paul Fabian. "We used to work together."

Mary said, "Really?"

Jim snorted. "Yeah, then he got the bright idea to buy a business."

"Sebastian's dad handled the deal and we've been friends ever since. My daughter's a flower girl." He glanced around. "Where are you sitting?"

Her dad pointed. "Here."

"So are we. I'll go get my wife."

He was back in the blink of an eye, but Autumn barely noticed. Jack entered, kissed Ivy's mom's cheek, shook hands with her dad and moved on to Sebastian's parents.

He looked amazing in a dark suit with a white shirt and a blue tie. The night she'd met him, she'd felt like she'd been struck by lightning. Tonight, a lot of those same feelings came tumbling back, but so did respect and an odd kind of empathy. She knew what it was like to fight her way through life. Now, she knew he did too.

The small room filled quickly, and Sebastian's dad announced that everyone should find their seats. She eased to the bridal table and wasn't surprised that she and Jack were seated next to each other.

"Hey."

He pulled his seat closer to the table. "Hey."

He seemed uncomfortable so she said the first thing that popped into her head. "How was your week?"

He glanced at her as if to remind her they'd spent bits and pieces of that week together, including the hour-long rehearsal only a few minutes before, where they'd learned their part for the wedding ceremony.

Eventually he said, "Exhausting."

She ignored the one-word answer that might have been a sign that he didn't want to talk. Their entire relationship had been built on drama. First, the lightning strike when they met. Going home together. Him getting a call that his mom was in the hospital, only to discover she was already gone. Her waking up alone. Then not seeing each other again for five years.

Maybe it was time to drop the drama and behave like normal people. "Mine was exhausting too." She faced him fully. "I spent most of it wondering about that dinner I had with my boss."

Obviously glad she wasn't going to talk about what he'd told her at the coffee shop, he perked up. "Oh, yeah. Why?"

"He told me he didn't exactly know my job." She paused, took a breath. "I should probably start at the beginning. Gerry is retirement age. When he told me we needed a private conversation, I thought he was going to tell me he was retiring and I was in line for his position."

Jack's brain clicked with a new memory. He'd remembered she'd talked about her job but couldn't remember everything she'd said. Now, he recalled her mentioning to him that someday she wanted to run the charity where she worked. She wanted to be CEO. She wanted to prove herself.

He waited for the recollection from that night to sour his stomach or make him feel guilty. Instead, it felt like a breath of fresh air—or like a clearing of the uncomfortable air that always hung between them. Maybe what they needed was a little more normal conversation about inconsequential things to whisk away the power that night seemed to hold over them.

He shifted on his chair to face her. "I sort of remember that. But I take it that wasn't why he'd wanted an out of the office meeting."

"No. I got the impression he felt odd about not know-ing exactly what I do."

"What do you do?"

"Lots. My job overlaps. I plan and execute all events, but I also monitor the mentors and the cases they han-dle. That way, I know exactly what we're doing and can also be the PR person."

"Wow. You raise the money, talk to the press and handle clients?"

She inclined her head. "Yes."

"Do you have any accounting experience?"

A white-coated waiter stopped to fill his glass with champagne before he filled Autumn's. As if wanting privacy, she waited until he had moved on to the next couple in the bridal party before she said, "I took classes at university but never did the job."

He considered that. "Your boss might have been feel-ing you out to see if you are a candidate to replace him. You know the business. You have a basic understanding of the accounting." He shrugged. "I wouldn't worry too much about the meeting."

"Thanks."

He barely had time to say, "You're welcome," before the toasts began.

Ivy's toast to her future husband was funny. Sebas-tian's toast to Ivy was sentimental and romantic.

After the meal, the rehearsal dinner went on in an al-most ordinary fashion, with people leaving their tables and mingling. He talked with Sebastian's best man Gio then Sebastian's dad. Then found himself in a group of laughing people. Autumn stood in the circle, enjoy-ing the crowd, and the mixed feelings he had about her when they first sat down together dissolved even more. She loved to laugh, and he loved hearing her laugh.

She didn't seem crushed or embarrassed or even guilty at having heard the story of his mom. But he supposed she shouldn't. They hadn't really known each other that night. And though she'd been sad about his mom's passing and truly had seemed concerned about him, the way she'd spoken so normally to him had soothed wounds he didn't even remember he had.

Suddenly he could put a name to the feeling he had around her.

Normalcy.

She made him feel normal.

He'd spent his entire life being slightly off center. After his dad had abandoned him and his mom, there were only the two of them and they'd formed a team. At little league and soccer, he hadn't been an outcast. There were lots of single parent kids. But he'd always been *that* kid whose father had left and started another family, as if Jack and his mom were somehow substandard. Then he'd become a chef and quickly rose to be everybody's boss at the business his mom owned. Then she'd died and *he'd* owned the business. Hundreds of people depended on him for a living. Plus, he'd had a dream to fulfill. His mom's.

He'd never had a minute to breathe and just be himself.

She let him be himself.

People began to leave. Sebastian and Ivy stood at the door, excited for the big day and telling everyone they would see them at the wedding.

As the crowd thinned, Jack also walked to the door, telling Ivy and Sebastian he would be at the townhouse first thing in the morning, and ambling over to the coatroom.

An older man and woman were sliding into jackets beside Autumn who already wore her black wool coat.

As he stepped inside, Autumn said, "Mom, Dad, this is Jack. He's my partner in the wedding."

He shook Autumn's dad's hand and said, "It's nice to meet you."

Her mom said, "So you're Autumn's partner?"

"Yes. For the wedding. She knows Ivy. I know Sebastian."

Her mom beamed. "It's going to be so beautiful."

"Ivy has impeccable taste," he agreed.

Autumn gathered her parents and headed for the door. "Time to go. You still have a long drive ahead of you."

Jack said, "You drove?"

Autumn's dad puffed out his chest. "I've been driving into this city for forty years. No reason not to."

Impressed, Jack nodded. Autumn said, "We'll see you, Jack." Then got her parents out the door.

He grabbed his overcoat, slid into it and walked out of the restaurant to the sidewalk, where Autumn stood alone.

He frowned. "Where are your parents?"

"Walking to their car."

He peered down the street. "Where'd they park?"

She laughed. "I don't know."

"Are they coming back to pick you up?"

"No. They live in Hunter. I live in Queens."

He glanced down the street again. "Oh."

"Don't ask me if I need a ride. I have a car coming."

He almost chuckled. She was so predictable in her need to be her own person. But he supposed he understood that now that she'd reminded him about her desire to rise to the top of her organization. She was capable and didn't want anyone to minimize that. "Okay."

"And you can go. I don't need a babysitter."

His lips lifted. She was so adamant in her independence, it never occurred to her that he wanted to stay to get some time with her. "What about someone to keep you company?"

She frowned as if that confused her.

"Come on. It could be fifteen or twenty minutes before your ride gets here. It's better to have company. I can give you my opinion on what your boss was thinking at dinner the other night."

"You already did."

"Okay. We can talk about the wedding."

"You want to talk about flower girl dresses and silver decorations that sparkle?"

He grimaced. "Probably not."

"How about the decision that the bridesmaids should wear champagne-colored dresses?"

He laughed. "Lord, no."

"I didn't think so."

"I am curious about what you've been doing the past five years."

She stiffened defensively. "Why? Because I'm still in the same job?"

"No. Because five years is a long time, and you aren't the same, but you aren't really different either."

She shrugged. "It would be odd if I hadn't changed at least a bit in five years."

"Yeah. I guess."

He looked up the street and down again, trying to think of something to say. What came to him surprised him, but he knew he had to say it. "When we're together like this, you know, kind of by ourselves, I realize that I missed you over the past five years. Just never really knew it."

"You couldn't miss me. You didn't know me. And

you were mourning your mom as you worked your butt off. There was no room for me."

"That's just it. I always had this little tweak way deep down inside. I think that was the memory of you trying to surface but not being able to because of all the other things bogging me down."

She laughed but her heart almost exploded from the romance of it. The night they'd met he'd swept her off her feet with simple sincerity. He had a way of looking at things, phrasing things, that was so honest she knew he truly believed what he said.

Not accustomed to anyone having that kind of feelings for her, she brushed it off. "That's silly."

He took a step closer. "Really?"

Her breath stuttered. Memories of their first kiss tumbled into her brain. How much she'd liked him. How eager she'd been for him to kiss her. The same feelings coursed through her now. Stealing her breath. Prickling along her nerve endings.

"I'd never met anybody like you before. Never experienced the love-at-first-sight feeling." He edged closer. "I was so smitten, and you were so perfect." He slid his hands to her shoulders. "How could you not have known only a real disaster would have blotted you out of my mind?"

He bent his head and brushed his lips across hers. Just like the first time he'd kissed her, she totally melted. He eased his mouth along hers a few times, raising goose bumps and igniting something hot and sweet deep inside her. Memories of their past drifted into nothing, as the present drove away everything but the feeling of him against her and the way their mouths fit so perfectly.

Dangerous longing woke in her soul. She'd felt this before and he'd left her. But right now, he was very solid under the hands she had gripping his biceps, as his tempting mouth teased her into believing every wonderful word he said.

The honk of a horn broke them apart. She glanced up to see the light blue sedan from her ride share request.

She pulled away but had to swallow before she could say, "That's my ride."

"You sure you don't want me to take you home?"

And have another goodnight kiss? One that might lead her to invite him inside? For a night of wonderful sex, deep, personal conversations and a dollop of silliness?

Her heart stumbled. Fear of rejection battled with yearning.

The car honked again.

She'd made this decision lightly once. She would not make it lightly again.

"I want to be rested for the wedding."

He laughed, then ran his hand along her hair. "If past experience is anything to go by we'd be walking zombies tomorrow if we went home together."

She held his gaze almost wishing they could have another night. That she could be strong enough to face the inevitable rejection.

But she knew she couldn't.

She headed to the ride share. "See you tomorrow."

His smiled, but his eyes filled with regret. "See you tomorrow."

CHAPTER NINE

SEBASTIAN AND IVY'S wedding was the most beautiful Autumn had ever seen. Men always looked resplendent in tuxes. But with four gentlemen as handsome as Sebastian, his brother-in-law, the best man Gio and, of course, Jack, she would bet the pulse of every woman in the room had scrambled.

Ivy's mom had forgone the typical pink for the bride's mother and had chosen a rich burgundy dress in a simple A-line style that cruised her tall, slim figure. Sebastian's mom wore an icy sapphire dress that suited her skin tone and white hair to perfection.

Add all those black tuxes and the champagne-colored dresses of the bridesmaids to the Winter Wonderland theme of the reception venue and Autumn truly felt she was in an enchanted forest. Well placed lights dramatized the small evergreens that had been sprinkled with silver glitter and scattered throughout the room. Round tables covered in linen cloths as white as snow held centerpieces of frosted evergreen adorned with blue and aqua Christmas ornaments. A huge white wedding cake sparkled in the center of the room. Accent lights of blue and aqua took turns illuminating the glittering confection, making it look like magic.

But the real beauty was Ivy. Wearing a simple white

velvet gown and white floral fascinator with netting that angled down one side of her forehead, she looked like a princess or the heroine from a fairytale. Slim, tall, regal. Her face glowed when she looked at Sebastian.

Jack slid his hand along the small of Autumn's back. "How long *is* this reception line?"

Though the feeling of his palm on her bare back sent shivers through her, she casually replied. "I don't know. Every time I turned around the guest list changed. I have no idea how many people are here."

He chuckled and temptation to look at him overwhelmed her. She glanced at him and let her breath stall at how sexy he looked in a tux. But just like the night of the gala—when he had been the most gorgeous man in attendance—she didn't feel less than. That night she'd worn one of Ivy's gowns and knew she looked as good as she felt. Tonight, she wore a backless dress. The high collar in the front was slenderizing. The dip of the back that slid the whole way down, stopping only three or four inches above her bottom, was sophisticatedly sexy.

If there was ever a night she truly felt his equal it was tonight.

For a few minutes there was chaos as the reception line continued and guests found their seats. Autumn shifted the beautiful bouquet the florist, Hailey, had made from her right hand to her left and back again, accepting hugs and greeting guests as they walked from the bride and groom to the bridal party.

When the line slimmed to thirty or so people, she and Jack skirted the edge of the room to go to the bridal table on a platform on the far end. Working to keep the confusion to a minimum, they sat as soon as they reached their chairs. Sebastian's sister and brother-in-law did too. And soon Gio and the maid of honor followed.

Ivy and Sebastian walked into the noisy room, a spotlight finding them for guests and following them. The room fell silent. They walked up an aisle created in the center of the round tables that led to the bridal table, while a version of "Silvery Moon" played. It was both a nod to Ivy's dad who loved old music and the theme of the room. Autumn marveled at the beautiful job done by wedding planner Alexandra.

The bride and groom seated themselves at the bridal table, laughing, holding hands. Gio immediately took his glass of champagne and delivered his toast.

But Autumn's gaze kept sliding to Jack, and his arm kept sliding to the back of her chair. They were like a magnet and metal. If they were close, they wanted to touch. She'd fought it the night before, through the ceremony and the wedding photos. She could be strong now too.

Gio finished his toast and to everyone's surprise Sebastian's sister rose to give a toast to her brother. Her comments were light and silly, making Sebastian laugh and his parents sit like two proud peacocks.

Champagne flowed like water. The whole room shimmered as if it had been touched by an angel.

Dinner was served, then Ivy and Sebastian cut the big white cake in the center of the room and it was distributed to the guests along with a small box containing the cakes made as a favor for each guest.

The room buzzed with appreciation and happiness. Ivy and Sebastian left the bridal table and mingled for a minute as the band returned. Then the MC announced their first dance and Ivy and Sebastian glided onto the floor.

Autumn sighed. "They look made for each other."

Jack said, "They are."

"When her dad retires, her life's not going to be easy."

"Sure, it will," he said, refilling her champagne glass from a magnum left by one of the waiters at Jack's request. "Sebastian's already working on software that will do most of her work."

She laughed and drank a little more of the delicious champagne before she turned to him. "We can't drink too much of this. We have a dance to do. In fact, I promised we'd practice before our performance."

"No need. Thanks to YouTube. Plus, there's no time for practice."

"True. We should probably head to the dance floor now to be ready once Ivy and Sebastian's dance is over."

Jack rose and pulled out her chair. "Let's go."

They eased off the raised platform of the bridal table and walked along the edge of the room until they were parallel with the dance floor.

The song shifted to the bridal party dance and Jack and Autumn hurried to get to the rim of the dance floor.

"And now here's the bridal party." The MC motioned for them to come forward. "First, bridesmaid Autumn Jones and groomsman Jack Adams."

Jack expertly twirled her out onto the floor. Then they faced each other, looked left and looked right. She twirled to stand beside him. They did five perfect Charleston steps and then he slid his hand across her bare back again, putting them in the waltz position to dance them over to Ivy and Sebastian.

Remembering Greg's training, she linked her gaze to Jack's and everything inside her stilled. Every time she touched him, every time she looked into his eyes, she felt a connection so strong she wondered if they hadn't been lovers in another life.

The music flowed and Jack smoothly led them around

the floor, his hand resting on the bare flesh of her back. She tried to focus her attention away from the way her nerve endings sparked, sending desire through her. But it was no use. Their chemistry was off the charts.

And maybe it was foolish to ignore that?

With their gazes locked, and whirling around the large dance floor as if they were made to be partners, it definitely seemed foolish to ignore it. What would it be like to roll the dice and see where this would go?

They finally reached Ivy and Sebastian. Their steps slowed, then stopped as they settled in beside the happy bride and groom, and Sebastian's sister and brother-in-law took the floor. After their few fun dance steps, they waltzed over to Jack and Autumn, stopping so close, they nudged Autumn up against Jack's side.

As if it were the most natural thing in the world, he slid his arm across her shoulders, making room for Sebastian's sister and brother-in-law.

Gio and his partner took the floor, did their steps and waltzed over. The dance ended. The MC introduced them again and they took a bow, before the band began playing a song designed to get people out of their seats and onto the dance floor.

It filled in seconds. Ivy and Sebastian headed into the crowd to mingle. Sebastian's sister and brother-in-law danced their way back to the floor. Gio disappeared.

Jack slid his arm from around her shoulders, as someone walked up to him. Clearly a business acquaintance, he motioned for Jack to move to a quieter area and then he was gone.

It seemed odd at first that he'd left her side. Being partners meant they'd been together all day. But this was the party portion of the program. They were no longer obligated to be together.

Her heart tweaked with disappointment, but she took a breath and found her parents who were still seated at their table. She asked her dad if he wanted a drink and plucked two glasses of champagne off the tray of a passing waiter.

"So fancy," her mom said reverently.

Her dad mumbled, "I'd rather have a beer."

"Let me take you over to the bar. I'm guessing Ivy has everything any guest could want."

He rose from the table.

"Wanna come, Ma?"

"No. I think I'll just sit here, sip my champagne and enjoy how beautiful everything is."

Temptation rippled through her. She nearly told her mom that Ivy's wedding might be top of the line, but she planned galas every bit as elegant for Raise Your Voice.

Still, she knew her mom didn't want to hear that. She walked her dad to the bar and after he got his favorite beer, they turned to go back to his seat. But Ivy stopped her.

She caught her hand and pulled her toward the dance floor. "I love this song. Come on. Dance with me."

Her dad motioned for her to go. "If I can find my way in this enormous city, I can find my way back to the table."

"You're sure?"

"Your mom and I aren't dorks."

Ivy laughed. "Your dad has a point."

"Okay. I'll be back after this song, Dad."

"No. You go have fun."

For once his words didn't sound condescending. Though she watched him as he returned to his table, he easily found his way.

She threw herself into the dance with Ivy and one

dance turned into three before Sebastian joined them. Feeling like a third wheel, she eased away and bumped into Gerry and his wife.

"Such a beautiful wedding!" Gerry's wife gushed. "And you look perfect! Wonderful!"

She blushed. "Thanks. Ivy has good taste."

"And you have good bones," Gerry's wife said. "I always knew that outside of that office you went from a duckling into a swan."

"Matilda!"

"What? Lots of women dress down for their job. It's a matter of being respected for the work they do. Not how they look." She reached out and pinched Autumn's cheek. "But outside the office? She's a glamour girl."

Autumn snorted. "Not a glamour girl."

"Ha!" Matilda said. "You cannot say that with a straight face tonight. I'm doing the same thing when Gerry and I move to Florida. I might have been dowdy here, but once we get our condo I'm going to dress up. We'll be the youngest of the old people down there and I will be fabulous."

Gerry groaned and shook his head.

Matilda frowned. "What? I'm talking about when you retire."

Though she laughed at Matilda's enthusiasm, the mention of Gerry's retirement caused Autumn's eyebrows to rise.

Gerry groaned again. "This is neither the time nor the place."

Matilda shrugged. "Whatever."

Gerry leaned into Autumn and said, "She's had a little champagne."

"It *is* good champagne."

"Marvelous champagne," Matilda said.

Gerry motioned to the door. "I think we might be leaving early."

Autumn said, "Have a safe trip home," watching them as they made their way through the crowd out of the ballroom to the coatroom. When she added Gerry's surprise dinner at the Italian restaurant to Matilda's happy thoughts about retiring in Florida, her breath stuttered with hope. What if he was in the planning stages for retirement? What if all of her career goals were about to materialize?

She told herself not to get ahead of things.

Still, she could almost see her name on the door to the CEO's office. This time next year, she could be running the charity that meant so much to her.

Her shoulders shifted back. Her chest filled with excitement.

She was doing it. She was accomplishing what she'd set out to do. She was the woman she'd always wanted to be.

She spent more time with her parents, even persuading her mom to dance. Then, drifting through the room, she chatted with other members of the Raise Your Voice staff who had been invited to the wedding, a new confidence rippling through her.

Her gaze found Jack in the crowd a few times. Once or twice their eyes had met. And he'd smiled at her as if they had a secret—

Well, technically they did. She hadn't gotten around to telling Ivy they already knew each other. And from the lack of comment from Sebastian or Ivy she suspected Jack hadn't either.

She returned his smile before she was pulled away by some employees of Raise Your Voice to dance. Far too soon, Ivy and Sebastian did their final dance, then took the microphone to thank everyone for coming and he carried her out of the venue and to a waiting limo. Everyone applauded and the band continued playing, but the night was drawing to a close.

She helped her parents get their coats and waved goodbye to them from the entryway as they waited for the valet to get their car.

She raced back to the big ballroom, hoping to dance the last few songs, and almost ran into Jack. "Hey."

"I thought you might be leaving."

"Nope, just sending the parents off."

"They're nice people."

"They told me you found them and had a chat."

He winced. "Nothing serious."

The band announced the last song of the evening and her heart sunk but Jack said, "Wanna dance?"

New, confident Autumn who'd been lurking under the surface all along said, "Sure. I'd love to."

He pulled her into his arms for the slow song and she melted into him. The connection was stunning. They didn't merely have chemistry. They truly liked each other…and she was a little tired of fighting something she wanted.

"I stayed away from you through the night to give you a chance to mingle."

She leaned back to look at him. "Really?"

"Sure. People from your office were here. So was your board of directors."

She wrinkled her nose. "I steered clear of them."

He chuckled. "I thought you'd take the opportunity to suck up to them."

She laughed joyously. It felt ridiculously wonderful that the universe seemed to be lining up for her. Career plans materializing. The man she wanted gazing at her adoringly.

If there was ever a time to be herself, to take instead of wait, this was it.

To hell with worry that she couldn't handle another rejection. If she looked at this as a one-night stand, a chance to be with a wonderful man again, she wouldn't get hurt.

She wasn't that naive anymore.

She sucked in a breath, marshalled her courage and said, "Want to come back to my apartment?"

He smiled hopefully. "Mine's closer."

Anticipation built then exploded. Her life had never been so perfect. No man had ever been so perfect.

"Sounds good to me."

CHAPTER TEN

JACK SHOT A quick text to Arnie and his limo was outside the wedding venue in a few minutes. He and Autumn slid into the back. He raised the partition between the driver and the passengers, then pulled her to him for a long, lush kiss.

Everything inside him told him this was right. He'd considered making the suggestion himself, but he needed to be sure this was what she wanted. Having her ask—without even a dropped hint from him—proved they were on the same page.

When they arrived at his building, he ushered her through the ornate lobby and into the elevator, where he kissed her again. The doors opened on his penthouse and they kissed their way through the living room and down the hall to the bedroom where they tumbled onto his California king bed.

It amazed him that a dress that essentially had no back, also gave no clue as to how he was supposed to get it off.

She broke their kiss, reached up and undid three almost invisible buttons that fastened in the back of the high band around her neck. Then she let them go and the front of the dress billowed down, exposing her creamy skin.

His breath caught. Reverence for the moment wrestled with need.

She didn't give him time to think. She slid her hands under his jacket, over his shoulders and slipped it down his arms. He shucked it off, then undid his tie and began to unbutton his shirt.

She slapped his hands away. "That's my fun."

"I let you unbutton your dress…"

"Yeah, because you couldn't find the buttons!"

"They were craftily hidden." He laughed, then kissed her as she worked her way down the buttons of his shirt. When she reached the last one, she yanked the shirt out of his trousers and he rose, reaching for his belt.

"If you want to get fancy, we can do it another time. I've waited too long. Remembered too many wonderful things." He slid out of his pants and sat beside her on the bed. "I want you now."

Longing shuddered through Autumn. She wanted him too. But it was more the things he said that filled her with need. How could she not be comfortable with a man who called their last night together wonderful?

The best of his life.

He pushed her back on the bed, then gave one quick yank that slid her dress off. His lips met the sensitive skin of her neck as his hand fell to her breast and she groaned with pleasure, smoothing her hands down his back, enjoying the solidness of the muscle and flesh.

But everything seemed off somehow and she realized they were too sedate. They'd played like two warring tiger cubs their last night together. And that's what she wanted. She wanted them desperate and assertive. So eager to have fun that politeness was not invited into their game.

With a quick jab against his shoulder, she shifted him enough that he rolled to his back and she straddled him. Before he could react, she brought her mouth to his neck. He groaned, but she bit and teased until a quick move from him reversed their positions again.

She laughed. This was what she wanted. The raw honesty.

He ran his hands over her quickly, hungrily, as he suckled her breast. The crazy need that had cruised her nerve endings burst into fire. Putting her hands on his cheeks, she lifted his face for a kiss that went from hot to scorching so fast she didn't even realize he'd positioned himself to take her.

The unexpectedness of it sent lightning through her. Their scorching kiss ramped up another notch. His pace became frantic. Need swelled to a pleasure pain that exploded into almost unbearable joy. She felt his release immediately after, as ripple after ripple of aftershock stole her breath.

He rolled away and she closed her eyes savoring the sweet feeling of complete satisfaction and the happiness at realizing she had not imagined the intensity and fun of their first night all those years ago.

As if to reinforce that, he angled her to him and kissed her deeply.

"That was nice."

She disagreed. "That was explosive."

Their legs tangled. She smiled. He smiled, then kissed her again. He broke the kiss and nestled her against him. The simplicity of it warmed her, as they all but purred with satisfaction. Her ridiculously high comfort level with him relaxed her to the point that she could have fallen asleep. After the long day that they'd had, sleep seemed like a good idea. Cuddled next to him, with his arm around her protectively and his whole body brushing hers, she felt like she was in heaven.

His hand skimmed her spine. Her hands trickled up his chest. Desire began to hum and build until the next thing she knew they were making love again. Kissing deeply, their bodies gliding against each other sensually. The slower movements suited them as well as the frenetic lovemaking had. But as the need grew, light touches became caresses. Inquisitive hands became bold. They only needed to roll together to connect again. The arousal so deep and profound it rose to a pitch that couldn't be sustained. It burst like a hot bubble that rained pleasure through her. She gasped for breath and let it take her.

This time when they cuddled, she swore she could feel his happiness. Everything about their first night together came into focus again. Why she'd been so sure they were about to become an item. Why it had been so devastating when he hadn't called.

Her eyes closed. She told herself none of that mattered. She did not want to fall into that pit again where her expectations didn't match what actually happened. Especially since her own life was up in the air right now.

He ran his lips from her neck to her belly button. "We are ridiculously hot together. And fast. That could be construed as a bad thing, but I've never felt anything so intense that I couldn't control it. And I liked letting go."

"Me too."

His lips grazed the sides of her belly. "You know how I mentioned the other night at the coffee shop that there were *things* I wanted to tell you?"

His question was so unexpected, she opened her eyes. *Talk about expectations being off-kilter.* The last thing she'd envisioned right now was conversation.

She opened her eyes to find him staring at her. "I remember."

He lifted himself away from her and lay down on his pillow again. "Essentially I told you only one of them."

"You sort of intimated a couple of other things in that one admission, like how you had to take over your mom's business...which made you very busy."

"Yeah." He hesitated. "But there were other...things."

With her life up in the air right now and too many complications from that warring for her head space, she wished they'd go back to pillow talk. "Did you rob a bank?"

He laughed. "No."

"Then why are you so glum? We're dynamite, heaven and fun all rolled into one. You should be savoring that."

"I like to be honest."

She liked that he was honest too. It was one of his best traits. As much as poetry and kisses, silliness and fun would have made things easier for her, she couldn't discourage that. "Okay."

"The other things aren't pretty."

She sat up and peered down at him. "I'm getting the feeling your last five years were very different from mine."

"I guess it all depends on your dating history."

She didn't think he'd been celibate for the past five years, but she had to admit she was curious enough to give him a few details of her own life, so he'd be comfortable giving her his.

"My dating history wasn't extensive. Three short relationships. A few dates scattered in between them."

"I had three longish relationships."

"Five whole years did pass."

"The first woman stole things from my house and sold them."

Once again, his comment was so far from what she expected that she couldn't control her reaction and she gasped. "What?"

"We had a miscommunication about her place in my life. In her mind, the things she took and sold were her attempt at balancing the power."

"She told you that?"

"I recognized it as her way of saying she got angry with me and sold things to buy herself something to make up for what she considered to be neglect."

Definitely someone who couldn't possibly be right for a serious guy like Jack. "That's…interesting."

"Honestly, that was easier to deal with than girlfriend number two who cheated on me and girlfriend number three who burned down my beach house."

Her eyebrows rose so high she swore she lost them in her hairline. "Is this your way of telling me that you don't have good luck with women?"

"No. This is my way of telling you that I'm so busy I often forget things like dinner plans."

"I get that."

"Because you also work?"

"The other loves of your life didn't?"

He snorted at her reference to his girlfriends as loves of his life. "No."

"Well, no wonder number one stole from you. Unless she was an heiress, she probably needed money."

"She was a trust fund baby. She didn't need money. She needed attention. I never saw it." He reached up and stroked Autumn's face. "I don't want to hurt you again."

Ah. Now she understood. He wasn't exactly fishing

to get her take on things. But he was trying to make sure they were on the same page with where they were going.

He held her gaze. "I'm committed to my company. Technically the first five years was the testing ground for the idea. The next five years will tell the tale of if the idea is strong enough that it can be replicated on a large scale in different markets and maintain a high level of success."

"I know you're busy. So am I. Raise Your Voice had only been in existence two years before I came on board. It's why I could wear so many hats and almost pick and choose my jobs. But in our infancy, I had to be a jack of all trades. Everybody did. We were always all-hands-on-deck. But as the charity got older and established itself, things settled down, our mission found its focus and we hired more people. Still, in those first few years I wouldn't have had time for a boyfriend."

"True."

"It also means, if I take over Gerry's job, I may want to look at reorganizing some things. I may want to find ways to improve services. Add services." She took a breath. "If Gerry really does retire—and his somewhat tipsy wife more or less confirmed he was considering it earlier tonight—I'll be as busy as you are. And I don't want to blow this chance. My mom could have never had a job outside the home. She threw herself into her family. She has the happiest husband and children on the face of the earth. So, I'm grateful. But it's not what I want. In my heart and soul, I am a businesswoman."

He rolled her to her back again. "So, we'll be like this wonderfully busy power couple who understand each other."

Relief poured through her. "Yes."

"We'll rule Manhattan."

She laughed. "I wouldn't go that far, but I will tell you that we'll understand each other. We won't push for things that can't be. And maybe we'll both simply be happy for what we have."

He smiled. "I like that." He kissed her. "And I like this. And I like you."

"I like you too." The power of honesty surged through her again. But so did the power of being his equal. She wasn't her mom, the little woman who ran the household. Though she knew it took more skill and strength to be a stay-at-home mom than most people realized, she wasn't made to stay home. She was made to be in the workforce, negotiating, building, mentoring. He understood that.

She ran her toe down the back of his leg. "Remember that thing we did as soon as we got to my apartment five years ago?"

He chuckled. "How could I forget?"

"Let's do that."

CHAPTER ELEVEN

THEY WOKE THE next morning to the sound of his phone chirping. He groaned, rolled away from Autumn and answered with a groggy, "Hello?"

"Hey, Jack!"

"Sebastian, why aren't you on a honeymoon?"

"We leave Wednesday, remember?"

He ran his hand down his face. He'd had about thirty seconds of sleep. He was lucky he could remember his last name. "Sure."

"We're sitting here wondering where you are. You're supposed to come to the townhouse for the after-wedding brunch."

He sat up. Another brunch. At the townhouse. It had all been in Ivy's last memo to the bridal party. "I forgot."

"Don't worry. Looks like Autumn forgot too."

He nudged her with his foot, his eyes widening as he pointed at his phone to let her know they were in trouble or at the very least about to get caught spending the night together.

"Anyway, Ivy's going to call her now. We'll keep the blintzes warm for you."

With that he disconnected the call.

Jack had only time enough to say, "Ivy's about to call you," before her cell phone rang.

She sat up, her pale skin glowing in the morning sun that poured in through the wall of window facing east. "Hey, Ivy," she said, catching Jack's gaze. "Oh, darn. I slept in." She bit her lower lip and shook her head, as if embarrassed by the lie. But she had a look of devilment in her eyes.

"I'll get there as soon as I can."

She hung up the phone and looked at Jack. "How the heck am I going to get to a brunch when the only clothes I have are a bridesmaid's dress and heels that are way too high."

He leaned in and kissed her. A discussion about dresses and shoes was not the appropriate way to greet the woman who had rendered him speechless the night before. Holding her gaze, he pulled away and said, "Good morning."

She smiled. "Good morning. I don't suppose you have a size eight dress and seven and a half shoes in your closet?"

"No. But I have a neighbor about your size who might be willing to lend you a something."

"I'll take it."

He hit a speed dial number on his phone to ask Regina if she had anything Autumn could borrow. Then he called Arnie and asked to have the limo outside in fifteen minutes.

When he was done with his calls, she bounced out of bed and they headed for the shower. Luckily, they knew Arnie was on his way with the limo and Regina would soon drop by with a dress and shoes or the sight of her all soapy would have delayed their trip to Ivy and Sebastian's even more.

She got out first, towel dried and slipped into one of his robes as the elevator bell rang.

He leaned out of the all-glass shower. "That's probably Regina. I gave her today's code. She'll be standing in the entry when you get out there."

She saluted and ran off. He finished his shower and when he walked into the bedroom, she stood by the bed, wearing an ivory sweater dress and black high heels.

"Luckily, I had emergency lipstick and mascara in my purse."

He slid his hands around her from behind and kissed her hair. "Yes. Luckily."

She laughed and pushed him away. "If we want our arrival to be realistic, we need to arrive separately."

He took a regretful breath. "Okay. Fine."

She opened the little black evening bag she'd taken to the wedding to get a credit card and book a ride share on her phone.

He dressed in casual chinos and a sweater, topped with a black leather jacket. They walked outside together, and her car awaited her. She got into the black SUV. He got into his limo.

Despite their efforts at concealment, they arrived at Ivy's simultaneously and walked up to the door together. When Sebastian opened it, he frowned.

"Her ride share pulled up the same time that Arnie and I did."

Sebastian said, "Convenient."

Jack smiled at Autumn. "Yeah. It was."

They ambled into the dining room behind Sebastian. Food warmed on the buffet on the back wall. Ivy's parents and Sebastian's parents sat at the dining room table talking. Plates pushed away and coffee cups brought forward, they'd obviously finished eating and were chatting.

"Where's everybody?"

"Not everybody showed up and of those who did most zipped off when they were done eating," Ivy said with a wince. "I got the impression lots of people are sick of us."

"Couldn't happen," Jack said, as Autumn said, "You did have a boatload of events."

"It's just so much easier sometimes to have everybody meet here," Ivy said petulantly.

Trying to appease her, Jack said, "The rehearsal dinner was nice."

Sebastian's parents said, "Thanks."

"And the wedding was even prettier," Autumn jumped in, seeing what Jack was trying to do. "Everything about this wedding was elegant and perfect," she said, taking a plate from the buffet and dishing out some eggs and breakfast potatoes.

Ivy laughed. "I loved your dance. You two were amazing."

"Jack had to look up the Charleston step on YouTube."

Everybody laughed.

"Hey. I might have had to do research, but I ended up doing a good job. And, admit it, you liked it."

"I loved it," Sebastian said. "Very manly."

"That's because Autumn told me to pretend that I was the extra-point kicker for the Giants."

The room fell silent as everyone thought that through, then a general rumble of laughter followed.

The tension of the room eased. While Jack and Autumn ate and Ivy and Sebastian's parents drank coffee and chitchatted, Ivy wound down. Sebastian relaxed on the seat at the end of the table.

At noon, Jack and Autumn left, forgetting to assume any kind of pretense that they weren't together. They reached the sidewalk where Arnie awaited, and Jack winced. "We forgot to get you a car." She pulled out her phone, but he stopped her with a hand over hers. "What if you didn't get a ride share?"

"You mean, let your driver take me to Queens?"

"I mean stay another night. It would be much easier to get to work tomorrow from my house than yours."

"Yeah."

She said it wistfully and he laughed. "You know you want to."

"I do. But you do realize that we'd have to run to my apartment now to pick up clothes for work and something that I can hang out in at your house today?"

"We could. Or we could call my personal shopper and ask her to pick up a few things."

She considered that. "Unless *we* did some shopping this afternoon?"

"Shopping?"

"I still have to get that sweater for my dad for Christmas."

He laughed as Arnie opened the limo door for them. "You know… I haven't been Christmas shopping in five years."

"Then it's time."

She climbed in and he slid in beside her. Arnie closed the door. Jack swore he felt the earth shift, as if something significant had happened.

But it hadn't. It couldn't.

He'd learned his lesson about relationships. He was no good at them. Mostly because he had nothing left to offer at the end of the day.

And Autumn didn't want a relationship. If her boss retired and she was promoted, she'd be as busy as he was—

Technically, they were the perfect couple.

He frowned. *Maybe something profound had happened?*

He'd found someone as busy as he was, who wanted what he did.

Why did that suddenly make him feel uneasy?

Arnie dropped them off at the entry to Macy's. The place was decorated to the nines with a dramatic Christmas tree on the back wall of the mezzanine above them. Covered in blue lights, it dominated the space. Evergreen branches were everywhere, highlighted with lights, colorful ornaments or pinecones.

He glanced around like an alien on a new planet. He hadn't been shopping in forever and the whole experience of the store amazed him.

Autumn had no such problem. She led him to the women's department, quickly chose a dress for work the next day, yoga pants and a big T-shirt for hanging out and some undergarments. They walked out and Arnie drove them back to the penthouse.

But when they stepped inside the lobby, he noticed the ornate decorations of his admittedly fancy building. Silver tinsel framed the huge windows facing the street. Small red bells looped across the front of the lobby desk. A silver tree decorated with oversize red ornaments sat in the corner. Candles with evergreen branches as bases adorned tables and the credenza leading to the elevators.

He looked at it all, his head turning right and left as he and Autumn made their way to the private elevator that would take them to his penthouse.

"You act like you haven't seen Christmas decorations before."

He didn't want to admit he hadn't paid any attention since his mom died, but her comment hung in the air, leaving him no choice.

"Truth is I hadn't really noticed Christmas decorations the past few years. But the decorations in Macy's were so eye-popping I couldn't help seeing them and they sort of opened my eyes to decorations everywhere."

"You've been hit by the Christmas bug."

He laughed. "There is no such thing as a Christmas bug."

"Sure, there is. It's like the flu except instead of wanting to spend the day in bed until you feel better, you want to spend the day looking at Christmas decorations and be around happy shoppers."

"I have never in my life wanted to be around a happy shopper." He caught her gaze as he carried her packages back to the main bedroom. "I'm not even convinced shoppers are happy. They all looked intense and driven to me."

"That's the look of a person trying to get the right gift."

"Much easier to use a personal shopper."

She shook her head, rummaged through her bags until she found the yoga pants and T-shirt and slipped off Regina's dress. He stared at her, his mouth watering. After all the things they'd done the night before, he shouldn't have the desperate urge that whooshed through him. But he did.

Too soon she slid the T-shirt over her head and jumped into the yoga pants.

"What do you want to do now?"

He wanted to go back to bed. But that sounded a little heavy handed. Besides, after the morning with Ivy and Sebastian and an afternoon of shopping he probably should feed her. "We could order dinner and watch a movie. Or if you're not hungry yet, we could watch a movie and order dinner after."

"How long will it take for dinner to get here?"

"Depends on what we order. Steak from Gallaghers

would probably take an hour because they generally get busy. Pizza could be here in twenty minutes."

"I'm hungry enough to wait for a steak."

He smiled. "Yeah. Me too."

They ordered, watched a movie, eating the steak and French fries when they eventually arrived. He found another movie for them, but she began to yawn.

"Neither one of us had much sleep last night. So rather than tough it out, what do you say we go to bed?"

She yawned again. "Good idea."

Getting ready for bed, exhaustion began to claim him too. Still, once they crawled under the covers, they gravitated like a magnet and steel and fell into bliss.

She drifted off to sleep first and he settled on his pillow. But instead of sleep, an odd feeling of doom filled him. He knew it was because the last time he and Autumn were together terrible things had happened. He told himself to forget their first night, his mom's heart attack and being overwhelmed with work. But even after he drifted off, the sensation invaded his dreams in the form of reminders of the failures and difficulties of the past five years.

He woke almost as tired as when he went to sleep, with the command running through his head that he couldn't get comfortable with this thing he and Autumn were doing. He couldn't get passive. He couldn't let it run them. He had to keep control of this so neither of them got hurt.

Autumn awakened in Jack's bed, though he was nowhere around. She took a second to listen and realized he was in the shower. Naked and happy, she rolled out of bed. After laying out her new work dress, she made her way into the bathroom. Jack was toweling off, but he paused long enough to give her a good morning kiss.

She got into the shower as he left the bathroom to dress.

She should have felt odd. At the very least uncomfortable. They'd known each other a couple of weeks, but they were comfortable naked, comfortable living together.

In fact, her heart slipped a notch when she thought about going home that night. Not because she liked his gorgeous penthouse. Because home was empty. He was here.

If that wasn't a red flag that she was getting in too deep, Autumn didn't know what was. Which meant she was going to have to go home after work that night. She couldn't let things get serious.

She took her time drying her hair and styling it. When she came out of the bathroom, he was nowhere around. But she smelled toast. She slipped into her dress and found him in the kitchen. White cabinets surrounded a huge island with Carrara marble countertops. She pulled out one of the tall stools with black wrought iron backs.

"Toast?"

She sat on the stool. "I'd love some."

"Coffee is there," he said, pointing at a one-cup brewer.

She got off the stool and headed over. "Can I make you a cup?"

He pointed at a half-filled mug by the toaster.

Her fears that they were getting in too deep dissolved into nothing because it appeared things weren't so perfect between them after all. Her heart jerked. Would this have been what it would be like if he'd stayed with her the night of their one-night stand?

Awkward? Silent? That just-get-out-of-here feeling in the air?

He set a small plate containing two pieces of toast in front of her. "Can Arnie and I drop you off at work?"

"I can easily get there from here."

He turned back to the toaster. "Okay."

She ate her toast in silence as he read his phone. Then they went their separate ways.

She tried to be chipper and happy at work, answering everyone's questions and even accepting Gerry's apology when he called her into his office to explain that his wife didn't get out much.

"Well, she certainly intends to fix that when you retire," Autumn replied with a laugh.

He squirmed in his chair. "Yes. About that. I wasn't going to announce until the first of the year but since my wife let the cat out of the bag, I'll be announcing my retirement at tonight's board meeting."

Her heart perked up. "That's…great? I mean, is this what you want?"

"Absolutely. We've been vacationing in Sarasota for years. It's where we want to be."

"Then congratulations!"

"My early announcement means everything will speed up. I'll start interviewing candidates now and probably the board will have someone chosen before the first of the year."

"Oh."

He frowned.

New confident Autumn couldn't stay silent. "I didn't think you'd need to interview." She almost wimped out and stopped with that statement but forced herself to move forward. "I thought I'd replace you."

"You might," he agreed, shifting on his chair again.

"Is there something wrong? Something that makes you think I wouldn't be a good replacement."

He took a breath. "It's not that. Exactly." He winced. "Seriously, you're so tight with Ivy, a board member and major contributor, that nobody's really looked at what you were doing in years."

"I was doing a lot!"

"Of course. And if you apply for the job, you'll have plenty of opportunity to show us all that."

Her heart sunk with disappointment—not that she should have been a shoo-in for the job, and no one noticed, but that no one seemed to have recognized everything she did. Still, she put her shoulders back and decided to take charge of getting the position she wanted.

The only problem was, she wasn't sure how. She'd done mountains of work, solved problems, helped clients…and no one had seen.

Plus, she'd already had one shot at impressing Gerry and, obviously, she'd failed or this conversation would have gone very differently.

She rose. "Thank you for letting me know."

"You're welcome." He smiled at her. "And if you really believe you're a good candidate for the job, I look forward to getting your resume and giving you a chance to interview."

CHAPTER TWELVE

JACK DIDN'T RETURN from work until after eight that night. That fact alone told him that he was correct in keeping things simple with Autumn. He set his takeout dinner on the big island, grabbed utensils from a drawer and settled in the living room to eat.

He turned on that night's basketball game as he ate his chef's salad, but neither held his attention. The entire penthouse seemed cold and dead. The day had been too long. After weeks of Autumn popping in and out of his life, damn it, he was bored.

He picked up his phone. She answered on the third ring.

"What are you doing?"

"Don't you mean what are you wearing?"

He laughed. "This isn't an obscene phone call." But the exhaustion of the day fell away.

"Too bad. I'm on the subway. I'm bored."

"Still on the subway?"

"Stayed late."

"Lots to catch up on after the wedding?"

There was a pause. A long one. Finally, he said, "Autumn?"

"My boss told me today he's retiring. I must have been under consideration to replace him because he took me to dinner and asked me questions about my job. But I don't think I passed muster."

He settled in on the sofa. "That's ridiculous."

"Not really. He already told me no one knew what I did, but he also mentioned my friendship with Ivy... as if being her friend made me untouchable and they couldn't have that."

"That's a tad insulting to both you and Ivy."

"He told me I could apply for the job. I'd have to interview, etc."

"Which is the perfect opportunity to prove your worth."

She went silent again. Jack waited. Finally, he said, "But you don't want to."

"I wish. The real problem is I don't think I know how. I've worked my ass off for these people for seven long years and no one noticed me?"

"No. No one gave you credit for what you did. Do you have a team that works for you?"

"I have a couple of assistants I delegate to—"

"Do you think one of them might have been taking credit for your work or ideas?"

"I don't know. I can't seem to analyze this situation properly. I never thought I'd have to apply for this job and the comments about my relationship with Ivy just add to the confusion."

"I think the real bottom line is that you didn't make sure your superiors saw what you were doing."

She said nothing.

"Autumn?"

She took a breath then glanced at him. "I don't like to brag."

"There's a difference between bragging and taking credit." And she didn't seem to know that, almost as if there was something holding her back.

"How about this? How about if you bring your re-sume to the penthouse tomorrow and let me look at it?"

"My resume?"

"We'll tackle this together. Since your resume is the first thing they'll see. That's where we'll start."

"Okay. But the only resume I have is the one I got this job with. I haven't updated it."

"That's okay. Starting from scratch gives us a good opportunity to write something strong. You want your resume to speak for you. You want it to demonstrate your worth. It's your first opportunity to show them your worth."

Her voice brightened. "Right. That's true."

"How does a person who works at an agency that helps women rise through the ranks of corporate America not know this?"

"I planned events, talked to the press, monitored the office, found mentors, assigned clients to them. I never actually *was* a mentor."

"Oh. Okay."

She sighed. "You could have knocked me over with a feather when Gerry told me he didn't know what I did, then criticized my relationship with Ivy. I always believed I knew the system. Now, I'm beginning to see what a lot of our clients go through. It was like a punch in the gut to realize I wasn't a shoo-in for the position. Which is exactly what our clients encounter in their day jobs when they're passed over for promotions. I'm as shellshocked as I'll bet most of them are."

"You do realize that after you go through the process to get that job, you'll be the perfect candidate to run the organization that helps them."

"I guess I could look at this as a good thing."

He smiled. "A learning experience. You will be going through what your clients go through every day…and what better person to guide the organization created to help them than someone who knows their struggle?"

"Yes."

He heard the strength return to her voice and pride expanded his chest. He liked that they were friends and that she didn't hesitate to let him assist her. There wasn't any doubt in his mind that she would get the job. She simply needed to see that for herself and expand the confidence she would get when they ran through mock interviews.

Which meant their spending time together had purpose—

Her coming to his penthouse the following night wouldn't be about them inching toward a relationship that couldn't happen. She needed a boost and an objective opinion, and he could provide it.

So, their getting together wasn't about expanding their relationship.

But that didn't mean they couldn't have some fun.

His voice casual and logical, he said, "Bring clothes and stay over. That way you won't have a subway ride home or to work the next morning."

She laughed. "So, I'm sleeping in the guestroom?"

"Not hardly." Because she couldn't see him, he rolled his eyes at her silliness. "Arnie and I will pick you up about six."

"I might have to stay late—"

"No. Your work now is getting that CEO job. That's where your focus should be."

When she stepped out of the office Tuesday evening at six, the limo awaited her. Jack exited the backseat and held the door for her. She slid inside and he slid in behind her, caught her shoulders, turned her to him and kissed her.

"Hey."

"Hey." Their gazes locked and all the weird feelings she'd had that day disappeared. Not merely the confusing bubble of excitement over seeing him again, but the billion things that popped up all day. Especially wondering how anybody could have missed the level of work she did. She didn't want to be angry...but damn it, how could she not be? The comments about Ivy, as if Ivy had gotten her her job and helped her keep it, were infuriating.

Still, deep down inside she worried that this was her fault. Her parents had always been so focused on her brothers' success, downplaying anything she did, that she'd become accustomed to staying in the background.

Was she actually downplaying her part in the charity's success because she was afraid of success...or afraid she didn't deserve it?

She didn't know, but she did recognize she had to grow beyond any feelings of self-doubt she had because her parents hadn't seen her as a businessperson, the way they had her brothers.

"Thanks for helping me. I'm starting to think I don't know how to take credit for what I've done."

He laughed. "I'm happy to help you see the light."

"I'm serious. This might sound horribly old fashioned, but my parents worked very hard to assure my brothers were educated enough that they could conquer the world if they wanted to. They helped me as much with tuition as they did my brothers, but they motivated my brothers more." She shook her head. "I know it sounds crazy, but I think I might have ended up believing I didn't deserve the career they did."

When she said it out loud, there was no might about it. She'd fought her whole life against becoming a "little woman" the way her mom had been. But she'd never anticipated the subtle damage that had occurred because her parents didn't see her as an equal.

Yet here it was. She'd downplayed her accomplishments. Hadn't sought recognition.

"Those are easy fixes."

Doubt tried to overwhelm her, but she fought it. "I hope so."

They drove to the penthouse and she changed into the sweats and T-shirt she'd brought. When she came out of the bedroom, he was by the stove. Something sizzled in a frying pan.

She sniffed the air. "Oh, man. Whatever that is, it smells great."

"It's the makings of Step Inside's famous fajitas."

"I've had those!"

"Everyone has. This was one of the recipes I created when Mom opened her first restaurant."

Resume in hand, she slid on the stool.

"It's been hacked and put on the internet."

She gasped, but he laughed. "Imitation is the greatest form of flattery."

He motioned to the resume. "Start with your education and move to the job history."

"I don't have much of a job history. I've been at Raise Your Voice since graduating university."

"Then we're going to have to make sure that you highlight everything, and I mean every darned thing you do for the company. Because your accounting experience is limited, we'll have to make sure we set out the classes you had at university and what you learned."

He motioned again for her to read and turned to stir the sizzling fajita makings.

She read her education, which basically said the school she attended and when she graduated. Sliding the fajita makings from pan to platter, he said, "You need to beef that up by listing important classes—especially the accounting courses. When you wrote this, you were applying for an assistant's job. Now you want to run the place. Even if it seems like overkill, you have to list the things that demonstrate that you have the knowledge to do that."

He talked as he warmed the tortillas and filled them with steak, peppers, onion and avocado and she made copious notes. Then he told her to put away the resume and join him in front of the television to eat the fajitas.

He picked up the remote. She picked up her fajita. She expected the TV to spring on. Instead, he stood watching her, waiting for her reaction to her first bite.

She groaned. "Oh, my gosh! That's good."

He grinned. "I know." He sat beside her on the sofa and turned on a basketball game. "Someday, I'm going to make you an omelet."

"Lucky me."

"You are lucky. And so are the Pistons. Have you ever seen them have a year like this?"

"No. But I don't watch basketball as much as I used to before I started working."

He peered over. "Do you like it?"

She shrugged. "I love basketball. I'm on the subway when the games start. I mostly see the second half."

"I have season tickets. Rarely use them."

She gaped at him. "Oh, that ends now."

He laughed. "I usually give the tickets to vendors, employees I want to reward or friends. But if you'd like to be courtside—"

Her eyes widened. "Courtside?"

"Yelling at refs, cheering for the Knicks, I suppose we could arrange it."

She set down her fajita, twisted to face him and

kissed him. Her simple thanks turned into something hot and spicy and they did things on his sofa that made them both breathless.

Their fajitas were cold before they got back to them, but neither cared and the next night they were court-side, watching the Knicks, yelling at refs and cheering on players.

She finished her resume on Thursday and turned it in to Gerry, who smiled and said, "Thanks."

She didn't know how a person could convey cool-ness in one word, but Gerry pulled it off, zapping her confidence enough that she called Jack.

"He didn't seem thrilled when I gave him my re-sume."

In his office, looking over yet another draft of the new five-year plan his financial staff had given him, Jack leaned back in his chair. Autumn needing assistance coupled with their mutual love of the Knicks had bal-anced out their relationship. It wasn't just romance and hearts and flowers and sleeping together. They were becoming friends.

Those were good reasons to continue to be involved. Casual reasons. Nothing serious happening between them.

"I think that means we're going to have to practice your interview skills."

She sighed. "Really?"

"Hey, it's not a big deal. I'll ask you a few questions and then tell you if any red flags pop up in your answers."

"Red flags?"

"Things that make boards of directors cringe. When you become CEO, the Raise Your Voice board becomes your boss. You have to know how to deal with peo-ple who will be criticizing your performance and your ideas. If you get huffy or say something that makes you seem difficult, they won't promote you."

"I'm never huffy or arrogant."

"Let me be the judge of that." He waited a second, then said, "You didn't happen to bring extra clothes to work, did you?"

"I have those spare yoga pants I used for our dance lessons."

"Let me call my personal shopper and get you something to wear to work tomorrow. That way we can go over your interview skills tonight."

"Tonight?"

"Yes. This is too important to leave to chance. Plus, because you work in that office, I worry that Gerry will call you in for an impromptu interview and you won't be ready."

"Impromptu interview?"

"Just trying to cover all the bases. He asked you to dinner to question you about your job and never gave you a hint that was coming. It wouldn't surprise me if he didn't just call you into his office someday and start asking interview questions."

"We do tend to lean toward a more casual office."

He relaxed. "Okay. We'll prep you tonight and he can call you into his office tomorrow and you'll be ready."

She laughed. "You bet I will."

"That's the spirit. Size eight on the dress, right?"

"Yes."

"Okay, Arnie and I will pick you up at six."

CHAPTER THIRTEEN

NOT MORE THAN five seconds after Autumn disconnected the call from Jack, her phone rang with a call from her mother.

"Hey, Ma. What's up?"

"I just wanted to tell you how much we enjoyed the wedding."

She leaned back, relaxing in her chair. "It was beautiful."

"And everyone was so friendly."

"Ivy and Sebastian both have lovely families."

"We spent the longest time talking with your friend Jack."

That made her sit up again. He'd said he'd spoken with her parents, but her mom made it sound like a marathon session. She very carefully said, "He's a nice guy."

"Very nice. Do you know he owns Step Inside?"

"Yes."

"He was a chef."

"I know."

"And now he runs the place. Just like your brother Aaron."

"Aaron's not a chef."

"No. But he started off as an entry-level accountant and now he runs the investment firm."

Excitement over interviewing for the CEO position coupled with hating the way her mom bragged about her brothers and before she knew it, she said, "I might someday run *this* place."

"Raise Your Voice?"

The confusion in her mom's tone boosted the sense that it was time to come clean with her mom and admit she had ambitions. Up until this point it had been easy to pretend she was an average office worker. But with Gerry retiring and a potential new job on the horizon, it seemed right to get this out in the open.

"Yes. My boss made it official that he's retiring. I've been supervising most of the general work of the charity for years. I know more about what goes on here than anyone."

Even as she said the words, she felt her confidence building. To hell with Gerry's skepticism. She could do this, and she would wow that board of directors when it came time to interview with them.

She simply had to wow Gerry first. Jack's coaching would make that possible.

"I'll be interviewing for the job before the end of the year."

"Well, that's lovely," her mom said slowly as if she'd never considered the fact that her daughter might make something of herself. "But don't you want to get married and have kids?"

"You chose to devote your life to your family," Autumn said, not getting upset about the question because she knew her mom's opinions were the result of living a different kind of life, having different goals and purposes. Still, this wasn't the time to have the discussion about *her* choices. That would only lead to an argument or a sermon. She wasn't in the mood for either.

Being deliberately vague, she said, "There are other ways to live."

"Sure. But having kids and running a company would be difficult."

"I'm a strong person," she said, steering clear of a real answer again, though her relationship with Jack popped into her brain. Neither of them was commitment oriented. Both wanted to be the best they could be in their careers. That's why their arrangement would work.

"Yes, you are a strong person, Autumn. You always have been a strong person. And you march to your own drummer."

Autumn cringed, but she recognized her mom meant that as a compliment.

"I also know," her mom continued, "that if you set your mind to do something, you will. And I'm proud of you."

The unexpected praise almost stopped her breathing. "Thanks, Ma."

"You're welcome. Now, the second reason I called was to remind you that I'd love to have you come to the house on Christmas Eve and Christmas Day, but both of your brothers bowed out until Christmas Day. Both said something about visiting in-laws on Christmas Eve." She sighed. "This is what happens when someone gets married. There are two families to accommodate."

"True," she said, biting the inside of her lip, suddenly confused. Maybe it was the talk of her brothers and their in-laws, but she realized she and Jack hadn't talked about the holiday. And she almost didn't think it would be appropriate to bring it up. If he said he had plans, that could get awkward. If he said he didn't but didn't want her around, that could be worse. Both of which meant it was too early to make an issue of it. If he said something, good. If he didn't…she'd be fine.

"Anyway, that means we'll just be doing Christmas Day. Also, you can bring your friend, Jack. Your dad and I like him."

It might be too soon for her to make an issue of it, but it was never too soon for her mother to matchmake.

"He was my partner for the wedding. He wasn't my date."

"Yeah, but he is a nice guy. It would be okay to invite him for dinner."

She squeezed her eyes shut, thinking this through, trying to come up with the response that would stop her mom before she got on a roll.

Her mom sighed. "If there's a reason *you* don't want to invite him, *I* can call him…"

She blanched. Not only would it be weird for her mom to call Jack, but there were eight million ways Jack could misinterpret that kind of call from her mother.

Oh, Lord. Even after all their discussions about not wanting a commitment, her mom could make her look like a bride on the auction block.

There was only one way to handle this. "Okay. If you want me to call him, I will." She'd never talk her mom out of inviting him, so at least if she asked Jack if he wanted to come to dinner, she could control the narrative. "The thing is, just because he and I were partners in a wedding, that doesn't make us friends. If he chooses to come to dinner it will be as *your* friend. Not mine."

"You don't like him?"

She adored him. He was smart, funny and whimsical. But his coming to her parents' home for Christmas dinner wasn't part of their deal. "He's a very nice person. But I can read between the lines. *You* like him and *you* think he'd be a good match for me. If you try to make something happen between us, it will be embarrassing for all of us and ruin Christmas dinner."

Her mom said, "Mmm. Okay. I get it. But he can still come for dinner."

"As *your* friend?"

"Sure. Ask Jack to come to dinner as *my* friend."

After a few more comments about gifts, Autumn disconnected the call shaking her head. If Jack came to Christmas dinner, even if she explained it was because her parents liked him—not an invitation from her—it was going to be awkward. Complicated. Especially if he accepted the invitation and her mom went against her word and tried to matchmake.

She would literally have to warn him that matchmaking was a possibility. Then at dinner, they'd have to pretend they weren't already in a romantic relationship.

And exactly how would that work?

Would they feign a growing interest in each other as dinner went on to keep her mom happy?

Or should they pretend disinterest in each other so her mother would back off?

It seemed…too complicated.

And embarrassing.

And wrong.

Not in their deal.

She lowered her forehead to her computer. Now she remembered why her mom never met any of her boyfriends.

Jack's limo pulled up to the building housing the offices for Raise Your Voice and Autumn came racing out. She slid into the backseat but didn't give him a chance to kiss her hello before she said, "My mom wants you to come to Christmas dinner."

Tired from a long day of work, he wasn't sure he'd heard that right. "What?"

"My mom called me today. She and dad love you. They want you to come to Christmas dinner."

"Because they like me?"

She winced. "Yes and no. They like you but I'm pretty sure my mom is matchmaking. The bottom line is they like you enough to think you're good for me."

He considered that. "That's a compliment, right?"

"Yes. I'm sorry. It *is* a compliment. But it's also confusing. I don't want my parents to get the wrong idea about us. Meaning, the dinner will be complicated."

The stab of disappointment he got when she said she didn't want her parents to get the wrong idea about them surprised him. Still, he saw her point. It would be weird to be at a matchmaking dinner when they already sort of were a match, but not really, and they didn't want anyone to know they were seeing each other.

He couldn't remember when they'd decided that, except they'd pretended they weren't a couple with Ivy and Sebastian the day after their wedding. He supposed they'd set that trend right then and there.

A family dinner with her would also set a precedent.

It almost seemed smarter to come clean and admit things—

Except, they didn't even know what they were doing together. How could they explain it to her family? Her *parents*?

"Give them my regrets and apologies. Say I have a prior commitment."

She met his gaze. "Do you?"

He glanced out the window and saw the happy red and green lights that shimmered in the falling snow. Reminders of Christmases with his mom flitted through his brain. She'd had so many friends that there wasn't a Christmas that wasn't filled with entertaining. He'd cooked. She'd schmoozed. Wine and laughter had flowed like water.

He hadn't missed that until now...because shopping with Autumn had reminded him that he hadn't noticed Christmas for five years. Now he couldn't seem to stop noticing it.

Realizing she was waiting for his answer, he smiled and said, "It's a big city. I always find something to do."

The way her eyes shifted told him she was remembering that his mom had passed, and he was an only child. He hadn't mentioned not having other relatives, but he supposed he didn't have to.

He slid across the seat and put his arm around her, changing the mood by changing the subject. "I've thought of a hundred really good interview questions to ask you tonight when we practice for your big day."

"Really?"

"Yes. And I'm going to cook for you again."

That made her smile. "That sounds promising."

"I thought I'd make something simple tonight. Chicken, sweet potatoes and garlic green beans."

The limo stopped in front of his building as she said, "Yum."

He opened the back door. "I'm using food to make you comfortable as I grill you. It will be like a mental anchor. When you think of interviewing, you'll be reminded of eating my delicious dinner and instantly be in a good mood. Which will make you positive and upbeat with Gerry."

They exited the limo and she cuddled against him as they entered the lobby. "I'll take it."

He kissed her cheek and they walked toward the elevator, Christmas decorations blinking at him, as if they had to work to get his attention. They didn't. Since his mom died, he hadn't felt alone on Christmas. He'd ignored the holiday. Why his subconscious suddenly wanted to be part of it again, he had no idea. But he couldn't it shake it off.

As he prepared the sweet potatoes to go into the oven, she pulled up the notepad app on her phone and sat at the center island. When she was settled, he didn't waste a minute and began asking interview questions.

"You've been working for us for over five years, but no one seems to know what you do... Can you explain that?"

She smiled craftly. "I've actually thought about this question and I realized no one understands what I do because I'm good at my job."

He shook his head. "Be careful. There's a thin line between confidence and arrogance."

She nodded, made a note in her phone, then looked up and tried her answer again. "I've actually thought about this question and I realized no one understands what I do because I work independently. I've been with Raise Your Voice almost from its inception. Back then, everybody pitched in and helped with everything. There were no job descriptions, but we all found our niches. I gravitated toward event planning and public relations, but I also love working with mentors. Those three jobs more or less became mine. Having done them for so long I don't often have questions or need assistance. The broad scope of my duties also gives me a very good feel for the organization. I know the mentors. I can handle the media. I understand our mission."

"I don't see any accounting in your background."

"I took courses at university. I can read and interpret

reports made by the accounting department. In my current position, I also set budgets and meet them."

The questions went on like that as the sweet potatoes baked and the chicken grilled.

They paused long enough to set the island with dishes and utensils and even begin eating. Then the questions started again.

Amazed at her knowledge, Jack couldn't find a way to stump her. She really did know almost everything about Raise Your Voice. She'd lived through most of the history of the charity. She could speak with authority about the Raise Your Voice mission, but also their mistakes. Their learning experiences.

When they were done, he stared at her in awe. "There's a part of me that wonders if you don't know more than your current CEO does, if only because you have this ridiculous ability to remember details."

She laughed. "I think it's all about loving the charity."

With the dishes in the dishwasher, they plopped down on the sofa. "I think you're right. Nothing serves a company better than a leader who loves the company's mission."

"Is that the secret to your success?"

"Yes and no. I know food. I know people. I know how much people like to get together over a good meal. So, I work to assure that our meals are festive and happy."

"From behind a desk?"

"When my mom first started Step Inside, I was the chef. I created our menu. I was supposed to form a whole new division of research and development to ensure our menu was always top of the line." He shrugged. "My being in touch with that end of things is like you understanding how a good event doesn't merely raise money, it raises awareness of your charity's mission."

She nodded, then nestled against his side as they watched a movie. They showered together, laughing and playing, making love under the shower spray before climbing into bed and discovering new and more interesting ways to tease and pleasure each other.

The next morning, he made her an omelet for breakfast and the kiss of thanks she gave him when he dropped her off at the building housing Raise Your Voice almost had him dragging her back to his penthouse to spend the morning in bed.

But he didn't. They both had jobs. They were a power couple. That's what he liked.

Still, he couldn't keep himself from calling her at noon. She no longer seemed surprised by his calls, and he loved hearing the smile in her voice when she said hello.

But when she sighed and told him she'd mentioned to her mom that he was unavailable for Christmas, he got a funny tweak in his heart.

"She's disappointed. She said Daddy will be too. But she certainly understood."

He remembered talking to her parents at the wedding, sitting at their table, feeling at home, drinking a beer with her dad.

They were nice people. Salt of the earth people, his mother would have called them. If he wasn't trying to hide his affair with their daughter, he might have actually taken them up on their invitation.

Which would only complicate things.

He had to remember that. What he and Autumn had was perfect. He did not want to ruin it.

CHAPTER FOURTEEN

FRIDAY NIGHT AFTER WORK, they drove to Queens. He went inside with her while she gathered clothes—including one of the gowns she wore to Raise Your Voice events because he had a Christmas ball to attend and had invited her to join him.

As she packed, he walked around the living space. The kitchen and dining room were combined, but the living room was large enough to accommodate a sectional sofa and oversize chair with an upholstered ottoman. The place was exactly as he remembered. Same furniture. Clean in a way only a single person could accomplish. The faint scent of lavender wafting through the air.

He waited for sadness to settle over him. When it didn't, he decided enough time had passed that he'd disassociated Autumn and his tragedy, but he also realized he'd barely known her the first time he'd been here. Now, they'd spent a couple of weeks together. His only connection to her wasn't a one-night stand. It was more like a friendship that had nothing to do with that one-night stand.

Satisfied with that explanation, he smiled as she walked out of the bedroom and said, "Ready?"

He took the bag from her hand. "Yes." He gave her a quick kiss. "Should be a very fun weekend."

Arnie drove them back to Manhattan. They ate at a cute Italian restaurant near his building, then they walked home through the falling snow.

Saturday afternoon, he asked her a few interview questions, but he was in the mood for lunch out, and they went to the first Step Inside restaurant.

She smiled when they entered. "So pretty. Christmas with a twist. Like Ivy's wedding reception."

"We let every manager decorate their own store." He looked around at the aqua and purple decor and decided he liked it. "We also have a contest. Every employee of the restaurant with the best decorations gets an extra week of vacation."

She turned to him with wide eyes. "Wow. That's incentive!"

"A little something to remember when you're the boss."

Knowing they had an event that evening that included dinner, they ordered only tomato soup and toasted cheese sandwiches. She groaned with pleasure over her sandwich.

"The secret is just a hint of chili powder."

She gaped at him. "Seriously?"

"It goes well with tomato soup."

A weird feeling shuffled through him. The way he kept slipping into chef mode confused him. Of course, Autumn loved his cooking and seemed to love his tidbits of information—

He had to be making too much out of nothing.

They strolled through Central Park in the falling snow, and when they returned to the penthouse it was time to dress for the ball.

A couple hours later, he was in his tux in the living room, watching college football, waiting for her. When she came out of the bedroom, his heart skipped a beat. Wearing a sparkly red gown, with her hair pinned up and dangling earrings that highlighted her long, slender neck, she stole his breath.

He slowly rose from the sofa. "You look amazing."

She walked over and straightened the bow tie, then the lapel of his tux. "You do too." She rose to her tiptoes to kiss him. "Some men were made to wear a tux and you are definitely one of them."

Her praise filled him with pleasure, but as quickly as he realized it, the odd sensation he kept getting all day prickled along his nerve endings. He wasn't the kind of person who needed accolades or compliments. He supposed it was the fact that the praise was from *her* that made it noteworthy.

But it confused him. He didn't behave like this. Usually, he was more disinterested. Almost like more of an observer of life than someone living—

He nearly rolled his eyes at his thoughts. Who cared if he was pleased that she thought he was handsome? It actually worked very well for two people involved romantically. And it was nothing more than that.

They drove to the Waldorf and checked their coats before taking their place in the receiving line.

Autumn had attended her share of charity balls, but there was something about this ball that filled her with awe. The size and scope alone were mindboggling. But the decorations and atmosphere were almost hypnotic.

"I don't know who your friend's party planner is, but…wow…" She glanced around at silver and gold decorations, fine china trimmed in gold on blindingly white linen tablecloths and candy cane lilies in arrangements for centerpieces. All of which were accented by red and silver lights that alternated around the room.

"This is lovely."

"Yeah."

He said it calmly, as if the hundred round tables set up around a turntable bar was something he saw every day, and she suddenly realized he might be accustomed this kind of ball. He might not go to one every week or even every month. But he'd been to his fair share—

Meaning, she'd stepped out of her world and into his. Her breath stuttered at the thought. She might plan high class events, but not this big. Her guests might be the cream of the crop in the city, but this party reached another level. Movie stars casually milled about. Two tech geniuses headquartered on the West Coast chatted by the bar. She swore she saw a prince and two Middle Eastern kings.

They reached the hosts, and Jack introduced her to Paul and Tilly Montgomery. At least eighty, with silver hair set off by a blue gown, Tilly took Autumn's hands in both of hers.

"Oh, my dear, how lovely to see our Jack has finally brought a woman to one of my parties."

Afraid Jack might have been insulted, Autumn hid a wince. "Thank you… I think."

Tilly chortled. "Seriously, Jack. You might have actually found a keeper this time."

Jack leaned in and kissed Tilly's cheek. "I'm still waiting for you."

Her husband, Paul, sighed. "I'm standing right here, Jack. If you're going to flirt with my wife at least have the good graces to do it behind my back."

Jack shook his hand, his face blossoming with fondness for the older couple. "I want you to be aware that your wife has options, so you step up your game."

Chuckling, Paul slapped his back. "It's good to see you happy again, kid."

Jack said, "I'm always happy."

Tilly and Paul exchanged a look that Autumn saw. They truly liked seeing Jack happy. And they didn't for one minute buy his claim that he was always happy.

Jack put his hand on the small of her back and led her into the ballroom, but Tilly's and Paul's comments stayed with her. They liked Jack and loved that he was happy—

She made him happy.

Or their arrangement did.

A waiter walked by with champagne and Jack plucked two glasses and handed one to her.

"Thank you."

"We don't have to stay long."

"Are you kidding?" Maybe she was a little high on the power she seemed to have to make Jack happy, but there was no way she wanted to leave. "This room is gorgeous. There's a band. And movie stars!"

"And here I thought you were happy to be with me."

She leaned in and kissed him. "You're the icing on the cake."

He laughed.

"You know I love being with you." Remembering how it felt to realize she made Jack happy, she said, "You make me happy. I always have fun with you."

He smiled as if he didn't have a care in the world, but Tilly's and Paul's comments came back to her. He might be the Jack she remembered from five years ago. Fun, easygoing. But Tilly and Paul had seen another side of him. They'd seen him grieving his mom. They'd seen him alone. They might have also seen him after his fiancées stole his ability to trust.

No wonder Tilly and Paul were pleased to see him happy.

A couple greeted Jack and stopped to wish him a merry Christmas. He turned to Autumn and said, "Tom, Grace, this is Autumn Jones. You might remember her from her work with Raise Your Voice. Autumn, this is Tom and Grace Howell. Tom's on my board of directors."

Autumn shook hands and said, "It's nice to meet you," as the strange feeling rippled through her again. But this time she recognized it. She might have stepped out of her world and into his, but she fit. She didn't feel out of place. She belonged at Jack's side. Not as arm candy, but as herself. She made him happy. She *loved* making him happy.

And he made her happy.

Seated with a group of Jack's friends, they enjoyed lively conversation at dinner. After dessert, Tilly walked up to the microphone and said a few words thanking everyone for coming and encouraging them to celebrate the season with her. Then the band began to play, and she and Jack took to the floor.

Just two short weeks ago, they'd been muddling through dance lessons with Greg, awkward with each other. Now, they fit in each other's arms, laughed when he swung her around, and enjoyed the night.

Then they were taken home in the limo she'd gotten very accustomed to.

When they arrived in his penthouse, he took her into his arms again, this time to kiss her. He looked her in the eye with his beautiful blue orbs and the horrible truth hit her. She didn't merely fit into his world. She loved him.

Again.

This time when he slipped off her gown and she undid the buttons of his shirt there was a familiarity that opened her heart like a blossom in the sun. Touching him took new meaning. Their connection breathed life into her soul. When she kissed him, she wanted him to know that. She wanted him to realize how special he was.

His kisses felt different too. They still played like two happy puppies. But when they were tingling and needy and he rolled her to her back and entered her, their gazes caught and held. Everything she'd been thinking at the ball came into focus. He'd brought her into his world, and she'd belonged there.

Because she belonged with him and he belonged with her.

She made him laugh.

He cooked for her.

She loved touching him.

He stole her breath every time he looked at her—

They were now officially in too deep. Much deeper than they'd intended to go.

And as soon as he saw that, he would be gone.

Sunday, after breakfast and a try at the *Times* crossword puzzle, she walked into the bedroom and came out dressed in jeans and a sweater.

"If you don't mind, I need to finish my shopping."

Tossing the paper to a sofa cushion, he rose. "I don't mind. I'll come with you."

She pulled gloves out of her purse. "That's okay. You don't have to."

He headed for the bedroom to get his coat and shoes. "I want to."

He wanted to see what she looked at in stores. Because he wanted to buy her a Christmas gift. It made him feel equal parts of happy and confused. He'd spent the past five years delegating his Christmas gift buying to his personal shopper, but he suddenly wanted to choose Autumn's present himself, even though he had no idea what she might want or need.

But her search for the perfect sweater for her dad and housecoat for her mom did not help him in the slightest. Neither did the thirty minutes she spent listening to a toy store owner discuss the merits of one train set over another.

"It's for my nephews," she'd told Jack as they walked out of the store with a starter set and onto the busy street again. "I promised my brother I'd get the train that they'll put under their tree. It had to be perfect. Something they can easily add to every year."

He snorted. "I know the importance of the right train. It took me and my mom an entire fall to find the one we eventually bought for under our Christmas tree—"

He stopped himself. The memory didn't hurt, but it did surprise him that he and Autumn had a shared experience. She wanted the right train for her nephews. He understood why.

They'd lived such different lives that it threw him for a second. But he shook his head to bring himself back to the present. Before his mom started Step Inside, he'd been raised in a blue-collar environment. Just as Autumn had been—

Maybe their lives weren't so different after all?

He froze, but quickly started walking again. The

conversation had thrown him back in time for a few seconds, back to roots he'd all but forgotten he had because his life had changed so much, but also because he'd been very busy.

It was not a big deal.

Monday, he didn't even tell Autumn he'd be picking her up at six. Arnie simply pulled the limo in front of her building and she raced out, using her worn briefcase like an umbrella because today's snowflakes were huge and wet.

She jumped into the limo saying, "You were right! Gerry called me in today. We did my interview."

"And?"

She set her briefcase on the floor a few feet away from her boots. "And Friday at two I have a second interview with the board."

"The twenty-seventh?"

"Yeah."

"I thought they said they wanted somebody in place by the first of the year?"

"Looks like they're cutting it close."

"Technically they have until Tuesday."

She laughed. "I guess. But we get out at noon on New Year's Eve—in case anybody has big plans, the charity gives us time to take a nap and get dressed. If they want someone in place when we return to work on January second, that means they have to announce their decision that morning."

He hugged her. "Doesn't matter. You got the second interview! That's great!"

She pondered that a second then said, "It is."

He frowned. "You seem to have lost your enthusiasm."

"There are four people interviewing with the board."

Arnie pulled the limo into traffic, heading for home.

He squeezed her hand. "You'll ace it."

"I think so. But it's difficult for me to get over the fact that I have to jump through hoops for this job."

He shrugged. "That's part of life."

She just looked at him.

"I'm serious. Things happen. And dreams don't fall from the sky. You have to work for them."

"I've been working for this for over five years."

"Look at this as your final push."

"Okay." She grinned at him. "So, what's for dinner?"

"What do you want?"

"First of all, I need to make sure you don't mind cooking."

The fact that she would even ask that shocked him. "I love to cook! I actually miss cooking."

"How good are you with soup?"

"I am *the man* when it comes to soup!"

"Turkey noodle?"

He winced. "Now, see… I have a problem coming up with that on the spur of the moment. I like to start with a carcass. You know, make my own broth."

"Seriously?"

"Think of me like an artist when it comes to food. Just like Picasso didn't do paint-by-number…, I'm not a fan of recipes. Unless I create them. I make my own broth. Make my own sauces."

"What can you come up with for a spur of the moment dinner tonight?"

"Steak. Spaghetti—"

Her face brightened. "Oh, let's have spaghetti!"

"Okay. But tomorrow I'm getting a turkey. I'll brine it and stuff it—"

"That could be Christmas dinner!"

"You're having Christmas dinner with your parents."

Her voice turned pouty. "My mom makes ham."

"And you like turkey?"

"I *love* turkey."

The way she said it made him laugh. "Maybe we could eat the turkey on Saturday. By then you'll be sick of ham. I can spoil you."

Autumn liked the sound of that. As long as he was happy, she was happy. And planning dinners was a far cry from the emotionally charged night they'd had after the ball. It almost seemed like a return to normal. The kind of relationship they could handle.

They changed out of work clothes and into casual clothes and she watched him make spaghetti. He pulled out a bag of frozen noodles that he'd prepared from scratch and a bag of frozen sauce.

The whole time he thawed and prepared things, he talked about creating the dishes for Step Inside.

"It was like having a couple thousand anonymous judges. People don't hesitate to criticize you on social media...or compliment. I loved the challenge of it."

She took a sip of wine. "You sound like me when I need to choose the perfect floral arrangements for a summer gala. I never minded the criticism I got on the samples. I use it to make the arrangements better."

He gave her a taste of sauce. "What do you think?"

"I think your abilities are wasted running the company."

He chuckled and turned away, but the truth of that settled into her brain. His food was amazing and he was clearly happy cooking—

"How did you go from being the creative soul of the

company to being the guy who looks at numbers? That couldn't have been easy."

"It was an adjustment."

"I'll bet." But he didn't say anything else. He didn't say, *It was an adjustment but now I love it.* He'd simply acknowledged the adjustment. He also wasn't enthusiastic about his job. Not the way he enjoyed cooking for her.

But he didn't seem to see it.

Just as she'd suspected, the spaghetti was so good, she groaned. "I can't imagine being this talented," she said, pointing at the spaghetti with meat sauce.

He ladled more sauce on her spaghetti as if he thought she hadn't taken enough. "I studied here in New York. After that I was working as a sous chef when Mom decided to open her restaurants. At first, it was just the one, but she had a dream."

"Have you ever considered that you inspired her dream?"

His eyebrows knit together when he frowned. "What?"

"You clearly have talent. She must have seen that and decided to create the vehicle you could use to skyrocket to stardom."

He laughed. "You have such an interesting way of looking at things."

She studied his face, seeking signs that he saw what was going on in his own life. None came. He was clueless. "Or maybe I see things that you missed?"

He shook his head and dug into his spaghetti, the conversation dying a natural death as they talked about myriad other things as they ate.

When they were done, he rose to clear their dishes. She motioned him back down. "I'll clean up."

"You're a guest."

After the way they'd made love on Saturday night, that hit her funny and she stopped halfway to picking up his plate. She'd felt the difference in their feelings, the connection, the commitment to each other. Maybe he hadn't. But she had. If she looked at it that way, she knew his calling her a guest was meant to be positive, complimentary.

And, really, she wasn't supposed to be looking at this any other way than casual. That's all he wanted. That's all *she* wanted—

Wasn't it?

She took a breath and reached for his dish again. The short amount of time they'd known each other made his way of categorizing the relationship the smarter one. No matter that their crossover into stronger feelings had happened naturally. It was not in their plan. She had to get herself in line with him or she'd say or do something she'd regret.

She stacked the dishes in the dishwasher and tidied the kitchen while he checked his streaming service for a movie. They stayed up later than usual because neither one of them had work the next day, Christmas Eve. Remembering that, she also realized he didn't have a tree or any sort of Christmas decorations.

It didn't seem right that she'd be waking up Christmas morning in a house that didn't even have a nod to the holiday.

She woke early on Christmas Eve. Leaving him sound asleep in his comfortable bed, she tiptoed into the bathroom. After showering and dressing, she went out into the marshmallow world of accumulating snow. Fat, fluffy flakes tumbled around her as they billowed to the ground, toppling on piles of snow scraped off the sidewalk to the fronts of coffee shops, restaurants and boutiques.

Two hours later, with a small artificial tree and two boxes of ornaments, she had to call a car to take her home. Jack wasn't anywhere around when she stepped off the elevator into the penthouse but that simply made her surprise even better.

Halfway through assembling the tree, her phone rang. She plucked it from the sofa, saw the call was from her mom and answered. "Hey, Ma."

"Hey, yourself."

She'd never heard that discouraged tone from her mom and knew something had happened. "What's up?"

"Oven broke. No one's working on Christmas Eve. I can't get it fixed. And it's too late to go out and buy a new stove. It wouldn't be here by tomorrow. Which by the way is Christmas…so no one is working then, either."

She pressed her lips together to keep from laughing. The problem might be bad, but it wasn't the end of the world. "I'm sorry. I know this ruins your plans for Christmas dinner."

"I wanted a big dinner, but we can make do. I'm thinking tomorrow's lunch could be cold cuts and a cake, if there's a shop that still has a cake this close to Christmas." She sighed. "I should have baked the pies yesterday."

"It's not a big deal, Mom. Cold cuts will be fine."

The elevator door opened, and Jack walked out. He carried two huge bags into the kitchen and put them into the refrigerator before he strolled over to the sofa and bent to kiss her cheek. She smiled up at him.

"The family's accustomed to my brown sugar pineapple ham."

"No one cares about the ham, Ma. Everybody just wants to be together. Besides, without having to spend your morning in the kitchen you'll have more time to play with your grandkids."

"I suppose."

Frowning, Jack sat on the sofa beside her.

"Maybe I could hunt around Manhattan for a cake?"

"Manhattan? Are you at work? It's Christmas Eve! Don't you take a day off?"

She winced, realizing she'd nearly spilled the beans about being at Jack's. "I meant Queens."

"Okay. With all the shopping I have to do to change dinner, I'd appreciate it if you could bring dessert tomorrow."

"Consider it done."

"Thanks. I'll see you tomorrow around noon."

Autumn disconnected the call and Jack pulled her to him for a long, lingering kiss.

"I take it that was your mom."

"Yeah. Poor thing. Her oven broke. She can't bake the family ham and mashed potatoes…or her world-famous pumpkin pies."

"World-famous?"

"Well, maybe not world-famous. But the whole family loves them. They're a tradition. Still, I think she'll be okay with having sandwiches and cake tomorrow." She shrugged. "Not the big dinner she likes to make, but the point is getting the family together. She knows that and she'll be fine."

He nodded, then inclined his head toward the half-assembled Christmas tree. "I was going to ask you where you were when I finally rolled out of bed, but I figured it out. You should have woken me."

She laughed and kissed him again. "I knew you needed the sleep."

He chuckled.

She rose from the sofa and began inserting fake evergreen limbs into the pole that made up the spine of the artificial tree. "I also thought your house could use some holiday spirit."

He picked up one of the branches and examined it. "I haven't had a tree in forever." He caught her gaze. "Not even a fake one."

She'd bet he hadn't had a tree since his mom's passing, but she decided not to mention that. "Where did *you* go?"

"I did some shopping too. Got a turkey."

"Oh, for turkey noodle soup!"

"Yep. Also got a ham. Thought I'd make that for myself tomorrow—"

Jack stopped midsentence. In the butcher shop, choosing a turkey, he'd seen the ham and the Christmas decorations around the display case and suddenly wanted it. But there was a much better purpose for that ham.

"I could make your family's Christmas dinner."

"What?"

"Your family could come here, and I could make Christmas dinner."

Her eyes widened in horror. "Fate stole my mother's chance to make a ham. She's not going to agree to having Christmas anywhere but at her house."

He realized that in his spontaneity he'd forgotten they'd be outing themselves to her parents. She'd be too familiar with his house. He'd be too comfortable having her there. But he wanted to do this—

"Okay. I'll bake the ham here and we'll take it to your parents' house tomorrow."

"That's very nice of you, but—"

"Hey, your mom invited me to dinner. I know I'm welcome."

"Of course, you are! I just don't want you to go out of your way."

"It's not out of my way. We can get up early. I'll bake the ham and make some side dishes." The happy feelings he'd had standing in the butcher shop returned full force. The joy of really celebrating the holiday rushed through him. "It will be fun."

She bit her lower lip. "I should call my mother and tell her you're going to do that."

"You don't want it to be a surprise?"

"I don't want my mom and dad to be eating deli meat from their freezer until August." Happiness suddenly filled her eyes, as if the merit of his idea finally sunk in for her. "Thank you. You're right. This could be fun."

He laughed as she picked up her phone to call her mom, but warmth filled him, as the spirit of Christmas warmed him. He'd liked her parents. It felt good to be able to do something nice for them.

He hadn't felt this way since he was nine, anticipating gifts and a special dinner. Candy in a stocking. Cookies left on the doorstep by neighbors. Carolers going from floor to floor of their apartment building, singing.

Crystal clear memories swept through him. Instead of brushing them away, he smiled and began planning the menu for Christmas dinner.

CHAPTER FIFTEEN

THEY WOKE EARLY the next morning, as Jack had said they would. He prepared the ham for baking then began making side dishes, sliding each one into storage containers as he completed them, then putting those containers into a thermal carrier.

"You're certainly prepared."

He peeked up at her. "Because I have storage containers?"

"No. The thermal thing. I didn't even know those existed."

He leaned across the center island and kissed her. "Because I'm guessing you don't cook, let alone take things to your mom's."

"Hey, I bought the cake."

"You and I are going to be the hit of the day."

He carted things to his Mercedes in the basement of the building. She scurried after him with the cake box, setting it beside the thermal container in the trunk. He'd baked the ham in an electric roaster not merely for ease of transport but to heat it before lunch. He took that to the car, then returned to the penthouse to help her carry the train for her nephews while she held a shopping bag of presents for her parents.

When they were finally settled on the front seat, she

thought he'd start the car. Instead, he sat there for a few seconds, then reached into the pocket of the leather jacket he wore over a sage green sweater.

He handed her a small gift, obviously a wrapped jeweler's box. "I bought this for you. Merry Christmas."

Her heart stuttered. "Oh, I'm sorry. I didn't think we were doing presents."

He laughed. "If you're saying you didn't get me anything, I'm sort of glad. We've only been in each other's lives a few weeks. Presents might have been premature at this point." He paused to suck in a breath. "But I just wanted to buy you something." He peeked at her. "Myself." He sniffed a laugh. "It sounds weird when I say it out loud."

It sounded wonderful to her. It sounded like a man who was getting real feelings for her. Maybe even a guy who hadn't had real feelings for so long he didn't recognize them.

But she did. As long as she didn't push, he'd eventually come to the right conclusions.

He nudged his chin in the direction of the box. "Open it."

Her fingers shook slightly as she ripped the red foil paper from the box then opened it to reveal a diamond solitaire necklace. She wasn't an expert, but she'd seen one and two-carat solitaires. This one was bigger.

Her gaze jumped to his. "Oh, my God."

"You like it?"

She took it out of the box. When she held it up, the diamond caught even the dim light of the basement garage and sparkled like the sun. "It's beautiful."

"I just kept thinking that you have such a pretty neck, and this would be perfect nestled right there."

He tapped the little dip at the base of her throat before motioning for her to give him the necklace.

She handled it over and pulled her hair off her neck before turning around so he could fasten it at her nape. When he released the chain, the diamond fell exactly where he wanted it.

She faced him again and he smiled approvingly, proudly. "Just as I thought. It's perfect. Merry Christmas."

She'd never seen him so happy. Tears filled her eyes. "Merry Christmas." Such an ordinary thing to say, and an ordinary thing to do on Christmas Day, but the moment softened her bones and found a home in her heart. He might not realize it, but he loved her.

He started the car, but she put her hand on his forearm to stop him from putting it in gear. Then she leaned in and kissed him. "Thank you."

He smiled. "You're welcome."

They arrived at her parents around eleven, an hour before the other guests were to arrive. He pulled the Mercedes into the driveway of a white two-story house with black shutters. Very modest and traditional.

Carrying the roaster first, he followed Autumn to the front door. She entered without knocking. "Ma! Pop! Jack and I are here with lunch."

Her mother scrambled down the stairs as her dad lifted himself out of a recliner in a living room made small by the enormous Christmas tree in the corner.

"I've got the ham," Jack announced trailing Autumn as she led him to the kitchen. "We can plug in the roaster and it will be perfect by the time guests arrive."

Autumn's mom pressed her hands to her face. "This is wonderful!"

Unbuttoning her coat, Autumn leaned in and kissed her mom. "It's fabulous to live with a chef."

Her mom's head tilted in question.

Realizing what she's said, Autumn quickly covered her mistake. "I meant have a chef in your social circle." She shook her head as Jack exited the front door again to get his thermal bag of side dishes.

She quickly faced her mom. If her mom said or did the wrong thing, Jack could react badly. He wasn't skittish. He was careful. And they hadn't known each other long enough for him to endure her mom's well-meaning but pushy comments. This perfect dinner could end their relationship or at least send them back to square one.

"You promised no matchmaking. That also means no making something out of nothing."

Her mom straightened indignantly. "Well, I'm sorry for wanting the best for my daughter."

"And I would like the chance to choose my own partner."

Her mom rolled her eyes. "You've been making up your own mind since you were four. I do not think I'll change you now."

Her mom sauntered away as if she wasn't going to let anything ruin her good mood, and Autumn breathed a sigh of relief. She'd killed two birds with one stone in that short exchange. Her mom had been warned about matchmaking and Jack had been out of earshot.

Things were going well.

As Jack took care of business with lunch, her dad ambled into the kitchen, opened the refrigerator and pulled out two beers. He handed one to Jack, then twisted the cap on the second for himself. Jack reheated side dishes and tended to the ham, and Autumn's dad chitchatted with him about the Knicks.

Aaron soon arrived with his wife Penny and two boys, Mark and Donnie, who bounded over to Autumn, hugging her around the thighs.

She laughed with them, then chased them from the living room, through the dining room, into the kitchen and the foyer and back into the living room again. They shrieked with laughter when she caught them and tickled them, then the whole process started again until Autumn was so tired she had to sit.

Pete and his wife arrived late. But once they were out of their coats and settled in the living room, the opening of gifts began. Autumn sat on the floor beside the recliner, while Mark and Donnie distributed gifts. At six and four, neither could read, so they brought the packages to Autumn who read the tags before the boys took them to the appropriate receiver.

With the gifts opened, they moved to the dining room, where they ate the ham, hot potato salad, peas and pancetta, herb and garlic linguine, and creamed kale and mushrooms.

Her mom said, "This is fantastic."

"I didn't want to overstep by making your pineapple ham and thought this would be a good replacement dinner until next year when your cooking will be the star again. Autumn tells me no one makes a pineapple ham like yours."

Mary blushed. "Well, I don't know about that."

"Your ham is great, Ma," Autumn said.

Aaron said, "Best around," as Pete said, "Absolutely the best."

Autumn smiled across the table at Jack, who winked at her, and she suddenly realized how modest he was. He didn't need to steal the show. He'd helped out— saved Christmas dinner—without making it a big deal.

Four-year-old Donnie strolled over to him with the car he'd gotten as a gift from Pete and Sasha. "It doesn't work."

Jack shifted on his seat and took the car from Donnie. Turning it over, he said, "Ah. You know why? It needs a battery."

Shaggy-haired Donnie blinked up at him.

Jack said, "It's a power source," then realizing who he was talking to he said, "It's what makes the car run."

Autumn bit back a laugh as her heart about exploded in her chest. She adored her nephews and having Jack be so kind to Donnie filled her with pleasure—then something else that made her swallow hard.

She could see Jack as a daddy.

No. She could see Jack as the father of *her* children. In this house for holidays. Laughing with her mom, talking about the Knicks with her dad.

She *loved* him. Deeply. Profoundly. So much her heart swelled to its breaking point.

It wasn't what she wanted.

But more than that, he wasn't ready.

Mary scrambled from her seat. "We have some batteries in the junk drawer."

Autumn's dad waved her down. "I'll get them. You eat."

Autumn did a doubletake as her dad rose from his chair and headed for the kitchen. He returned in a minute and handed the batteries to Jack who nimbly installed them and gave the car to Donnie.

"Press that little button there."

Donnie grinned, pressed the button and giggled when the toy car's engine came to life.

"Put it on the floor," Pete encouraged.

Donnie stooped down, placed the car on the floor

and gasped when it raced from the dining room into the kitchen, stopping only when it hit the center island.

Everyone laughed. Donnie ran into the kitchen. Jack set his napkin on his plate and followed the little boy to the car. Mark quickly joined them.

Jack showed the two little boys the clear path for the car to run and they took turns hitting the start button, setting it on the floor, letting it run to the back door, then scooping it up and repeating the process.

Autumn watched them through the twenty minutes they played, wondering if Jack realized how good he was with kids.

And that he wanted a family?

Oh, he'd never say it. And she'd never even hint to him that his longing and joy were evident on his face and he played with her nephews…but it was there. She could see it. He wanted a family and she didn't.

Instead of watching the football game, as Jack assumed they would, the family cleared the table then set it up again for a game of Yahtzee.

At Jack's puzzled expression, Pete caught his elbow and dragged him a few feet back.

"Ma doesn't like football. So we play an hour or two of Yahtzee before we settle in like slugs."

"Okay."

They took seats around the dining table again. This time, instead of being across from Autumn, he found himself seated beside her. He remembered her warning about her mother and matchmaking, but he didn't have the sense that her mom had pushed them together. All he saw was what he believed to be the normal activities of family.

He and his mom had never been alone on Christmas. She had too many friends. But they'd never had the simplicity of connection that he found here with the Jones family.

Kindness and laughter interspersed with teasing that usually led to more laughter.

Not familiar with the game, he'd come in dead last. Autumn's mom won, even letting Donnie roll her dice most of the time. Jim drank more beer, clearly unconcerned with positioning his dice rolls for maximum score. But Pete and Aaron had something of a competition that led to Pete coming in second and Aaron third, but only by three points.

Everybody laughed and joked, but by the time they were in the living room the Yahtzee scores were forgotten.

Around seven that night, it struck him that he hadn't once thought about leaving. He liked it at Autumn's parents' house. It wasn't the Christmas he was accustomed to with his mom. It was Christmas the way he'd imagined it when his friends talked about their holidays. What he believed "real" Christmas should be like.

He knew he was quiet as he drove back to the penthouse and realized neither he nor Autumn questioned where she'd spend the night. He pulled the Mercedes into his parking space. Autumn carried her gifts from her parents, and he carried the roaster which was big enough to hold the empty storage containers and thermal carrier.

They stepped off the elevator into the penthouse, totally silent. He assumed she was exhausted, maybe too tired to talk. It had been a long two days. But he was quiet because it all felt too normal.

Too, too normal.

Technically, he'd known Autumn for five years. But he had really only been in her life a few weeks. He'd met her parents three times. He'd only met her brothers that day.

How could this feel normal?

And why was it he hadn't missed his mom?

Hadn't *thought* of her except in passing all day.

Hadn't even considered going to the mausoleum with flowers as he did some Christmases.

Guilt overwhelmed him. His mother had been the center of his world. She had also provided him with an opportunity to be the creative center of Step Inside. He didn't believe, as Autumn had said, that she'd opened a restaurant to give him a place to showcase his talent. But he did see that those years he'd spent planning menus and creating recipes for her company had been a gift of a sort.

And he'd forgotten her.

It rattled through him, made him feel odd, itchy like he couldn't reconcile it in his brain.

"I think I'll shower," he said as they stepped into the bedroom. He walked toward the bathroom, pulling his sweater over his head, not waiting for Autumn's reply.

In the bathroom, he turned on all the jets and grabbed his bodywash. The shower steamed enough that he didn't see Autumn enter until she opened the glass door and walked inside to join him.

Without a word, she slid against his soapy torso, put her arms around his neck and kissed him. He fell into the kiss like a drowning man, which only confused him more. When the diamond solitaire at her throat winked at him, something sensual and possessive raced through him and he kissed her hotly, greedily, as he ran the luffa down her back, then let it fall to the shower floor, replacing it with his hands.

Laughing, she slid away, but he caught her wrist and brought her back, so he could nuzzle the shiny spot at her throat and let his hands touch every inch he couldn't reach with his lips. Sliding both palms up her sides, he let them meet below her breasts, lifting them for his eager mouth. She moaned as he pulled on each one, then she wrapped one leg around his thighs.

Power coursed through him when he realized she'd positioned them perfectly. He angled himself to enter her, then shifted their positions so that he could sit on the shower bench with her straddling him. When they were settled, he let his lips roam from her shoulders to her stomach and back up again. She tensed, trembling and began the rhythm that brought them both to a fever pitch of need.

Her release came first, rippling around him, bringing him to the point of no return.

After that they showered for real, and he'd never felt more energized and yet more exhausted. The crazy push pull between guilt and happiness happening in his brain had been silenced while they were in the shower, but it seemed to be back again. Guilt wanted to drag him down. Even as happiness bubbled through him.

Telling himself to stop thinking, he toweled off Autumn's back and she returned the favor, which led to kissing again.

Wonderful kisses that reached the entire way to his soul and filled up empty places he always knew were there but couldn't reach himself. They kissed their way to the bedroom and fell into bed where they made love again and eventually drifted off into an exhausted sleep.

But in the last seconds of consciousness, it struck

him that even the fleeting thoughts or memories he'd had of his mom had always evaporated into nothing that day.

It was like he couldn't hold on to them.

Like losing her again.

Which made him wonder how in the hell he could allow himself to be happy, when he was forgetting the person who hadn't merely raised him; she'd given him a wonderful life.

CHAPTER SIXTEEN

He woke the next morning to find Autumn gone. He rolled out of bed, slid into sweatpants and a sweatshirt and headed for the main area.

When he reached the living room, he saw her in the kitchen, toasting bagels.

She walked over and kissed him. "We had so much rich food to eat yesterday, I thought we should go back to basics...bagels."

Scrubbing his hand across the back of his neck, he laughed. He loved having her with him and wished he could figure out, and to make his peace with, his guilt and sorrow. Especially when Autumn herself was one of the reminders of his remorse. He'd been with her the night his mom had died.

In fact, being with her had taken away his opportunity to change the outcome of that night.

If he hadn't been with Autumn, he might have gotten his mom the medical help she needed—

"I also wanted to thank you for being so good to my parents yesterday. My whole family really."

He fought the guilt, the memories of the night his mom died, and forced himself into the present. "Your family is very easy to get along with."

The toaster popped. She took out two sides of the

first bagel and offered them to him. "You have cream cheese, right?"

"Of course, I have cream cheese."

She laughed, then kissed him again.

The world righted for a few seconds then quickly fell off-kilter again because he could not understand how all this could feel so perfect, so right, when inside he was angry with himself. He stood in the center of his fancy kitchen, holding two halves of a bagel, looking like a tourist in Times Square, not sure which way to turn.

She opened the refrigerator, retrieved the cream cheese and set it on the center island.

He shook his head, hoping to clear these feelings, as he prepared his bagel.

"Of course, we could eat them plain to give our stomachs the chance to balance out."

He said nothing, simply took his bagel to the side of the center island that offered seating, set it on a napkin and then walked to the coffeemaker. Silence hung in the air as she put cream cheese on her bagel and his coffee brewed.

When both were finally seated at the island the silence wasn't merely obvious, it was telling.

He knew he couldn't get himself out of his own head. Couldn't fight the guilt over having had such a good day.

He had no idea why Autumn was quiet.

She took a breath. "Okay, look. I know yesterday had to be hard for you."

"You just said you appreciated how good I was with your family. Now, you're saying you could tell the day was difficult for me?"

"You didn't get quiet until we were in the car. Then you were odd when we got home."

"You didn't seem to think so in the shower."

She laughed and caught his gaze. "You were your normal self then."

He couldn't reply. Not because she was wrong. Because he hated that she wanted to talk about this when he wasn't even sure what to say.

"I think it's perfectly normal for someone to decompress after meeting so many new people, but there's more. You really seemed to enjoy cooking dinner for my parents."

"I did."

"And they loved it and you loved that they loved it."

"What's wrong with that?"

"Nothing. That's my point. You've been cooking and talking about cooking so much that it struck me last night that I think you might be missing how cooking is becoming part of your life again."

That was far, far away from what he'd been thinking last night, but for some reason or another it resonated. Which was stupid considering all the misery and guilt he'd been experiencing. "You think I miss cooking?"

"Yes."

Suddenly, the truth of that rippled through him. Experiencing grief and guilt had tried to drown it out, but she was right. He'd enjoyed making Christmas dinner. He'd enjoyed cooking in a way he hadn't in years—

He blocked the thought, but it wouldn't go away because these feelings weren't new. He'd been having them since he'd begun cooking for Autumn. He'd gotten so good at blocking them he didn't even feel them pop up anymore.

That thought spiraled into more thoughts. He could see himself cooking for her forever. But he could also see that though that might be fulfilling for a while, it was not a permanent solution—

Solution?

To the guilt? That didn't make sense.

"You know, you haven't spoken a lot about your mother, but you've said enough that I've guessed some things."

He glanced over at her.

"You've told me that you're keeping her dream alive. Maybe building her dream."

He cautiously said, "I am."

"And you believe her dream was to have a bunch of really great restaurants."

"A business. Not necessarily restaurants. My mom wanted to run a business. She was incredibly smart. She took night classes at community college, thought things through and ultimately wanted to create a successful business."

Her face softened as she put her hand on his forearm, as if comforting him. "When did the desire to start a chain of restaurants come up for her?"

"After I did some apprenticeships, we both saw that I had some unique abilities and she realized that was her chance."

"What if that wasn't what happened?"

He peered at her.

"What if she saw your potential as a chef and she started her business as a way to give *you* a platform?"

She'd mentioned something like that before, but it didn't fit. "My mom had always wanted to start a business. Because she'd been a waitress and hostess and even a general manager of a diner, restaurants seemed like a good fit."

"Jack, I know I may be overstepping here. But watching you cook for me all week and how you enjoyed it… I felt like I understood what your mom felt watching you. She might have always wanted to start a business, but she didn't even try until you showed promise."

He stared at her.

"I think what she really wanted was for you to continue research and development. To make Step Inside extraordinary because of your talent."

His temper hummed below his skin. "Are you saying Step Inside wasn't her dream?"

"It was very much her dream. Her dream *for you*. I think that when you lost her, you got it backwards. I think she wanted you in R&D. Not taking the place she had."

The hum became red hot anger. "Stop. Just stop. That wasn't how it was."

She held up her hands. "I'm not saying this to make you mad. I'm not saying that you have to change. I'm just giving you something to think about, something to consider."

"Because I've been moody?"

"Sort of. But more because you're wasting your talents."

"Well, thank you very much." He rose from the stool, his anger so hot and so potent he could have easily said something he would regret. Heading for the bedroom, he said, "I'm going in to work today. I'll text Arnie's number to you and you can have him drive you home." He turned and faced her. "Unless you'd rather take the subway. Isn't that what you do? Resist everybody's help or opinion. Even though you don't hesitate to share your own."

"That's not fair! Especially since you all but coached me for the CEO position."

He said, "Hmmm." And headed for the bedroom again. She was right. She had taken his help and now she was offering hers and it infuriated him. Not because he didn't like assistance or opinions but because she was wrong! She thought she had his whole life figured out when he didn't even have his life figured out!

He dressed quickly and was returning to the main area before she'd finished her bagel.

Without a word, he walked past her, shrugging into his leather jacket. Knowing no one else would be in the office, he'd worn jeans and a sweater, so the jacket worked.

And his Mercedes keys were in the pocket.

Autumn watched him go. A million questions swam in her head. She could think their disagreement small, meaningless, a blip, something they would laugh about that evening when he returned.

Except—with his offer of a ride from Arnie—he'd kicked her out.

She bit her lower lip, thinking this through. Technically, they'd been living together. Without getting to know each other they'd fallen into a serious living arrangement and with their first fight hanging in the air, she realized she needed time as much as he needed time.

Whether he saw it or not, he was changing. His life was changing. What he wanted was changing.

And she might be getting her big break. A break that didn't mesh with the new things he wanted.

She didn't call Arnie. Instead, she gathered her things with an eye toward carrying them on the subway. She left behind the dresses and items he'd bought her. Not just because they wouldn't fit into the duffel bag she'd used, but because they weren't hers.

When all the clothes and cosmetics she'd brought were stuffed in the duffel, she touched the solitaire at her throat.

He'd given that to the woman he had fun with. Not the one who'd tried to get him to see that he might have taken his life down the wrong path.

She reached behind her to undo the clasp, slid it off and set it on the table in his walk-in closet. He liked fun Autumn. He didn't seem to like more serious Autumn or maybe he didn't like *anyone* questioning his life choices.

She couldn't say. They hadn't been together long enough for her to know that.

Rolling her duffel behind her, she headed for the main room and the elevator. They definitely needed some time apart. If he called her and they smoothed things over, the solitaire would be on the table in the closet.

If he didn't—

She refused to think about that.

Jack returned home from work, half expecting Autumn to be there. As he rode the private elevator, nerves skittered through him. He didn't want to have a fight, but he didn't want her in the penthouse. No one had the right to question his decisions about Step Inside. Someone who didn't know his mother had even less right to an opinion.

Plus, that morning at work, his world had seemed to right again. All those crazy feelings he'd had at breakfast had disappeared.

So what if his penthouse seemed cold and empty without Autumn? So what if he missed cooking for her, missed the eager expression on her face before she took her first bite of whatever he'd made her? Something about being alone felt right.

* * *

Friday morning his staff returned to work and even more order came to his world. Contracts arrived, resumes for new chefs were stacked on his desk, blueprints for the new restaurants to be built in Pennsylvania were delivered.

He dove in eagerly, but by eleven he'd looked at the details on the drawings so long his eyes crossed. Telling himself that was normal, he called the architects, and they came to his office to meet with him. As they spoke, it struck him that they were competent enough that he shouldn't be making decisions that they were more qualified to make.

Worse, after the architects were gone, he tried to read the five-year plan, but it bored him so much, he stuffed it in his briefcase to read over the weekend while watching a game.

An itchy feeling trembled along his nerve endings. He refused to try to identify it.

Autumn had had her interview with the board of directors for Raise Your Voice Friday afternoon, and as Jack had said, she aced it. She should have been happy. Instead, she kept getting weird thoughts about whether or not a CEO had enough time to raise children.

The very thought shocked her. Never in her life had she thought she'd want to have kids. She loved her nephews, but they hadn't made her long to have her own child until she'd seen Jack with those rambunctious little boys.

Thinking about Jack made her catch her breath. He'd arranged for her to leave Thursday and all of Friday had gone by without a word.

She'd noticed that they were both changing. He

wanted more out of life than to run his mom's company. He wanted a family and suddenly she wanted kids. Not to accommodate him but because it seemed right.

But he wouldn't talk about it. He hated when she mentioned his returning to research and development. What would he think if she brought up kids?

He'd probably explode as he had the morning after Christmas.

Had she pushed him? Had she believed she'd seen something that wasn't there?

She knew she hadn't. She knew what she'd seen. She'd been trying to help, but he didn't want help. So now she knew his boundaries. She wouldn't breach them again. She'd forget about having kids. Forget about Step Inside. Not second guess anything about his life.

Because he would call. He was a smart guy. They had a casual relationship. Eventually, his anger would cool, and he'd remember how much fun they'd had.

But when he didn't call Friday night, she knew this wasn't a blip in their relationship. Like five years ago, he'd simply walked away from her. Every time she glanced at her silent phone, every time she peered out the window, hoping to see his Mercedes pull in her driveway, she felt the awful ache of reality.

He'd left her once and never looked back.

He had done it again. He might have asked her to leave his apartment, but he'd done the asking and now he was ghosting her.

Saturday morning, she woke knowing she had to get her thoughts off Jack. Her comments at breakfast the day after Christmas hadn't been an accusation but were meant to be the start of a discussion. But that wasn't how he'd taken them, and she couldn't turn back the hands of time.

She forced her thoughts to her interview with the Raise Your Voice board. Not one person on the board had a problem with her until Quincy Fallen had asked about her relationship with Ivy. She'd kept her response brief, then shifted the conversation to her knowledge and experience with Raise Your Voice and most of the members had nodded with approval—

But what if Quincy was a holdout? Could one negative vote ruin her chances of being appointed CEO?

And what would it be like not to be able to tell Jack? To commiserate. To have him remind her there would be other opportunities?

She groaned. She'd circled back to Jack! Why did she want a guy who had no problem leaving her?

And why did it hurt so much that he'd simply told her to leave his apartment? No discussion. No chance for her to think it through and apologize—

Because that's how their last foray into a relationship had ended. With him simply deciding it was over. And never calling her again.

Angry with herself, she grabbed her jacket and mittens, as well as clothes for an overnight stay and called a ride share to take her to her parents' house.

When she finally arrived after lunch, she hoisted her duffel over her shoulder and headed for the front door. It opened before she could reach it and her mom frowned at her.

"What are you doing here?" She eyed the duffel. "Are you planning on doing laundry?"

"No. I thought I could watch a little basketball with Pop and maybe we could play a game tonight."

"Your dad's at Tony's with his friends. But he'll be

back in a few hours." Her mother took the duffel from her shoulder and guided her inside the foyer. "So if this isn't laundry, you must have brought clothes to stay overnight?"

She shrugged.

"You're not going out with Jack tonight?"

She peeked over at her mom. "No." She struggled with tears. She was tired. She was hurt. But more than that, she couldn't escape the feeling that she'd over-stepped her boundaries and hurt *him*.

And that was what was really bothering her. She'd missed something. They'd had other discussions of his mother's death and vague discussions about his taking over Step Inside. Not enough for her to know his entire story, but enough that she should have known not to speak until she could do so intelligently.

But she'd pushed ahead.

Because she'd been so sure she was correct about Step Inside.

It hurt that she'd lost him. But she ached over the realization that she could have hurt him.

Avoiding her mom's eyes, she said, "Let's go make cookies or something."

Shaking her head, her mom walked to the kitchen. "Okay. Don't tell me. I'm happy to distract you with cookie making. You're also lucky that the oven is fixed. Your nephews will be here tomorrow afternoon. They like snickerdoodles and chocolate chip. We'll make both."

Relief rippled through her until watching her mom mix batter reminded her of watching Jack cook. She grabbed the recipe and began locating ingredients for her mom to add. That made her feel marginally better.

But when her dad came home, the cookies were cooling and the game was at halftime, the achy, horrible realization that she was alone rolled over her again. Not because she didn't have someone but because *she* hurt Jack.

She was going to have to go to his penthouse and apologize.

Of course, that didn't mean he'd take her back.

But at least she'd have the chance to admit she'd been wrong.

She sucked it up, retrieved her duffel from her old bedroom, called a car and said goodbye to her parents.

She didn't like the idea of carrying her duffel bag into his penthouse, then realized if things went well, it would be good to have clothes for tomorrow morning.

With a deep breath to encourage herself, she walked into the lobby.

Josh, the doorman, stopped her. "Miss Jones."

She smiled. "Yes… Oh, wait! I probably don't have today's elevator code."

He chuckled. "You're also out of dress code."

"Excuse me?"

"It's a party, remember?"

It took a second for that to sink in. When it did, she swore her heart exploded. While she'd been upset for days, worried that she'd overstepped her boundaries and hurt his feelings, he'd been planning a party?

She forced herself to smile at Josh. "You know what? I forgot." She took two steps backward, toward the lobby door. "And I'm not going up in jeans."

Josh laughed. "There's some pretty fancy dresses in that penthouse right now."

She smiled again, but she had to grit her teeth to keep it in place. "I'll bet."

She turned and raced out into the frigid night. The

cloudless sky was inky black. The marshmallow snow had become dirty gray from days of pedestrians walking on it. She picked up her pace and told herself to call a ride share but the humiliation cut too deep.

When would she learn that Jack Adams wasn't ever going to love her?

And why did a realization that should have been common sense hurt so much?

Jack woke the next morning to silence so thick and so total it reminded him of the day after his mother's funeral. He'd lived alone, but he'd stayed in his mother's penthouse that night, simply to make things easier.

But he'd woken to the reality that he was alone. Truly alone. He'd woken to the realization that his selfish desire to spend the night with Autumn might have caused her death. Her cardiologist had told him that her condition had been severe and that his getting her to the hospital sooner *might* have saved her…but his professional opinion was that a few extra minutes probably wouldn't have made a difference.

So he'd woken in her penthouse, knowing she was gone, knowing he was in charge and so tired he wasn't sure he could think.

Today, he didn't have that problem. The party the night before had been filled with executives who were happy to give him their opinions. He had a million possibilities floating around in his head about how to expand Step Inside, and no desire to work toward fulfilling any one of them.

He rolled out of bed, strolling to the kitchen in a navy-blue silk robe that cost more than his mother had made in a year when she was raising him on a waitress's salary.

He made a cup of coffee, and read the *Times*, which had been brought to his penthouse by whoever was manning the lobby desk. He didn't think about Autumn; just as he had after his mom died, he'd blocked her from his thoughts.

But his heart hurt, and his head about exploded from the waterfall of good ideas that had been presented to him the night before…and behind all that was guilt.

Not that his mom had died but that he was living her dream and he didn't appreciate it.

He ran his hands down his face, showered and dressed in jeans, a leather jacket and sunglasses. Without clouds, the sun was a ruthless ball in the sky that didn't provide warmth this frigid Sunday. It only glared down at him.

Arnie awaited at the curb. Holding the back door of the limo, he said, "Good morning, sir."

"No *sir*," Jack growled. "Just Jack…remember?"

"Yes, sir… I mean, Jack."

Jack slid inside. Arnie closed the door. When he was behind the steering wheel, he said, "Where to?"

"New Jersey… The mausoleum."

Arnie caught his gaze in the rearview mirror. He'd been Jack's driver for years. He knew exactly what Jack was talking about. "Okay."

Jack stared out the window as they drove to his mother's resting place. Almost an hour later, they pulled onto the winding road. Trees typically thick with green leaves stood bare and empty.

When they reached the building, Arnie stopped. Jack got out without a word.

He walked into the silent space. Beautifully appointed with murals in the domed ceiling and gold trim, the echoing room spoke of peace and tranquility.

He ambled to the bench closest to his mom's space and sat.

"I haven't been here in a while." The quiet of the room greeted him. No reply. Not even his own imaginings of what his mother might say.

He sat in the silence. Sorrow for her loss and faded memories filled the air. But he couldn't hold them. They all withered away.

Into nothing.

Alone in the cold bleak room, he wondered what he was doing there. There were no answers in the mural. There were no answers in the silence of the room.

He lifted himself from the bench, walked over and touched the gold-plated square that held his mom's name.

He longed for her to be in his life, but he didn't cry. She'd been gone five years. He missed her laugh. He missed her crazy sense of humor. He missed her smart-as-a-whip way of running Step Inside.

But she wasn't here and nothing about the past could be changed—

And life had gone on.

Arnie drove him home and Jack handed him the tickets for the next Knicks game to thank him for working on a Sunday.

Arnie beamed. "Jack! Thank you. You don't have to do this…" He laughed. "You do pay me."

Jack shook his head and walked toward the lobby doors. "Take your son."

As the word *son* spilled out of his mouth, his chest tightened. He always thought of himself as a *son*. But the way the word rippled through him was different this time.

He waved at the doorman as he ambled to the elevator, then rode it up to the penthouse.

The place was as sterile and empty as he remembered. He walked through to the bedroom, into the closet where he hung his jacket, took off his sweater and exchanged it for a T-shirt.

Turning to go, he saw a wink of light and stopped. Sitting on the counter of the closet table was the necklace he'd given to Autumn.

If he closed his eyes, he could feel the soft skin his fingers had grazed as they fastened it around her neck. He could see the look of surprise on her face. He could her the whisper in her voice when she thanked him. He could feel her kiss.

His heart stumbled.

He lowered himself to the bench beside the table.

His mother was gone.

The life she wanted was over.

He'd fulfilled her dream.

But *his* dream had frozen in time.

And Autumn had seen that.

He hadn't gotten mad at her because what she'd suggested was absurd. He'd gotten angry because it wasn't. The time had come for him to move on and he didn't want to see it.

He should have seen it. Having Autumn walk into his life again, bring him joy, should have been a clear sign. The way she'd filled the empty spaces in his soul felt like he'd been waiting for her.

But he was too busy trying to have the future *and* the past—too busy working at something that was wrong for him—to see he'd been waiting for Autumn to somehow come back into his life. She hadn't been Cinderella waiting for the Prince to find her again. He'd been the Prince, working through his grief, straightening out his life. So that when she came back into his life, he'd been ready for her.

The love of his life.

The love of his life...

Oh, God. She was the love of his life. The rest of his life. But having dumped her again, he'd blown their second chance.

She'd be crazy to even answer a phone call from him, let alone love him.

CHAPTER SEVENTEEN

AUTUMN HAD SPENT the Saturday night and most of Sunday crying. She couldn't believe it was possible to fall in love in four weeks, but she had. And losing Jack this time was worse than waking up to find him gone after a one-night stand.

After four weeks together she knew he was wonderful, kind, smart and imaginative. They were meant to be together.

But how could they ever be together? How could Fate possibly believe they were meant to be together when they kept screwing things up?

First, he ghosted her.

Now she'd hurt him.

And he wouldn't talk about it. Everything wrapped up in his past seemed to be off limits.

They were doomed. And she decided it was time she accept that.

Jack Adams might not want her, but someone would. She was a catch.

She might not have seen that before he'd waltzed back into her life, but she did now. Not just because she had a shot at becoming a CEO—and even if she didn't get it, there were other charities in New York City that could use her expertise—but because she finally realized she wanted a family.

She strode into work on Monday morning so confident she could have fought a tiger. She hung her coat on a hook and tossed her purse into her old metal desk, knowing that if Raise Your Voice didn't want her, she was ready to job hunt.

She would forget about Jack—eventually. She simply had to plow through a few weeks of a broken heart, knowing she'd caused it herself.

But Monday went by without Gerry making an announcement about the new CEO. Still, she calmed herself with the reminder that they had one more day, December thirty-first, to make their decision.

Tuesday, she dressed for work in a somber mood. If they didn't offer her the job that day, she'd be reading the name of the new Raise Your Voice CEO in Thursday's *Times*.

So she walked into the office with her head high, reminding herself there were other charities who needed CEOs. She might not get the job as the CEO for Raise Your Voice, but she would begin her quest for a CEO position somewhere. And she would someday be running a charity.

"Can I see you for a minute?"

Autumn glanced up to see Gerry standing in her doorway. She rose from her seat. "Sure."

He led her down the hall to his office and closed the door behind her. Her heart stopped. He was so somber he could be about to tell her that she didn't get the job.

Motioning for her to take a seat, he walked to his desk chair. "As you've probably guessed, we've made a decision about the CEO position."

Her breath stuttered. This was it. She got the job, or she moved on. It almost didn't matter either way. She'd lost Jack but she planned on getting back out into the dating pool and looking for someone who would really love her. She could lose this position. She would apply for other jobs.

She had found herself as a woman and a worker. She would not lose that.

Gerry said, "Congratulations! You've got the job."

Her mouth fell open. Here she was, ready to start making copies of her new resume, expecting the worst. Getting good news shocked her.

"I'm…"

"Speechless." Gerry laughed. "We would like to announce on January second, so that gives you about twenty-four hours before we need your answer."

She burst out laughing, even as her heart tweaked with longing to call Jack and tell him she'd gotten the job. Maybe to thank him for his help. Probably because she still loved him. He was a great guy. And she wasn't entirely sure how she'd gotten everything wrong, but she had and she had no one to blame but herself for losing him.

Knowing that didn't help. It only made her heart ache. But she pulled herself together and forced herself into the moment.

She might have lost the man she loved, but she'd gained the job she'd been working for forever. She had to get her head back in the game.

Gerry handed a folder across the desk. "This is the full benefit package and the formal written offer." He rose. "I hope you'll accept."

She stood. "You know what? I don't need twenty-four or thirty-six hours. I've wanted this job forever." She reached across the desk to shake his hand. "I'm your new CEO."

"Congratulations!"

She took a breath. "Thanks." But despite her bravado, her chest hollowed out. She was getting what she'd worked for since the day she walked into the Raise Your Voice offices. But she wasn't getting what she wanted.

The only reason she wanted to be a mom was because she wanted Jack's kids. She wanted to raise kids with Jack. To instill in them his sense of humor and drive. And hope they got a thing or two from her too.

Getting the job didn't exactly feel meaningless, but she now knew there was more to life than work, and she wasn't sure what to do about that.

She turned to go but Gerry stopped her. "Oh, I almost forgot." He reached into a desk drawer and handed her two tickets.

"Those are tickets for Audrey Brewbaker's annual New Year's Eve party tonight. I'm not CEO anymore." He smiled. "You are. Because we're not announcing until January second, you can't actually talk Raise Your Voice business. But you can go, look around, figure out who you need to schmooze. You never know when you'll have to replace a board member or need a benefactor to fund a special project."

He laughed and she smiled, looking at the tickets as if they were foreign things. But she'd longed for this challenge, and she was up to it. She simply might need the whole day not just the afternoon to get ready for her first party as newly appointed CEO.

She walked out of Gerry's office, directly into hers, grabbed her purse and coat and headed home, refusing to let herself think about the fact that she'd gotten what she'd always wanted but she wasn't complete. There was a hole in her heart.

Still, she would fix it. Without Jack. He'd rejected her twice. She got the message.

CHAPTER EIGHTEEN

JACK WALKED INTO the ballroom for Audrey Brewbaker's annual New Year's Eve party, not feeling very much like schmoozing or dancing or even eating dinner. But he'd RSVP'd for two, when he believed he would be taking Autumn. He couldn't back out completely. He would say hello to the hosts, eat dinner and then race home.

After greeting Audrey and her daughter Marlene in the reception line, he walked farther into the ballroom and saw a swatch of red. The same color as the gown Autumn had worn to the Montgomerys' Christmas party.

She was here?

Telling himself he was crazy, he edged over to the bar, but he saw the red again and *knew* it was the same gown.

His heart did a flip. But as the bartender poured him a bourbon, he reminded himself that her being here was a long shot. She needed a ticket to get in.

Still, when he turned from the bartender, his bourbon in hand, he couldn't stop himself from scouting for the red again. He found it and saw her, and his stomach fell to the floor, but his brain clicked in. If he genuinely believed Fate had brought her back into his life because he'd been waiting for her and was finally ready, then he had to have the guts to face her.

He worked his way through the crowd that milled around the linen-covered tables and after ten minutes of following her from one group of people to the next, he finally caught up to her.

"Hey."

Obviously recognizing his voice, she turned. "Hey."

"I'd really like five minutes to talk to you."

She smiled…that same smile that she'd given him at Ivy and Sebastian's the night they'd all had dinner together. The fake one.

"That would be fun," she said, not meaning a word of it. "But I'm not really here as a guest." She winced. "Well, I am a guest. But I'm also CEO of Raise Your Voice."

She'd gotten the job! "That's great!"

"Yes. And I know I owe it to you. But I'm also here to make connections." She stepped to the right. "If you'll excuse me."

And just like that, she was gone.

He started after her, but she really was talking with people Jack knew were benefactors for charities. Good business sense kept him from interrupting her or joining her groups, making her nervous on what was—technically—the first day of her new job.

Dinner was served and he tried to find Autumn but couldn't. Audrey Brewbaker's New Year's Eve party was the party of the year in Manhattan. There had to be four hundred people in attendance and lots of women wore red gowns.

After Audrey's thank-you-for-attending comments and wishes for everyone to have a wonderful New Year, the band began to play.

As people ambled onto the dance floor, the crowd thinned, and Jack spotted Autumn. He was not leaving without apologizing or better yet, explaining.

He'd run out on her the first time. Though he had a good excuse, he would not run out on her a second time. He would explain. He would apologize.

He eased through the tables toward hers. Four steps before he reached her, she rose and headed to the right.

Close enough to reach her, he caught her wrist and stopped her. She turned and looked at him.

Everything inside him melted with need. He could see their future. But he didn't deserve it and even if he did he had no idea how to tell her that. He released her wrist but couldn't resist the urge for one final dance.

"Dance with me."

"I don't know—"

"Please. I need to apologize."

The surprised expression on her face confused him. She glanced left then right, then caught his gaze. "I thought I needed to apologize. I was hoping, though, to see you in a more private place."

"No one even cares we're here." He waited a second then said, "Dance with me."

This time when she smiled at him, he saw the real Autumn. He held out his hand and she took it. They reached the dance floor as one song ended, and another began.

"A waltz."

She shook her head. "Looks like the heavens are smiling down on you."

He laughed. "Yeah. I literally get to put my best foot forward."

He took her into his arms and glided them out onto the dance floor. Autumn's heart lurched. Nothing had ever felt so right as dancing with him. She'd never had the feelings for another man that she had for him. To be this close physically and so far away emotionally was a pleasure-pain too intense to describe.

"I just…" He paused. "I need to tell you that I'm sorry. What I was going through on Christmas Day was nothing like either one of us thought. I thought I was feeling guilty that I had forgotten my mom. But the truth is I think Fate was trying to tell me it was time to move on."

She pulled back so she could see his eyes. She hated that he had gone through that. Hated even more that she'd made it worse. "And I'm sorry I said those things about your mom's real plan."

"No. You might have been right." He swung them around the dance floor in a flawless waltz. "It's been five years. I did everything my mom had planned, but I'd gotten bored with it. Cooking for you nudged me to remember how much I loved it."

Surprised, she said only, "Oh."

"And that's not all I want to say to you… What made me realize I needed to move on was how much I missed you."

Their gazes caught and clung. "I missed you too."

"The night we met, I knew I'd found the person I wanted to spend the rest of my life with."

Her heart stuttered.

"Then everything went wrong, and I almost forgot you."

"I thought you had forgotten me."

"I sort of had until I saw you at Ivy and Sebastian's. You came out the door when I was waiting by Sebastian's limo and I couldn't believe it."

Not sure what to say, she only held his gaze.

"I'd hardly thought of you in five years and suddenly there you were. I realized today that Fate hadn't brought you back into my life until I was ready for you…ready to move on. And in the five years we were apart, I chose the three worst women to have a relationship with because I think deep down I knew I was waiting for you."

She blinked up at him. "I'm not sure if that's the craziest thing I've ever heard or the most romantic."

"Make it the most romantic thing you've ever heard because I really believe we're a match. I've never felt about anyone what I feel about you. I don't want to."

Her heart swelled at the romance of it, but she had to be sure they were on the same page. "Now it's my turn. I realized on Christmas Day that I didn't just want to be the CEO for Raise Your Voice. I want to have kids. *Your* kids. I want the whole thing. I don't want to be the second half of the power couple you envisioned. I want more. I want it all. I want the fairytale."

He whirled her around. "Really?"

"Think that through because you will not get a chance to leave me a third time. There will be no charm in your life if you ghost me again."

"How many kids are you thinking?"

The interest in his voice gave her enough courage to say, "How many kids are you thinking…"

He considered that. "One of each I guess."

"Seriously? You saw how much fun Mark and Donnie have. You need two of each so they can be friends."

He laughed. "We do have enough money that we could hire help."

"A nanny? My mother would shoot me if we shut her out."

"Looks like we're going to need a bigger penthouse."

"Or a house in Hunter."

He frowned. "Near your parents?"

"Why not?"

He looked at her for a few seconds, then smiled. "Why not?"

The music stopped but instead of pulling away, they stepped closer and kissed.

Dancers walked by them, couples exiting or entering the floor.

They kept kissing.

When the music began again, he pulled away and they headed for the coatroom. She texted Arnie as he found their coats.

A half hour later, they were kissing their way to the bedroom. When they reached it, he stopped. "Hold on a second."

She frowned. "What?"

He held up one finger. "Just give me a second."

She shook her head, but he returned quickly. "Turn around."

Confused, she only stared at him.

He held up her necklace. "You must have forgotten this the day after Christmas."

She smirked. "Must have."

He laughed, fastened the necklace around her neck and gave her a little nudge that tumbled her to the bed.

"I love you."

She froze. Her eyes filled with tears. "I don't think we've ever said that."

"Well, now that we have, let's not stop."

She smiled. "I love you, too."

EPILOGUE

THEY WERE MARRIED on Valentine's Day two years later. Believing Ivy and Sebastian had brought them back together, they asked Ivy to be maid of honor and Sebastian to be best man.

They held the wedding in the same venue Sebastian and Ivy had, Parker and Parker. The castle-like building stood tall in the thick February snow, as Autumn raced inside, Ivy holding her long lace train. Her entire dress was lace and her headpiece a tiara that sparkled in her reddish-brown hair.

In the bride's room, her mother fussed, but her dad grinned. He loved the new addition to their family. Not just because Jack had Knicks season tickets but because he was a great guy. They waited in the quiet room with four full-length mirrors and ornate French Provincial furniture until the wedding planner opened the door and announced it was time for Autumn's mom to be seated and for Autumn to position herself to walk up the aisle.

Her parents scurried out, along with the wedding planner and suddenly Ivy and Autumn were alone.

Ivy's eyes pooled with tears. "I'm so happy for you."

"I'm so happy for me too. You don't know how close we came to losing each other twice."

"I've heard the story about the night you met." Ivy winced. "Jack told Sebastian."

"He thinks we're destined to be together."

Ivy straightened the veil beneath the glittering tiara. "I agree."

"Then let's go get me married."

They left the bride's room and headed to the chapel area. Autumn's dad, looking dapper in his black tux, walked her down the aisle.

When it came time to say their vows, Jack took her hands and smiled at her. "Autumn Jones," he said, beginning the vows he had written for the ceremony. "I think Fate saved you for me and I'm grateful. You're smart and funny and you love my cooking. But I think our adventure is just beginning."

Staring into his blue eyes, she whispered, "I do too."

The minister laughed. "Was that your vows?"

She blushed. "No." She swallowed then said, "Jack Adams, you're the strongest, smartest person I know. And I love you in a way I didn't know existed before I met you. We're going to have the best kids ever and the most fun showing them the world."

He nodded slightly, then leaned in and kissed her cheek.

The minister sighed. "It's not time for a kiss."

"I didn't kiss her lips."

A chuckle ran through the crowd.

The minister shook his head. "May I have the rings?"

Ivy and Sebastian stepped forward and the ceremony proceeded normally from there. They ate a rich, delicious supper prepared by Step Inside chefs and then danced the night away.

With their family.

And their friends.

So many wonderful people now populated his life.

Jack took it all in and every once in a while glanced heavenward, knowing his mother would approve.

Especially since he'd resigned as CEO of Step Inside and now devoted himself to creating new dishes and new menus.

Autumn had been right. As soon as he shifted back to the job he loved and settled in with the woman he adored, his life had blossomed.

He didn't think he could be happier…but Autumn's dad had told him to wait till the first time he held his newborn baby. That moment would steal his heart.

He was looking forward to it.

* * * * *

COMING SOON!

We really hope you enjoyed reading this book.
If you're looking for more romance, be sure to
head to the shops when new books are
available on

Thursday 1st
December

To see which titles are coming soon, please visit

millsandboon.co.uk/nextmonth

MILLS & BOON

THE HEART OF ROMANCE

A ROMANCE FOR EVERY READER

MODERN — Prepare to be swept off your feet by sophisticated, sexy and seductive heroes, in some of the world's most glamourous and romantic locations, where power and passion collide.

HISTORICAL — Escape with historical heroes from time gone by. Whether your passion is for wicked Regency Rakes, muscled Vikings or rugged Highlanders, awaken the romance of the past.

MEDICAL — Set your pulse racing with dedicated, delectable doctors in the high-pressure world of medicine, where emotions run high and passion, comfort and love are the best medicine.

True Love — Celebrate true love with tender stories of heartfelt romance, from the rush of falling in love to the joy a new baby can bring, and a focus on the emotional heart of a relationship.

Desire — Indulge in secrets and scandal, intense drama and plenty of sizzling hot action with powerful and passionate heroes who have it all: wealth, status, good looks…everything but the right woman.

HEROES — Experience all the excitement of a gripping thriller, with an intense romance at its heart. Resourceful, true-to-life women and strong, fearless men face danger and desire - a killer combination!

To see which titles are coming soon, please visit

millsandboon.co.uk/nextmonth

MILLS & BOON

Coming next month

VEGAS WEDDING TO FOREVER
Sophie Pembroke

There was safety in numbers. And Toby was alone.

Or he had been, until he woke up married.

Still, now the time came to actually put his plan to her, the words seemed stuck in his throat. Was this crazy? Probably. But it was still the only plan he had.

"I've been thinking." In between the pounding hangover and the being shouted at. "About this marriage thing. I know it might not have been exactly planned on either side, but you are my wife." The marriage certificate had shown up in the pocket of the trousers he'd been wearing the night before, already creased and crumpled.

"If this is you about to offer me money again—"

"It's not," Toby said, quickly. Now he'd had some more coffee, he could see the flaws in that plan. He'd never paid for sex, he wasn't about to start paying for marriage. Not to mention that scandal it would cause if it came out. His father would be revolving slowing in his grave already, but if anyone else found out what had actually happened here he'd probably go into a full on spin.

"Then what?" Autumn asked, impatiently. "I've got to go and clear out my room after this. And, you know, find another job." She waved her phone at him too fast for him to make out anything more than the vague impression of a text message. "My roommate says the boss is about to throw my stuff out into the street if I don't go and collect it. I mean, I travel lighter than most, but I'd still like to not lose everything I possess, if you don't mind?"

"I think we should stay married." The words flew out unbidden, sending Autumn's eyes wide and her mouth clamped shut. "I meant to build up to that a bit more," he admitted, rubbing a hand across his aching brow. "Explain my reasons and such. But in essence, I think we should stay married, and you should come to Wishcliffe with me. For a time."

Continue reading
VEGAS WEDDING TO FOREVER
Sophie Pembroke

Available next month
www.millsandboon.co.uk

MILLS & BOON
MEDICAL
Pulse-Racing Passion

Set your pulse racing with dedicated, delectable doctors in the high-pressure world of medicine, where emotions run high and passion, comfort and love are the best medicine.